What do voodoo and love have in common?

The rules aren't written down.
Both involve strange rituals.
Neither are for amateurs.
If you aren't careful,
someone will get hurt.
You don't know what's hit you . . .
until it's way too late.

STEPHANIE
BOND

By Stephanie Bond

IN DEEP VOODOO
WHOLE LOTTA TROUBLE
PARTY CRASHERS
KILL THE COMPETITION
I THINK I LOVE YOU
GOT YOUR NUMBER
OUR HUSBAND

STEPHANIE

BOND

In Deep Voodoo

AVON BOOKS
An Imprint of HarperCollins*Publishers*

This is a work of fiction. Names, characters, places, and incidents are products of the author's imagination or are used fictitiously and are not to be construed as real. Any resemblance to actual events, locales, organizations, or persons, living or dead, is entirely coincidental.

AVON BOOKS
An Imprint of HarperCollins*Publishers*
10 East 53rd Street
New York, New York 10022-5299

ISBN-13: 978-0-06-082057-2
ISBN-10: 0-06-082057-8
www.avonromance.com

First Avon Books paperback printing: October 2005

Printed in the U.S.A.

10 9 8 7 6 5 4 3 2 1

Acknowledgments

Many thanks to David and Grace Waldrop for the title brainstorming session over margaritas on the beach at Captiva—*In Deep Voodoo* is my favorite title ever. Thanks to my husband, Christopher Hauck, who listened to my oftentimes nonsensical ramblings as this story and these characters came to life in my head. A shout-out to gal pal Joan Hug for giving me the idea for my character's secret vice, and to Christy Brown for entertaining "taxing" questions for all of my books. Thanks to my writing critique partners, Carmen Green and Rita Herron, for their constant support. And many thanks to my logistics men, Willis Bond and Tim Logsdon. Thanks also to my agent, Kimberly Whalen at Trident Media Group, for encouraging me to write this series, and to my editor, Lyssa Keusch at Avon Books, for buying it (and making it better). And to my readers, whose e-mail notes to "write faster!" keep me going when the words don't want to come.

Stephanie

1

Start with a dangerous dose of curiosity . . .

"I could *kill* Deke for this," Penny Francisco said, peering with a tiny pair of binoculars through the mini-blinds that covered a window of her health food store, The Charm Farm.

The normally sleepy two-lane Charm Street bustled with early traffic for the annual Voodoo Festival. But in between the passing cars, Penny had managed to get a good look at the Victorian house heavy with ornate cast ironwork that she had bought, refurbished, and lived in with Deke Black, attorney-at-law, until their explosive breakup a few months ago. A painting crew was methodically covering the rich color of Vanilla Milk, which she had lovingly chosen from thousands of paint chips, with what looked to be Pink Nightmare.

She ground her teeth until her jaw ached. "Just look at what he's doing to my house!"

"Let me guess," Marie, her quirky employee of six months, said from behind the juice bar, where she was refilling canisters of vitamin additives. "He's painting it."

Penny looked at the woman suspiciously—many people in town had insinuated that eccentric Marie Gaston with the electric blue hair had a "third eye." "How did you know that?"

"I saw Lou Hall's painting van pull up as I was coming in this morning."

Penny frowned and looked back out the window. "Deke's not just painting my house—he's painting it Puke Pink."

"But it's his house now."

"Still. I can't believe the historical society would allow him to paint my house *pink*."

"It helps that his mother is mayor," Marie offered dryly. "And it's *his* house now, boss."

"But I have to look at it every day." Penny jammed her hand into her coarse auburn curls as frustration billowed in her chest. Moisture gathered in the corners of her eyes, but she quickly blinked it away—no more tears over Deke Black. "He did this just to annoy me."

"Probably." Marie cleared her throat. "Although I heard down at the Hair Affair that, um, Sheena was planning to redecorate."

Penny stiffened, pain knifing between her shoulder blades. Deke's mistress. Girlfriend. Tart. Practically everyone in the town of Mojo, Louisiana, knew about Deke's fooling around. The fact that he had moved litigious Sheena Linder into the home he and Penny had bought together was the ultimate humiliation. "I can't believe that I have to live over the doughnut shop and that woman will be living in my house."

"You live over a *beignet* shop. And it's his house, boss."

"The bastard could have waited until the ink was dry on the divorce papers."

"Uh-huh. Well, maybe Sheena will fall in the shower and sue him. Lord knows she's sued almost everyone else in town."

"And Deke defended her the last few times she *allegedly* injured herself."

"If it's any consolation, I heard she slipped on a spilled Yoohoo in the Quickie Mart last week and is laid up again."

"As if the woman needed a reason to be on her back," Penny muttered, her blood boiling.

The soaring pin oak tree that had first drawn her to the Victorian on Charm Street was ablaze with deep red foliage typical for early October. The glorious ruby color clashed horrifically with the vicious pink hue the painters were rolling onto the wood siding—another insult. The last time the leaves had been red—this time last year—she had been happy . . . mostly.

Last summer had been fraught with stress as she had debated whether or not to clear the land they owned behind The Charm Farm to plant an organic vegetable garden. Deke had been vehemently opposed to the idea, saying he had other plans for the empty half-acre lot, but Penny had had the distinct feeling that her husband had been trying to undermine her business, which he had pooh-poohed from the beginning. When she'd first suggested that they convert the small rental house across the street that his father had given him into a retail business, Deke had made her feel foolish.

"A health food store in Mojo?" He'd laughed until

his eyes had run. "Maybe a fish and chips joint. In case you haven't noticed, honey, the deep south really means the deep *fried* south."

Hurt, but determined to put her rusty nutrition degree and homeopathic know-how to good use, Penny had persisted. After a rocky start, her enterprise had taken off. As it turned out, the residents of Mojo preferred home remedies to fancy doctoring, and The Charm Farm's inventory of roots, herbs, and vitamins fit the bill nicely.

But while her business had grown steadily, the law practice that Deke had taken over from his father had started to slide. Two of his big manufacturing clients had jumped to more tony law firms in nearby New Orleans. Deke had begun to supplement his client list with personal injury cases, and supplement his diet with bourbon.

The downturn in his business had coincided perfectly with a midlife crisis. One day he had driven home a new fire engine red two-seater Lotus Elise. That was about the same time Penny had found brochures for hair transplants in his briefcase. With new lingerie and lots of TLC, she had tried to head off what had seemed to be an inevitable affair, but in the end, terminally tanned and ferociously feminine Sheena Linder had been too much for a simple man like Deke to resist.

Penny and Sheena weren't complete strangers. The women had met once when Penny had visited Sheena's Forever Sun tanning salon and asked that Sheena give her customers a flyer on the dangers of tanning so they could make a more informed decision before roasting themselves. Sheena had called her the "c" word and had thrown her out of Forever Sun, threatening to sue for trespassing and mental anguish. Penny found out later that her trip to the tanning salon had prompted Sheena to see Deke about possibly filing a lawsuit against some crazy woman named Penny Black. Apparently Deke had overlooked Sheena's inability to figure out that her new attorney and her intended defendant shared the same last name and might be related or, in this case, married. Thankfully, Deke hadn't filed a suit against Penny on Sheena's behalf. Instead he'd started porking Sheena, and now Penny's last name was no longer Black.

Life was nothing if not ironic. Penny had secured the barracuda of an attorney from the city who had handled her friend Liz's divorce. After much legal wrangling, Deke had gotten the Victorian and the property it sat on, and Penny had gotten The Charm Farm and the property it sat on. When the final papers had been signed earlier in the week, Penny had staked out the premeditated garden with pink flags. Those flags symbolized her own growth and filled her with a sense of purpose.

And she also gained satisfaction in knowing that one day, Sheena Linder would crawl out of one of her tanning beds looking like a dried-apple-head doll. Penny's skin, on the other hand, would still be lily white and unwrinkled . . . but lightly veined . . . and . . . freckled. She frowned suddenly, trying to remember why she had felt so victorious.

Across the street, a faded green sedan pulled into her former driveway behind Lou Hall's painting van. Probably another workman hired to do something else unconscionable to her beloved house. She started to turn away when the car door opened and a tall man she didn't recognize climbed out. With the binoculars she could see he was long-limbed and well built. Unbidden, a spark of appreciation flared in her stomach. The man was dark-haired, dressed in boots, brown leather coat, and faded jeans that he tugged higher as he approached the steps leading to the front porch of the house. His loose-hipped walk suggested an affinity for . . . something other than Pilates.

Penny's tongue lodged firmly in her cheek. What was a handsome man doing at the house at an hour when Deke was at his office and Sheena was purportedly indisposed with an injury from the Yoohoo spill? Maybe Sheena was already bored with Deke's fumbling foreplay and dense back hair and had decided to call in reinforcements.

The fact that the thought cheered her immensely proved just how much the nasty divorce had changed her; before she wouldn't have wished evil on anyone, no matter what they had done to her, but now . . . well, now she had fantasies about Deke getting his comeuppance in a manner worthy of a regional headline. She glanced toward the phone and seriously toyed with the idea of calling Deke and inventing an emergency to bring him running home. How fitting if Deke walked in on Sheena doing the nasty with another guy in the same bed in which *she* had caught Deke and Sheena going at it like two greased pistons.

She would probably never be able to get that horrific image out of her head. Now, ten months later, the detail she remembered most vividly was that the bottoms of Sheena's feet (stuck up in the air) were dirty, and the fact that she was sullying Penny's organic cotton sheets in the process of shagging her husband was just . . . well, unforgivable, really.

Penny pressed the binoculars closer to the window, her mind spinning gleeful scenarios, all of them ending with Deke crawling back to her—not that it would do any good, but oh, the sweet satisfaction.

The stranger's body language was definitely suspicious as he climbed the steps, stabbed the doorbell, and waited in the shadows of the covered porch. He looked from side to side, his gaze seeming to catch and linger on the antique metal glider that she had painstakingly stripped of countless layers of peeling paint and refurbished for the porch. His good taste in furniture apparently did not extend to women, Penny thought sourly. The door opened and Sheena stood there in a pale, voluminous peignoir, a la Zsa Zsa Gabor, her orange skin glowing like a jack-o'-lantern, nary a back brace or neck cast in sight.

Penny waited for the man to scoop Sheena into his arms, or for her to flash him some leg—or an orange boob. Instead, his posture went rigid and he appeared to say something she didn't like. Sheena's blond head tilted, her hip cocked saucily, and her face contorted. Then she tried to close the door, but the man wedged his foot in the opening long enough to add something. When he withdrew his foot, the door closed, and Penny imagined the *thwack* of the dead bolt turning as she had turned it many times herself.

The man retraced his steps to the car, every footfall exuding frustration. Penny couldn't get a good look at his face as he swung into the driver's seat. Exhaust blasted out of the tailpipe when he started the car engine. He backed out of the driveway onto Charm Street and sped away in the direction of downtown Mojo. For some reason, though, she doubted the man was in town for the Voodoo Festival.

Penny's pulse spiked. Who was the mystery man to her ex-husband's shack-up honey? A relative? A debtor?

A lover?

2

Add a dash of weakness . . .

Suddenly Penny realized that Marie was speaking. The mini-blind snapped back in place. "I'm sorry. What did you say?"

Beneath her blue pixie haircut, Marie frowned and leaned into the counter. "I said are you going to let a bad paint job ruin tonight's party?"

Penny pulled her mind back to the moment and made her best attempt at a smile. "No. It's sweet of you to throw a party to celebrate my divorce." In truth, she dreaded it like a pelvic exam. People used to mourn a broken marriage—now greeting card companies offered "you're better off without him" poetry. It all felt very sordid to her, but she knew Marie was only trying to lift her spirits. "I've never been to a divorce party—what will we do?"

"Well—"

The phone rang and Penny held up her finger. "Hold that thought." Praying that Marie's thought was of canceling the party, Penny shoved the binoculars into her pocket, then walked to the front counter and picked up the handset next to the cash register. "Charm Farm, Penny speaking."

"Penny, it's Gloria Dalton. Is this a bad time?"

At the sound of her divorce attorney's voice, Penny grimaced. "Only if this is bad news."

"No," Gloria said quickly. "Actually I was just . . . checking on you."

Penny blinked. "Checking on me?"

"Call me a mother hen. I know that sometimes the finality of signing the divorce papers can pack an emotional punch." She cleared her throat. "I just wanted to let you know that if you ever feel like talking . . ."

"I'm fine," Penny rushed to fill in the pause, realizing in flushed embarrassment that Gloria hadn't bought all those excuses about allergies when her eyes had watered and her nose had run during consultations.

"I know things between you and Deke ended on a sour note," Gloria said. "If he harasses you, Penny, I'll help you to get a restraining order."

The vehemence in her voice made Penny wonder if Gloria had firsthand experience with restraining orders. Penny gave a hoarse laugh. "He painted my old house pink—can you do anything about that?"

Gloria sighed. "You know I can't. I wish I could have gotten you the house, too."

"I'm happier with my business. He only wanted this place so he could shut me down, you know. All that talk about his father giving him this place and it having sentimental value was bull."

"Still, I'm sorry that he's being so childish about painting the house."

"Well, I couldn't care less," Penny lied, then glanced

up. Her gaze landed on Marie. "In fact, I'm having a party tonight to . . . celebrate my freedom."

"Oh. That's . . . great." Gloria made an approving noise.

"If you don't have plans, join us. We'll be at Caskey's bar on the square. The Voodoo Festival is going on, so Mojo is hopping with activity for once."

"Sounds tempting," Gloria said. "I'd love to drive over, but I already have a . . . commitment . . . of sorts."

A date? Penny wondered. Gloria Dalton was beautiful, but emitted a general disdain for men. "Okay. Well, thanks for calling," Penny said, trying to sound breezy.

"Sure. And Penny . . . that offer to talk is always open."

"Thank you," Penny said somewhat woodenly. She felt so pathetic—her own attorney pitied her. "Goodbye, Gloria." She hung up the phone and thought not for the first time that the woman was very good at her job; she had, after all, blocked Deke's vigorous attempt to keep the rental house. Yet it seemed to Penny that Gloria Dalton carried out her duties of legally dividing married couples with a certain sadness—Penny sensed the attractive New Orleans attorney had a story.

She pursed her mouth. But then, didn't everyone?

"Bad news?" Marie asked across the room.

"No," Penny said, then exhaled and donned a cheerful expression as she walked over to the smoothie counter where Marie was working. "You were about to tell me what to expect tonight at the party?"

Marie's smile was secretive as she pushed a glass of yellow-colored juice toward Penny. "I have a few surprises planned."

Penny picked up the glass with a wry smile. "No offense, Marie, but I've had enough surprises to last a lifetime. I'm ready for my life to settle into a nice, quiet rut."

"*Good* surprises," Marie amended. "We'll have fun."

Penny sipped from the glass and murmured when the citrusy, almost floral-flavored juice washed over her taste buds. "Mmm, this is good."

"It's my own blend. I was thinking about adding it to the menu for the festival crowd."

Penny narrowed her eyes. "As long as you didn't sneak in some suspect ingredient."

Marie grinned. "Can I help it if my juice boosts sex drive?"

Penny reluctantly swallowed the mouthful of tangy stuff she'd been savoring. "What's in this?"

"Just a little bee pollen and some ginseng." Marie's eyes twinkled. "And a secret ingredient or two."

Penny wagged her finger. "We have to divulge our recipes to our customers, Marie. And I'm afraid you wasted your love potion on me."

Marie sighed. "Penny, Deke put you through a horrible ordeal, but don't let him keep you down." She gestured wide. "Just look at your success."

Penny pivoted her head to take in the two large rooms they'd created when they'd gutted the rental house. She tried to view her business as a stranger might. The high ceilings had been fitted with two skylights to allow natural light to flood the space. One room housed shelves and racks of bottled vitamins, minerals, and a plethora of other natural additives in powder, liquid, crystal, and solid form, plus books, magazines, and other packaged products aimed at attaining a healthy lifestyle.

The second room featured the juice bar, plus bins and baskets of colorful organic produce, including dried and fresh herbs, roots, barks, teas, edible flowers, and other goods harvested from their tiny herb garden and from other sources. The wide-plank oak floors had been left alone, the distressed finish adding to the homey feeling of a general store. With the soothing sounds of nature playing through overhead speakers, The Charm Farm was a fragrant, welcoming place. Pride swelled her chest at the thought that from the germ of an idea, she had built a profitable business. Yet a tiny pang managed to slice through her satisfaction: She had hoped to share her success with Deke.

The idea that they were no longer a couple still hadn't completely sunk in. Oh, her mind was processing the information rationally, but her heart seemed to be lagging woefully behind.

"And soon you'll be expanding with your garden," Marie pointed out. "You'll probably make a killing this week with the festival. You're sitting on a gold mine here—and you did it all without freaky Deke."

Penny sighed. "Actually, in spite of him. Deke was never particularly supportive of the business."

"I wish all men were like my Kirk," Marie said dreamily. "He always encourages me to try new things."

Penny tried not to roll her eyes. Ever since Marie had begun working at The Charm Farm, she had regaled Penny with the virtues of Kirk, her long-distance boyfriend. The man was, among other things, a real estate baron, pilot of his own private plane, an accomplished sailor, a martial arts expert, a big-game hunter, a world-class chef, and a poet. Marie was vague about how they'd met, and they corresponded via e-mail.

Penny had begun to believe that, at best, "Kirk" was simply a figment of the young woman's imagination or, at worst, a predatory con-man. But she tamped her skepticism and murmured, "Lucky you."

"What did you do before you had this business?" Marie asked.

"I worked in Deke's law office."

"Ah."

Penny could see the words going through the young woman's head—the business had contributed to her marriage breakup. Words that Deke's mother, Mona Black, had uttered often enough in Penny's ear: *"If you don't give up on this fool notion of running your own business, you're going to lose Deke. You should be working to build his business, or go home and have children, like a proper wife."*

One upside of the divorce, Penny acknowledged, was breaking familial ties with the overbearing woman. Of course, since Mona was also the mayor of Mojo, Penny couldn't escape her grasp completely.

"I don't think our marriage would have lasted even if I hadn't opened this business," she said in her defense, which was ridiculous because she didn't have to convince Marie. Was she trying to convince herself? "Deke and I were so different, all the way down to our diet."

Marie laughed. "I'm not sticking up for Deke, but I don't know anyone who eats as healthy as you do."

"Junk in, junk out." Penny knew she sounded prim, but it was important to her that she lived the lifestyle that she touted to her customers. She'd always been health conscious, but little by little, since she'd opened the store, she'd given up red meat, white meat, trans fats, caffeine, refined sugar, alcohol, and dairy products. Now she took a multi-vitamin, calcium, extra vitamin B, C, D, and E, fish oil, St. John's Wort, and grape seed extract, along with downing flaxseed, steel-cut oats, bran, tofu, and green tea. She ran three miles a day and did Pilates five times a week and slathered on sunscreen with SPF 40 even on cloudy days. By all rights, she should live forever . . . if the stress of divorcing Deke didn't kill her. She walked back to the window and fingered open the blind.

Marie grunted. "Okay, so you'll have the last laugh because you'll outlive Deke by forty years. But the important thing is now that the divorce is final, you have to get on with your life."

Penny bristled and turned her head. "I *am* getting on with my life."

"No—you're standing at the window and spying on your *former* life."

Penny stepped back, and the blinds rattled. Her cheeks flamed as she avoided the gaze of the younger woman. She suddenly wished she had maintained more of a professional distance with her employees. They knew too much about her affairs; conversely, she knew very little about their personal lives. . . .

Marie made a sympathetic noise in her throat. "I know it's hard, but that's why I'm throwing you a party—to celebrate a new phase of your life. New digs, new business . . . new man."

"Whoa—slow down."

Marie wiggled her blue eyebrows. "Rebound sex is the best."

Penny gasped, then tried to look haughty. "How do you know I haven't already *had* rebound sex? Maybe

I'm rebounding every single night." In truth, Deke had been the last man she'd slept with, and that had been over a year ago.

Marie gave her a pointed gaze. "I'll bet you ten dollars that the next person who walks through the door is having more sex than you."

Once again, the thought flitted through Penny's head that Marie had ESP. A chime sounded, signaling the arrival of a customer. Penny turned, then bit back a smile when she saw Jules Lamborne—Mojo resident and oldest woman in the state of Louisiana at one hundred and nine years—stride in sporting a walking stick, her white, wispy hair floating around her smiling, leathery face beneath a tattered bucket hat. So much for Marie's ESP.

It was Jules who had put their business on the map a few months ago when the *New Orleans Post* had reported that Jules stopped by The Charm Farm on her daily walk and chugged a cup of Vigor Juice, claiming it made her feel like a spry ninety-nine-year-old again. The juice and smoothie bar, which Penny had hoped would appeal to tourists on their way to visit the Instruments of Death and Voodoo Museum next door, had become an overnight sensation.

The article in the *Post* had also caught the eye of a New Orleans celebrity chef, Ziggy Hines, who was looking for a source for unusual herbs and spices. Shortly after the article had run, he had arrived at The Charm Farm unannounced, sporting his tall chef's hat. After much nodding and humming, he had bought every ginseng root and cinnamon fern fiddlehead that woodsman Jimmy Scaggs had foraged for Penny, plus all the fresh sulfur shelf and dried porcini mushrooms she'd had on hand, with an order to call him the minute she had more. Word had spread like warm cocoa butter, and soon professional chefs and fledgling gourmets from all over had made The Charm Farm a buying destination, all thanks to the ball that Jules had started rolling.

"Good morning, Jules," Marie said.

"*Bonjour,* ladies," Jules said, her voice warbling, but strong. She was a wrinkled slip of a woman, dressed in jeans, a flannel shirt, and white Adidas high-top athletic shoes. Time had robbed the centenarian of every feminine characteristic; her creased face, narrow figure, gnarled hands, and baritone speech were all androgynous. As she climbed up on a stool and leaned her intricately carved walking stick against the counter, she appeared more mythical than human. "I came for my morning elixir."

"Coming right up," Marie said.

Jules slanted her chin toward Penny. "Don't you own the house across the *rue*?"

Penny could follow Cajun expressions as long as they were in context. "I used to. But now it belongs to my ex-husband, Deke Black."

"Is he blind?"

"Pardon me?"

Jules tapped her temple. "I said, is the man blind? Must be, considering the god-awful color he's painting that poor house. There should be a law against ugly-ing up the town like that."

"There is," Marie said, pulling a lever to dispense a greenish liquid into a glass. "But when your mama is mayor, laws don't apply."

"I know who his mama is." Jules snorted, then took the glass that Marie extended, leveling her vibrant gaze on Penny. "How come you and that Deke Black to split up?"

Penny hedged with a little smile. "Our marriage had run its course."

"He was fucking around on you, was he?"

Penny blinked. "Well—"

"Yes," Marie declared.

Jules swirled the liquid in her glass. *"Fils de putain."*

"Son of a bitch," Marie explained, grinning.

"Want me to put a hex on him?" Jules asked.

"Yes!" Marie said excitedly.

"*No,*" Penny said, giving Marie a stern look.

Marie pouted. "Oh, come on—get into the spirit of the festival."

"Thanks anyway," Penny said to Jules with a little laugh.

Jules looked disappointed, then raised the glass of fibrous Vigor Juice. "To the old days, when women had a remedy for cheating men."

Her mind churning, Penny watched as the woman chugged the vitamin-packed liquid. Jules sat the empty glass on the counter, wiped her mouth on her sleeve, then heaved a satisfied sigh. "Guess I'd better be going. Thanks for the tipple."

"Um, Jules," Penny said, her curiosity burning a hole through her common sense, "what did you mean when you said 'a remedy for cheating men'?"

Jules grinned. "In my day, when a man got out of line, the wife put the voodoo on him as *punition.*"

"As punishment," Marie whispered.

"Put the voodoo on him?" Penny asked.

Jules leaned in, her aged eyes flashing with an eerie

light. "You know—put a hex on him. Before long, the woman's problem was solved. You should think on it."

A chill skittered up Penny's back, sending goose-flesh over her arms. "But Deke Black isn't my problem anymore. I'm over him."

Jules studied her until Penny felt jittery, as if the woman could see into her soul and see what a big, fat liar she was. Finally, Jules shrugged her frail shoulders. "Whatever you say."

"Are you going to stay in town for the festival, Jules?" Marie asked.

The old woman made a face. "No. Bunch of fools playing with black magic—they'd better watch themselves. Voodoo is not for amateurs." Jules pushed away from the counter, then gathered her walking stick and reached in her pocket to withdraw a leather change purse.

"Put your money away, Jules," Marie said. "Penny gave you a lifetime supply of Vigor Juice on the house, remember?"

Jules chuckled, then lifted a crooked finger in Penny's direction. "You're going to be surprised when I'm still coming in here twenty years from now."

Penny laughed, although it came out sounding a bit strangled because she half-believed the woman.

Then Jules's eyes constricted and she appeared to turn inward, as if she were remembering back . . . or maybe remembering *forward*. "In fact, a lot of people around Mojo are going *mourir* before me."

Penny looked to Marie for translation.

Marie swallowed, then whispered. "To die."

"Some of them soon," Jules added.

At the hoarse intensity of the woman's prediction,

Penny's pulse picked up. She exchanged a wide-eyed glance with Marie, then she hugged herself, feeling silly, as the old woman turned to go. Jules loved to scare people with her stories of the supernatural. "See you tomorrow, Jules."

"*Bon Dieu* willing," the woman said, throwing up her hand.

"Jules," Marie called, "we have a new juice to improve your sex drive—want to try some?"

Jules cackled. "Mr. Fielding is only allowed one conjugal visit a week at the nursing home. I don't want to kill the man." The old woman was still laughing as she left.

Penny looked at Marie, her mouth open in disbelief. "No way."

Marie pursed her mouth and nodded. "Yep. My cousin Eddie is an orderly at the nursing home and says that Jules shows up like clockwork on Tuesday afternoons to get it on with Mr. Fielding."

Penny grimaced. "So you're telling me that a one-hundred-nine-year-old woman is getting more action than I am?" Too late, she realized she'd told on herself.

Marie held out her hand and fluttered her fingers. "You owe me ten dollars."

"Okay, okay, you'll get your money." Penny rubbed her hands up and down her arms, trying to dispel the peculiar chill that had settled into her pores. She needed to turn on the heat. "Marie . . . you don't really believe all that stuff about hexes, do you?"

Marie shrugged. "Why not? Lots of people do. I've told you how many people come in asking for voodoo dolls. We could probably sell a thousand this weekend alone!"

Penny frowned. "People can buy all they want at the souvenir shop at the Voodoo Museum. And there will be booths full of them on the square."

"Some people don't want the ones made in Taiwan. They're looking for the real ones made out of human hair and tar."

Penny shook her head. "Well, they won't find them here. I don't believe in all that hocus-pocus, and I refuse to promote it."

Marie gave a wry laugh. "Just remember that the power of suggestion is a tremendous force." She nodded pointedly toward the glass of "love potion" juice that Penny had abandoned, then picked up an empty cardboard box and headed toward the stockroom.

Penny nodded thoughtfully, then picked up the glass of juice, staring into the clear yellow liquid. Marie was right—it was time she started getting on with her life . . . and her sex life. She had allowed Deke to destroy her confidence and her libido, while the pink house was a public symbol of his prowess—and rejection. In a sudden burst of defiance, she lifted the glass to her mouth and drained it. Inexplicably, the image of a long-limbed, dark-haired man in a brown leather jacket and faded jeans came to mind, but she pushed it away.

The last thing she needed in her life was another man connected to Sheena Linder.

She rinsed the glass. At a sudden tingling on her tongue, she swallowed hard and looked over her shoulder to see if Marie was still occupied. She was. Penny wet her lips and tiptoed through the vitamin room into the bedroom she had turned into her personal office. She stared at the locked bottom drawer of her desk, her mouth watering now. The stress was making her weak.

She shouldn't . . . she couldn't.

The door chime sounded, announcing a customer. Penny exhaled, grateful for the distraction.

She wouldn't. For now.

3

A pinch of revenge . . .

As Penny walked toward the entrance of the store, she heard a man call, "It's only me!"

She smiled when Guy Bishop came into view. He had been working for her since the store opened. He kept the books, helped her find vendors, and dealt with salespeople. Although Guy was nearing forty, he could pass for a college youth, dressed as he was in slim corduroys and an untucked button-up shirt. His hair was blond, gelled, and lofty, his funky wire-rimmed glasses sparkling clean. He was buff and handsome and everyone in town seemed to know that Guy was gay . . . except Guy. He'd had several long-term relationships with gorgeous, cosmopolitan women who lived in nearby New Orleans, but for one vague reason or another, the relationships had seemed to . . . peter out. Still, Penny humored Guy when he exhibited uber-hetero behavior and didn't comment on the more feminine manners that seemed to leap out of him involuntarily.

"Good morning, Guy."

He stopped and angled his head. "Have you seen the train wreck happening across the street?"

She nodded, biting her tongue.

He sighed. "It looks like a decorating reality show gone bad."

She attempted a nonchalant shrug. "Maybe we can use it in our advertising—Located Across from the Tacky Pink House."

He pursed his mouth, nodding. "I like that."

Marie stuck her head out of the stockroom. "Guy, are you coming to the party at Caskey's tonight?"

"Won't Caskey's be packed with the festival crowd?"

"We have a private room reserved."

"Oh. Well, is it okay if I bring a date?"

"Sure."

"Great. I met this new babe named Carley." He grinned sheepishly. "We've only gone out a couple of times, but I think she might be the one. She's really hot, was first runner-up in the Miss Louisiana pageant a couple of years ago."

Penny avoided looking at Marie. "That's . . . great. But are you sure that you want to bring her to a divorce party?"

His eyebrows climbed. "Why not? Are you planning to do something cheesy, like have half-naked guys dancing around?"

"No," Marie said.

His disappointment was apparent. "Oh. Well, then everything should be fine. It's just a regular party, right?"

"Ask Marie," Penny said, pointing. "She's the organizer."

"It's not *just* a party," Marie declared. "It's to celebrate Penny's liberation. She's a single woman again!"

"She is?" a man's voice said behind them.

Penny startled, then turned to see Jimmy Scaggs, the

man who sold her goods he scavenged from the woods, standing inside the door, wearing brown camouflage gear. It wasn't the first time he had managed to slip in without triggering the door chime.

"Jesus," Guy said sourly. "Sneak up on people, why don't you?"

Jimmy grinned. "It's what I do best, Gay."

Guy scowled. "My name is Guy."

"Jimmy," Penny said to intervene, "do you have something for me today?"

He smiled at Penny and removed his hat, revealing long, flattened hair. "Yes, ma'am."

She gestured to the dry sink along the wall. "Why don't you show me?"

Jimmy Scaggs was a wiry, rawboned man of indeterminate age. He lifted a green canvas sling bag over his head and walked to the area where he always showed her his finds. Jimmy wet his thin lips. "Did I hear right—that you're . . . single now?"

Penny hesitated. The man had nice teeth and interesting, if spooky, pale blue eyes, and underneath the layer of perpetual dust he might be a passably good-looking man. But Jimmy Scaggs took the survival gig just a little too far for her comfort level. "Um, yes. I'm divorced. Did you bring more ginseng?"

"Yeah, a couple with interesting shapes." He spread out several orange-brown roots and picked out one about five inches long that looked like a human leg. "Some people say the root will cure the part of the body it most resembles."

"Is that so?" Penny asked, noticing that despite the dirt caked beneath the man's fingernails, he had well-shaped hands.

He nodded and picked out another root that was the size of her palm and shaped remarkably like a human heart. "I brought this one for you," he offered gently. "Your ex is a no-good polecat, running around with that nasty Sheena Linder."

Penny bristled at the personal topic and raised her gaze to his. A mistake, she realized, when she saw affection shining in his eyes. "Thank you, Jimmy, but actually, Toby Madeer was in last week asking for ginseng. He lost his wife over the summer and he's still in a bad way. I think he could grind up this root and use it more than I."

Jimmy stared at her for a few seconds, then something akin to frustration flashed in his eyes. "Whatever you say, Miss Penny."

She smiled. "I'll buy all of these. Did you bring anything else?"

"Some oyster mushrooms," he said, lifting them out of his bag and spreading them on the table.

Penny nodded. "I'll take them. Anything else?"

He scratched his temple. "Got any interest in truffles?"

Penny's eyes went wide. "Truffles? You mean the underground kind?"

He nodded.

"But truffles grow only in the Pacific Northwest and in France."

"And here," Jimmy said with a mischievous smile.

Penny gave a little laugh. "How is that possible?"

Jimmy leaned in closer and lowered his chin. "My granddaddy was a Frenchie and knew something about truffles. He started messing around with growing them when I was just a boy—even if they catch in the ground, it takes ten years or so before they're ready to harvest." He made a rueful noise. "Granddaddy died a few years back, but I've kept watch over the area. Trained my dog Henry to sniff 'em out."

He opened his hand to reveal two dark lumps of what looked like large animal droppings, but their fishy pungency wafted through the air. She had never seen a whole black truffle before—just precious shavings over pasta or baked in puff pastry. She carefully picked up one of the spongy lumps and knew instantly that she was holding gold. "H-how many do you have, Jimmy?"

"Probably a pound or so. And there's more where they came from."

She felt giddy. "Let me make a phone call." As she made her way back to the office, she glanced over to see Marie and Guy both tending to the first customers of the morning. She closed the door to her office, checked her Rolodex, and dialed the number for Ziggy's in New Orleans, her pulse clicking higher. When a woman answered on the second ring, Penny identified herself and asked for Ziggy.

"*Chère,* Penny! How are you?"

"I'm fine, Ziggy. I called to see if you would be interested in homegrown truffles."

"Grown where?" he asked, sounding dubious.

"According to my woodsman, right here in Mojo."

He made a dismissive noise. "That's impossible."

"That's what I thought . . . until he showed them to me. It's possible to grow them commercially, right?"

"Yes, but the conditions have to be perfect, and even then it's iffy. Are you sure they aren't morels?"

She held up the truffle between forefinger and

thumb. “I’ve only seen pictures, but they look like the real thing to me, Ziggy.”

“What color?”

“Black.”

He was silent for several seconds, but Penny could hear the wheels turning in his head . . . or maybe it was his saliva glands pumping. “How much of these homegrown truffles does your man have to sell?”

“A pound.”

“*Bon Dieu.* Is he trustworthy? People have been known to dye cheap Chinese truffles and try to pass them off as authentic black ones.”

“That’s not how this guy works,” Penny said. “But if you’re not interested, I’ll call someone else—”

“Okay, okay.” He sighed dramatically. “I’ll come up and take a look at these so-called truffles. What time do you close?”

“Six P.M.”

“I’ll be there just before six.”

She frowned. “Won’t that cut it close for you getting back for the dinner hour?”

“There’s a water line break on our street—it’s chaos here and we can’t open tonight. The city is trying to put me out of business!” Ziggy cleared his throat delicately. “And Penny . . . just in case there is some truth to these homegrown truffles, let’s keep this between you and me and your woodsman, shall we?”

She smirked. “For now, Ziggy. But I can’t make any long-term promises.”

He grunted and hung up.

Penny laughed, then hurried back to Jimmy, who stared warily at the activity around him. The man was antisocial and a bit of a conspiracy theorist. She leaned in and whispered, "Jimmy, I have someone coming from the city to look at the truffles. Do you trust me enough to leave them with me?"

He withdrew a bulging cheesecloth sack and handed it to her. "I trust you."

She smiled. "I'll check the Internet for market prices and get you the best deal I can."

He nodded. "Thank you kindly."

"Meanwhile, I'll pay you for the other items." She weighed the ginseng and oyster mushrooms and jotted figures in a notebook.

Two more customers had arrived, including Steve Chasen, a clean-cut guy in his twenties who worked as a paralegal in Deke's office and who dropped in occasionally to get a fruit smoothie. Penny didn't completely trust the man, and from the probing nature of his questions, she'd sometimes wondered if Deke had sent him to spy on her . . . although admittedly, that could have been a manifestation of her fantasy that Deke cared what she did.

She also suspected that Steve had a crush on Marie, although the young woman seemed to have nothing but disdain for the man who looked as if he'd been scrubbed with a brush and spit-shined. Steve waved, and Penny smiled hello. Voices buzzed, and the smoothie machine whirred busily in the background.

"Um, Miss Penny, I was wondering . . ."

She looked up. "Yes, Jimmy?"

"Want to go out with me sometime?"

Suddenly the room fell dead quiet—conversation halted, the smoothie machine stopped, and in a moment of what could only be described as unfortunate timing, the sounds of the nature CD on the overhead speakers played crickets chirping. Penny glanced around, and everyone stared at her, wide-eyed, mouths twitching. Heat scalded her neck as she cast around for a polite way to turn down the man's pass.

"I'm very flattered, Jimmy, but I'd rather keep our relationship professional."

"Oh." His shoulders fell.

She gave him a cajoling smile. "What would I do if I lost one of my best suppliers?"

He seemed unconvinced of her sincerity, but he didn't argue.

"Um, Guy," she said quickly, tearing the sheet of paper from the notebook, "would you cut a check for Jimmy, please?"

"Sure thing," Guy said, although he and Jimmy moved around each other like repelling magnets as they made their way toward Guy's cubicle inside the stockroom.

Penny carried the bag of truffles to her office and glanced around for a secure place to store them. Her gaze dropped to the locked bottom desk drawer, but she quickly dismissed it as a temporary stash. The drawer, after all, was her survival kit behind glass—to be breached only in an emergency.

Instead she located a lockable file cabinet drawer that was half empty. Penny opened the bag in her hand and stared at the dozens of valuable little lumps of fungus that sent chefs around the world into fits of orgasmic pleasure. She tucked the bag into the drawer, then slid it back into place and locked it.

When she emerged, she saw that Jimmy and Guy were still in his office. She waited on a mousy woman dressed in running clothes who was a regular customer, but whose name always slipped Penny's mind. After the woman purchased a box of energy bars and left, Penny turned to Marie, who was studiously ignoring Steve Chasen while he finished his smoothie. "Why can't I remember that woman's name?"

"It's Diane," Steve offered. "Diane Davidson."

Penny nodded. "Oh, right. She's a teacher at the high school."

Marie leaned on the counter. "*Was* a teacher—I heard she was fired."

"Yeah," Steve said thickly, then swallowed. "For being a witch."

Marie rolled her eyes. "She's Wiccan—that doesn't mean she's a practicing witch. And even if she is, that's religious discrimination."

"She wanted Deke to file a lawsuit against the school system for wrongful dismissal," Steve said, "but he didn't take the case."

Penny straightened, loathe to discuss anything having to do with Deke.

But Marie had no such qualms. "Why not?"

"I don't think—" Penny began.

"Deke said he was afraid of her," Steve said, his voice low and expressive.

Penny frowned. Deke was the least superstitious person she knew.

Marie put her hand to her mouth. "I asked her to stop by the party tonight—I hope that's alright."

Penny shrugged. "I don't mind, although I don't know her very well."

Marie looked embarrassed. "There weren't a lot of people to invite."

Penny's skin tingled with humiliation. Deke had

gotten most of their friends. Deke and Sheena. The more she said their names together, the more it sounded like the title of a redneck Tarzan movie.

"Kirk was going to fly in for the festival and the party," Marie said, "but he was called to Canada on business at the last minute."

Of course he was, Penny thought wryly.

"Who's Kirk?" Steve asked.

"My rich, older boyfriend," Marie said emphatically.

Steve's mouth turned down. "Oh. What party?"

"We're having a divorce party for Penny tonight at Caskey's," Marie said, then picked a piece of lint off her apron. "You can come if you want."

Steve straightened. "Really? Okay."

"Bring a gag gift," Marie said.

"That's not necessary," Penny said with a frown. She considered calling her friend Liz in New Orleans and inviting her, but something stopped her . . . embarrassment maybe. Despite their proximity, she hadn't seen her friend in ages—Liz didn't even know that Penny had used her divorce attorney. Liz had gone to school with her and Deke and had never approved of Penny's being with Deke. Since the breakup, Penny had wondered if Deke had cheated on her in college and Liz had known about it. That would explain a lot. . . .

Marie nudged Penny playfully. "Want me to invite Mountain Man?"

Penny looked over her shoulder in the direction of Jimmy and Guy, then looked back to Marie. "I don't think that would be a good idea."

Marie angled her head. "He might not be too bad if he had a bath."

Penny ignored the others' chuckles, then retrieved three pieces of mail for the museum that had been misdelivered. "I think I'll drop off Hazel's mail."

"Good excuse to leave," Marie murmured.

"Hey, Penny," Steve said as she was leaving. "What do you think about the color Deke's having the house painted?"

His eyes seemed cool, almost mocking. Again Penny was assailed by the feeling that she didn't trust him. And the thought that Steve would report to her ex-husband that her best prospect for a postdivorce affair was with a man who could find water with a forked stick made her shrivel inside. But Penny managed to feign a look of disinterest. "Is he painting the house? I hadn't noticed."

Marie gave her an approving smile. Penny turned and strode to the front door of the store and out, underneath the hood-shaped red canopy that welcomed customers to The Charm Farm, and into the small parking lot in the breezy sunshine. It was a perfect fall day—blue sky, drifting white clouds that made one want to look for animal shapes, and just a hint of crispness to the air.

In the parking lot sat Marie's red bicycle with its wire basket, leaning benignly on its kickstand. Locks were unnecessary in Mojo. Steve Chasen's white BMW sat next to Guy's impeccable black Lexus and Jimmy's battered blue Chevy pickup. Jimmy's bloodhound, Henry—the mighty truffle hunter—stood up on his hind legs in the bed of the truck, whining for attention. Penny walked over and scratched his elephantine ears. He closed his eyes, and one leg started to jerk spasmodically. Penny laughed; maybe she should get a pet. Deke had a bizarre aversion to animals—she'd bet it had something to do with having Mona the Stone for a mother. Remembering her errand, she gave the dog a final pat.

In the distance to her left, the steeply pitched roof of the hulking three-story Archambault mansion that housed the Instruments of Death and Voodoo Museum was barely visible through the trees. Penny checked her watch—ten minutes before eleven. Hazel Means, the manager of the museum, wouldn't be in yet, so Penny would just drop the mail through the door chute. Hazel wouldn't have time to chat anyway, not with readying the museum for tourists, the number of which would balloon for the weeklong festival and remain steady through Halloween.

Which would, in turn, be good for her own business.

The house that she had renovated for The Charm Farm faced east, toward downtown Mojo, with her former house to the right, facing the side of her business. She held off looking at it, instead staring out over the small town where she'd lived for the past eight years. Nestled in a little bowl the size of six city blocks by six city blocks, Mojo was the perfect town for a Disney movie . . . or a horror flick.

Once populated by families with long, peculiar lineages (like Deke's), the brick-sidewalk community with matching streetlights and little nylon banners that changed with the seasons (and now heralded the festival) had been gentrified by New Orleans upper-class, double-income couples who gladly traded the thirty-minute commute for safer, smaller classrooms for their children and safer, larger homes for themselves. Vintage houses in town had been gobbled up, sending property values skyrocketing and displacing locals who could no longer afford the taxes. Storerooms and attics over businesses had been turned into pricey apartments.

The one-bedroom hovel she leased over Benny's Beignet shop in the center of town three blocks away was easy to spot because of the giant spinning brownish square speckled with white paint that was supposed to resemble a beignet—a gob of fried dough sprinkled with powdered sugar . . . a French doughnut. She lifted her sleeve for a sniff and grimaced—the sickeningly sweet scent had permeated the rugs and the curtains of her apartment, and now her clothing. Even if someday doughnuts were miraculously declared to be healthy, she would never eat another one the rest of her life.

The rest of her life. The phrase sounded so benign, but the rest of her life was going to be so different now, she thought with a twinge of sentimentality. Deke . . .

A sudden gust of cold wind blew over her, raising a chill. Penny hugged herself and lifted her gaze to the new subdivisions carved into the hills around Mojo proper. The palatial, modern homes stared down at her and the town like predators with huge glass eyes. Even in the daylight, the creepy feeling of being watched was inescapable.

Penny inhaled deeply to calm her frayed nerves with clean, pumpkin-scented air, but instead she got a head full of paint fumes. Unable to deny her curiosity any longer, Penny pivoted to her right and gasped at the sight of her beloved home, now almost completely covered in the dreadful pink color, like the stomach being coated in the Pepto-Bismol commercial. She covered her mouth with her hand to smother the choking noise that erupted from her throat. Unbidden, tears sprang to her eyes.

"Ain't it something?"

Penny blinked. Her feet had carried her to the sidewalk on their own volition. And to her horror, Sheena Linder stood across the narrow two-lane road, dressed in tight jeans and a tighter sweater, sporting a white neck brace and smirking at Penny behind enormous gold sunglasses.

Penny's tongue lodged against the roof of her mouth. She'd seen the woman come and go from the tanning salon on the square, but the last time she'd seen her face-to-face (so to speak) had been when Penny had caught her having sex with Deke. She'd relived that scene a thousand times, wishing she had done or said something so profound that both of them would have begged for forgiveness—or at least disengaged from each other. Instead, they had paused to stare at her stupidly only long enough to curse before resuming their slapping, heaving screw. She had heard them climax as she had stumbled out into the hall, their squeals and moans mingling to create a noise as unnerving and unforgettable as the screech of a computer connecting to a modem. It was the single most degrading moment of her life.

During the divorce, Penny had somehow managed to avoid the woman's company, although she had secretly fantasized about writing something nasty on the windows of the Forever Sun tanning salon or running into Sheena at the grocery store and saying something wicked and clever over the public address system.

But whatever clever words she had dreamed up escaped her now as the woman looked both ways and teetered across the street on hooker high heels. Penny could not have been more terrified if a car had been careening toward her. Her feet were rooted to the spot as she estimated the distance back to the front door of her store. And yet some small, realistic part of her knew she was going to have to deal with the woman sooner or later.

Although later was definitely more appealing.

Traffic literally stopped for the curvaceous woman as she crossed the two lanes. Catcalls ensued as Sheena beamed and waved at the male drivers in both directions, stroking the brace around her neck, managing to look sexy and sympathetic at the same time. Penny watched in stupefied awe, taking a couple of steps backward as Sheena joined her on the sidewalk. The woman's skin was the color of a scorched sweet potato, her hair platinum blond. Next to Sheena's trendy, tight clothing, Penny felt like a plain, pale pioneer woman in her wrinkled denim overalls, flat, chunky-heeled sandals, and long-sleeve hemp shirt.

"I wanted to see the house from over here while the painters were taking a break," Sheena said with a toss of her head. Indeed, the workers and the van were gone. She peeled off the sunglasses, stared at the house, and sighed. "It's perfect."

Penny straightened. "Pardon me, I was just leaving."

"You don't like it?" Sheena asked with an innocent smile.

Penny set her jaw. "It's none of my concern. It's Deke's house."

"And mine, soon enough," Sheena said, holding out her left hand. On her ring finger, a huge, dazzling diamond nearly lasered Penny's corneas. "I thought you should know that Deke and I are getting married." She grinned, meanly. "No hard feelin's."

Hurt and rage rose in Penny's chest like a tide, overwhelming her. Scenes from the past several months swam in her brain—the betrayal, the heartbreak, the attorneys, the arguments, the upheaval, the loneliness, the VD tests. She had found Deke's fumbling foreplay amusing, his back hair endearing. She had loved him despite his faults, yet he had exposed her to ridicule and speculation. The mail in her left hand rattled as her arm began to shake. It was one thing to bear the humiliation of her husband's kicking her to the curb for this . . . this . . . this *cliché*, but having to endure the woman coming over to her side of the street to rub it in was simply too much.

Something dark and sinister came over Penny, filling her with vengeance. She put her hand on Sheena's bulbous chest and shoved her hard, off the sidewalk and in front of oncoming traffic.

4

A liberal dose of theatrics . . .

In slow motion, Sheena clawed at the air as she stumbled backward, her kohl-lined eyes wide with fear when she realized she was going down on asphalt. On the sidewalk, Penny stood frozen, part of her unable to believe that she'd just pushed the woman, part of her morbidly fascinated as she watched the action unfold. A dark SUV was barreling down Charm Street toward Sheena. The driver held a cell phone to his ear and hadn't yet noticed the woman flailing in the street. From the other direction came a station wagon, but it slowed: The driver seemed to be distracted by the horrid pink house.

Alarm overrode self-preservation, propelling Penny into the street. She dove and tackled Sheena, then rolled them both to the center line and braced to be struck and torn into a dozen bloody parts. She hadn't planned to die in the arms of her husband's girlfriend. Their joint demise would spark scandal . . . headlines . . . folk songs.

Tires squealed and horns blasted the air, although Penny could barely hear over Sheena screaming in her ear. She was lying underneath the woman, pinned by Sheena's pendulous breasts, unable to breathe. Her body sang with pain, especially where the mini binoculars in her pocket bit into her hip, but slowly Penny realized that they hadn't been pulverized. She opened her eyes, squinting into the sun.

"Holy freak, are you ladies okay?" A wide-eyed teenager leaned out of the driver's side window of the SUV. He still held his cell phone to his ear. "Dude," he yelled into the mouthpiece, "I nearly mowed down two lesbians!" Then he moved the phone away from his mouth. "Seriously, are you two okay?"

"Get off me!" Sheena screeched at Penny.

"You're on *me*," Penny muttered, pushing to free herself.

Sheena flopped onto her back, her white neck brace and hair a stunning contrast against the dark asphalt. She looked dazed, and she'd lost a high-heeled shoe, but otherwise, she seemed fine. Well, other than the mad-as-hell part.

"I could have been killed!"

The teenager gave a dry laugh and pointed to Penny. "Yeah, she saved your life, lady. I would've splattered you for sure if she hadn't knocked you out of the way."

"Me, too," shouted the lady driving the station wagon. "That woman is a hero." Sporadic applause and cheers burst out from drivers who had rolled down their windows.

Penny pushed up on her elbows, looked at where the young man's SUV had finally come to a stop, and swallowed hard. Sheena's sunglasses lay in a thousand pieces behind one of the big tires. He *would* have splattered Sheena if she hadn't decided to act.

Of course, if she hadn't pushed Sheena, she wouldn't have had to save her.

Penny clambered to her feet and brushed herself off, feeling shaky at the close encounter with death, and guilty that she was being heralded a hero. She reached down, grasped Sheena by the arm, and, with considerable effort, pulled the stunned woman to her feet. As soon as Sheena was standing, she slapped at Penny's hands like a windmill.

"Get away from me, you lunatic!"

Penny shrank back, turned to give the teenager a wobbly smile, and called, "We're fine here. Thanks." He pulled away and other cars followed slowly, staring at Penny and Sheena standing on the center line. The pieces of mail that Penny had held flapped on the ground like wounded birds. She glanced toward The Charm Farm and saw Jimmy Scaggs jogging toward them.

Great.

"Let's get out of the street, Sheena."

"Where is my shoe?" Sheena bellowed, hobbling in one high heel.

"It's over there," Penny said, pointing to the curb in front of her former house, avoiding curious stares from drivers, growing more frantic by the minute. She had almost *killed* the woman—no matter what sins Sheena had committed, she didn't deserve to die. Penny gulped air. What had she been thinking? Shaking noticeably, Penny touched Sheena's elbow. "I'm sorry. Come on, I'll help you across."

Sheena swatted at Penny again, her face mottled as she limped ahead, stopping cars with a mere lift of her hand. "Don't *touch* me. I told Deke you were going to blow, but he swore to me that you were a doormat."

Penny recoiled as if she'd been slapped. She stumbled, then stepped up on the curb beside Sheena, mere feet from what used to be her own driveway. That crack in the concrete—she had pulled weeds out of that crack more times than she could count. "Excuse me?"

Sheena glared, then leaned over to scoop up her shoe. "You've got Deke snowed—he thinks you're a meek little mouse without the backbone or the brains to retaliate." She shook the shoe, wielding the stiletto like a blade. "You jealous little *bitch*—you can't stand the thought of me marrying Deke, so you tried to kill me!" She shoved her face close to Penny's. "You're going to pay, Granola Girl."

Penny's body flamed with humiliation, both at the knowledge that Deke so thoroughly ridiculed her behind her back, and at the woman's vicious tone.

"Is everything alright, Miss Penny?" Jimmy asked as he loped up next to them.

Penny turned, floundering for words. "F-fine, Jimmy. There was a little accident, but everything's under control."

"Accident, my ass," Sheena said with a snort. "Did you see her push me in front of those cars?"

Jimmy narrowed his eyes at Sheena, then spat on the ground. "No. I didn't see a thing."

But when he looked at Penny, she had the feeling that he was lying to protect her. "Jimmy," Penny said calmly, "please . . . leave us."

He frowned, but nodded and waited until two cars went by before crossing the street, thankfully distracted by Henry, who had escaped from the truck bed and looked as if he might run after Jimmy. Penny turned back to Sheena, fighting desperation. "Sheena,

I'm sorry. I was angry, but I didn't mean for you to get hurt."

"Right." Sheena lifted her dirty foot—did the woman ever wash her feet?—and shoved it into her shoe. "I'm calling Chief Davis to have you arrested for assault."

Penny's stomach bottomed out. Jail . . . prison. So after a lifetime of scrupulous behavior, she had finally succumbed to her family destiny. All of her well-kept secrets would be revealed. . . . Deke would be extra glad he'd left. . . .

"It'll be my word against yours," Penny said on an exhale.

"Not when you fail a polygraph."

Penny felt the blood drain from her face.

The blond looked triumphant. "Then I'll file a civil suit for every piddly dime that Deke let you keep!"

Penny's throat constricted. Not only had she pushed a woman in front of a car but she'd also pushed a woman *who would sue her own mother* in front of a car.

Sheena adjusted her neck brace with a savage twist. "You attacked an injured woman—a jury will give me anything I want." She emitted a harsh laugh. "Just wait until Deke hears about this."

Penny's mind raced. God help her, the thought of Deke and everyone in town believing that she was so jealous that she would try to kill his mistress made her ill. She could lose her freedom, her business . . . not to mention what was left of her tattered pride. Sweat beaded on her hairline. But what could she do? She was guilty, and she had nothing to bargain with, no way to convince Sheena to keep quiet.

Then a memory chord stirred. Or did she?

Penny pulled herself up and summoned strength while giving Sheena her most level stare. "Speaking of Deke, wait until he hears about your visitor this morning."

At the stiffening of the woman's spine and the panicked look in her eyes, relief zigzagged through Penny's chest—leverage. *Thank you, God.*

"What visitor?" Sheena asked lightly.

"You know—tall, dark, and handsome, brown leather jacket. Driving a green sedan. I assume you were good friends since you answered the door in your nightgown." Penny angled her head. "Oh, and you weren't wearing your neck brace then."

Sheena's jaw dropped. "You were *spying* on me?"

"I, um, just happened to be looking out the window."

Sheena's red mouth tightened, and Penny steeled herself for a verbal onslaught. Then magically, Sheena's mouth curled into a repentant smile.

"Maybe I overreacted just a tad." She emitted a hollow little laugh as she smoothed her hand over her stiff platinum hair. "After all, no one was hurt when you accidentally stumbled and pushed me off the sidewalk." Sheena studied her nails. "So maybe I'll just forget this little episode happened . . . if you forget that I had a visitor this morning."

Entering into a pact with the woman sent a finger of unease up Penny's spine, but she had no choice. "Agreed."

Then Sheena's eyes narrowed. "Just so that we're clear—this doesn't mean that you and I are friends, Granola Girl."

Penny nodded. "Clear."

"And spying on me is really pathetic," Sheena added. "You need to get a life."

Penny's mouth watered with the words *You got my life,* but she swallowed them.

Sheena turned on her high heels and marched toward the pink house, her full hips swaying. Penny watched her go, flooded with relief but fighting an undertow of frustration and sudden, mounting fear.

Not fear of Sheena Linder but fear of herself, of what she was capable of. Deke's description of her timidity wasn't flattering, but it was more true than not, she admitted. Growing up in a family of hell-raisers, she had learned that the best way to escape notice was to fly below the radar. She was generally the kind of person who lived her life and let other people live their lives, because she'd learned that sticking her neck out usually led to messy situations . . . like confronting Sheena Linder about the dangers of her tanning beds.

The woman still had her tanning beds—and now had Penny's husband to boot.

But pushing Sheena in front of a car . . . that was more than sticking her neck out. That was submitting to dark impulses that she entertained only in the wee hours of the morning. . . .

A horn blasted, stealing her breath. Penny jerked her head around to see that Lou's painting van had returned and she was blocking the driveway. She was being honked like a stranger out of the driveway that used to be hers. She stepped aside, then looked down as one of the envelopes that she had been going to take to the museum blew across her sandal. She spotted the other two pieces of mail just off the sidewalk, dirty and damp. She picked them up as she made her way back to her side of Charm Street, her pulse thudding in her ears as realization bled through her about how differently the pushing incident could have ended, and how a person's life could be forever changed by one impulsive decision.

This time she'd been lucky.

"Excuse me, Red."

Penny startled from her musings and turned her head, then nearly swallowed her tongue. Sheena's mystery man sat in his faded green car with the window rolled down, his head and one arm leaning out. Now that she was in a position to get a good look at his face, she immediately identified his relationship with Sheena: lover. He was breathtakingly handsome, with a darkened, chiseled jaw and glittering black eyes that hinted at danger despite the fact that he was smiling. No one had called her "Red" since grade school. Ridiculously, she shoved a strand of unruly hair behind her ear, thinking she must look frightful after rolling around in the street.

"Y-yes?" she managed, darting a nervous glance toward the pink house. If Sheena was watching, the woman might think she was gathering information to take to Deke.

He angled his head in a way that made her think he was used to getting what he wanted out of people—women, in particular, she guessed. "I was wondering if you could recommend a decent motel." His smooth Cajun cadence made him sound as if his jaw was double-jointed.

So, whatever Sheena said hadn't scared him away—apparently he was settling in . . . with plans to harass

Sheena? Penny wet her lips and stared at the long, blunted fingers of his hand draped casually next to the side mirror. A man's hands always fascinated her, and she liked the look of his—powerful . . . capable . . . ringless. Sexual awareness sprang to life in her midsection and she wondered crazily if Marie's love potion had something to do with her bizarre reaction to this stranger, or perhaps her body was playing tricks on her because she already had him so firmly entrenched in her mind as a playboy.

"It doesn't have to be fancy," he added with a wink, "but clean sheets and a firm mattress would be nice."

Her mind spun off into wild tangents, conjuring up visions of him tangled in clean sheets and performing erotic gymnastics on a firm mattress. She could feel the heat climbing her cheeks and the amused look on his face told her that he'd noticed her blush. Giving herself a mental shake, she tried desperately to be composed and act as if she were immune to the libidinous vibe he emitted.

"Try the Browning Motel," she said, pointing in the opposite direction of downtown Mojo. "Stay on Charm Street, go past the interstate, and it's on the left."

He nodded curtly and gave her a savagely sexy grin. "Much obliged." Then he pulled away from the curb, although she caught his reflection as he drove away when he glanced at her in his side mirror.

Penny tingled like a teenager over the chance encounter. The man had no idea that she knew of his connection to Sheena. Worse, *because* of his connection to her ex-husband's girlfriend, she should have been repulsed by him . . . instead of standing there feeling as if her fuse had just been lit. Pushing aside her uncharacteristically wayward thoughts, she puffed her cheeks out in a cleansing exhale and turned her mind to something much less hazardous: delivering Hazel's mail.

Instead of walking along the sidewalk past her store to the corner and down a half-block to the locked museum entrance, she retraced her steps to The Charm Farm parking lot, turning left past the tiny herb garden, to the new area that had been staked off for her planned expansion. She could take a few enjoyable minutes to imagine what the new garden would look like, then cut through the rusted opening in the iron fence along the tree line that separated her property from the property on which the museum sat.

Penny surveyed the area with pride and anticipation. She'd marked the boundaries herself with limber wire stakes topped with pink plastic flags. The flags danced in the wind, waving happily. The staked-off area, about a half acre, was covered in thick underbrush, thorny blackberry bushes, and waist-high weeds. Deke had sworn the soil underneath was rocky, clay-filled, and useless, but she was determined to make it work. He'd also warned her that the zoning commission would never allow a garden to be planted, but she'd learned a little while working in Deke's office. She knew how to decipher city ordinances . . . and to find loopholes that even her ex-mother-in-law the mayor couldn't deny. When the land next to her had been rezoned to mixed use to allow the museum to open, the land that Deke's father had given him had been zoned for mixed use as well, which meant that gardens and buildings were supposed to peacefully coexist.

She picked up a long stick and made her way through the brush, keeping an eye out for copperheads, which, Deke had warned, nested in the thicket. They would be slow-moving in the lower temperatures but deadly nonetheless. At the edge of her property there was a shoulder-high cast-iron fence, which was almost completely obscured by vines and heavy foliage. She had found the break in the fence when she had staked off the garden. There was an opening in the barbed hawthorne trees just large enough to squeeze through to the other side. It was her little secret, a shortcut to visit or just to study the house that had morbidly fascinated her ever since she'd moved to Mojo. It seemed like fate that she had wound up owning the property adjacent to the museum.

Part Victorian, part Tudor, part Gothic, the massive house was slate blue and dreary gray and faded black in various places, the kind of house that Penny imagined in the story of Hansel and Gretel. Surrounded by a tangle of trees and vines, the mansion was spooky enough to fuel all kinds of musings about secret passageways and hidden dungeons and, considering the rumored history of the Archambault family, the perfect setting for the Instruments of Death and Voodoo Museum.

From the back, the mansion was a peculiar-looking structure. Over the years, owners had built onto the monstrosity, uncaring about the appearance from the rear since it was seldom seen, leaving it with jutting, uneven roof lines, mismatched windows, and hodgepodge siding. Protruding off the back was a large garage for the three employees—Hazel and her mentally deficient son, Tilton, who did odd jobs around the museum and drove an old hearse for his occasional freelance work with the town's two funeral homes; and Troy Archambault, the last remaining Archambault, a dermatologist who lived in New Orleans and oversaw the museum's trust, stopping in occasionally to check on his family landmark. Alongside the almost medieval house, the contemporary garage, with its driveway and gate exiting to a side street, seemed an unfortunate but necessary appendage, like a colostomy bag.

A few feet inside the breached fence, among fallen leaves, she located stepping stones that were nearly hidden from years of leveling into loamy ground. The air was quiet here, except for the creak of ancient, ropy vines and the whisper of leaves overhead, which sent ghostly voices swirling around her. A cold chill skated over her arms. She might have been the only person in the vicinity, but she had the unearthly feeling that there were many souls about.

She attributed the sensation to the spooky lore surrounding the Archambault family—that old Dr. Archambault, Troy's great-grandfather, had conducted bizarre experiments on transients and anyone who needed extra cash . . . and that some reportedly never left the house to spend their hard-earned money. At least those were the stories that Hazel Means embellished for tourists who paid six dollars for the forty-minute tour, and the tales were fodder for local gossip at Caskey's bar when a homeless person disappeared, although migration to the city was the far more likely scenario.

The phantom moans continued as she stepped onto the footpath that ran along the side of the house and followed it to the crooked stone walkway that meandered in front.

The Instruments of Death and Voodoo Museum had become quite the attraction since it had been added to an interstate sign a couple of years ago (Troy's brainchild). Dark and hulking and surrounded by the same shoulder-high, iron fence that she had slipped through, the structure resembled every haunted manor in every classic horror movie. The many additions over the decades had left it looking like an architectural experiment gone wrong, with accidental arches, railed walkways, mismatched gargoyles, landings that went nowhere, and occasional stained-glass windows. The asymmetrical structure was topped with various turrets and finials and a cupola worthy of Rapunzel, except for the fact that bats had taken up residence in its ceiling and could be seen flapping around at dusk. The tourists loved it.

In honor of the festival, a large sign had been posted near the steps announcing when voodoo rituals would take place in the main parlor—harmless fun and child friendly in comparison to the more serious rituals that would take place in a specially constructed *peristil*, a shelter of sorts, in the town square. For a week at least, the town would be steeped in voodoo.

A noise startled Penny. A man dressed in a dark business suit emerged from a set of stone steps that appeared to lead to the museum's basement, which housed, if she remembered correctly, the tools of torture display, like the chair of nails and the human stretching machine, complete with a sound track of inhuman screams.

The man mopped at his forehead with a handkerchief, his gaze down, his movements jerky. Penny blinked in astonishment. "Deke?"

5

A spoonful of surprise . . .

Deke lifted his head, and surprise replaced the worry lines on his forehead. "Penny . . . hi."

Emotions stabbed at her. She hadn't seen him since the divorce papers had been finalized at a brief courthouse meeting with little eye contact. He looked lean and artificially tanned and, thanks to the hair transplant, much the way he had looked in college when they had fallen in love ten years ago. But the laid-back, smiling young man who had convinced her to sneak him into her dorm room on hot, steamy nights was long gone. These days he seemed alternately anxious and arrogant. Instead of his usual slacks and sport coat, his suit had a European cut and the tie, a funky, trendy print. His business must have picked up, she thought wryly . . . or maybe Sheena's many personal injury settlements were providing extra cash flow for the designer duds.

By comparison, she felt ugly and awkward in her overalls and wet sandals, silently wishing she'd taken the time this morning to smooth a flatiron over her curls and put on a little mascara. Feeling self-conscious under his gaze, she gestured to the building behind them. "What are you doing here?"

"Business," he said abruptly, tucking a blue folder under his arm.

She knew that the museum kept him on retainer, but she couldn't resist a jab. "Let me guess—Sheena took a tour and is suing for mental anguish?"

"Jealousy isn't becoming to you, Penny."

A flush ran up her neck, spreading over her face. She had asked for that one.

He turned to walk away, and she shook her stick at his back in mute frustration, then followed him, blurting out what was really on her mind. "Did you have to paint the house pink, for God's sake?"

His shoulders drooped. "That damned *house*." He turned to face her, suddenly looking tired. "It's my house now, remember? I wanted the rental property, but you wouldn't budge. Besides, the color isn't that bad."

"Are you smoking crack? The color is revolting."

"It's what she wants."

He sounded so protective that a lump formed in Penny's throat. *What about what I want?*

Then Deke glanced at the padlocked front gate and back to her. "How did you get in here?"

She squirmed. "I found an opening in the fence when I staked off the garden."

He rolled his eyes. "Not the garden again." He pinched the bridge of his nose. "Look, I have to warn you—Mother is rallying the city council for a zone restriction. She said a garden in the downtown area will look out of place and will attract rodents."

Penny frowned. "Can she do that?"

"You know Mother."

Penny set her jaw, then swallowed her pride. "Deke, can't you help me out here? I'm trying to grow my business."

He shook his head, as if the matter was inconsequential. "Sorry, I tried to tell you the idea wouldn't fly."

Her throat closed, and she averted her eyes lest he see how his casual dismissal—again—hurt her.

"Anyway," he admonished, "you shouldn't be snooping around over here. The back gate was vandalized last week. Chief Davis added an extra patrol, and I'd hate to have to bail your bony ass out of jail for trespassing."

Anger pinged through her chest. "I wasn't snooping. I was dropping off mail that landed in my box by mistake." She held it up, and the tire imprints across the envelopes reminded her of the incident with Sheena and how close she'd come to having to call Deke to bail her bony ass out of jail for murdering his fat-ass hussy.

Folding the letters into her hand, she forced a smile. "I understand congratulations are in order."

His eyebrows shot up. "Congratulations?"

"I, um, ran into Sheena. She told me that the two of you are going to be married."

"She did, did she?" He gave her a pitying look. "You're going to have to get used to the idea of me being with another woman, Penny."

She gritted her teeth at his conceit, but the thought that Sheena might already be fooling around on Deke flashed through her mind. Deke was going to get his . . . eventually. She leaned forward, invading his personal space and catching a whiff of noxious cologne. "I was trying to be nice, but forget it. By the way, I'm having a party at Caskey's tonight to celebrate our divorce. I'm over you, Deke." She wheeled and walked toward the front entrance of the museum.

"Penny!" he called.

She had one foot on the bottom step, but something in his voice made her turn around.

"You were too good for me," he said, his expression suspiciously sincere.

His words were nirvana to her ears, the closest he'd come to saying that he was sorry for the way he'd behaved, for the misery he'd put her through. For a split second, something in his eyes reminded her of the old Deke, the Deke she'd quizzed for exams while he'd been in law school, the Deke who had defied his mother's plans for a big wedding in favor of the private ceremony that Penny had wanted, the Deke who had promised to find a way to buy and help her renovate the Victorian house on Charm Street that she adored. Penny's throat tightened in profound sadness for what he'd thrown away as carelessly as a toy that had fallen out of favor. She opened her mouth to respond, but he had turned on his heel and was striding away from her.

"No, I wasn't," she whispered to his retreating back, acknowledging that as hurt and humiliated as she'd been by their breakup, some very small part of her was relieved that she no longer had to feel guilty about the secrets she'd kept from Deke during their marriage. She inhaled a cleansing breath and realized suddenly that she was looking forward to the divorce party

Marie was throwing tonight in her honor. What had Marie said it would be—liberating?

God, she hoped so.

She turned back to the museum and was seized by a sudden bout of vertigo as she stood at the bottom of the steep flagstone stairs, the gloomy house towering over her. A low, moaning sound floated on the wind, seeming to come from the house itself. For the span of two heartbeats, she was paralyzed with the crazy sensation that the house was alive and might consume her. Her pulse echoed in her head, while her gaze bounced around. She took a half-step backward, leaning on the stick she held to keep from falling. The moaning sounded again, but just when she was ready to bolt, she looked up and saw a large tree branch rubbing against an eave, scraping paint and making the noise that had spooked her.

Feeling foolish, she laughed at herself and climbed the steps, crossed the creaky porch boards, and stood before the ten-foot-tall wooden door stained blood red—another of Hazel's wild tales, that the door had been stained crimson with blood from tortured victims. Penny lifted the brass mail chute in the door and dropped the envelopes through.

From the rear of the house came the sound of a sports car leaving in a big hurry—Deke, driving like a teenager in his penis-extending red convertible. Penny walked back down the steps, replaying what he'd said just before he'd left, wondering why she was still willing to give him the benefit of the doubt, why she wanted to believe that he harbored some amount of remorse for what he'd put her through: Because she wanted not to doubt her judgment for falling for him in the first place, or because she was so starved for love that she was willing to accept crumbs?

A movement in the window on the third floor of the museum caught her eye, sending a zing of alarm through her chest. Was it a flash of a cape? A curtain? She had assumed that the house was empty, that Deke had simply dropped by to pick up a file, but perhaps he'd been meeting with someone. Or maybe Hazel had arrived early to clean and had heard Penny and Deke talking. Penny stared at the window but saw nothing; she dismissed it as sun glare . . . or her overactive imagination. Still, she couldn't shake the feeling that she was being watched as she trespassed her way back to the opening in the fence and across the tangled field next to her shop.

She tossed down the impromptu walking stick, then spotted a police car on Charm Street turning onto Voodoo Street—Chief Allyson Davis, no doubt, cruising for troublemakers like Penny, according to Deke. As if the woman had anything better to do. The only crime in Mojo was the occasional bar fight at Caskey's and misdemeanor mischief like the recent break-in at Primo Dry Cleaners during which a roll of quarters had gone missing.

The Charm Farm parking lot was full of cars, so Penny picked up the pace to give Marie and Guy a hand. Yet at the corner of the lot, Penny was unable to resist one glance back at the Archambault mansion. From this vantage point, only the turrets and the cupola were visible . . . and a person standing *in* the cupola?

Penny blinked to focus, then pulled out her binoculars, but whatever she thought she'd seen was gone. She shook herself and wondered if Marie had put something in that so-called love potion to make her paranoid.

She wet her lips and acknowledged that she *was* feeling . . . self-aware. Maybe tonight at Caskey's she'd run into a stranger who wasn't *too* strange.

The day passed quickly because business was hopping. The Voodoo Festival brought out three types of people: tourists who wanted to buy souvenirs and have their palms read, the cautious believers who came with cash and hopes of learning black magic tricks, and the hard-core *vodou* crowd who came from New Orleans and beyond to ensure that the festival maintained a level of authenticity. Robes and costumes abounded, along with headwraps, charm pouches, and colorful language—a mixture of English, Cajun, and voodoo speak. The smoothie machine ran constantly, herbs flew off the shelves, and, just as Marie had predicted, several customers asked for voodoo dolls and various bizarre items.

"Do you have tarantulas?"

"Um, no."

"Powdered bones?"

"No."

"Goat blood?"

"No."

"We should start giving classes on voodoo potions and spells," Marie said. "We'd make a killing."

"Please stop saying that," Penny said, bagging a handful of dried nasturtiums. "You're giving me the creeps. Besides, you heard what Jules said—that voodoo isn't for amateurs." She walked over to the smoothie bar and smiled at the next customer. "May I help you?"

The woman nodded. "I'll have the hot voodoo sex."

Penny blinked. "Pardon me?"

Marie leaned in and whispered, "That's what I named the new juice—Hot Voodoo Sex. It's selling like mad."

Penny gave her a withering look, then put a glass under the dispenser and pulled the lever for Marie's love potion. She shook her head at the woman's nonsense, but when some of the yellow juice splashed onto Penny's hand, she licked it off when no one was looking . . . just in case.

Foot traffic had begun to slow just before closing when Ziggy Hines arrived, larger than life, wearing his chef's hat.

"*Chère*, Penny!" he cried, turning on the charm and the accent for the customers. "Ziggy has arrived."

"I see," Penny observed with a smile.

The dimpled, black-haired man walked over and kissed her on both cheeks, then angled his head close to her ear. "Where are the little treasures you told me about?"

"Follow me." She went into her office and closed the door, then unlocked the file cabinet and withdrew the bag of truffles.

"*Mon Dieu*," he muttered when he opened the bag. He lifted a truffle and scrutinized it under the light, then inhaled its pungent odor and rolled his eyes in ecstasy.

Penny laughed. "So do these Mojo truffles pass muster?"

He nodded, then stroked his chin. "I am amazed. Are there more where these came from?"

"So he says."

"How does this man grow them? I must meet him."

"I'm not sure that's a good idea," she said. "He's a very private person." Plus she had the feeling that Ziggy was trying to cut out the middleman—her. She didn't mind, but she would have to talk to Jimmy first.

"Does he use a pig to sniff them out?"

"A dog, actually."

"Ah. Dogs are preferable because they won't eat the truffle when they dig it up, but they are difficult to train." He sighed. "Now . . . how much?"

"Four hundred for the pound."

"Two hundred," he countered.

"Three hundred."

"Two hundred fifty."

"*Three* hundred," Penny repeated firmly. "And you know that's a great price."

"That's a great price for imported *French* black truffles," Ziggy corrected. "We do not yet know what the market will be for Mojo black truffles."

Penny crossed her arms. "Perhaps I should find out."

"Three hundred," he agreed, then removed his wallet with a sigh. "And as many more as he and his wonder-dog can find." He counted out one-hundred-dollar bills into her palm. "And this is our little secret?"

"I can't make any promises on the part of my woodsman."

Ziggy frowned. "Your woodsman had better be quiet for his own safety. The minute the word gets out that he's sitting on black truffles, he will be descended upon."

Penny gave a little laugh. "You're joking."

"No, I'm not. If he and his dog can forage a pound of truffles a day for the season, that's excellent money—especially if he can avoid the tax man."

She nodded solemnly. In an area like Mojo, where jobs were scarce, it was the equivalent of drug money, without the risk of jail time.

Penny led Ziggy back out into the store, and he nodded approvingly at the customers milling around. "I see the festival is bringing in the tourists."

"Yes, it's been very good for business."

His gaze latched onto a couple of fetching young women who were looking through the magazines but glancing at him under their lashes. "Hm. I might find somewhere to get a drink before I return to the city."

"Try Caskey's," Penny said. "It's right on the square." She hesitated, then added, "We're having a little party there tonight if you want to stop by."

His eyebrows went up. "And what are we celebrating?"

Warmth crept up her face. "My divorce."

"Oh? I didn't know. I've talked to Deke a couple of times and he didn't mention it."

Penny blinked. "I remember the two of you meeting here once, but I didn't realize that you . . . were friends."

Ziggy's face reddened. "I was having a little personal problem, and I needed an out-of-town attorney to handle it."

"Oh."

"I'm sorry to hear your marriage didn't work out."

She still didn't know what to say when people told her that. That she was sorry too? That she wished she'd never met Deke Black? That she had lost faith in marriage as an institution and in the idea that she would ever trust someone again? "Thanks."

"I might see you at Caskey's," Ziggy said, then hurried to open the door for the women he'd been ogling.

"I'll lock up," Marie said, then gave Penny a pointed glance. "So you can go home and change into something more . . . festive."

Penny looked down at her overalls and wrinkled shirt, which still bore skid marks from her earlier encounter with the asphalt. "You think?"

"I think."

"I'm not sure I have anything . . . festive."

"Look," Marie said. "Hard."

"Okay," Penny agreed with a sigh. "I'll meet you there in, say, a half hour?"

"Why don't you take a full hour to get ready?" Marie suggested. "Maybe even break out the lipstick."

Penny frowned. "See you there."

After retrieving her coat and waving to Guy, she slipped out the front door and turned right, out of habit. She had reached the sidewalk and stood face-to-face with the house in all of its pink misery before she realized what she'd done. Self-pity washed over her.

Some people were like rubber bands—willing to stretch but eager to snap back into place at the first opportunity.

It was a Freudian slip, she decided, to walk back to her former home just before she celebrated her divorce. Shaken, she abruptly turned and strode toward her apartment over the odorous doughnut store. She scanned the faces of the pedestrians trickling toward the downtown square, hoping no one who knew her had seen her gaffe.

Penny frowned—she had done a lot of things today she hoped no one had seen. And the day wasn't even over yet.

6

A cup of celebration...

The three-block walk to Penny's apartment was typically a quiet, meditative time of the day. But as she neared downtown, the murmur of drumming and chanting rode on the still air. The voodoo rituals were about to begin and would continue on the town square all evening and well into the night. The sharp scent of burning wood stung her nostrils, leading her gaze to the plume of lavender-colored smoke rising in the air, marking the site of a makeshift temple. Her bedroom window would give her a bird's-eye view of the activity and, for once, a good reason to miss sleep.

She threaded her way through the crowds, which became heavier the closer she got to her apartment. Dusk was falling, and as the daylight faded, she could feel a spike in the energy. She was jostled by enthusiastic visitors who danced as they walked, flinging their arms and swaying their hips. Perfume, spices, and perspiration mingled for an erotic aroma. Yet as she rounded the corner, the sickening sugary smell of doughnuts managed to cut through every other odor.

Ugh—she was home.

Benny's Beignet shop was overflowing with bodies, and across the square, Caskey's bar was also enjoying a brisk business, as were the food and drink vendors set up around the perimeter of the square, selling sausage kabobs, crawfish etouffee, spicy pickles, hot peppers, and Creole coffee. In another area, booths draped in multicolored lights offered jewelry and vibrant clothing, voodoo dolls, and thousands of trinkets. Since she had left for work this morning, a covered shelter had been erected to house the voodoo rituals and readings, with a hole in the roof to allow smoke from the ceremonial fire to escape. The structure itself could barely be seen for the crush of bodies vying for a good viewing spot. The energy was contagious, and Penny's pulse synched to the rhythm of the drums, her muscles jumping to the jingle of tambourines, flutes, and rattles.

The door leading to her apartment was next to the door of the beignet shop. She excused and pardoned herself through the crowd, working up a claustrophobic sweat by the time she unlocked the door and closed it behind her. A dim light overhead provided just enough illumination for her to get her bearings. The narrow, steep stairway in front of her disappeared into darkness. She felt for the light switch and flipped it, but the bulb on the landing above popped and fizzled futilely.

Penny groaned in frustration—it was the fifth lightbulb to burn out in a matter of weeks. When she'd complained to Elton, the landlord, he'd said something about a high-voltage pull running through the building, that she needed 130-volt bulbs instead of the standard 120-volt. Which wouldn't be a problem if the local hardware store actually *carried* 130-volt bulbs.

The fine hair on the back of Penny's neck prickled in dread as she slowly climbed the worn steps, which listed slightly to the left. She was being ridiculous, she knew, but since she had moved out of the house that she and Deke had shared, her childhood fear of the dark had returned. It was understandable, she assumed, since she was living alone for the first time in her life, but justification didn't make her phobia any easier to deal with. The drone of the noisy crowd at her back didn't help—in fact, it made her feel more isolated. If something happened, no one would hear her screams.

She gripped the handrail all the way up, stumbling once on the landing before catching herself. The stink of burnt bulb hung in the musty air. She turned left and felt for the door to her apartment, fumbling for what seemed like an eternity to find the keyhole with her key. The landing was large enough and the air black enough that someone could be standing behind her and she wouldn't even know it. Her skin crawled as perspiration gathered at the small of her back. At last, she turned the dead bolt and practically fell into her apartment, lunging for a light switch as she pushed the door closed behind her.

The light flickered but caught, illuminating her tiny dining room to the right and part of the kitchen behind it. She exhaled to relieve her pent-up tension and walked a few feet to her left, hitting another light switch to reveal the living room, which led into a bathroom straight ahead and into the bedroom around the corner. All five rooms could have fit into the master bedroom suite in the Victorian on Charm Street. The upside was that they'd been easy to furnish—one delivery from Furniture Galaxy and she'd been set:

miniature dining table and chairs, two bar stools, sage green leather couch and butter yellow leather chair, side table, lamp number one, hooked area rug, television cabinet, television, queen-size bed, chest of drawers, and lamp number two.

She tried not to think about the luscious antiques that had stayed with the house, all of which she had handpicked, refurbishing many herself. On her way out the door, she had stolen a plant, a ficus tree sitting in the foyer that had thrived under her care. She couldn't imagine Deke missing it; in hindsight, he hadn't been particularly attached to *any*thing in the house that was living.

The one thing that she most regretted leaving was a lovebirds tree ornament that Deke had given her the first Christmas they were together in college at Louisiana State University. He hadn't been able to understand why she'd cried, and she'd been too embarrassed to confess that as a child she'd always longed for a twinkling Christmas tree with lots of ornaments. That kind of admission would have led to questions about her family that she hadn't wanted to address. As far as Deke knew, she was an only child and both of her parents had died.

Which was partly true.

When she'd been gathering her clothes and personal effects, she had forgotten about the ornament, which she had kept wrapped in tissue paper in a chest in the attic. On some level she wanted the ornament as a reminder that she hadn't imagined Deke's love for her, but a stronger motivation was envisioning Sheena running across the ornament and having a belly laugh at Penny's sentimentality. The thought of that woman—

or Deke—tossing the ornament as if it meant nothing kept Penny awake at nights. Someday she would figure out a way to get it back without either one of them knowing. She was too ashamed to let anyone know the ornament still meant something to her.

Penny glanced around her little apartment, conceding that it wasn't without its own charm: tall plaster ceilings, waist-high white bead board that ran throughout, worn, honey-colored wood floors that were always pleasingly warm because of the heat generated beneath her in the doughnut shop. And the windows—the windows were magnificent. Two in the living room, two in the bedroom, nearly floor to ceiling. The pair in the bedroom opened onto a Juliet balcony, encased by an intricate cast-iron railing.

If only she had a Romeo to gaze down upon, instead of a giant revolving square doughnut.

Penny shrugged out of her coat and dropped it onto the quilted coverlet on her bed. For a few seconds, she stared at the coat with envy—she'd had a long, disturbing day, and she'd rather have curled up on her bed and listen to the crowd through an open window than attend this party that Marie had planned. She stretched high on her toes and exhaled noisily. She couldn't back out now—it was nice of Marie to have planned it. And maybe the party *would* help her put some closure on her relationship with Deke.

First things first. She phoned her landlord and left another message about the lightbulbs. The plain yogurt and dried bananas she'd eaten for lunch were long gone, and Caskey's would have few to no healthy choices on the menu, so she made a quick spinach and tofu salad and washed it down with mineral water and lemon. A long, hot shower would have felt great, but her water heater was on the fritz more often than not, so she settled for a long, lukewarm shower. Afterward, she took special care to smooth on scented lotion, dab almond oil on her pulse points, and make an attempt to tame her auburn curls with a round brush.

Frowning into the mirror, she studied her reflection, something she'd been doing more of lately, she acknowledged. She wasn't about to accept blame for Deke's sleeping around, but after being tossed aside as carelessly as she had been, she did have her moments of self-doubt.

Okay, make that *hours* of self-doubt. At thirty-two, her features were beginning to sharpen as youthful lipids left her skin. Sometimes when she looked in the mirror, she felt old; at other times, simply mature. Her face was unremarkable, although she'd always believed her green eyes were her best attribute. Deke seemed to prefer her smile, but she thought she showed too much gum.

"That's when I know you're really happy," he'd said once. *"When I see a lot of gum."*

She couldn't remember the last time she'd shown a lot of gum.

With a sigh, she withdrew her dusty makeup case and poked around for any products that weren't dried up. A dusting of powder would have to suffice as foundation. Too late, she remembered why she didn't use the powder more often—it contained skin "brighteners," which sounded scientific but were, in effect, ground-up glitter so difficult to remove, it practically had to wear off a person's skin. She lucked out and found an unopened wand of mascara and a pinkish lipstick that did double-duty as blush. Then she gave up while she was ahead.

With much trepidation, she opened the door of her closet, Marie's not so subtle suggestion to dress up ringing in her mind.

"Festive, festive, festive," she murmured, flipping through jeans, corduroys, chinos, painter's pants, overalls, jumpers, and sweaters. In a near panic, she reached into the back of her closet, and her hand closed over a forgotten dress, one she'd purchased at a local boutique when she'd first detected Deke's restlessness. She withdrew it and held it in front of her, the tags dangling. The sleeveless emerald green wrap dress was fitted through the bodice, tied at the waist, then fell to a long, swishy skirt edged with a thick row of embroidered gold trim. The lustrous fabric was finely cut and flattering to her lean figure. She had paid more for it and a pair of gold wedge-heel sandals than any ensemble since her wedding gown, but she hadn't gotten the chance to wear it and had been too embarrassed to return it . . . afterward.

She removed the tags, then slid into the dress and stepped into the shoes, turning this way and that way in the mirror, remembering Deke's reference to her "bony ass." She looked, she decided, as good as she was ever going to look. She added dangly earrings and a few ethnic bracelets, tied a yellow shawl around her shoulders, and dropped essentials into an appliquéd canvas shoulder bag, including a flashlight so she wouldn't have to climb the stairs in the dark again.

At the last minute, she glanced in the mirror and panicked at her made-over reflection. Did she look as if she was trying too hard?

Then she winced. Trying too hard to do what? To forget about Deke? Wasn't that the plan?

She walked to the window and looked out across the people milling in the square—couples holding hands, friends arm in arm, children running wild. The main crowd still gravitated around the shelter, where the dancing had grown more frenzied. Small groups of dancers had erupted on all sides, and everyone seemed to be getting into the spirit of the festival. From her vantage point, she scanned the crowd for anyone familiar and spotted Marie's blue hair as the young woman hurried in the direction of the bar.

Penny smiled wryly—time to stop stalling and go celebrate her failed marriage.

She started to turn away from the window when she noticed a tall, muscular man standing next to a streetlight, casually inspecting the crowd. Something about him struck her as familiar. . . .

The man who had visited Sheena!

She took an involuntary half step back from the window, then peeked around to see if Sheena was lurking about. If she was, she wasn't making herself known . . . or maybe the man was waiting for her.

Penny picked up her purse, her chest bursting with curiosity. She left the light over the dining room table burning and prayed it would last until she got home. The new shoes made getting down the dark stairs precarious, especially when she had to use one hand to hold the flashlight. When she opened the door onto the street, the noise blasted her. The volume had increased twofold since she had gone inside. Night had fallen, but the square was awash with pink and yellow light. The lamp under which the mystery man had been standing illuminated emptiness. Penny glanced around but didn't see him anywhere.

A child ran by and Penny jumped back, laughing, to avoid being plowed by a train of shrieking children holding sparklers high. She worked her way through the crowd, past the trinket vendors. She fingered glass bead necklaces and velvet charm pouches and smiled over jars of crushed "bones" like the ones on sale at the souvenir shop at the voodoo museum. (Close scrutiny of the label revealed the contents as "rock bones," or in layman's terms, crushed limestone.) Jars of "spider legs," "poison frog skin," and "fish eyes" were equally bogus but were being snapped up anyway.

The booth selling voodoo dolls was the busiest by far. Factory-stamped "stick it to your boss" fabric dolls were prevalent, as were cartoonish "love" and "revenge" dolls of ambiguous sex and miniature novelty dolls in bright hues. High in the rafters of the tent, however, she spied more authentic versions of the dolls, some of them grotesque, made from black cloth or wax, wrapped in scraps of fabric. The woman running the booth saw her studying the dolls and made a move to get one down for her, but Penny waved her off.

She made her way toward Caskey's, marveling over the intensity of the atmosphere. She had experienced the festival every year that she'd lived in Mojo, but she'd never seen so many people, so much energy. It had the feeling of Mardi Gras without the beads and the nudity. The strong aroma of incense and cloves cleared her sinuses and stung her eyes. The air throbbed with the beat of the three drummers of the *batri* playing for the ceremony, and the ground vibrated with the force of pounding feet.

As she walked past the shelter, she noticed wooden cages of white chickens lined up. Their frantic squawking added to the din, as if they knew their fate. The priests and priestesses had met animal control halfway by agreeing to kill the birds humanely in their sacrificial ritual, and only at a time when children most likely would be home in bed.

Penny shivered and pulled her shawl higher on her bare shoulders as she wound through the crowd waiting at Caskey's. Marie was smart to have reserved a room for the party. Penny only hoped that enough people showed up. When she finally made it to the hostess stand, she shouted to be heard above the noise, and the young girl directed her to the party room. On the way past the bar, Penny did a double take; the mystery man sat alone, nursing a long-neck beer.

Still dressed in the brown leather coat and clothes she'd seen him in this morning, he was as long-limbed as he had appeared from a distance, and broad-shouldered, but slouching in a "screw everyone" posture. His black gaze latched onto her in puzzled recognition, then darted to her cleavage. Penny realized with a flush that she looked radically different than when he'd stopped to ask for directions. She quickly averted her gaze and hurried toward her destination.

But poor Deke—even with the hair transplant, he didn't stand a chance against the guy.

She grinned and was pretty sure she was showing gum.

Suddenly she felt like celebrating. She found the room and smiled at the sign reading Congratulations on Your Divorce, Penny! She rapped on the door that was ajar before sticking her head inside the nearly empty room. Rollicking zydeco music blared from a boom box in the corner. "Is this the divorce party?"

Marie turned, and her eyes widened. "Wow, Penny, you look . . ." She squinted. "Your skin is all glittery."

Penny smirked. "You said festive."

"You look awesome, boss, really."

Penny thanked her, then laughed as she walked into the room festooned in streamers and balloons. "The decorations are awesome, too," she said, picking up a noisemaker and giving it a spin. "But it looks like this is going to be one dead divorce party."

"Then maybe we should go," said a voice behind her.

Penny turned, and at the sight of the two women standing in the doorway, she let out a happy cry and broke into a run.

7

Toss in some unexpected spice . . .

"Liz, Wendy . . . what are you doing here?"

"We came to liven up this dead party," Liz said with a laugh.

Penny embraced the women one at a time, then angled her head at Marie. "You set this up."

Marie looked pleased with herself. "So I snooped in your address book."

"Marie called me," Liz said, "then I called Wendy."

Penny pulled her two friends forward, glad that her employee had made the call that she herself had been too embarrassed to make. "Marie, meet my two best friends from college—Liz Brockwell and Wendy Metzger."

Still tingling with shock and pleasure, Penny observed the sleek women as they shook hands with Marie and said hello. They were just as attractive as when they'd all met at Louisiana State University—maybe more so. Liz was a vivacious blond, twice divorced, who lived in New Orleans and ran a chain of chiropractic clinics. She had always been the personality of the trio, as well as the fashion plate—and still was, as evidenced by her Dana Buchman tweed jacket over Decca jeans and the Judith Leiber bag—things that Penny recognized from the Saks ads in the *Post*.

Wendy was a quiet, petite, raven-haired beauty from Atlanta who had never been married. She ran an art gallery—perfect for her reserved nature and refined taste. Only Wendy could look so feminine in her tiny Versace glasses and tailored boyish clothes, her long hair pulled back into a simple ponytail.

Liz lifted a gift bag. "Where do you want the gag gifts?"

Marie pointed to a gaily decorated table just inside the door. "Put them there and Penny can open them later. I'm going to get a round of drinks." She grinned at Penny, then skipped out of the room, leaving the three of them alone.

Penny flushed under Liz's direct gaze. "What—you couldn't call and tell us that you and Deke were getting a divorce?"

"You didn't call me when you got your last divorce," Penny pointed out.

Liz shrugged. "You'd only met Richard once. Besides, I wasn't exactly torn up about it."

Penny lifted her chin slightly.

"Not that you're torn up about it," Wendy said quickly, then winced and touched Penny's arm. "Are you?"

"She's having a party, isn't she?" Liz said, swatting at an errant balloon.

"What happened?" Wendy asked, her voice laced with curiosity and concern.

Penny shrugged and tried to sound philosophical. "Deke found someone else."

Liz rolled her eyes. "How young is she?"

"Young," Penny admitted. "And . . . voluptuous. I caught them together . . . in our bed."

"I'm so sorry," Wendy said, giving her a hug.

"Well, I'm not," Liz declared to Penny. "You've never looked better in your life, so the divorce must be agreeing with you."

"You're gorgeous," Wendy agreed.

"Thanks," Penny said, knowing they were trying to make her feel better, and letting them.

"I assume you got the house," Liz said, tapping her foot.

"No, but I had a good attorney—I called Gloria Dalton."

Liz's eyebrows climbed. "Gloria is a great attorney—she didn't get you the house?"

Penny smiled. "Deke got the house, but I got the rental property across the street."

"Which is your health food store," Wendy said.

"Right."

"Liz pointed it out to me when we drove in—it looks terrific."

"Thanks, I really love it. And business is good, knock on wood."

Wendy's dark eyes widened. "But you're across the street from Deke in the house—that's kind of icky, isn't it?"

"It hasn't been easy," Penny conceded. "His girlfriend moved in."

"Well," Liz said dryly, "that explains the pink paint job. I knew that wasn't your handiwork."

Penny made a face and shook her head. "I confronted Deke about it this morning and he said it's what *she* wants."

Wendy frowned. "Who is this woman?"

Penny sighed. "The town bimbo, unfortunately. And she owns the local tanning salon."

Liz snorted. "Couldn't Deke at least have been original?"

"Did the two of you just grow apart?" Wendy asked.

Good question, one that Penny had asked herself a hundred times. "We must have," she said carefully. "We were happy for the first few years we lived here, but I was bored working in his law office, so I suggested opening the health food store. Deke was against it, but in the end he gave in—I think he believed it would go under within a couple of months and I'd come back to work with him." Penny made a rueful noise. "I thought it was a good thing, that maybe we were spending too much time together, but that's when things started to go south."

"Is his mother still alive?" Liz asked.

Penny nodded. "And she's still the mayor. She always tried to interfere in our marriage, but Deke stood up to her." Penny frowned. "At first. Then his practice started to slide. When I left to start the health food store, his business dropped off even more, and his entire personality changed. I think he blamed me for leaving him without an office manager. He was jumpy and irritable, and . . . paranoid."

Liz crossed her arms. "Paranoid?"

"Paranoid might not be the right word—stressed. He was stressed all the time, working longer and longer hours. That's when I began to suspect that something was wrong."

"Sounds like drugs," Liz muttered.

Penny bit down on the inside of her cheek. She had considered the possibility, and it would have explained a lot of things, like his erratic passive-aggressive behavior. "Nothing so dramatic—he was just having a good old-fashioned midlife crisis."

"Penny, are you doing okay, really?" Wendy asked.

Penny nodded. "Some days are harder than others, but overall, yeah, I'm fine."

"Did you consider leaving Mojo?" Liz asked.

Somehow Liz always managed to find Penny's sore spots. "I might have if my business wasn't doing so well." And the sad truth was, she had nowhere else to go. She clasped their hands, eager to change the subject. "How long has it been since we were all together?"

"Two years," Liz said. "Your thirtieth birthday."

"How long can you stay?"

"We have to go back to the city right after the party—Wendy's flying out at the crack of dawn."

Penny groaned. "So, catch me up."

"Same old, same old for me," Liz said with a languid smile.

"Still rich and single, in other words," Penny said dryly.

Liz's laugh tinkled. "It's a great life, isn't it, Wendy?"

"Don't ask me. I've got the single part down, but the rich part has eluded me."

"Not true," Liz said, then looked at Penny. "She just bought a fabulous loft in an artsy section of Atlanta."

"Really?" Penny asked, surprised. Wendy had always said she wanted to wait until she married Mr. Right before taking on a mortgage. "That's wonderful. Your career must be going gangbusters."

"She's been asked to curate an exhibit at the High Museum of Art," Liz said, then slanted a glance toward their doe-eyed friend. "*And* she has a mystery boyfriend."

Penny lifted her eyebrows. "Do tell."

Wendy gave Liz an exasperated glance. "Liz talks too much."

A cell phone rang, and Wendy glanced toward her purse.

"Speak of the devil," Liz said.

"Answer it," Penny encouraged.

But Wendy seemed nervous and shook her head as the phone continued to ring. It stopped, only to start ringing again a few seconds later.

"He's persistent," Liz declared.

Wendy bit her lip as she reached into her bag and withdrew the phone.

Liz leaned over to steal a glance at the screen, and Wendy yanked it back. "Liz, mind your own business!"

Liz laughed and looked at Penny. "He must really be important—maybe he's a famous artist."

"I need to take this," Wendy said with a frown, then hurried out the door.

Liz smirked. "I think she's doing her boss, Mr. Shepherd."

"Why would she want to keep it a secret?"

"Because he's married."

"Oh." Penny swallowed. Having been cheated on gave her a different perspective of an affair. If Wendy was seeing Mr. Shepherd, that made her Mrs. Shepherd's Sheena.

"I think he bought her the loft," Liz murmured, "but she won't talk about it. She's been as jumpy as a cat since I picked her up at the airport."

"It seems out of character for Wendy to get mixed up with a married man."

"People change." Liz glanced after Wendy, then

sighed. "Besides, love makes people stupid. You should know that, Penny."

Penny looked up. Was Liz talking about her stupidity for marrying Deke, or were the feelings she still had for Deke so transparent?

Liz's gaze probed hers. "Look at how Deke has behaved, for instance."

"Oh. Right."

"Of course, no offense, Penny, but I always thought you could do better than Deke anyway."

Penny gave a dry laugh. "Apparently not, since he's who I wound up with."

"You settled."

Funny, but Penny had felt lucky at the time, and most of the time since. In fact, she had sometimes wondered if Liz was jealous—not of Deke, but of their relationship. "He was the one who ended the marriage," she felt obligated to point out.

Liz gave a dismissive wave with her manicured hand. "You're so much better off without him. Cheating bastard."

"Who?" Wendy asked, rejoining them, her cheeks flushed.

"Deke, of course," Liz said lightly. "Who did you think we were referring to?"

Wendy adjusted her glasses—a nervous habit, Penny recalled. "No one. What did I miss?"

Liz smiled. "I was just telling Penny that she was too good for Deke Black and that when she falls in love again, she shouldn't settle. Right, Wendy?"

Wendy paled. "Right."

Penny felt a rush of sympathy for gentle-hearted Wendy. If she'd fallen in love with a married man, she was probably feeling tormented. "And I was just getting ready to tell Liz that—"

The door opened suddenly, and Penny turned her head. Her pulse jolted at the sight of Sheena's mystery man standing in the doorway, his broad shoulders spanning the opening, his dark gaze tantalizing. The man was built for carnal sport, and she had no doubt he could . . . score. Penny wet her lips and murmured, "Sometimes . . . sex is enough."

8

Top with a few sour grapes...

A few seconds passed before Penny's words registered in her own brain. Where had that inane comment come from? She groaned inwardly, blaming Marie's Hot Voodoo Sex concoction for the misfirings of her nether regions—and her mouth. Meanwhile, the mystery man was giving her the once-over with those heavy-lidded black eyes that glinted with suppressed laughter.

"Sorry," he said in a low, smooth rumble. "I was looking for the men's room." He glanced down, then bent and retrieved the Congratulations on Your Divorce, Penny! sign that had fallen off the door. "I didn't mean to crash the party." He looked up and grinned in her direction. "Are you Penny?"

She nodded, feeling ridiculous.

"Thanks for the tip on the Browning Motel this morning."

A flush climbed her neck. "No problem."

He extended the sign. "And congratulations on being single again."

She stood, frozen, staring at his long-fingered hand

until Liz bumped her from behind. "Thanks," Penny mumbled as she took the sign.

"My pleasure."

She had the absurd feeling that if he'd been wearing a hat, he would have tipped it. He gave a curt nod and disappeared.

After a few heartbeats of silence, Liz bumped her again. "Was that the best you could do—*thanks*? That man was *hot*. And he was *interested*."

Penny acknowledged with an exhale that yes, he was indeed hot, then she turned. "Don't get any ideas. I don't know his name, but he's mixed up with Sheena somehow."

"Who's Sheena?"

"Deke's girlfriend."

Wendy squinted. "Deke's girlfriend has a boyfriend?"

"I don't know—maybe they used to be involved. I saw him drive up to the house this morning. Deke wasn't home. When Sheena answered, she was wearing something slinky, and it looked like they were arguing."

Liz's eyebrows shot up. "You were spying?"

Penny's cheeks flamed. "No. I just happened to be looking out the window." She didn't miss the look that Liz exchanged with Wendy. "I'm over Deke," she assured them, although her voice came out strident and thin. "I . . . I just couldn't believe he'd paint my house pink, that's all."

A lazy smile curved Liz's mouth. "I don't know, I think it would be kind of poetic if you hooked up with the woman's ex-boyfriend. If Deke can have a plaything, so can you. What's good for the goose, and all that jazz."

Before Penny could respond, the door opened again

and Marie walked in, all smiles, carrying a tray of jewel-toned martinis. "I got an assortment of plain, cherry, and apple, so everyone can help themselves. And I found some of our group!"

Steve Chasen walked in behind her, followed by two young women whom Marie introduced as friends of hers—Jill and Melissa, both of whom worked at the Hair Affair, and both sporting hairdos as riotous as Marie's. Diane Davidson arrived a few minutes later, and Penny hardly recognized her because she wasn't wearing a running suit. The woman seemed hesitant, so Penny went out of her way to make her feel welcome, introducing her to Liz and Wendy. She tried not to let Steve and Marie's comments about Diane being a witch color her perception of the quiet woman, but she had to admit that she saw her through new eyes. Diane was dressed in a black skirt that swept the floor and a black tunic belted with a long sash embroidered with silver pentagrams. Perhaps coming to the party and wearing a Wiccan symbol was her way of fighting back, of standing up for herself.

Penny felt a sudden surge of kinship with the woman and vowed to herself that she would try to get to know her better. After all, any woman who scared Deke was worth befriending. Besides, she couldn't imagine that the Wiccan religion was any more terrifying than the frenzied, snake-handling Pentecostals in the small Tennessee town in which she'd grown up. Every religion, including voodoo, had its exaggerations and misinterpretations by outsiders.

"Drink up, boss," Marie urged, handing her a brimming martini glass.

Penny eyed the liquid warily, trying to gauge her alcohol tolerance based on how long it had been since she'd indulged and the fact that tofu didn't coat one's stomach as well as buttered toast did.

"Oh, no, you don't," Marie said, wagging a finger. "I don't want to hear anything about free radicals spinning through your body, or how bad alcohol is for your skin."

"It dehydrates you," Penny muttered.

Marie sighed. "Just for tonight, let go a little." She leaned in, her eyes sparkling. "I have a feeling that something really exciting is going to happen to you tonight."

Again, the rumors about Marie having ESP flitted through Penny's mind. Then, inexplicably, her mind bounced to the mystery man and the sexual spark she'd seen in his dark gaze. Was he, by chance, the exciting thing that Marie was forecasting? Penny glanced toward the open door and took a sip of the cold, fruity drink. She winced at the afterburn, but the second sip went down more smoothly . . . and the third sip more smoothly still.

By the time that Guy arrived with Carley, his gorgeous "date," Penny had emptied her glass and was starting to feel the minty tingle of the alcohol swimming toward her brain and extremities. Marie replaced Penny's empty glass with a full one, and she had finished half of the second drink when Hazel Means stuck her head inside the room.

"Hazel!" Penny said happily, gesturing wide. "Welcome to my party!"

The trim, middle-aged woman smiled, but she looked uncomfortable and fingered her hearing aid; Penny suspected that loud, public places were distracting for her. "I can't stay long, I just came by to wish you the best and to drop off a little something from the souvenir shop." She set a gift bag on the now overflowing table and winked.

Penny was touched. "Thank you, Hazel. I realize that you've known Deke and his family for years, and that it's difficult for you to take sides. I appreciate your friendship."

Hazel leaned in. "Mona is here, and she knows you're here. But Chief Davis is out there checking I.D.s, so maybe Mona will leave you alone."

Penny winced—she didn't want to face her ex-mother-in-law tonight of all nights. "Thanks for the warning."

"Don't mention it." Hazel patted Penny's arm and turned to go.

"Oh . . . Hazel, did you get the mail I dropped off this morning?"

"I wondered where that mail came from—it looked like it had been trampled."

"Sorry . . . I, um, dropped it on the way over."

"No problem. Thanks."

"Hazel—who was at the museum this morning meeting with Deke?"

Hazel shrugged. "No one that I know of. When was Deke there?"

"I ran into him when I dropped off the mail."

"Well, he has a key to the office. He comes and goes as he pleases."

"I know, but I thought I saw someone in the window as I was leaving." Penny pressed her lips together, knowing they were growing looser by the second but unable to stop. "And someone in the cupola."

Hazel laughed. "You must have been seeing things. The door to the cupola was boarded up years ago for security reasons. Nothing up there but bats and fog."

Relieved, Penny nodded, but the movement gave her a head rush. "Of course. You're right—it was foggy this morning."

"I have to run. The tourists will be lined up at the museum early tomorrow."

Penny waved good-bye, then smiled happily when Ziggy Hines strolled into the room, holding a tall drink and looking well on his way to being sloshed. "You made it, Ziggy."

"Not yet," he said suggestively, his gaze roaming the room. "But I still have high hopes for the evening." His head stopped. "Who is that woman?"

Penny turned, not surprised to see him nodding toward Liz on the other side of the room. She was deep in conversation with Wendy.

"Liz Brockwell," Penny said. "She was my roommate at LSU, and she lives in the city."

He turned his back and rubbed his hand over his mouth. "I've seen her in my restaurant. Striking woman."

"I can introduce you," Penny offered.

"No," he said quickly, moving toward the door. "In fact, I should be going—I have to meet someone."

Penny smiled—one of the young women he'd left her shop with, no doubt. "Good night, Ziggy. I'll call you when I have more truffles."

He nodded absently, then glanced toward Liz and left abruptly.

Penny frowned after him and shook her head. The man was Mr. Macho until faced with the prospect of meeting a woman on his own level. She sipped from her glass and studied Liz and Wendy from across the room, warmth infusing her chest. At one time the three of them had been inseparable, sharing their dreams and aspirations. Yet they had fallen out of touch . . . grown apart . . . just like her and Deke. It was funny that she prided herself on having a green thumb, on being able to nurse any plant back to health, yet she allowed her personal relationships to wither on the vine.

Moisture gathered in her eyes. The alcohol was making her weepy.

But the energy level of the small party was definitely ratcheting higher as drinks flowed and a waitress brought in trays of greasy appetizers. Friends of friends arrived, some of whom Penny recognized as customers, and soon the room boomed with music and laughter. Penny made the rounds and tried to behave like a happy divorcée. Her mind kept straying to the mystery man who had crossed her path more than once today, but she reasoned that he had probably already hooked up with someone, or maybe he and Sheena had made up.

"Someone told me you were here."

Penny had time to school her face into a pleasant mask before turning to face her ex-mother-in-law. Mona Black was a tall, imposing woman with piercing eyes and a pile of black hair on her head, divided by a shock of white in the front. She didn't wear makeup, although admittedly she didn't need it. She was an attractive woman in her sixties, her uniform a black pantsuit, her only ornament a small silver cross at her throat.

"Hello, Mona," Penny said cheerfully. "Welcome to my divorce party. Can I get you a drink?"

Disgust filled the woman's eyes. "A party? Don't you have any class?"

"Too much for your son, apparently. Or haven't you met your new future daughter-in-law?"

Mona's jaw hardened. "What are you talking about?"

"Haven't you heard? Deke and Sheena are engaged."

Mona tried not to react, but Penny knew the woman had been taken by surprise.

Penny lifted her glass. "Congratulations, Mona. Maybe Sheena will give Deke those grandkids you've always wanted, and they'll have a beautiful tan."

Loathing glinted in Mona's eyes before she recovered. "I didn't come to discuss Deke. I wanted to warn you that the city council is going to file a restraining order to stop you from turning Mojo into a damn cornfield."

Penny tensed as years of resentment toward the woman came to a head. "Really? Where was the restraining order, Mona, when Deke painted my house the color of a vagina?"

9

Then slice with a sharp object . . .

As luck would have it, her outburst coincided with a lull in the conversation. Gasps sounded, followed by giggles. The look of horrified indignance on Mona's face was worth the transgression, Penny decided.

"You're drunk," Mona hissed, then nodded toward Diane Davidson. "I'll leave you to your misfit friends."

After Mona left, Penny was still reeling over her own behavior. Guy gave her a thumbs-up across the room. Liz and Wendy came over and gave her high fives.

"Well done," Liz said. "Consider that bridge burned."

"I can't believe you said that to his mother," Wendy said, laughing.

"It was false courage," Penny admitted, then drained her glass. "But did it ever feel good."

Pleased with herself, she went in search of another martini, feeling for the first time since she'd seen the bottoms of Sheena's dirty feet on her white sheets that things were going to work out. That not only would she survive, but she just might thrive. She was stirring another drink when Marie came up to her. "Boss, I need to talk to you."

"Oh, Marie, this is a great party. Thank you so much for putting it together. I wasn't so sure at first, but I'm really enjoying myself."

"Good." Marie's smile was tight as she pulled Penny into a secluded corner. "Listen, I just found out something that I thought you should know."

"That Deke's getting married? I already know."

Marie frowned. "Deke's getting married? No—this is different . . . but related, I suppose."

Penny used her teeth to pluck an olive from the martini stirrer. "What?"

"Um . . . apparently Deke hid assets during the property settlement. He put some things in Sheena's name and some in her company's name. Cash . . . a boat . . . other things."

Denial sprang to Penny's chest that Deke would purposely cheat her, then she remembered the investments that had allegedly gone bad, how their savings had dwindled. The strange phone call she'd received at home before this had all started about a boat she'd known nothing about and that Deke had sworn was a mistake. Suddenly his tan and designer suits made sense. Anger and dismay rolled over her in waves. "Did Steve tell you this?"

Marie sent a worried glance his way. "Yes, but he'll be fired if Deke finds out. I thought that maybe your attorney could do some research and keep Steve's name out of it."

Penny was struck mute, but she nodded. Would the betrayal ever end? Would she ever stop feeling stupid? Had her entire marriage been a sham? She felt light-headed. "I . . . need some air," she said, then walked out of the room.

Not that the air out in the bar was clearer. A haze of smoke hung above the throng of bodies jammed into the space. The scent of blackened meat burned her nose. The music was loud, and voices were raised to near crescendo. The alcohol had keened her senses, but she felt numb from the stimulus overload. She turned away from the noise and walked down a hall in search of the ladies' bathroom. Her neck felt sticky from perspiration, and her mind reeled as Marie's words reverberated in her head.

Deke had plotted to cheat her out of assets they'd built together. Throughout the divorce, she had regarded him as weak when it had come to matters of the flesh, and stubborn when it had come to going after the assets he'd wanted, but she wouldn't have dreamed he would stoop to this . . . to robbing her . . . to breaking the law. She felt so small and so . . . used.

At the end of the hall she spotted the line for the bathroom and opted to wait by the pay phones until the line died down. She needed space around her and time to think, to regroup. She'd call Gloria, of course, but just the thought of several more months of wrangling with Deke was enough to sicken her. Maybe she should have let him have the rental property and given up her business in exchange for cash . . . moved somewhere else and started over . . . nearer to her mother . . .

God, if she was thinking about her mother, she *must* be drunk.

Penny inhaled and exhaled, realized she was still holding her drink, and took a cooling sip. She leaned against the wall and wondered briefly if anyone would miss her if she didn't return to the party . . . or if she left Mojo.

On the opposite wall, a white flyer among the dozens stapled and tacked into the wood paneling caught her attention.

MISSING:
Jodi Reynolds, age 17,
last seen in New Orleans, September 12.

In the color picture, the bespectacled woman looked bookish . . . ordinary. Only her curtain of long blond hair set her apart. Penny looked into the woman's sad eyes and wondered if the person who had created the flyer was a concerned relative, or someone else—an abusive parent, an obsessed lover?

Penny leaned forward and murmured, "Did someone take you, Jodi Reynolds, or did you disappear on purpose?"

"Is this a private conversation, or can anyone join in?"

She swung her head around, and the mystery man was standing there, holding a bottle of beer. And he was still breathtakingly sexy . . . all muscles and male, leather and Levi's.

"I, uh . . ." Her brain was pickled.

He looked at the flyer she'd been studying. "Do you know her?" His smooth Cajun cadence was like a down pillow for her ears.

"No. I was just . . . wondering what might have happened to her."

He took a drink from the bottle, still reading. "Looks like a good kid, I hope she's found safe."

"Or not."

He arched one eyebrow. "You hope she isn't found?"

Penny shrugged. "She's seventeen. Maybe she doesn't want to be found."

He pursed his mouth. "Is that the voice of personal experience? Do you have secrets, Penny?"

Her mouth went dry as his gaze bored into hers. One minute in and he was already too close for comfort. "No," she croaked.

"Ah. So it's the cynicism of someone newly divorced." He grinned and took another drink. "You left your own party?"

"I just stepped out for a few minutes."

"I'm ready to leave, too. So why don't we leave together?"

She blinked, wondering if she'd misheard him, but the sexy glint in his eyes and the curve of his mouth was unmistakable—he wanted to get busy . . . with her. A tug on her midsection answered his call, and her breasts tingled, but her good-girl training kicked in. "I don't even know your name."

"It's B.J.," he said. "And don't worry—I'm not a serial killer."

She smirked. "I'll bet that's what all the serial killers say."

He laughed, a pleasant noise that stroked her curiosity. "I promise that as long as you're with me, nothing will ever happen to you . . . that you don't want to happen."

She swallowed hard. Strangely, she believed him, trusted him . . . with her body anyway.

He leaned forward. "You smell good."

"Thanks . . . it's, um, almond oil."

"Really? Smells like doughnuts."

She pushed her tongue into her cheek. She had to find a new place to live.

He grinned. "I love doughnuts."

"I don't," she said firmly, and started to push away from the wall.

"Hey," he said with a little laugh. "Relax. What *do* you like?"

She lifted her chin. "Tofu."

"Tofu?" He made a rueful noise. "Lady, I'd sure like to try to change your idea of fun."

She couldn't help but laugh at his Cajun masochism. The man was appealing in a base sort of way.

He nodded toward the exit. "So how about it, Penny? Let me take your mind off . . . whatever."

Penny started to shake her head no, but something took hold inside her chest that she recognized as power. Feminine satisfaction swelled in her belly, and her thighs pulsed with pleasure. It had been a long time since she'd been pursued by a man. It had been over a decade since she'd even seen a man other than Deke naked, and she suspected that B.J. here would measure up . . . and then some. Besides, if she were very clever, maybe she'd find out something about Sheena that would help her to apply pressure when she took Deke back to court.

She wet her lips, testing the words silently. *"Okay . . . let's go . . . your place or mine?"* She tried desperately to remember what kind of underwear she'd worn—black lace bikini, or full coverage cotton?

"Penny!"

Down the hall Marie motioned to her and shouted, "Come on—it's time to open the gag gifts!" then disappeared back into the room.

Penny straightened, remorse and . . . relief? . . . bleeding through her. "I guess I'd better get back to my party."

He tore a corner off a faded flyer and wrote something on it using a pen that was attached to the wall. "I have to take off," he said, extending the paper. "But here's my cell number. Why don't you call me when you're finished here and we'll . . . see what happens."

Penny took the piece of paper but decided not to commit. He didn't press her for an answer, just inclined his head and left. She shoved the slip of paper deep into her pocket and watched him disappear into the crowd. He didn't act like a player—he wasn't scouting the bar for another score, and he didn't have an entourage. She made her way back to the party, her heart thudding with apprehension.

Everyone was in high spirits when she returned, although she spotted Liz checking her watch a couple of times and felt guilty; her friend had probably traded a night of sophisticated entertainment to come to Mojo and have watered-down drinks at a hole-in-the-wall bar. Wendy looked equally out of place, stabbing at her glasses and checking her cell phone. Guy, too, looked restless, and Diane Davidson appeared ready to bolt at the first chance. Determined to put everyone out of their misery, Penny went to the gift table and clinked a fork against her glass to get everyone's attention. Guy turned down the music.

Penny inhaled and cleared her throat. "Thank you so much for coming tonight and thanks to Marie for putting this together." The alcohol was pumping through her body, unhindered by food. As she looked over the motley crew that had assembled on her behalf, she suddenly felt sorry for herself, and for them for being dragged into her personal drama. Unbidden, revulsion for Deke and what he had put her through welled in her chest. Tension whipped through the room as everyone waited. Marie pressed her lips together and averted her gaze.

In a desperate attempt to ward off tears, Penny decided to play the sarcasm card. "Most of you know the circumstances of my divorce. For those of you who don't—my husband was a lying, cheating, son of a bitch."

Everyone erupted in laughter, relieving the tension in the room and thankfully, in her chest. "But I got the last laugh because he has to live in a pink house and I got all these presents!"

Marie handed her a gift bag. "I asked everyone to keep the gifts anonymous."

"Ooh, mysterious." She pulled out a box of condoms, and cheers broke out. A flush warmed her face, and B.J.'s number seemed to burn through her clothing into her skin.

Subsequent bags and boxes revealed a ball cap and T-shirt that espoused the virtues of divorce, a roll of ex-husband toilet paper (Guy's gift, she suspected), a bottle of champagne that was speedily opened, an inflatable husband (from Liz and Wendy?), a couple of Happy Divorce chocolate bars (although she hadn't eaten chocolate in over a year), a charm kit to bury the past (probably from Hazel), and a vibrator (definitely from Marie).

The last box, however, got the biggest laugh—an eight-inch voodoo doll dressed in a little suit. A red Hot Wheels sports car had been glued to his hand. Penny shrieked with laughter at the likeness to Deke.

"Stick him!" someone shouted, then everyone started chanting, "Stick him! Stick him!"

Caught up in the moment, she removed one of the black hat pins and considered sticking the doll in the crotch. At the last second, she settled for stabbing his cheating heart, to the sound of enthusiastic cheers. The force dislodged the little car from his hand, sending it crashing to the floor, crumpling the front end. Groans and chortles chorused around the room, then everyone applauded heartily.

"A prick for a prick!" Liz shouted.

Penny took a little bow, flushed with the exhilaration of retaliation—even if it was meaningless. Then unbidden, Jules's words of warning came back to her about voodoo not being for amateurs. Staring down at the mortally wounded doll, Penny experienced a blip of panic: She didn't truly wish Deke harm.

Although she wouldn't lose sleep if the thieving bastard came down with his own bad case of heartache.

10

Allow everything to ferment . . .

"I can't thank you enough for coming," Penny said, hugging Liz, then Wendy. They had stayed behind for farewell drinks. Everyone else had left Caskey's in various stages of inebriation and celebration to enjoy the festival that was still going strong. "It was wonderful to see you both."

"I wish we could stay longer," Wendy said, "but I have to be back tomorrow to get ready for a show. Maybe we can all get together during the holidays."

"Liz, we can have lunch," Penny said, "when I come to the city to see Gloria Dalton. I invited her to come tonight, but she said she had a commitment."

Liz lifted her hands. "I've tried to get to know Gloria, but she's so private. I've heard that her house is like a fortress." Then she scowled. "I can't believe that on top of everything else, Deke hid assets during the divorce." She nodded to Penny's bag of gag gifts. "You should have torn the head off of that voodoo doll!"

At Liz's vicious tone, Penny laughed nervously. "Were you the one who brought it?"

"No, but it was brilliant. That man deserves to be taught a lesson."

Wendy nodded fervently. "He can't get away with this."

Touched that her friends were so angry on her behalf, Penny set her jaw. She was definitely going to call B.J. and begin laying her plan of attack against Deke and Sheena. (*Lay* being the operative word.) "Don't worry—I have plans for Deke. He's going to regret screwing me over." She stood and grabbed the table to steady herself.

Liz frowned. "Are you sure you're okay to walk home? Maybe you should get some coffee first?"

"No, I'm just across the square," Penny said, then inhaled deeply before turning toward the exit. "I'll be fine." Besides, if she sobered up, she might not make that phone call.

"You're going to feel like hell tomorrow," Wendy said.

Penny winced and put her hand to her head. "I think I will go to the ladies' room before I leave."

"Want us to wait?" Wendy asked.

"No, go ahead. Drive safely."

They embraced again, then the women left the bar. Penny watched them, her chest squeezing with fondness. But as she watched, Liz wheeled on Wendy and said something sharp, her expression angry, her finger accusing. Wendy seemed to shrink under the verbal attack before responding. Then Wendy strode ahead, her body language jerky. Liz glared after her before following.

Penny frowned at the exchange, wondering what they were arguing about—Wendy's mystery friend? Penny's predicament? Liz's ability to drive home? Then Penny dismissed it; the two women had always bickered when they'd all hung out, but they'd somehow managed to stay friends.

In the ladies' room, she wet a paper towel and dabbed at her neck and forehead. Her reflection in the mirror was fuzzily attractive—she finally understood the concept of "beer glasses." But her hands were covered with the damnable glitter from her makeup. Everything she touched sparkled . . . and B.J. didn't seem like the kind of guy who would appreciate waking up tomorrow with sparkles on his—

"Granola Girl—I thought that was you."

Penny looked up to see Sheena standing next to her, her hip cocked and her neck hitched in an unnatural position, a huge python-skin bag over her shoulder.

Sheena snapped her gum. "Did Deke get ahold of you?"

Penny sighed and tossed the soggy paper towel in the trash. "I don't know what you mean."

Snap, snap, cock, hitch. "He's lookin' for somethin' in the house and thought you might know where it is."

"What's he lookin'—I mean *looking*—for?"

"Search me," she said with a shrug.

"Considering how few clothes you're wearing, that wouldn't take long."

Sheena narrowed her eyes. "He's been tryin' to reach you. He seemed kinda worried, so you should give him a call at our home."

At *their* home. "Okay." And then she'd spend the night with Sheena's hottie boyfriend.

"What's so funny?"

"Nothing. See you around."

Penny left the bar and strolled across the square to her apartment. With alcohol buzzing through her system, the climb up the stairs was precarious at best. Twice she dropped her bag of gag gifts and had to go back to retrieve items—the ex-husband toilet paper, she had to admit, was a hoot. By the time she reached the top of the stairs, she was exhausted, but the flashlight helped dispel the darkness.

Once inside, she set the bag on the dining table and picked up the phone, wondering what Deke had misplaced that was so important (other than his accurate financial records), and how she was going to get through a conversation with him without tipping him off that she was on to him.

The display said she had four messages. She pushed the button.

"Penny, it's Deke." His voice was low and angry. *"I've lost something and thought you might know where it is. Call me."*

Penny frowned.

"It's me again. Why don't you get a cell phone like the rest of the world? Call me as soon as you get in."

"Call me." Heavy sigh. *"It's important."*

"Damnit, Penny, where the hell are you?"

His tone startled her—no matter what a bonehead he was, he never raised his voice to her. Whatever he'd misplaced, it must be important. With her heart thudding in her chest, she dialed the number to the house, but the line was busy.

Her hand brushed against her pocket, rustling the piece of paper inside. She withdrew the scrap and studied the phone number that B.J. had scrawled there. Her thighs quickened at the memory of his dark, interested gaze raking over her, but on the heels of the excitement was apprehension. She hadn't been with a man for a long time . . . she couldn't even remember the scant lovers she'd had before Deke. What did men like these days—meat and potatoes sex, or whipped cream and cherries? And what was *she* supposed to like? Freaky positions? Flavored lube?

She really should read a magazine once in a while.

Deciding that she needed a boost before dealing with Deke, she dialed the number B.J. had given her and inhaled for courage. After two rings, she panicked and started to hang up.

"B.J. here."

His voice sent a rumble through her midsection. "Um . . . hi. It's Penny." She swallowed. "We met at Caskey's."

"I remember," he said cheerfully. "The redheaded lady with the secrets. I didn't think you were going to call."

"Well . . . I did." She winced—that was bright.

He laughed. "So you did. Where do you want to meet?"

She debated the safety and privacy of her apartment versus a hotel room and decided that her apartment was probably better on both accounts. "My place. I live over the beignet shop on the square."

"Benny's?" He laughed. "Well, that explains your perfume."

She flushed hot. "Where are you?"

"Not far," he said vaguely. "What time do you want to meet?"

"I need a few minutes to take care of something," she said, glancing at her watch. It was a little past ten o'clock. "How about eleven? It's the door to the right of the shop. Just ring my bell. I mean . . . *the* bell."

"I'll be there," he promised, his voice thick and full of other wicked promises.

A silly smile crept up her face. "Okay. Good-bye." She hung up the phone and squealed like a teenager. She was going to have hot voodoo sex tonight.

Impatient and horny, she called Deke's number again, but the phone was still busy. Sighing in frustration, she worked her mouth from side to side. She could walk to the house, ring the doorbell, and be done with it faster than waiting for him to get off the phone. And maybe this was her chance to get back her lovebirds ornament under the pretense of finding whatever he was looking for. She moved toward the door a little too quickly, and a sharp pain stabbed her temples. Maybe the short walk would sober her up just a tad, too.

If she was going to spend the night with a long, hot Cajun, she wanted to be able to remember some of it.

She retrieved her purse, then grabbed her flashlight and headed back down the stairs, slowly. Out in the square, she blinked against the bright lights—fireworks were being set off in the fire department parking lot. The festival had grown even more frenetic, with the crowd around the *peristil* chanting, whirling, and twirling to the increased tempo. Lulled by the earthy rhythms, Penny relaxed and moved through the crowd at a leisurely pace, enjoying the weightlessness of her buzz and the hum of noise around her, womblike and comforting. On the far side of the shelter, she spotted Jules Lamborne performing some kind of dance in slow motion, her eyes closed and her movements fluid. She seemed to be stepping and waving to a song in her head.

Penny smiled, thinking she'd have something to tease Jules about in the morning—that she'd decided to put in an appearance at the festival after all. A sharp, whacking sound close by startled Penny. She turned and winced to see a chicken's head fall to the ground mere inches from her foot, its body spirited away to be offered to whatever *lwa* was being celebrated. A robed priestess was leading the ceremony, wearing an eerie mask that resembled the front of a human skull, minus the lower jaw, and topped with a spray of feathers. She held the headless chicken in one hand and a bead-covered rattle in the other hand.

Fascinated, Penny watched as the priestess began to spin, slowly at first, then faster and faster, more times than what seemed humanly tolerable. When she finally stopped, she was facing Penny. Suddenly the woman lifted the rattle in Penny's direction with an arm so rigid that it shook from sheer effort. Penny stood rooted to the ground, mesmerized by the rattling noise and the jingle of the bell attached to the handle, unable to move. Cold fear trickled down her back, like ice water. Was the priestess singling her out, casting a spell to rid her of—or to infuse her with—evil?

The moment was broken when the priestess abandoned her rattle to snatch another squirming chicken from its cage and relieve it of its head, this time with a savage twist of her bare hands, leaving a long white neck bone exposed. Penny winced—the sacrifice was even more bloody than the first, and in violation of an agreement with animal control. But the crowd seemed energized, cheering when the priestess set the headless chicken on its feet and the carcass ran around, flapping its wings, exhausting adrenaline in its muscle tissue.

Penny shuddered and backed away, eager now to finish her errand. The dark side of voodoo did not amuse her.

The streetlights were bright, illuminating the sidewalk during the three-block trek back to the Victorian on Charm Street. Away from the main crowd, though, the temperature had dropped into the low fifties, she guessed as she pulled the yellow shawl tighter around her shoulders. And something else warmed her—the anticipation of spending the night with the sexy, mysterious B.J.

The Victorian fairly glowed with its new pink paint job—if possible, the color was even more ghastly at night, and it emitted a damp, fusty odor. The porch light was on, as were the light in front of the garage and a few strategic landscape lights that she had installed herself. From the street she could see lights on inside the house—the kitchen, Deke's office, and the master bedroom. She climbed the steps to the porch and glanced at the metal glider before ringing the doorbell. After a couple of minutes passed, she cupped her hands around her eyes and peered into the small square window on the door. The pressure made the door swing inward. Deke still hadn't adjusted the plate on the frame so that the door would catch without leaning a shoulder into it.

She stuck her head inside. "Deke?" She stepped into the foyer and closed the door behind her. "Deke, it's Penny!"

She took a few seconds to enjoy the stunning entryway that she had been so proud of, trying not to notice the things that were out of place or the cobwebs hanging from far corners illuminated by the rose-colored, recessed lighting. She inhaled the comforting scent of old plaster and Bri-Wax, and her heart squeezed with homesickness. She knelt to straighten a rug whose corner had been upturned, then frowned at a stack of unread newspapers by the door and brightly colored high-heeled shoes casually lying about, blazing a trail to the kitchen doorway on the left. Mail was piled up and falling off the Duncan Phyfe side table. A zebra-print jacket had been tossed carelessly over the silk flower arrangement adorning the table.

She hated to think what she might see in the daylight.

Seeing Sheena's things strewn about the house she loved made bile rise in Penny's throat, but she tried to push the thoughts out of her mind. Deke had made his choice and Sheena was his problem now. Apparently, the woman was still at Caskey's, dressed to kill.

Penny swallowed hard, antsy to leave. "Deke! It's Penny!"

From the darkened entryway, she could see his office door on the second floor, just beyond the landing. The door was slightly ajar, spilling light into the hallway. The muffled noise of the television sounded. She could picture him reared back in his chair, his feet on his desk while he talked on the phone with one eye on a ball game.

She worked her mouth back and forth in sudden inspiration—if she was careful, she could get to the attic and remove her lovebirds ornament before he even realized she was in the house.

She slipped off her sandals and carried them as she crept up the wood stairs in semidarkness. Because she knew where all the creaky spots were, she was able to make her way up silently, although the floor felt gritty beneath her bare feet. Her heart rattled against her breastbone, but she conceded a thrill of excitement to be doing something so illicit.

When she reached the second floor, she held her breath as she stole by Deke's office door, sure that any second he was going to emerge and blast her for snooping around. But she made it past the door undetected. Next was the master bedroom. She couldn't resist a glance inside, but she grimaced at the unmade bed and piles of clothes on the floor. Their framed wedding picture on the dresser had been replaced with a picture of Sheena and Deke.

"He could have at least bought a new frame," she muttered. On impulse she walked in and picked up the picture, hurt and anger bubbling in her chest anew. The picture had been taken on a carriage ride—in New Orleans, no doubt.

Deke had never taken *her* on a carriage ride.

In the photo, Sheena looked pouty, and Deke looked . . . pained, as if his balls were in a bind.

Feeling malevolent, she placed the picture frame on the floor, then slipped her foot into her sandal and ground her heel against the glass until it cracked, sending a splinter across their faces. Then she positioned the photo facedown so that it appeared as if it might have been knocked off by an errant tube top.

With her ears piqued, she stepped back out into the hallway. Hearing nothing but the television, she turned toward the narrow stairway leading to the attic. A pull chain to a bare lightbulb provided just enough light to climb to the top. Penny jiggled the glass knob to the attic door and pushed it open, wincing when it groaned loudly. She waited a few seconds, but when she didn't hear Deke pounding her way, she stepped into the attic.

Every woman should have an attic, a place to put things that were special and not for public display. Unfortunately, she hadn't had the family keepsakes and heirlooms that would have filled up the large space beautifully. Instead she'd had an old calico chair losing its stuffing that she'd never gotten around to reupholstering, a large framed mirror that was cracked in the corner but had been too nice to put in the Dumpster, and a chest of drawers painted pale blue that had never seemed to fit anywhere in the house.

She stepped onto the linoleum she'd laid down, thinking her feet would be black by the time she left. She'd have to take a shower before B.J. showed up . . . but then if he had bedded Sheena, he probably didn't mind dirty feet.

The top drawer of the chest held mostly linens she'd bought at estate sales. She rummaged until her hand closed around the tissue paper holding the lovebirds ornament. For old times' sake, she unwrapped the pewter ornament and ran her finger over the white enameled birds holding a ribbon in their beaks that said Deke and Penny, forever.

Biting her lip at their naiveté, she conceded that they'd been happier then . . . before they'd had grown-up problems. With a sigh, she rewrapped the ornament and put it in her purse, then retraced her steps to the darkened hallway, where she tiptoed past Deke's office door to the top of the stairs. Then she stepped back into her sandals.

"Deke!" she yelled, stomping as if she were only now coming up the stairs. "It's Penny! I got your messages and thought I'd just stop by. Deke?" She walked to his office door and rapped loudly. "Deke?"

She pushed open the door. "Deke, it's P—"

Her voice died as her brain tried to process the scene before her. The television was on, airing a cheesy beer commercial. The phone on the desk was off the hook, ergo the busy signal.

And Deke . . . Deke was on the floor on his back, arms and legs askew. He still wore the European-cut suit and the trendy silk tie, but his white shirt was now red . . . from the wound caused by the object sticking out of his chest:

A wire stake topped with a pink plastic flag . . . just like the ones she'd used to stake off her new garden.

11

Until it boils over . . .

For several surreal seconds, Penny had the most bizarre feeling of déjà vu, as if she'd dreamed this incident, or had lived through it before. . . .

No—the voodoo doll.

She gasped and stumbled into the room, overwhelmed and confused. Terror pulsed through her veins as she fell to her knees next to Deke. Blood speckled the beige carpet.

"Deke," she murmured, choking. She was certain he was dead—his eyes were open in a blank stare. His skin was chalky. He lay in an unnatural position. But she made herself press her trembling fingers against his neck to check for a pulse. Nothing.

The sulfurous smell of blood enveloped her. Her stomach heaved, and despite her best efforts to move, she fisted her hands in the material of his jacket and threw up all over him. The alcohol burned her throat even worse on the way up than it had on the way down. By the time she had emptied her stomach, she was sobbing. She wiped her mouth with the edge of her shawl and stared at the unholy mess she'd made.

Deke was dead. Not just dead—*murdered.*

Shaking in disbelief, Penny scrambled to her feet, her mind reeling. What to do? Who to call? She hyperventilated until common sense finally kicked in—she had to calm down. Gulping for air, she picked up the phone to dial 911, and the situation slammed into her like a brick wall: What if the police thought she'd done it? Then another, more horrific thought hit her: What if whoever killed Deke was still in the house somewhere? Looting the spare bedrooms, rooting through the kitchen, prowling in the garage?

With trembling hands, she returned the receiver to the cradle and covered her mouth to smother the scream that hovered at the back of her throat. *Breathe*, she told herself. *Breathe . . . think.* Wildly searching the room for a weapon, she grabbed an antique cane from the umbrella stand near the door. First she had to get out of this house, then she'd flag down a car or call 911 from the store.

Desperation rose in her chest, threatening to paralyze her, but she forced herself to focus on her surroundings. With her heart thrashing, she stuck her head into the hall and frantically looked both ways. All clear.

Wielding the cane like a baseball bat, she stepped out into the hall illuminated only by the light from the office. She started for the stairs. A noise below, however, stopped her. She froze, her ears zoning in.

There it was again—the sound of quiet footsteps coming from the back of the house toward the foyer . . . as if the person was trying to mask their approach. Panic lodged in her throat—should she scream? Try to escape? Hide in the attic?

Her lungs worked like bellows. Perspiration dripped down her back. She was sure the intruder would be able to hear her fractured breathing. Her stomach was roiling again, and she swallowed hard to try to ward off another sick episode. From where she stood on the landing, she couldn't see down into the foyer, and she prayed that she, too, couldn't be seen. A few seconds of silence passed and her breathing slowed. Then she heard the noise again—the person was climbing the stairs, and they apparently didn't know the creaky spots.

Her pulse pounded in her ears as she fought the overwhelming urge to run. The light on the landing, she recalled, was blinding—if she could find the switch, she might have the advantage of surprise to get past the intruder or push them down the stairs. Pure fear spurred her into action. She lunged for the light switch and raised the cane, poised to kill if necessary. Or at least bruise.

A hot, white light flooded the landing. The intruder threw up her overtanned arms and screamed like a wounded hyena.

Sheena.

Penny's shoulders slumped in abject relief.

"I knew it!" Sheena said, stabbing her finger in the air. "I knew you and Deke were carrying on behind my back!"

Penny squinted. "What?"

"If you think you're going to get him back, you can think again!"

Penny glanced toward the office door—at this angle, the scene inside wasn't visible.

"How long has this been going on?"

"You've got it all wrong, Sheena. Stop talking—I have to tell you something."

"I want to hear this from Deke," Sheena said, then started toward the office.

Penny grabbed her arm. "Don't go in there, Sheena."

"What—is he naked?" Sheena shouted. "Still cleaning up the scene of the crime?"

"No," Penny said, squeezing the woman's arm harder. "Deke—"

"Let *go* of me." She wrenched her arm away, then ran to the door of the office. "Deke, how could you—" She covered her face and screamed, jogging in place. "Omigod, omigod, omigod. Is he *dead*?"

"Yes."

"You killed him! You killed my Deke!"

Penny shook her head and held out a hand to calm her. "No. I found him like this, Sheena. Just a few minutes ago."

Suddenly the blond's eyes widened at the sight of the cane Penny held. Sheena flattened herself against the doorjamb, her mouth a gaping red hole. "And now you're going to kill me, too!"

"Calm down," Penny said, holding up her hands. "See, I'm putting down the cane. We need to call the police."

In a flash, Sheena whipped her cell phone out of her snakeskin purse and pushed a button. Just as quickly she whipped up a few crocodile tears. "Hello? This is Sheena Linder. My fiancé, Deke Black, was just murdered by his ex-wife in our home."

Penny's knees buckled. *"What are you doing?"*

"Yes, she's still here. Her name is Penny Francisco.

We're at 110 Charm Street in Mojo. It's the pink house. Thank you." Sheena snapped the phone shut. "They're on their way." She narrowed her eyes. "You're going to fry for this, Granola Girl."

12

Let things simmer for a while . . .

Penny sat in a room at the local jail wearing baggy gray sweats borrowed from the supply room and feeling ready to come undone. At least an hour had passed since she'd been escorted to the room, since she'd left a voice message on Gloria Dalton's cell phone, two hours since she'd found Deke's body. By now word of the grisly murder had probably spread to every household in Mojo via Sheena's megaphone mouth. Penny alternately tapped her fingers on the table, hugged herself, and pinched herself, just in case this was all a long, bad dream. Unfortunately, she was very much awake.

And under suspicion.

Under suspicion for murdering Deke. The idea was so ludicrous that she had burst into laughter several times while waiting for Chief Davis to return. If anyone was watching on the other side of the darkened window, they probably thought she had lost her mind.

Her throat was parched, and her mouth tasted of stale vomit. Her head pounded from the countless vodka martinis. Her finger stung from the punch-needle the CSI tech had used to check her blood-alcohol level at the scene. Her pride hurt from having her clothing confiscated. And her heart had turned to lead over the fact that Deke was dead.

And that someone had either unwittingly or purposely made it look as if she had done it.

The door opened, and Penny's pulse jumped. Police Chief Allyson Davis, a tall, big-boned brunette, walked in, accompanied by a rocky-faced, suited man that Penny had never seen.

"Sorry for the delay," Allyson said, her face pale and drawn, making her look even more severe. With the festival going on, she'd probably had a long day. "This is Detective Maynard from New Orleans—he's going to be assisting in the investigation."

Penny nodded, although she had a feeling that the two of them were not overjoyed to be working together.

"Can I get you some coffee?" Allyson asked, setting a tape recorder on the table.

Penny eyed the machine warily. "Water, please. And maybe some aspirin?"

"No can do on the aspirin, but I'll be back with the water." She looked at the detective. "I'd appreciate if you'd wait to talk to *my* witness."

He nodded, but he made no promises, Penny noted.

When the door closed, he sat in one of the chairs and withdrew a packet of chewable aspirin from his coat pocket. "I take them by the handful. Just don't let her know I gave it to you."

"Thank you," Penny murmured, then tore open the packet and chewed the orange-flavored tablets.

"So . . . Ms. Francisco, how long have you lived in Mojo?"

"Eight years."

"What brought you to town?"

She shifted on the uncomfortable chair. "I moved here with my husband."

"You mean, your ex-husband?"

She bit her tongue. "Yes."

"Where is your family?"

She hesitated. "I grew up in a small town in Tennessee."

He nodded. "What town?"

"King . . . ston."

"Kingston?"

She coughed and nodded. "But I don't have any family left."

"What do you do for a living, Ms. Francisco?"

"I own a health food store."

"Across the street from the house where the murder was committed."

"That's correct. My husband—I mean, my ex-husband and I owned both pieces of property. When we divorced, he kept the home we lived in, and I kept the business."

"Why did you and your husband divorce?"

The door opened, admitting Allyson Davis. She handed Penny a bottle of water and glared at Maynard. "I thought I told you to wait."

"We're just getting acquainted," he said mildly.

Allyson lowered herself into a chair. It was then that Penny noticed that the woman's nose and eyes were red. Penny realized that Allyson had known the Black family for some time . . . that she and Mona, if not friendly, seemed to tolerate each other, that she and Deke had conferred on many cases. Penny suspected that this was the first homicide that Allyson had worked on since she'd arrived in Mojo; for the victim to be someone she knew must be doubly difficult.

"Are you doing okay, Penny?" Allyson asked gruffly.

Penny took a long drink of water, then nodded. "Considering."

"Do you want to tell us what happened?"

"I already told you," Penny said.

"For my sake," Maynard said, his voice apologetic.

"And I'd like to hear it again," Allyson said, "just to make sure I didn't miss anything."

Penny fidgeted with the label on the bottle. "Has Gloria Dalton arrived yet?"

"Your attorney? No."

Penny wet her lips. "Perhaps I should wait."

Allyson pursed her mouth. "Why do you need an attorney, Penny? I thought you said you didn't kill Deke."

The woman had already convicted her, Penny realized suddenly, and the knowledge pushed her sweat glands into overdrive. "I *didn't* kill him," she said evenly. "But until the evidence can be processed and I'm cleared, I want my attorney to be involved, and I'd rather not have to go through all of this again when she arrives."

"What if I told you that we already have enough to arrest you on?"

A rap on the door sounded. Allyson frowned and pushed to her feet. When she opened the door, Penny sagged in relief to see Gloria step inside. She was wearing a suit, but no makeup, and she looked flushed. Behind her glasses, her blue eyes were bloodshot. Penny squinted—Gloria's eyes were normally green, like her own. Her contact lenses must be colored.

"I'm Gloria Dalton, Ms. Francisco's attorney. What's this all about?"

"It's about murder," Allyson said dryly. "Your client's ex-husband is dead, and she was discovered at the scene."

Gloria looked at Penny, then back to Allyson. "Is she under arrest?"

"Not yet."

"Where are her clothes?"

"Her clothing was bloodstained, plus she threw up all over herself—and the body. We offered her something clean to wear."

Gloria blanched. "I'd like to talk to Penny alone."

"It's fine, Gloria," Penny said. "I don't have anything to hide, I just wanted you to be here when I gave my statement."

Gloria looked at Allyson. "A moment, please?"

Allyson signaled to Maynard, and they left the room. As soon as the door closed, Gloria strode over to the table, her expression pinched. "Penny, I'm not a criminal attorney!"

"I know. But relax—I didn't kill Deke. I just wanted someone here that I could trust."

Gloria pulled her hand down her face, clearly agitated. "Are you sure you don't want me to call someone who could better advise you?"

"Yes. The last thing I want is for Allyson to think I'm lawyering up on her."

"Allyson? Do you know the chief personally?"

"Everyone knows everyone in this town."

Gloria shook her head, but after a few seconds, she acquiesced. "Okay, but if I interrupt, you have to do what I say."

"Agreed."

Gloria squinted. "Do you know you have glitter all over your face?"

Penny rolled her eyes. "Yes. I may never wear makeup again."

"This is against my better judgment," Gloria declared, then asked Allyson and Maynard to return. Soon they were all crowded around the table.

"No recorder," Gloria said firmly.

"It's for your client's protection as much as ours," Allyson said.

"No recorder," Gloria repeated.

Allyson frowned but nodded curtly. "Okay, Penny, let's start at the beginning."

Penny shifted again—her rear end had gone to sleep sitting on the hard metal. "You mean when I arrived at the house?"

"Let's go back further. How did you spend your evening?"

"Friends gave me a party at Caskey's. I was there until about ten o'clock."

"And what was the party for?"

She clasped her hands around the water bottle, now speckled with glitter from her hands from touching her face. "To celebrate my divorce."

"From Deke Black?"

"Yes."

"Did anything unusual happen at the party?"

Penny thought of the voodoo doll episode, but it was just too, too ludicrous. "Not really. It was a small crowd. Everyone seemed to have a good time."

"We'll need a list of everyone who attended. What did you do after you left the party?"

Penny looked up to gather her thoughts. "I went back to my apartment and I had—let's see—four voice messages from Deke that he needed to talk to me." Then she winced. "No, wait, I need to go back . . . before I left Caskey's, I ran into Sheena Linder and she told me that Deke was looking for something at the house and that he thought I might know where it was."

"For the record, Sheena Linder is Deke's girlfriend?"

"Yes."

"And she's the woman that he had an affair with that ended your marriage."

Penny wet her lips. "That's . . . correct."

"Okay, so Sheena tells you that Deke wants to talk to you. Did she tell you he was home?"

Penny frowned. "I don't remember exactly. I guess I just assumed that he was home, since he wasn't with her."

"Where is your apartment?"

"Over the beignet shop, across from Caskey's, on the square."

"Uh-huh. So why did you decide to go to see Deke?"

"The phone was busy."

"Why didn't you just keep calling? Or let him call you back if it was so important?"

"Because I—" Penny stopped. *B.J.* She'd forgotten all about meeting him. A flush began to work its way up her neck. How long had he waited? "Because I . . . wanted to go back and enjoy the festival."

Maynard pivoted his head to address Allyson. "Do you mind if I ask a few questions?"

Allyson's mouth twitched. "Go ahead." Although it was clear that she did mind.

"So, Ms. Francisco," he said, "you decide to walk to the house to see what your ex-husband wanted."

"Right. It's only a three-block walk."

"Do you have any idea of what he was looking for?"

"None whatsoever."

"Can you venture a guess?"

"Knowing Deke, it was probably a cigar lighter, or something like that."

"Mighty helpful of you to be so worried about what it was he needed."

Penny took another drink from the bottle of water. "I've tried to remain cordial after our split."

"You didn't have any animosity toward your ex-husband?"

"No."

"None at all? I should warn you that we'll be questioning your friends and employees."

Penny swallowed hard. "Well, I wasn't pleased that he had the house we lived in painted pink."

"That's all?"

She wet her lips and glanced at Gloria—when they'd been alone, she should have told her attorney about the fact that Deke might have been hiding assets. Gloria must have seen something in Penny's expression, because she lunged forward in her seat.

"My client already said that she endeavored to remain cordial. Move along or this interview is over."

Maynard sighed. "Okay, tell me what happened when you arrived at the house."

"I rang the doorbell, but no one answered. I assumed Deke was still on the phone, and when I leaned on the door, it opened."

His eyebrows shot up. "So, let me get this straight—the door was open when you got there, and you didn't think it was strange?"

"Not really. The front door always swells until winter—you have to apply a lot of pressure to close it. I just assumed whoever had closed it last didn't take the time."

He leaned his chin on his hand. "So you just went into the house?"

Penny bristled. "I announced myself."

"Did Mr. Black answer?"

"No."

"Then what did you do?"

She decided to skip the fact that she'd snooped a bit. "I heard the television in his office—the door was ajar, and I could see that the light was on. I yelled a couple of more times from the foyer, then I went up and I . . . found him."

Maynard leaned back and crossed his arms. "Can you be more specific?"

She moistened her dry lips. "I opened the door and he was lying on the floor, with that thing coming out of his chest."

"The wire stake."

She nodded.

"We'll get back to the stake," he promised, "but tell me what happened next."

"I knelt over him to see if I could find a pulse, but there wasn't one." She closed her eyes briefly. "And that's when I got sick . . . I was just so scared, and I'd had a few drinks at Caskey's." She grimaced. "I don't usually drink."

Maynard sighed heavily. "So you threw up on the deceased. Then what? Did you call 911?"

"No. I thought about it," she added quickly. "But then it occurred to me that whoever had killed Deke might still be in the house. I heard a noise downstairs, so I picked up a cane to defend myself."

"But if you were afraid, why didn't you call 911?"

Because I was more afraid that this would happen. "All I could think about was getting out of that house. Then I realized it was only Sheena coming home."

"She said you were going to kill her with the cane."

Penny sighed. "I thought she was an intruder—I was trying to protect myself."

"Did you strike her?"

"No, I didn't lay a hand on her." Not since she'd pushed her into traffic, that is.

"So you're saying that Mr. Black was already dead when you found him?"

"Absolutely."

"Are you willing to take a polygraph?"

"Yes."

"Strike that," Gloria interrupted. "It's too early in the case to discuss a polygraph."

Maynard pressed his lips together. "Let's get back to the wire stake that was used to kill Mr. Black. Did you recognize the stake, Ms. Francisco?"

She bit her lip. "Yes."

"From where?"

"It looked like the same kind I used to stake off a garden next to my health food store." Next to her, she felt Gloria stiffen.

"And I understand that this garden was a bit of a contentious point between you and your ex?"

Penny sighed and massaged her temples, which still pounded. "Deke was never in favor of me starting the health food store, and when I suggested the garden to expand business, he was against it, yes."

"But you went ahead with your plans?"

"As soon as the divorce papers were final, and the land was mine."

"When was that?"

"Earlier this week."

"And do you have any idea why anyone would kill your ex-husband in such a bizarre manner?"

"No."

"Who had access to the wire stakes?"

"I bought them at the local hardware store. And there are several in the ground next to my business—anyone could have gotten one."

Maynard sighed. "Ms. Francisco, do you believe in voodoo?"

She felt the blood drain from her face. "No."

"But isn't your health food store called The Charm Farm?"

"That's because it's on Charm Street," she explained. "And because I sell organic products."

"We've heard a rumor about a voodoo doll at your divorce party."

Penny's stomach rolled, emitting an untimely gurgle. "It was a gag gift. One of many I received."

"Tell us about the doll," he encouraged.

She gave a little laugh to hide her mounting fear. "It was supposed to represent Deke."

"And what did you do to it?"

"I . . ." She swallowed. "I . . . stabbed it with a pin. But it was all a joke."

"Uh-huh. Where exactly did you stab it?"

She closed her eyes briefly. "In the chest."

"Uh-huh. And don't you find it coincidental that shortly after you stab a voodoo doll of your ex-husband in the chest with a pin, he's found dead with a stake sticking out of his chest? A stake from your garden?"

Panic rose in her chest like a choking tide. "I know how it looks," she said, her voice squeaky, "but I didn't kill him! That's why I'm here telling you everything."

"Who gave you the voodoo doll?"

"I don't know—all of the gifts were anonymous."

Allyson scoffed, clearly eager to jump back in. "That's convenient. Sheena told us that you were really upset earlier today when you discovered that she and Deke were engaged."

Had Sheena told them that she'd pushed her into the street? Penny gripped the empty water bottle so hard that it popped up in the air and landed on the floor. Maybe that polygraph wasn't such a good idea after all. She leaned over to scoop up the bottle. "I was surprised, but it didn't bother me." Another lie—God, she was pathological.

Allyson leaned forward, her eyes hard. "I think you're lying, Penny. Sheena also told us that she thinks you and Deke were fooling around behind her back." Allyson's anger was palpable, vibrating around the room.

"That's simply not true," Penny said, pulling back slightly from Allyson's aggressive posture. The irony was downright humiliating—she and Deke hadn't had sex very often when they were *married*, much less after they'd split.

"Chief Davis," Gloria said carefully, "since you were acquainted with the victim, perhaps Detective Maynard should handle the questioning."

Allyson sat back and seemed to regain her composure. "I apologize. But this happened on my watch—I'm sure you can understand my eagerness to get to the truth."

"Why aren't you questioning Ms. Linder?" Gloria asked. "She was the one who told Penny that Deke was looking for her. Maybe she set Penny up."

"Ms. Linder was at her place of business," Allyson said. "From there she went directly to Caskey's, and several people have vouched for her alibi." The chief looked back to Penny and took a deep breath, visibly trying to calm herself. "I think you killed him, Penny. I think it made you crazy to see Deke with another woman, so crazy that you'd rather he be dead than with someone else."

"That's not true," Penny said, exasperated. "If I were going to kill Deke, I certainly wouldn't have done it with a garden stake!"

"Oh? How would you have killed him?"

Penny opened her mouth to describe her fantasies but clamped it shut when she realized she'd been baited.

Allyson smiled. "I think you were obsessed with him."

Penny pressed her mouth together, suddenly close to tears. "I loved Deke, but when our relationship ended, I let it go."

"Really?" Allyson gestured to Maynard, who reached into an inner jacket pocket and removed a plastic evidence bag. Inside was the lovebirds ornament emblazoned with Deke and Penny, forever. "Do you always carry this around in your purse?"

Penny puffed out her cheeks in an exhale. "No. Deke gave it to me when we were first dating, and it was special to me. I forgot about it and left it in the house when I moved out."

"And when did you get it back?"

She bit down on the inside of her cheek. "Tonight."

"When tonight—before you murdered Deke?"

"Stop badgering my client," Gloria interjected.

"Answer the question, Penny."

She wiped her clammy palms on the thighs of her borrowed sweatpants and sighed. "When I got to the house, like I said, I thought Deke was still on the phone because he didn't answer when I called his name. I figured that while I waited for him to finish his call, I might as well go to the attic and get the ornament."

"Steal it, you mean."

"It was mine," she countered. "Deke wouldn't have cared—it just wasn't worth bothering him."

"But you didn't want him to know," Allyson said. "After all, he was engaged—you didn't want him to know that you were still in love with him."

"I wasn't in love with him, I just wanted the keepsake, that's all."

Allyson crossed her arms. "There's blood on your clothes, Penny."

She lifted her hands. "I must have gotten it when I leaned over him."

"The CSI tech says they look like projected bloodstains, not transfer stains, which means you were standing in front of him or over him when the blood was spurting out of him."

Penny winced and shook her head. "That's impossible. I didn't kill him. I wasn't there. He was already dead when I found him."

Allyson held up her fingers, counting off. "You had motive, opportunity, and you just happened to be the one who found the body. From where I'm sitting, this is practically an open-and-shut case."

Penny's stomach bottomed out. "But I *didn't* kill Deke."

Allyson pounded her fist on the table. "Then who did?"

Gloria stood abruptly. "Figuring that out is *your* job, Chief. Are you finished? My client is obviously exhausted from her ordeal."

"I'm finished, all right." Allyson's hand hovered over the handcuffs at her side, but Maynard cleared his throat.

"Give us a minute, Counselor." He looked at Allyson and nodded toward the hallway. She followed, looking none too pleased.

When the door closed, Gloria collapsed into the chair. "Penny, this is serious, and I have to tell you, I'm in way over my head here. If they arrest you, you have to get another attorney."

Penny bit her lip. "There's more."

Gloria held up her hand. "Whatever it is, I don't want to know."

"But this concerns you." Penny looked at the window. "Can they hear me?"

"No. They're not allowed to listen in when a suspect talks to their attorney."

Penny lifted her eyebrows. "I thought you knew nothing about criminal law."

Gloria sighed. "That's about the extent of it. What is this thing that concerns me?"

"Deke's paralegal told my employee Marie Gaston that Deke hid assets during the divorce settlement."

Gloria closed her eyes. "Oh, this is bad. And when did Marie give you this information?"

"During the party."

"Before or after you stabbed the voodoo doll?"

"Um . . . before."

Gloria mouthed a curse word.

The door opened and Maynard returned, alone. "Today's your lucky day, Ms. Francisco. We decided not to make an arrest until the crime scene evidence has been processed."

Penny almost wet herself with relief.

Then Maynard's eyebrows came together in a dark frown. "You're free to go, but don't take any trips. Oh, and a search warrant is being served on your apartment as we speak." He left the room, banging the door shut.

Gloria melted into her chair. "Tell me you burned that voodoo doll."

"It's at my apartment."

"Oh, God, we're in deep shit."

Penny winced. "More like deep voodoo."

13

Then stir things up again . . .

"Are you sure you'll be okay?" Gloria asked.

Penny tried her best to smile as she slid out of the passenger door of her attorney's car. "I'll be fine from here—my place is just around the corner. Thanks for the ride home."

"I'll call you tomorrow."

Penny closed the door and shivered against the lower temperatures. The police had confiscated her purse, releasing only her keys and driver's license. Without the flashlight, she felt vulnerable on the side street. She couldn't see her watch in the dim lighting, but she estimated the time to be about 3:00 A.M. The street was nearly empty, save for the people who were camped out for the night against the building, the tips of their cigarettes glowing in the dark. Hushed talk and low laughter floated out, along with the scent of incense and clove.

Spooked from the pictures of Deke's murder scene now burned into her brain, she walked as quickly as the borrowed flip-flops would allow, eager to be in her own bed. Her body was wracked with exhaustion, but she doubted she'd get any sleep. She just wanted to put the covers over her head for a few hours and absorb the absurd reality that Deke was dead.

And more absurd still, that the police thought she'd done it.

She rounded the corner and entered the square, not surprised to see the ceremonial fires still burning and a knot of people still chanting and dancing. But the crowds had dispersed and the chirp of cicadas had replaced the drums. And thank goodness, the masked priestess who had rattled Penny (literally) was nowhere to be found.

The giant revolving beignet had never looked so good to her. She stepped up to the outer door leading to her apartment, then inhaled sharply when she realized a man was sitting on the sidewalk, his head down, his back leaned against her door. Her startled cry made him stir. He lifted his head, raising his hand to shield his eyes from the street light.

"B.J.?" she asked, incredulous. How desperate was the man to get laid that he'd waited four hours?

"Hey," he croaked, pushing to his feet. "I heard what happened. Are you okay?"

She was instantly suspicious. "How did you hear what happened?"

"I was here when the police came—I guess they searched your place? One of the cops told me that your ex-husband was murdered."

"That's right," she said, wondering what else the cop had told him.

"So . . . did you kill him?"

Indignance puckered her mouth. "No."

He brushed off his backside. "Good. I usually can size up people pretty well, and I pegged you for a lover, not a fighter."

In the daylight, he might have been charming, but at this hour and considering what she'd been through, she wasn't amused. "Look, it's been a very long night. I'm not up for company."

"What? Oh, no, I didn't expect you to . . ." He made a rueful noise. "I just wanted to see if you were okay."

"I'm okay."

"Good." He nodded. "Then . . . I'll be on my way."

She watched him begin to walk away, remorse coursing through her chest. If only she had left Caskey's with him, she reasoned crazily, she wouldn't have been in the mess she was in. The next time she had the choice between fun and obligation, she would choose fun . . . assuming there would be a next time. "Hey," she said. "Wait."

He turned back.

"I guess I owe you an explanation."

He shrugged. "Not unless you want to talk about it."

She crossed her arms over her baggy sweatshirt. "Just who are you anyway?"

He gave a little laugh. "That's a fair question. My name is Beaumont."

"Why are you in Mojo?"

"I'm in town on business."

"What kind of business?"

He hesitated. "I'm a private investigator from New Orleans. I specialize in missing persons. I go where the crowds are—festivals, concerts."

Penny narrowed her eyes. "Why were you at Sheena Linder's house yesterday morning?"

"How did you know about that?"

"She's engaged to my ex-husband, the man who was murdered tonight. And she lives in the house I used to—only it wasn't pink when I lived there. I have a business across the street, and I saw you drive up in a green car."

He whistled low. "Not bad. If you got my license plate number, I'd like to offer you a job."

"Are you two involved or something?"

"No." He held up his hands. "I'd never met the Linder woman until yesterday, and it didn't take me long to realize that she's not my type."

Okay, so he was improving in her eyes. "Then why were you there?"

Another hesitation. "It was a dead-end lead. Wait a minute—did *she* kill your ex-husband?"

"That would be too simple." Immediately, guilt descended, and Penny sighed. "I'm sorry—that was a terrible thing to say. I'm tired."

"Right." He stuffed his hands into his coat pockets. "Look, I know it's late, but do you want to talk, maybe grab a cup of coffee at the diner?"

She looked down to the far left corner of the square. Sure enough, Ted's was still open. Penny wavered and looked down at her baggy sweats and flip-flops. "I'm not exactly dressed for it."

"It's a diner. There's mashed potatoes on the floor."

She smiled for the first time in what seemed like days.

"Come on—just a cup of coffee. Decaf."

Why did she gravitate toward this stranger? He

looked dark and potentially dangerous, yet there was no denying the fact that he exuded a vibe of strength that she needed . . . and wanted. She caved to curiosity and walked toward him. "That's the only thing on Ted's menu that's passable, and just barely."

They walked in silence, past the erected shelter and the vendor booths that had been closed up for the night, past bundles of people sitting on tarps around portable Coleman lanterns with blankets wrapped around them. Without being obvious, B.J. glanced at every face.

"Does the voodoo festival always bring out such a big crowd?" he asked.

"Never quite this big. The weather has helped."

He held open the diner door, and she walked under his arm. "What kind of business do you own?"

She frowned at the deadly desserts rotating in the refrigerator case as they passed. "A health food store."

He chortled. "That explains the tofu remark at the bar."

"Have you tried it?" she asked as she slid into a sticky red-and-white booth.

He shrugged out of his leather bomber jacket and tossed it on the seat before sitting opposite her. "No, I can honestly say I've never tried tofu."

"Well, don't knock it until you've tried it." She glanced around to see if she knew anyone in the diner and spotted the two friends of Marie's who worked at the Hair Affair, who had come to her party. One of the girls saw her and put her hand to her mouth, then whispered to the other one, who looked up, her eyes wide.

Penny turned away, wondering what she'd been

thinking to come here—in standard issue Mojo jail garb, no less.

"Friends of yours?" B.J. asked.

"Not really. But I guess word has gotten around about Deke."

"That was your ex's name—Deke?"

"Deke Black. I went back to my maiden name, Francisco."

"Penny Francisco," he said, as if testing it on his tongue. "Nice." Then he frowned. "His name sounds familiar—would I know him?"

"He's an attorney—" She stopped. "I mean, he *was* an attorney here in Mojo. Maybe your paths crossed at some point."

"Maybe."

Ted walked by and tossed two menus on the table.

"So," B.J. said, opening a menu. "What happened?"

She fingered the menu and told him about running into Sheena before she left the bar and the messages that Deke had left for her at her apartment. "After I called you, I kept getting a busy signal at Deke's." She lifted her hands. "Don't ask me why, but I decided to walk to the house to see what he wanted and get it over with. When I got there, I found his . . . body." A shudder overtook her, but she was determined not to break down. "And then Sheena came home and found *me*."

He was quiet, but from his eyes, she could tell his mind was racing.

"Made up yer mind yet?" Ted asked. His apron was stained every color in the rainbow and smeared with some chunky stuff that Penny didn't want to identify.

"Decaf coffee for me," she said, pushing away the menu.

B.J. looked up. "Do you mind if I get some food? I'll eat fast."

"No, go ahead." While he ordered, she studied his features, placing him in his late thirties. His square jaw had a day's growth, and his hair was long on top and windblown. His black Kenny Wayne Shepherd Band T-shirt had seen a few washings. She'd never met a PI, but she decided the occupation suited him and idly wondered about his background.

"Comin' right up," Ted said, then he looked at Penny. "Weren't you married to that Deke Black who was murdered tonight?"

She swallowed. "We were divorced."

"Word is that you stabbed a voodoo doll and did him in."

Penny tried her best to look outraged. "That's ridiculous."

B.J. looked at Ted. "How about that coffee?" When the man shuffled away, B.J. said, "What's all this about a voodoo doll?"

She sighed. "It's silly. I got a voodoo doll dressed like Deke as a gag gift at my party. I got carried away and . . . stabbed it."

He nodded thoughtfully. "And how was Deke killed?"

"Um . . . he was stabbed."

"Oh."

She started to get up. "Look, this was a bad idea . . . I'm in a lot of trouble . . . I shouldn't even be here . . . with you."

He put his hand on her arm. "Maybe I can help."

She looked down at his big hand, thinking how

wrong everything seemed—Deke was gone and another man was touching her, offering help. Her eyes welled with tears, and she was afraid to move or speak. Mortification rolled over her in waves.

"Shhh," he murmured. "Don't break down . . . not now. There are too many eyes."

He was right. She blinked furiously just as Ted returned to slide two mugs of coffee across the table. She sat back down and drank deeply from hers, feeling somewhat calmer. "Are you saying that I should hire you to help clear me?"

He shrugged. "Maybe."

"Are you any good?" The words hung in the air, thick with the implication of what might have happened tonight if she hadn't gone to Deke's.

A little smile curved his mouth. "The best in three states."

What was he going to say? Still, she believed him. Yet the urge to tell this man everything scared her a little. "Do you have some sort of ID or something that says you're what you say you are?"

He withdrew his wallet and showed her a card-sized registration for his agency. *Beaumont Investigative Agency.* "I started the business with my brother about five years ago."

Then he showed her his Louisiana driver's license—on top of everything else, he was photogenic. She nodded, satisfied.

"Are you still interested?" he asked, then smiled. "In my help, I mean?"

The idea of relying on him was unnerving simply because she was so physically attracted to him, which was a bit insane considering her situation. Regardless, it wouldn't hurt to have someone with his expertise on her side until things settled down. "Are you expensive?"

He winked. "Don't worry—you can afford me."

"Okay, you're hired."

He nodded, as if it had been a foregone conclusion. "Now, tell me more about this voodoo doll."

14

Keep stirring to prevent anything from sticking . . .

Penny took a deep breath, then told B.J. about the gag gifts and how everyone had goaded her to stab the voodoo doll. "It was just a joke, of course."

A half-smile curved his mouth. "But it probably felt good."

She nodded sheepishly. "Of course now I feel terrible."

"Was it a bad breakup?"

She shrugged, loathe to share all the sordid details. "I caught him with Sheena, I moved out, I filed for divorce."

"Rather recently, I assume?"

"It all started about ten months ago, and it was final this week."

He grunted. "So, his girlfriend tells you he wants something, you call and the line is busy, then you go to his house and find him dead."

"Right. In his office."

"You still have a key to the house?"

She pursed her mouth. "Probably a couple." One on the extra key ring in her purse that the police had, dammit. She told him about the door being open.

"And what was he stabbed with?"

"A garden stake."

"Come again?"

"A wire garden stake with a flag on the end. I, um, used them this week to stake off a garden next to my business."

He looked at her as he drank from his cup, as if he was wondering whether or not to believe her innocence. "I guess the police put you through the wringer," he said carefully.

"Yes."

"So why didn't they arrest you?"

"A detective from New Orleans was there—I think he believed me. It seemed to me that he didn't want to make an arrest until the crime scene was processed."

"What was his name?"

"Maynard."

B.J. nodded. "I know of him. He has a reputation for being fair. Did you have an attorney present?"

"Gloria Dalton. She's my divorce attorney."

He looked alarmed. "Divorce attorney?"

"She told me I'd have to find someone else if I'm . . . charged."

"The police must have set a record for obtaining a search warrant."

"Did I mention that Deke's mother is the mayor?"

"Ah."

Ted returned with a platter of sausages and bacon

swimming in brown grease, three fried eggs, and four pieces of toast drenched in butter.

Penny stared. "You're not going to eat all of that?"

He proceeded to cover everything with a layer of salt. "Want some?"

She made a face. "No. You're clogging your arteries."

"Probably." He shoveled in a huge amount of food and chewed heartily. "So, does your ex-husband have any enemies?"

"I don't know—maybe. He's an attorney, so I'm sure he's pissed off a few people along the way."

"Did he have any girlfriends other than Sheena?"

She flushed. "I don't know . . . wait. When Sheena first arrived at the house, she accused me of sneaking around with Deke behind her back. She said she suspected that something was going on."

"Was there?" he asked pointedly.

"*No*. But maybe he was seeing someone else."

"When was the last time you saw him?"

"Yesterday morning. I ran into him at the museum."

"Museum?"

"The Instruments of Death and Voodoo Museum. It's Mojo's claim to fame. And it's located next to my business. I walked over there yesterday morning to drop off some misdelivered mail, and I ran into Deke coming out of the museum."

"Is that unusual?"

"No, he takes care of the museum's legal affairs."

"Did he seem upset or preoccupied?"

"Stressed, maybe, but that's been the norm lately when we're together."

"Did you two have an argument?"

"Not really. I was irritated that he'd painted the house pink."

He winced. "Yeah, that's bad. So . . . maybe he has another honey on the side who was tired of being ignored."

Penny nodded, then another thought struck her. "Sheena and Deke just got engaged, so if he had another woman on the side, maybe that sent her over the edge."

B.J. studied Penny, and she knew what he was thinking—that the engagement could just as easily have sent *her* over the edge. But he simply nodded. "You think that whoever did it might have been trying to frame you by using a stake from your property and simulating the voodoo doll stabbing?"

When he said it, it sounded utterly ridiculous. "I don't know what to think. I'm a little numb."

He shoveled, chewed, and swallowed. "Who gave you the doll?"

"I don't know—the gifts were anonymous. But there were only a few people at the party, so it shouldn't be hard to find out."

He shoved a napkin in her direction, then fished a pen out of his coat pocket. "Write down the names."

She took the pen and wrote down everyone she could remember, pausing when she got to Liz and Wendy—she needed to call them, to break the news about Deke.

"Does anyone stick out in your mind as someone who would have done this?"

Penny turned her head to glance at the two girls from the Hair Affair, who had their heads together. One of them was biting her nails. Penny looked back and sighed. "No. But Deke hid a lot of things from me."

"There's always the possibility that it was a random killing—a stranger passing through for the festival."

She nodded, strangely buoyed by the fact that it could be someone who didn't know Deke . . . who hadn't killed him because they hated him. "What happens now?"

He finished the last bit of food and washed it down with a swallow of coffee. She stared at his empty plate as he wiped his mouth with a paper napkin. "Now I do the legwork that the police might not do."

She pursed her mouth. "If I lose my business over this, I might have to pay you in vitamins."

He winked. "We might have to think of something else."

She tried to laugh but found suddenly that she didn't have the energy. "I need to get to bed."

"Okay," he said, withdrawing his wallet. He threw cash on the table.

"Alone," she added, then instantly felt like an idiot.

His smile was sardonic. "You're in luck—I don't sleep with clients." He stood and picked up his jacket. "Come on, I'll walk you back."

Penny clamped her mouth shut lest she say something else brainless.

On the way out of the diner, he stopped at the public bulletin board. Reaching into his jacket, he pulled out a white flyer and used a pushpin to attach it to the corkboard.

MISSING:
Jodi Reynolds, age 17,
last seen in New Orleans, September 12.

Penny bit her lip. "So you're the one who posted the flyer."

He nodded. "I'm hoping someone in town for the festival might have seen her."

"Who hired you to look for her?"

"Her grandmother." He held open the door, and she walked under his arm.

She shivered when the cool, dewy air hit her face. "How many of them do you find?"

He opened his leather jacket and settled it onto her shoulders. She started to object, but honestly, it felt good. "About half. But even then, like you said earlier, some of them don't want to be found. I'm working on about a dozen missing person cases at the moment, some of them a couple of years old."

"Do you have a feeling about this girl?"

He nodded. "My feeling is that she ran away, then ran into trouble. And from what I know about her, she wouldn't last long on the streets."

A chill ran down Penny's back. Evil people were out there, just looking for an innocent to prey upon. "Do you have any leads?"

"The bartender at Caskey's said he thinks this is the girl who tried to pass him a fake ID a couple of weeks ago, but he wasn't sure. Truthfully, she could be anywhere."

"Or dead?"

"Yeah," he said in a voice that told her that if he were a betting man (and he probably was), he'd bet that the girl was never coming home.

The campers were more subdued when she and B.J. walked back through the square, with a few diehards kicking around a hackey sack. The fire in the *peristil* had petered out. Penny averted her gaze from the empty chicken cages.

"This festival seems to bring out an interesting crowd," B.J. observed.

"Interesting? I had a woman come in my store and ask for bat brains."

He laughed, a warm, throaty sound. "It takes all kinds."

When they reached the outside door leading to her apartment, her dread at seeing what the police had done to her place mounted. "Wonder how they got in," she murmured.

"Some guy let them in—short, stocky, smelly."

"Elton," she said. "My landlord. I hope he installed some lightbulbs while he was here." She opened the door and flipped the light switch—nothing. "Guess not."

"I take it your apartment is at the top of these stairs?"

"Right."

"I'll follow you up."

She didn't argue, glad to have company as she felt her way up. And she got felt up once when he reached forward and found her rear end.

"Sorry," he muttered.

She was sorry too—that such an accidental graze could leave her tingling all over. The sleep deprivation had left her vulnerable, she rationalized. Oh, and the looming murder rap.

At the top of the stairs, B.J. pulled out a penlight to help her find the keyhole. She pushed open the door, turned on the light over the dining table, and gasped. Everything was upturned, on end, or inside out. The gag gifts were strewn across the dining room table—the toilet paper unfurled, the condoms strung out accordion-style, the vibrator dismantled, batteries and springs hanging out.

She fisted her hands, on the verge of laughing maniacally . . . and gobbling down the Happy Divorce chocolate bars.

B.J.'s intent gaze didn't miss a thing, lingering on the erotic items a little longer than necessary. Then he walked over to remove a piece of paper taped to her refrigerator.

"What's that?" she asked, hugging herself.

"A list of what was removed during the search." He scanned the paper. "The voodoo doll you mentioned . . . a photograph album . . . an inflatable life-size male doll . . ." He looked up, eyebrows raised.

She squirmed. "Another gag gift."

His expression was dubious. "Whatever you say." He glanced back to the paper. "And a handgun."

Penny's eyes went wide. "What? That's impossible. I don't own a gun."

"It says here that you had a .45." He gave her a piercing look. "That's a pretty big handgun to forget about owning."

She frowned. "I'm telling you, I don't own a gun! There must be some mistake."

He pursed his mouth. "I suppose the police could have planted it, but that doesn't compute, since your ex-husband was stabbed."

"It's a mistake, that's all," she said, taking the paper. "Everyone who knows me knows how I feel about guns."

He gave her a little half smile. "Then you'd better stay out of my pants."

Surprise and arousal blazed across her skin. "Excuse me?"

He patted a bulge at his waistband, and her discomfort level ratcheted higher. Could she trust this man? Could she trust her own instincts anymore?

"Anyway," he said, drawing the word out into fourteen syllables, "you should have your attorney check out the gun report first thing in the morning."

She nodded and hid a yawn behind her hand.

"Is there someone you can stay with for a while? I'll drive you."

Faces of friends and acquaintances filed through her head—Marie, Guy, Hazel, Liz—but she discarded them one by one. She didn't want to get them involved, to implicate them in the ugly gossip that was already making the rounds. "Not really."

"Boyfriend?" he asked lightly.

Heat rushed her neck. "No."

He nodded curtly, as if filing that tidbit of information. "How about getting a hotel room?"

"The few places in town are probably full from the festival."

"There's my room—"

"I'd feel better here," she cut in. "Especially since the night is almost over."

He worked his mouth from side to side. "I could sleep on the couch."

She swallowed. "Th-that's not necessary."

He nodded. "Okay, then I'll take off so you can get some rest." He glanced around. "Is this door the only way in and out?" He opened the door they had just entered and checked the dead bolt with a frown.

"There's a Juliet balcony off the bedroom, but there's no access to it from the street."

"Will you show me?"

She nodded and padded through the mess. When they entered her bedroom, her stomach pitched—her bed linens were torn from the bed, her underwear was hanging out of drawers.

He opened the doors leading to the tiny balcony, then stepped outside and looked down before stepping back inside and closing the doors. "You should have new locks installed on both doors."

"Are you kidding? I can't even get lightbulbs installed."

He turned. "I'm serious."

She swallowed. "Okay. It's just that Mojo is so . . . safe."

"Except for the occasional murder?"

She winced.

"Whoever killed your ex-husband is still out there. Do you have something to protect yourself with?"

Her thoughts strayed to the box of condoms on the dining room table, but she forced herself to focus. "Um . . . no?"

He walked back through the apartment to her kitchen. She followed and watched as he pulled out drawers. At length he withdrew a butcher knife and walked back toward her. At the sight of the large knife in his hand, panic sliced through her chest as she once again questioned how much she should trust this man. She took a step backward.

He stopped, then extended the knife to her, handle first. "Sleep with this . . . and your cell phone."

"I don't have one."

"Get one. Do you still have my number?"

She looked around at the mess. "It's here somewhere."

He wrote it on a piece of paper and handed it to her.

"Call me if . . . something comes up. Will you be here tomorrow?"

She shook her head. "I think I need to be at work. I want to reassure my employees—and my customers—that everything is okay."

He nodded. "It's best that you stick to your normal schedule as much as possible . . . if you feel up to it."

At the concern in his eyes, her senses stirred . . . until she realized it was the same look he'd had when he'd talked about the missing girl from the flyer. It was B.J. Beaumont's job to rescue people, and she just happened to be in the wrong place at the right time.

She followed him to the door, her heart clicking in her chest as she reluctantly handed him his leather jacket. "Um . . . thank you . . . B.J. I barely know you, but . . ." She looked into his dark eyes and felt an entirely inappropriate urge to press her face into his chest. "Thank you for agreeing to help me," she finished lamely.

He donned his leather coat slowly. "I have to be honest," he said in his cottony drawl, "a business relationship isn't what I had in mind when I first saw you." Then one side of his mouth lifted. "But I'll take it . . . for now. Sleep tight, Red."

When the door closed behind him, Penny wanted to run after him. It was, she realized, desperation in the face of turmoil, the compulsion to cling to the most stable thing in sight. Her head buzzed from exhaustion and a host of emotions pulling on her, draining her. She couldn't bear climbing into the bed that the police had torn apart, so she grabbed her pillow and a blanket and curled up on the couch with her butcher knife and cordless phone, then stared at the shadows on the ceilings. Her mind would not be quieted.

Deke was dead. The finality of it simply wouldn't sink in. He was too young, too arrogant, too *special* to die. In truth, her own death would have come as less of a surprise to her, especially considering the environment in which she'd been raised.

A dark, niggling thought slid to the forefront of her mind: What if the police looked into her background, found out what kind of stock she came from?

She burrowed further into the couch, making herself as small as possible, closing her eyes tight. If that sordid bit of information came to light, it would virtually notarize her arrest warrant.

15

Make a generous portion, because everyone will want some . . .

Penny was jarred awake by a loud clanging noise. She sat straight up, sending the butcher knife and the cordless phone crashing to the floor, her heart in her throat. For a few disoriented seconds, she couldn't remember why she was so afraid . . . then it all came flooding back . . . Deke . . . dead. The phone rang, and she realized with relief that it was the noise that had awakened her.

She stood up, grabbed her aching head, and got to the phone on the fourth ring, wondering what time it was. Daylight was just beginning to filter through the lead glass windows. "Hello?" she croaked.

"Is this Penny Black?" a man asked.

"Penny Francisco," she corrected.

"You're on live with Kenner on WYNO news radio—will you give us a statement on the murder of your ex-husband?"

Her mouth opened and closed as her mind spun. Of course the media had gotten wind of Deke's bizarre death. In a small town like Mojo, murder was big honking news.

"Ms. Francisco, did you put a hex on your ex?" the man demanded. "Do you have some kind of mystical power?"

She squinted. "What?"

"Did the voodoo ceremony that you performed on your husband have something to do with the festival that's taking place?"

"*Ex*-husband," she muttered on an exhale. "And no!" She hung up the phone in a panic, but it rang again a few seconds later. She yanked the phone cord from the base unit, her chest heaving.

Rubbing her gritty eyes, she went to the kitchen for a drink of water. It was just after 7:00 A.M. She leaned into the sink, welcoming the cool of the stainless steel against her flesh, fighting nausea as the previous day's events came back with jarring clarity. Fending off the remnants of a hangover and dealing with the most shocking news of her life was not a good combination. She felt as if she'd been dragged by her heels over some very rough terrain; the last thing she wanted to do was go out for her morning run, but she knew it would help clear her head. For energy, she downed a tall glass of orange juice, then she went into the bedroom, trying to ignore the mess while she rifled for running gear. She dressed in record time.

When she opened the door and stepped onto the sidewalk, the scene was dank and depressing. Everywhere people lay sleeping, unwashed clumps covered with dew. Food containers littered the ground. From the shelter rose a sickening smell of chicken flesh and smoke. Penny swallowed and took off on her usual route, toward Charm Street. B.J. had said to act normal.

As her feet hit the pavement, her thoughts went to the man who so quickly and so willingly had come to her aid. She pondered her strong attraction to B.J. Beaumont and told herself it was because she was still stinging from Deke's rejection . . . and death.

As she bounded onto Charm Street toward the Victorian, she stayed on the side of the street of her business. Her store was quiet, and probably would be until Marie opened at 9:00. Business should be good . . . unless people decided to avoid her store because of the rumors that were bound to have spread about Deke's murder. The residents of Mojo were a suspicious, unforgiving lot—take Diane Davidson, for instance. In the same situation, Penny wasn't so sure she'd have the guts to stay . . . and she hoped she wouldn't have to find out.

She tried, but she couldn't resist a glance at the pink house as she jogged by. The yard was flattened and marred with muddy tire tracks from the many police vehicles that had parked wherever they could the night before. She wondered if Deke's office had been cordoned off with police tape, if Sheena had spent the night in the house. When the memory of Deke's staring eyes rose in her mind, she dug her heels deeper into the pavement. When the vision of the wire stake imbedded in his chest haunted her, she pumped her arms and picked up speed. Her brain couldn't dwell on those horrific details if it was occupied with processing pain signals from her straining calves.

She ran to the corner and turned right to jog past the

Instruments of Death and Voodoo Museum. The museum loomed ominously in the predawn light, separated from the sidewalk by the shoulder-high iron fence and the padlocked gate. As she ran by, a flicker of light in one of the stained-glass windows on the top floor caught her eye—a strobe of some kind? A fire? When she slowed, however, the light disappeared. She resumed running, deciding that the rising sun was playing tricks on her eyes. She shook her head, reminding herself that she had plenty of intrigue in her own life without imagining more.

She crossed a quiet street and inhaled deeply to prepare her body for Hairpin Hill, which led up into the new suburbs that surrounded Mojo. The curvy road was quiet and deserted, hemmed with thick hawthorne trees and white camellias at the peak of their perfume. With its three hairpin curves traversing the side of the small manmade mountain before looping back to the road on the other side, Hairpin Hill was the most challenging leg of her run, but also her favorite . . . usually.

This morning the darkness of the tree canopy seemed menacing instead of shady, the air stifling instead of aromatic. She blamed her unease on B.J.'s warning that a murderer was still on the loose, and on her own fatigue. Without proper sleep and nourishment, her energy was flagging, her muscles tightening, her lungs constricting. Halfway through the last hairpin turn, she stopped, gasping for air, and leaned over to grasp her knees.

A loud crack exploded in the air, startling her. From the echo, the noise sounded amazingly like a gunshot. She pivoted, thinking a car had backfired, only to find herself alone on the road as far as she could see in both directions. Another loud crack split the air. This time, whatever it was, was close enough for her to hear the whizzing noise as it sped by, and it caused wood to splinter on a tree next to her. In the fraction of a second that it took for her to register the fact that someone was shooting at her, her feet, thank goodness, had already figured it out.

An enormous surge of adrenaline sent her sprinting back down the hill faster than she'd ever run in her life. A couple of times the momentum alone nearly took her down, but terror kept her upright and moving, her arms and legs pumping. The stretch of road had never seemed so long. A frightened, keening sound erupted close by, then she realized the noise was coming from her throat. Someone was shooting at her, trying to pick her off like a duck in a carnival game. Her back burned with the overwhelming sensation that someone was bearing down on her.

At the bottom of the hill, she flung herself across the road blindly, her only thought getting to the other side and into town. A car horn blasted the air. She turned her head to see the blur of a white car and braced for impact. The driver locked the brakes, but the car still grazed her hip, knocking her to the ground. The tang of burned rubber filled the air. The driver's side door sprang open, and Steve Chasen jumped out. "Penny?"

Shaken, she picked herself up off the road. She was so relieved to see a familiar face, though, that she practically fell into him.

"Are you okay?" he asked. "My God, I almost didn't see you in time to stop."

"Someone . . . was . . . shooting . . . at me," she said, her teeth chattering.

"What?"

"On the hill," she said pointing.

He frowned, his expression wary. "It was probably someone playing with fireworks."

"No," she said stubbornly. "It was gunshots."

Steve was quiet for a few seconds. "Penny," he said gently, "I heard about Deke, that the police questioned you."

She read his expression. He thought she was guilty . . . and perhaps had snapped. "I didn't kill Deke, Steve. And I wasn't imagining things just now."

He nodded and led her to the passenger side of the car, as if she were a small child. "But you're understandably upset. You might have heard something and thought it was a gunshot."

Penny opened her mouth to object but recognized the futility of arguing. "Will you please just take me to my apartment?"

"Of course," he said, opening the car door and helping her inside. While he walked around the front of the car, she glanced back toward Hairpin Hill. Nothing seemed amiss. Had she mistaken the wild shots of a woodsman or a car backfiring for someone trying to kill her? She sank deeper into her seat, her mind racing.

Steve was quiet as he drove her back toward town, although she felt his gaze upon her. He slowed at the pink house and stared before driving on.

"I can't believe he's dead," he murmured.

"Neither can I," she said.

"Did he really die like everyone is saying?"

"If everyone is saying that he was stabbed, then yes."

"With a garden stake?"

His eyes glittered with excitement, and a finger of unease tickled the back of her neck. Steve had seen her stab the voodoo doll and might have had his own reasons for wanting his boss dead.

"That's right," she murmured.

"It's kind of spooky that you stabbed the voodoo doll at the party, and then Deke winds up dead the same way."

"Uh-huh. By the way, did you bring the doll as a gag gift?"

"No," he said quickly, then looked sheepish. "I didn't have time to buy a gift." Then his eyes widened. "Do the police think it was someone at the party?"

"They don't know," she said carefully. "The doll might be some kind of bizarre coincidence. Was Deke having trouble with any of his clients?"

Steve shrugged. "He was having trouble collecting fees from a couple of people, but otherwise . . . Wait— Diane Davidson threatened Deke."

Penny frowned. "Threatened him how?"

"She said he'd be sorry that he didn't take on her case."

"That's hardly a death threat."

"It was the way she said it," Steve said. "She was giving him the evil eye . . . and she was at the party. Maybe she brought the voodoo doll."

Penny didn't want to think the quiet woman had anything to do with Deke's death, but Diane, too, had seen Penny stab the voodoo doll, and Penny really didn't know her very well. "Are you going to open Deke's office today?"

"Yeah, even though I'm out of a job unless someone takes over the practice." He flushed. "I know that sounds selfish, considering what's happened."

"No," Penny said charitably as he pulled up in front of the beignet shop. "You have to take care of yourself." She opened the door, eager to get out of the car. "Thanks for the ride, Steve. I . . . maybe I was overreacting about the sound I heard. I didn't get much sleep last night."

Steve nodded sympathetically, and she climbed out of the car. "Penny, do you know anything about a funeral service for Deke?"

She swallowed hard and shook her head. The only tie she had to Deke now was as a murder suspect. "I'm assuming Mona will handle everything . . . or maybe Sheena. Bye, Steve." She closed the door before he could ask more questions. For some reason, she still didn't trust him. When she picked up the morning *Post* that had been delivered while she'd been out running, she realized her hands were trembling. Even if those gunshots hadn't been meant for her, they had come too close for comfort.

When she entered her apartment, the clutter only further reminded her of the chaos in her life. She took a few minutes to clear the dining room table of the gag gifts, shaking her head at the condoms and the vibrator, thinking she'd be using one before the other . . . if her life ever returned to normal.

She unrolled the newspaper and stared in horror at Deke's photo under the headline "Voodoo Festival Incites Murder." The story cited "official sources" as reporting that Deke Black, noted attorney in Mojo, had been stabbed in the chest with a long sharp object after his ex-wife, Penny Francisco, had purportedly stabbed a voodoo doll in a "divorce voodoo ceremony." The article went on to say that Penny owned a charm and spell shop in Mojo, and was, coincidentally, the person who had found the body.

She crunched the paper closed. From the newspaper account, *she* could almost be convinced that she'd killed Deke. She stood and paced, gnawing on her nails. This couldn't be good.

Hoping that food would help calm her jitters, she ate a bran muffin and plain yogurt. Unbidden, her thoughts went to B.J. Beaumont and what garbage he was consuming for breakfast. She tried to shake her thoughts of him, but they dogged her into the shower, where, as she ran soapy hands over her body, she kept remembering the interest in his dark eyes, replaying the evening they might have had if . . .

Penny sighed as guilt descended. How could she be thinking about being with another man when Deke wasn't even in the ground—especially when a lot of people thought she had put him there.

She showered and dressed quickly, then picked up the damaged phone cord to discover that her yank had disabled the base unit. The phone calls she needed to make—to Gloria, to B.J., to Liz—would have to wait until she could make them from her office. She glanced at her watch. Marie would already have the shop open, but she and Guy were probably worried sick about her. Penny frowned at the burned-out bulb on the landing as she left, then hurried down the stairs. When she opened the door leading to the sidewalk, she blinked at the woman standing there with a microphone that read WTNL. Behind her, a man held a camera on his shoulder, and it appeared to be rolling.

"Ms. Francisco," the woman said, "what can you tell

us about the voodoo ritual that resulted in your ex-husband's grisly death?"

"Nothing," Penny said, attempting to sidestep the woman.

"Ms. Francisco, how long have you practiced voodoo?"

"I don't," she replied.

"Are you some kind of priestess?" the woman asked, stepping on Penny's heels. "I understand that you sell charms and spells at your place of business."

"You misunderstood," Penny said, pushing past her and breaking into a jog. Hopefully the police would have some answers soon and would be able to clear her name. In the end, she was sure that science would win out over voodoo.

She walked briskly, glancing over her shoulder to see if the reporter and her crew were following her. Thankfully, it appeared that they had given up. She relaxed a bit . . . until she noticed a commotion up ahead in front of her store. A crowd had gathered, including two more TV cameras. Marie's blue hair shone like a beacon; she was standing under the awning, gesturing in what looked like an attempt to address the crowd. Penny picked up the pace, dread billowing in her stomach. What now?

She was a few feet away from the crowd of about fifty when someone shouted, "There she is!"

In one collective movement, the people turned to stare, then began to run toward her. Paralyzed, Penny stood rooted to the ground as women surrounded her, thrusting voodoo dolls in her face. "My husband needs a wake-up call—can you stick him in the hip?"

"In the foot?"

"In the crotch?"

"I want mine dead! Stick him in the heart, like you stuck it to your husband!"

16

Monitor concoction for deterioration . . .

Penny blinked, slack-jawed, as women pushed and pulled on her clothing, begging her to perform a ritual on their husband voodoo dolls. A doll popped her in the forehead, then fell to the ground. Suddenly she was pelted with dolls. Out of nowhere, Marie appeared and grabbed Penny's arm.

"Get a divorce lawyer!" Marie yelled to the crowd as she dragged Penny to the relative safety of the door. The cameras had captured everything.

"There are more inside," Marie warned, then she opened the door. Sure enough, Penny was rushed again by people clutching dolls and amulets, bones, and even a live chicken. Guy cowered behind the counter. "Everybody out," Marie shouted, "unless you plan to buy something."

"I'll pay for a voodoo session!" one woman yelled, holding her doll high.

"Me too"s chorused around the shop, and Marie

turned to Penny, eyebrows raised. Penny scowled, then shook her head, and Marie seemed dejected. "Sorry, folks, no voodoo sessions, but how about a nice tall glass of Hot Voodoo Sex?"

The question distracted the crowd enough for Penny to slip away and make a beeline for her office. She closed the door behind her and leaned against it, puffing her cheeks out in an exhale. How much crazier could things get?

Then she straightened and looked heavenward, her hands up in surrender. "I didn't mean that as a challenge."

She sighed and dropped into her desk chair, then stared at the locked bottom drawer, tempted to dive in. She needed the comfort, the flood of endorphins to calm her. Her mouth watered, and she was reaching for the desk key before she caught herself. She'd regret it later . . . she always did. The stash was there as a reminder that she could resist temptation, not as a quick fix. Recognizing the distraction as a delay tactic, she forced herself to pick up the phone and dial Gloria Dalton's cell phone number. Gloria answered on the second ring.

"Hello?"

"Hi, Gloria, it's Penny. Is this a bad time?"

"I just heard you on *Kenner in the Morning.* Please don't talk to the press, Penny."

"But I didn't!"

"When the man asked if you'd killed your husband with a voodoo hex, you said, '*Ex*-husband.' "

"So?"

"So that sounds like you admitted to killing your *ex*-husband with a voodoo hex!"

Penny winced. "It was taken out of context."

Gloria sighed and something rattled in the background that sounded like a pill bottle being opened. "How are you holding up?"

"I haven't fallen apart." Penny glanced at the bottom desk drawer. "Yet."

"Good. Hang in there. I have a call in to Detective Maynard for an update. Maybe he'll have good news."

"While you have him on the phone, ask him about the .45 handgun that was supposedly found in my apartment during their search."

"You had a gun?"

"No! That's the point—a gun is listed on the paperwork as being removed, but I don't own a gun and I never have."

"Okay," Gloria said, sounding nervous. "I'll look into it. Anything else?"

Penny hesitated, then said, "There was an incident while I was out on my regular morning run."

"What kind of incident?"

"I was, um, shot at."

"*What?* Are you sure?"

"I'm sure that two shots were fired that came very close to hitting me."

"Did you see where they came from?"

"No."

"Have you reported it to the police?"

"I will as soon as we hang up."

Gloria made agitated noises. "Okay, I'll let Maynard know when I talk to him."

"One more thing," Penny said. "I hired a private investigator."

"Why?" Gloria said, her voice suspicious.

"I thought he might be able to poke around where the police can't."

"Be careful. You don't want to step on toes at the police department."

With a pledge to talk soon, Penny hung up the phone and dialed the police station. "Chief Davis, please. This is Penny Francisco."

After a minute or two of silence, Chief Davis came on the line. "Hello, Penny. Is your conscience bothering you?"

Penny pursed her mouth. "No. I called to report something strange that happened this morning while I was running."

"What?" Allyson asked in a bored voice.

"I was shot at."

Allyson gave a disbelieving little laugh. "Shot at?"

Penny closed her eyes briefly. "That's right. On Hairpin Hill. Two shots were fired, and one came very close to hitting me."

"You must have been mistaken," Allyson said. "Maybe you heard a car backfire, or someone was playing with fireworks."

"I don't think so. A bullet hit a tree next to me."

"Then maybe someone was shooting at an animal and the bullet went astray."

Penny bit her lip. "I suppose that's possible, but don't you think you should look into it?"

Tension crackled across the line. "Don't tell me what I should look into, Penny, else I might think you're trying to send me on a wild-goose chase to distract me from Deke's murder case."

Penny ground her teeth. "I'm telling you, someone was shooting at me."

"Why would someone be shooting at you, Penny? Is there something you're not telling me?"

"No," Penny said through clenched teeth. "I was just on my normal morning run."

"And have you ever been shot at before while you were on your morning run?" Allyson's voice dripped with sarcasm.

"No. But considering the timing, it might have something to do with Deke's murder."

Allyson sighed. "Okay, I'll send an officer out there to sniff around. What time did it happen?"

"Around 7:15 A.M."

"And you're just now getting around to telling me?"

"My home phone isn't working. I'm calling you from the shop."

"I saw the crowd at your *shop* this morning when I drove by. I have half a mind to book you for inciting a riot for suggesting that what happened to Deke has something to do with voodoo."

"But . . . I didn't."

"Right. The paper is full of reports of hexes and voodoo rituals. It's bad publicity for Mojo, especially since Deke's mother is the mayor. Every half-baked witch in the tristate will be here causing trouble."

"I want this to be over more than you do," Penny said evenly. "Maybe if you were less intent on pinning Deke's murder on me, you'd find the real killer." She slammed down the phone, realizing she'd probably nixed any investigation into the shooting.

Penny inhaled and exhaled several times to quiet her racing pulse, then she picked up the phone to make another difficult call. She dialed slowly, almost hoping that Liz wouldn't answer, but she did.

"Hello?"

"Liz, hi, it's Penny."

"Hi, sweetheart. I'm taking Wendy to the airport—her flight was delayed a couple of hours. Are you hung over this morning, or did you manage to hook up with that hottie from the bar?"

Penny pursed her mouth. "I guess you haven't watched the news."

"No," Liz said suspiciously. "Why?"

"Liz, Deke is . . . dead."

"What?" Liz screeched, then moved her mouth away from the phone. "Wendy, Penny says that Deke is *dead*." She put her mouth back to the phone. "What on earth happened?"

Penny recounted the details for what seemed like the hundredth time.

Liz gasped. "Stabbed? But that's just like the voodoo doll."

Penny frowned. "I know . . . and people are drawing comparisons, including the police."

"Oh, my God, honey, how awful for you. What can we do—do you want us to come and stay with you?"

"Thanks, but that's not a good idea right now. Television reporters are following me, not to mention the crazies who seem to think that I have some kind of magic voodoo powers."

"That's downright spooky."

Penny cleared her throat. "Liz, the police are going to question you and Wendy because you were at the party. I have to ask again—did either one of you bring the voodoo doll as a gag gift?"

"No," Liz said. "We brought the blow-up guy. Wait a minute—are you saying that the police think that you killed Deke because of sticking that stupid voodoo doll?"

"That's about the gist of it."

Liz made an exasperated noise, then stopped suddenly. "You *didn't* kill him, did you, Penny?"

"No! How could you even ask?"

"Because . . . well, I wouldn't blame you if you did. After all, he was a lying, cheating bastard who deserved to die a slow, painful death."

Penny stuck her tongue into her cheek. "Still, I didn't kill him."

Liz made fretting noises. "Why don't you come and stay with me until this all blows over?"

"I need to stay in town." The unspoken words hung in the air: *I'm the primary suspect.* "I have my business to run," she added hurriedly.

"Right," Liz said slowly. "When is the funeral?"

"I'm not sure, but I'll let you know."

"I'll be there, and Wendy is saying that she'll come back, too. We're both so sorry, Penny."

Penny's eyes began to water. "Thanks."

"Promise that you'll call if you need anything."

"I will."

Penny hung up the phone, fighting a sudden bout of tears. Telling people that Deke was dead didn't make it seem any more real—only more unbelievable.

A knock on the door sounded. She wiped the corners of her eyes and took a deep breath. "Who is it?"

"It's me, Guy."

"Come in."

Guy poked his head inside, his expression forlorn. "You can come out now—they're gone."

She pushed to her feet. "Thanks."

When she walked out, Marie stood next to Guy, looking just as distressed.

"I didn't do it," Penny said quickly. "And I'm sorry, but the police will probably be questioning you. Do you know who brought the voodoo doll to the party?"

They shook their heads.

Penny sighed. "Okay, don't worry about me. The best thing is to try to conduct business as usual."

They both nodded, their expressions anguished, and she felt a rush of fondness and gratitude. "Guy, where's the best place to get a cell phone?"

While he went to write down some information for her, she turned to Marie. "I'm going to be in and out until this blows over. Can you handle things here at the store?"

"Absolutely."

"Great—thank you." Suddenly a thought popped into her head. "Marie, what about the two friends of yours who came to the party, the ones who cut hair?"

"Jill and Melissa? What about them?"

"Could one of them have brought the voodoo doll?"

She shrugged. "I can find out."

"Do you know if either one of them is connected to Deke?"

Marie squirmed and averted her gaze.

"Marie?"

The young woman sighed. "I don't know for sure, but Melissa bragged once that she'd, um, slept with Deke."

Penny felt the blood drain from her face. "When?"

"She said it was when Deke first bought his car—he gave her a ride."

And then she'd given him a ride. Penny fisted her hands at her sides—had the man exercised no restraint?

"I'm sorry, boss."

Penny inhaled to get a grip on her emotions. "Thanks for being honest."

"By the way, who was that man you were talking to last night at Caskey's?"

Penny hesitated. "Um . . . just someone I met. He's in town looking for a missing girl and was asking questions about Mojo."

"He looked mighty interested in you," Marie said lightly.

The door chimed, and Penny looked up to see the man they'd been talking about materialize.

"Good morning," B.J. said.

Penny straightened under Marie's probing gaze. "Good morning."

Good God Almighty, the man was in excess. He wore jeans and a holey sweatshirt. His hair was shiny clean but looked like it had been combed with barbed wire. And for someone whose specialty was finding things, he seemed to have misplaced his razor.

He lifted a bag from Benny's Beignets. The bottom half of the bag was transparent with grease. "Hungry?"

She licked her lips. "Um, no. This is a *health* food store."

"I'll take one," Marie said.

"Me, too," Guy said, emerging from the stockroom. He handed Penny a page of notes on where to buy a cell phone. "He's cute," he whispered.

Penny's mouth quirked to one side. She awkwardly introduced B.J. as "a person who's helping me" and left Marie and Guy to figure out what he was helping her with.

"Nice place," B.J. said, walking around.

Penny frowned. "You're getting powdered sugar on the floor."

He looked down and used the toe of his boot to scatter the white stuff, as if it would help. Marie and Guy both looked at him with dreamy eyes until Penny stared them down. She nodded in a "get lost" movement, and they scattered to straighten shelves.

"I tried to call you," B.J. said.

"My phone isn't working," she replied, then held up the sheet of paper that Guy had given her. "But I'm going to buy a cell phone."

"I'll go with you," he said. "It'll give us a chance to talk."

She nodded, although the dark tone of his voice made her chest tighten. What had he discovered?

The chime sounded as the door opened, admitting Jules Lamborne.

"Hi, Jules," Marie called loudly.

But instead of her regular cheerful greeting, Jules lifted her carved walking stick and pointed it at Penny. "I told you that voodoo isn't for amateurs."

Penny blinked and held out a calming hand. "Jules, I know what everyone is saying, but Deke Black's murder had nothing to do with me sticking that voodoo doll."

"That's what you think," Jules said, her voice crackling with strain.

"Maybe it was a random killing," Marie said, munching on her beignet. "Maybe someone here for the festival got carried away."

"Nothing is random," Jules declared, then looked back to Penny. "Someone put a hex on that doll, and used you as a carrier."

Penny frowned. "A carrier?"

"Or someone could have put a hex on *you*."

Penny started to deny Jules's words, then she remembered the masked priestess in the shelter who had singled her out. Penny asked Jules about the woman and the rattle.

"It's called an *ason*," Jules said. "It's a gourd filled with snake vertebrae, to honor Danbala, the Great Serpent spirit. Only voodoo priests and priestesses are allowed to use the *ason*. They can be used to bring forth good . . . or evil."

For a few seconds, Penny was riveted, then she shook herself. "I don't believe in voodoo, Jules."

"You should," the old woman said, backing toward the door. "I told you that people were going to die, but you didn't listen."

Cool air settled over Penny's arms, raising gooseflesh across her shoulders. "I'm listening now."

"Good," Jules said, then stabbed the air with her stick. "Because the dying isn't over yet."

17

You might need to test alternate formulas . . .

"She's a spooky old gal, isn't she?" B.J. asked, holding open the passenger door of his faded green sedan, which was parked in the store parking lot. Homemade and mass-produced voodoo dolls littered the ground, many with notes attached.

On impulse, Penny scooped up one of the dolls at her feet and nodded as she slid by him. The scent of strong soap tickled her nostrils, and she suddenly had doubts about being with him in such a confining space. The fact that she'd known him for such a short time niggled at the back of her mind. On the other hand, she'd known Deke for years, yet her trust in him had been utterly misplaced.

The crude doll was made from wax and straw, wrapped in a white cotton strip that looked to be part of a dingy T-shirt. The attached note read, "My husband is a pain in the neck—please give him one back." The T-shirt no doubt belonged to the annoying husband.

"Do you think there's any validity to what Jules Lamborne said—that Deke's murder has something to do with voodoo?"

He quirked a dark eyebrow. "There are a lot of things in the world that are unexplainable—love at first sight, vegetable pizza, and potpourri, for instance. But I doubt that your ex's murder is one of them."

He closed her door. She was immediately overcome with the stale scent of French fries and rolled down the window, then studied him as he walked around the front of the car and climbed inside.

"Sorry about the mess," he said, reaching over to remove the fast-food bags from the floorboard beneath her feet. He tossed them in the backseat, which was piled high with newspapers, manila file folders, and athletic equipment.

She fastened her seat belt, then reached beneath her hip and removed a woman's lime green stiletto pump.

He grinned. "Wonder how long that's been there."

She smirked. "I wonder."

He tossed it in the back, too, then started the engine. "Have you seen today's *Post*?"

She nodded. "And I talked to Chief Davis this morning—she wasn't in a good mood. She said this murder was bad publicity for the festival and for the town, and she blames me personally."

"She called to tell you that?"

"Er, no. Actually, I called her." Penny told him about the shooting incident.

B.J's expression darkened. "Why didn't you call me?"

"No phone at home," she reminded him. "And I was going to call you . . . soon. Anyway, I reported it to

Chief Davis, but I got the feeling that she thought I was making up the story for sympathy."

B.J. was quiet for a few seconds, and she wondered briefly if he also thought she was making up the story for sympathy. "Speaking of shooting, did you ask her about the gun that was removed from your place?"

"No, my attorney is going to handle it."

"That's probably best," he agreed. "What do you know about this Chasen guy who picked you up this morning?"

"He's worked for Deke for a couple of years. I don't particularly like him, but he's never really done anything to me."

"Just a feeling?"

Penny nodded. "At the party he told my employee Marie that Deke hid assets during our property settlement."

"So he wasn't completely loyal to your ex."

"Plus he could have been gossiping to cozy up to Marie. I asked him this morning if Deke had any enemies, and he said that Diane Davidson had threatened him."

"Her name was on the party list, too."

"Right. She's a customer of mine, but I don't know her very well. Apparently, she was fired from teaching at the high school because she's Wiccan."

"What's her connection to Deke?"

Penny told him about the lawsuit Diane Davidson had wanted to file.

He put the car into gear. "I say we pay Diane Davidson a visit. Do you know where she lives?"

Penny squinted, trying to remember. "In a new subdivision—all their names sound the same to me. Something Heights, maybe."

"Where?"

She stopped, then the realization hit her. "On Hairpin Hill, where I was running this morning."

"Okay, let's get that phone, then we'll start asking questions. Where can we find Steve Chasen?"

"He said he was going to open Deke's office today. It's just a few doors down from the cell phone place."

B.J. smiled. "I love small towns."

But Penny was having different thoughts, since another group of women bearing voodoo dolls was descending on The Charm Farm. She sank lower in the seat. "Get me out of here."

He obliged, and she told him which way to turn.

Deke's office was on the far end of the city limits, away from the square, past the new high school and the Bi-Lo grocery and the car wash, close to the interstate. Deke's parents had constructed a small strip mall with brick fronts and elegant entrances, primarily to house his father's law practice. The structure, which they had dubbed Charmed Village, had turned out to be a cash cow, however, when the other spaces had quickly filled up with Primo Dry Cleaners, Tam's Electronics, Lewis Taxidermy, S&C Upholstery, Quinto's sub sandwiches, and the Looky-Loo bookstore.

"Tam's Electronics sells phones," she said, pointing. They parked and walked in, armed with the notes Guy had given her. The clerk appeared to still be in high school. He stared at her, and his Adam's apple bobbed as he answered her questions. He'd obviously seen the article on Deke's murder in the newspaper.

"This is the one you want," B.J. cut in, setting a slim phone on the counter.

She looked up at the matter-of-fact certainty in his

eyes and was struck by his self-assurance. It was nice to have someone who made her life . . . easier. Deke had always been full of promises and good intentions, but in truth, he'd rarely made good on them. He'd bought the Victorian with assurances that he would help with the restoration, but when the time had come, he'd always been working late or too tired, or he'd needed to spend time with his mother. Meanwhile, Penny had worked at his office full-time, restored the house, and taken care of the details of their life, allowing him to concentrate on his career.

She frowned. And on his philandering.

"It's just a suggestion," B.J. said mildly. "I've had almost every model on the market."

"Thanks. I'll take it."

While she filled out paperwork to activate the phone, B.J. withdrew the flyer of the missing Reynolds girl and asked the young man if he'd seen her. The clerk squinted at the picture, then scratched his head. "Maybe."

"Maybe?" B.J. pressed. "Where?"

"I can't be sure, but I think she was in the sub shop one day."

"When?"

The young man shrugged. "Maybe a month ago." He flushed. "I remember a girl with long blond hair. It was almost white."

"Did you get a look at her face?"

More blushing ensued. "I wasn't looking at her face."

B.J.'s mouth quirked. "Did she have a good figure?"

"Yeah, she was stacked."

Penny smothered a smirk and kept her eyes on the form she was filling out. Missing persons flyers might be more effective if they showed the subject from the neck down.

B.J. grunted. "Did you notice her clothes? Did she have a backpack?"

The boy shook his head. "I don't remember, man."

"Was she with anyone?"

He shrugged again. "It might not even have been her, you know?" He handed the flyer back to B.J.

B.J. nodded. "Do you mind if I put this on your bulletin board?"

"Knock yourself out."

"There's a number to call if you remember anything else," B.J. said. "It could be very important."

Penny's heart squeezed at the intensity in B.J.'s voice. He desperately wanted to find Jodi Reynolds alive. He tacked the flyer and two others with much older dates—both women, both missing from the New Orleans area—to the bulletin board. Their families, she knew, were suspended in a nagging limbo. Most of her life she'd endured the ache of waiting for someone to come back. Was it worse, she wondered, when the missing person was suspected dead, or, as in her case, when she knew the person was still alive?

"Ready?" B.J. asked.

Jarred from her disturbing musings, Penny nodded, handed over the paperwork, and exited the shop. "I should call Gloria and give her this number," she said.

B.J. hooked his thumb to the left, in the direction opposite from Deke's office. "I'm going to step into the sandwich shop and ask a few questions."

"I'll wait for you here," she said, not keen on entering Deke's office alone.

He nodded as if he understood, then strode away.

Her gaze lingered on his broad shoulders, and she wondered how long he would stay in town, how long she would need his help. Would he be able to find something to exonerate her before the police lowered the boom? She still held out hope that the crime scene evidence would lead the police in another direction, but if the killer truly had gone to such lengths to frame her, he or she probably would have taken pains not to leave anything behind.

So she was back to hoping that Deke's murder was a random event by some unstable person whipped into a frenzy by the activities of the Voodoo Festival.

Praying that Gloria Dalton would have good news, Penny punched in the number using the tiny buttons. She must have done everything right, because the phone rang on the other end, although it rolled over to Gloria's voice mail. Penny left a message with her new cell phone number and disconnected the call with a sigh.

Standing in the cool breeze enveloping the lovely fall day, she closed her eyes and wished for the relative peace of her life twenty-four hours ago. She wasn't sure when the finality of Deke's death would sink in, but she dreaded the moment. She felt like the headless chicken she'd seen flapping around the voodoo shelter in the square—eventually the adrenaline was going to run out, and she'd be . . .

Well, hopefully not dead.

She looked all around, remembering her close call this morning. Her pulse spiked, but all seemed quiet and normal in Mojo. Pedestrians strolled on the sidewalk of the strip mall, and cars rolled down this section of Charm Street as if everything were perfectly normal. Then suddenly the cool breeze turned cold, sending dried, curled leaves scuttling across the ground, the sound conjuring up images of rattling bones.

Penny shivered. Everything wasn't perfectly normal. A murderer was in their midst, who, according to Jules, had not yet exhausted his or her evil.

"Ms. Francisco?"

Penny turned to see the young man who'd sold her the phone standing in the open door to the electronics shop looking . . . uncomfortable.

"Yes?"

"I was wondering . . . do you know how to cast a . . . a . . . l-love spell on someone?"

She frowned. "Excuse me?"

"You know," he said, gesturing vaguely. "Can you do or say something to make someone fall in love against their will?"

"I certainly hope not," B.J. said, striding up with a wink. He clasped Penny's elbow and steered her away from the inquisitive youth. "Can you?" he murmured.

"No," she said, her breath coming faster at his teasing grin and his warm proximity. Then she felt silly for even answering and straightened. "Did you find out anything?"

He shook his head. "Another dead end. This town seems to be full of them—no pun intended. Did you talk to your attorney?"

"I had to leave her a message."

B.J. stopped before a door bearing a black-and-gold sign that read Deke A. Black, Attorney at Law. A black mourning bow had been attached to the sign. Penny's lungs constricted painfully.

"Are you okay with this?" B.J. asked.

Her distress must have been written on her face. "I . . . I remember when Deke hung that sign. This was his father's practice, and Deke joined it when we moved to Mojo. Then his father died suddenly, and Deke said he felt as if he was betraying him by changing the sign."

"That's understandable," B.J. said. "Sounds as if they were close."

"You would think so," Penny said. "But actually there was always something between them."

"What?"

Penny frowned. "Deke's mother, Mona."

"That would be the mayor."

"Right. She ruled the roost, and both men accommodated her. And she wasn't above playing them against each other if it meant getting her way."

B.J. grimaced. "She sounds like a real piece of work."

"She is, but Deke is—was—devoted to her."

"I'm guessing you and Mona didn't get along."

"We tolerated each other while Deke and I were married."

"And since the divorce?"

Penny sighed. "Mona is dead set against me expanding the garden next to my business—she's trying to turn Mojo into a bona fide city, and she thinks a garden in the town limits is too provincial. When I saw Deke yesterday morning at the museum, he told me she was going to get the city council to invoke a zoning restriction, and she stopped by the party to tell me as much herself."

"Did you argue?"

"Yeah." She winced. "I'd had a lot to drink."

"I remember," he said with a little smile. "Does your ex-mother-in-law own a gun?"

Penny frowned. "What?"

"The woman doesn't like you, and she probably thinks that you killed her baby boy. Maybe she was trying to exact her own revenge."

Penny's eyes flew wide. "You think she was the person who fired those shots?"

He shrugged. "I'm just tossing out a theory. Does she know that you run in the mornings?"

"Sure . . . and anyone else in town who cares to notice."

"Is shooting at you something she would do?"

Penny's blood ran cold. "I . . . I don't know."

"But it's possible?"

She puffed out her cheeks in an exhale. "Yesterday, I would have said no, but today . . . anything is possible."

The door opened, and Penny blinked at the tall, robust man coming out. "Ziggy?"

Ziggy seemed surprised to see her, too. "*Chère*, Penny." Then he looked forlorn. "I am so sorry about Deke."

"Thank you."

"Don't worry—I don't believe the newspapers and all the talk about voodoo. I know you couldn't have killed him." But as he talked, he eyed B.J. up and down. "Sir, have we met?"

"I don't think so," B.J. said, extending his hand. "B.J. Beaumont."

"Hm," Ziggy said, as if he was still trying to place him.

"And you are?" B.J. prompted.

Ziggy pulled himself up. "I am Ziggy Hines."

B.J. seemed unfazed. "Nice to meet you, Zig."

Ziggy frowned, and Penny hurried to cover the awkward moment. "Ziggy is the chef of his own restaurant in the city."

"Ah," B.J. said. "I'm more of a fast-food kind of guy myself."

Ziggy scowled at B.J.'s disheveled appearance. "I wouldn't have guessed."

"Ziggy is a customer of mine," Penny cut in. "By the way, how did the, um, *you know* work out?"

Ziggy's eyebrows climbed in question, then his mouth rounded in realization that she was referring to the truffles. "Ah, the—" He cut off and glanced toward B.J. suspiciously. "They are perfection. When will you have more, *chère*?"

"I'll let you know," she promised, not sure when she'd get back to the day-to-day running of the store.

"Please do." He glared at B.J. "It was nice to meet you."

"Likewise," B.J. said cheerfully, inclining his head.

Ziggy turned and strode toward a black Mercedes in the parking lot.

"Why do I get the feeling that I didn't pass muster?" B.J. asked.

"Oh, that's just Ziggy. His ego was bruised when you didn't recognize him."

"Do you know why he's here?"

"He told me that he was working with Deke on a personal matter that required an out-of-town attorney. I don't know what it concerned." Then a memory slid into her brain. "Ziggy dropped by the party at Caskey's."

"I don't remember his name on the list."

"I'd forgotten," she murmured. "He was there for only a minute or two, just stuck his head in to say hello." She recalled the way he'd stared at Liz, then bolted.

"So what's the secret stash that Zig's been buying from you?"

She bit her lip. "I can't say."

B.J. quirked one eyebrow. "Oh?"

"It's not illegal," she rushed to explain. "It's something rare that my woodsman scavenges and Ziggy buys for his menu, and they don't want word to get out."

"Your woodsman?"

"A local guy—he collects roots and bark and . . . other things."

One side of B.J.'s mouth curved up. "Sounds intriguing."

"It's just business."

"If you say so." He nodded toward the door. "Are you ready to go inside?"

"Sure."

B.J. opened the door and held it while Penny walked through. She immediately remembered her number one complaint from when she had worked in the office: Despite the lush upholstered furnishings, the thick floor-length drapes, and the plush berber carpet, the place was as cold as a morgue. The desk that Steve Chasen normally occupied sat empty, and to the right, the door to Deke's office stood open. Instead of the easy-listening station that usually played over the intercom, a rock station reverberated from the speakers.

Penny walked to the doorway of Deke's office and was startled to see Steve sitting behind Deke's desk with his back to them, the telephone to his ear, his feet propped on the credenza running along the wall. His position struck her as irreverent, considering the fact that his boss had just been offed.

"I'll let you know if I hear from her," he said. "Later." When he turned to hang up the phone, he caught sight of them and jerked upright, dropped his feet to the floor, and sprang up. "Penny." His voice was squeaky and thin. "I, um, was just changing all the messages on voice mail and canceling appointments. What are you doing here?"

"We just came to ask you a couple of questions," she said, "about this morning." She introduced B.J.

"We're trying to figure out if the shooting incident this morning was deliberate," B.J. said. "Do you remember seeing anyone or anything out of the ordinary?"

Steve's face went blank. "No—just Penny running out into the road. I nearly ran over her."

"Where do you live?" B.J. asked.

"About a mile from Hairpin Hill, just inside the city limits."

"Do you own a gun?"

Steve squinted, then crossed his arms. "I'm sorry—tell me again how you're connected to this . . . situation." He looked back and forth between them.

"I'm an investigator," B.J. said casually. "Just trying to eliminate the obvious scenarios."

Steve wet his lips. "No, I don't own a gun." He reached down to pick up a stack of file folders. "Now, if you don't mind, I really need to call the courthouse and have Deke's cases postponed."

Penny exchanged a glance with B.J., then looked back to Steve. "Thanks again for your help this morning. And for answering our questions. We'll let ourselves out."

On the way through the lobby, Penny stopped by Steve's desk and hit the Recall button on the phone. She pursed her mouth, then looked at B.J. and jerked her head toward the front door. Once they were outside, he said, "What?"

"I pulled up the phone number of the person Steve was talking to when we walked in."

"Did you recognize the number?"

"It was city hall—to be more specific, the mayor's office."

18

Blood makes a nice colorant . . .

"It could have been an innocent phone call," Penny admitted as they climbed into B.J.'s smelly car. "It would make sense that Mona would be calling Deke's office and keeping tabs on me . . . *if* I was the 'her' Steve mentioned he'd be keeping an eye out for."

B.J. grunted. "Steve Chasen didn't seem to be that torn up about losing his boss . . . or his job."

"I noticed."

"Would he stand to gain anything from your ex's death?"

She lifted her shoulder in a slow shrug. "Not that I know of. He didn't have ownership in the practice, and he's not an attorney, so it's not as if he can take over Deke's clients."

"Is that BMW his?" he asked, pointing to the gleaming white car parked nearby.

"Yeah."

"Pretty snazzy ride on a paralegal salary." B.J. put his own not-so-snazzy car in gear. "Okay, let's see if we can find Diane Davidson."

Penny called directory assistance, but the number and address were unlisted. "I think we have it at the shop," she said, then dialed. After several rings, Marie answered breathlessly.

"Charm Farm, this is Marie."

"Marie, it's Penny."

"Penny! Thank goodness it's you," Marie whispered. "People have been coming in all morning and leaving voodoo dolls. We have trash bags full! And some detective has been tromping around in the garden, and now he's asking questions."

Penny swallowed hard. "Is his name Maynard?"

"Yeah, that's it," Marie said.

"What kinds of questions?"

"About the garden, about the party, about the voodoo doll. He's talking to Guy now."

"Don't worry," Penny said on an exhale. "Just be truthful."

Marie made a fretting noise. "I don't want to get you into trouble."

Panic darted through Penny's chest. How much had she complained to Marie about Deke? Had she said things that could be misconstrued? "Just . . . be honest," she said carefully. "Marie, you *know* I didn't kill Deke."

Marie's silence wasn't comforting.

"Marie? *Don't you?*"

"Well, of course . . . but I'd understand if . . . I mean, I'm not saying you *would,* but if I were in your shoes, I might."

Heat flooded Penny's chest and face. Good grief, if even Marie thought she'd killed Deke, she was sunk. She turned toward the window, angling her body away from B.J. and lowering her voice. "I didn't kill him, Marie, you *have* to know that."

"Okay," Marie breathed. "Should I tell him about my friend Melissa and Deke?"

"Yes," Penny said. "Absolutely. As soon as we hang up."

"Okay. The detective is looking at me, so I'd better go."

"I need for you to look up a customer address first."

"Let me step behind the counter." The computer keyboard clicked. "Okay, who?"

"Diane Davidson."

"Okaaaay." Marie's curiosity was practically burning up the phone line, but to her credit, she didn't ask questions. Marie rattled off the address, and Penny jotted it down. Then she gave Marie her new cell phone number. "Call me if . . . you think you need to." She disconnected the call, then shifted uncomfortably in the seat and handed the address to B.J., directing him where to turn.

B.J. cleared his throat. "Maynard is interrogating your employees?"

"It would seem so."

"How well do you know Marie and Guy the gay man?"

She pivoted her head. "You think Guy is gay?"

"Isn't he?"

"He says he isn't . . . and he has lots of girlfriends."

B.J's mouth quirked. "Yeah, well, then he's the only one who didn't get the memo. What do you know about Guy other than the fact that he's sexually delusional?"

"He's worked for me since day one—he's completely trustworthy. Why?"

"Well, if someone truly did try to frame you, it would have to be someone who knew about those garden stakes."

She gave a little laugh. "Guy's no murderer. Besides, anyone could have walked onto my property where those garden stakes are."

"What about Marie? How long has she worked for you?"

"About six months. And no way would she hurt anyone."

He lifted an eyebrow. "From listening to your phone conversation, it sounds like you trust Marie more than she trusts you."

Penny pursed her mouth. "I admit she's a little . . . quirky."

"You're referring to the blue hair?"

"That and she has this boyfriend, Kirk."

"And?"

"And he's a nebulous, superman phantom. She goes on and on about how much money he has, and all the different things he does. He's a pilot and a scientist and a big game hunter—"

"A hunter? Where does he live?"

Penny shrugged. "He supposedly has houses all over the country."

"But you've never seen him or talked to him?"

"No. I don't even know his last name. And they seem to correspond primarily by e-mail."

"So you think she's fallen for a pathological liar in a chat room?"

"That or maybe he doesn't exist at all."

"Ah. Does she have mental problems?"

Penny gave a little laugh. "Not that I'm aware of, although people have hinted that she has a third eye."

"ESP?"

Penny shrugged. "So people say, although I've never seen any evidence of it, and Marie doesn't talk about it." Tingling with embarrassment, she told him what Marie had said about her friend Melissa bragging that she'd slept with Deke. "Melissa was at the party, and she was in the diner this morning when you and I had coffee."

"The girl could have been lying about the affair," he said quietly.

She looked at him with gratitude . . . and resignation. "Maybe . . . but probably not."

He sighed. "Okay, so she's someone else who might have had a motive if she and Deke argued. Maybe she's pregnant."

Penny winced.

"Or maybe she's the other woman that Sheena seems to think Deke was involved with."

Penny touched her temple. "My head hurts. How do you do this for a living?"

He smiled. "It's easier when you're not in the middle of everything. Back to Marie—did you say that Steve Chasen has a crush on her?"

"I think so. He's been coming into the store regularly, and although she's always ignored him, they seemed to hit it off at my party."

"So he was only there because of her?"

She nodded. "In fact, I was surprised that he showed up, because others might have seen it as some kind of betrayal of Deke."

"Love trumps principle every time," B.J. said wryly. "What about you?"

"What about me?"

"Are you sure you don't have a boyfriend?"

The moisture left her mouth. "Not the last time I checked."

"Have you gone out with anyone since you and your husband split up?" He lifted his hand. "It might be important to the investigation."

Her face flamed. "I . . . no. I've been . . . busy." And she wasn't about to admit that the only man who had asked was scruffy Jimmy Scaggs.

"Were you still hung up on your ex?" he asked mildly.

"No," she said, too quickly.

"It's okay if you were. It sounds as if the split caught you by surprise."

She looked down at her hands. "It did," she admitted. "But I was trying to get on with my life." She had considered Sheena to be a cliché, but wasn't she a cliché as well? The signs were there, but she hadn't seen it coming.

"It must have been hard in a small town, running into your ex all the time."

She shrugged. "I didn't see Deke that much after I moved out, mostly when we were in court." And when she'd seen him come and go from the house if she happened to have been looking out the window of her store. With her binoculars.

"So I was going to be your ricochet lay?"

"Pardon me?"

He grinned. "You know—sex on the rebound."

She blushed furiously and her breasts tightened

against her will. Thinking about what might have happened between them couldn't be good for her cortisone level.

"That's a lot of pressure on a guy," he said, then mischief lit his eyes. "But I enjoy a challenge."

Desire danced in her midsection. Just talking about their missed opportunity raised her temperature. If only she'd followed her baser instincts that night. . . . Thrilled to change the subject, Penny sat forward in her seat and pointed. "This is Hairpin Hill."

"Compared to most of the flat land around here, this is a mountain."

"It's actually a landfill," she said. "For decades, Mojo was the repository for a lot of the trash coming from New Orleans. Several years ago, someone decided to cover it up, plant grass and fast-growing trees, then divide the land into lots."

"Amazing," he muttered.

She was quiet as they drove another quarter of a mile up the curving road, his earlier, provocative words winding through her head. She glanced at his rugged profile and felt a corresponding tug on her senses. The man was so damned appealing. With great difficulty, she forced herself to focus and pointed. "That's where I stopped running to catch my breath, then I heard the shots."

He slowed. "From what direction?"

She gestured, then he continued driving. A few turns later, they drove into Diane Davidson's subdivision, Garden Willow Heights. The houses were numbingly similar, the street names disorienting in their sameness—Willow Street, Willow Court, Willow Circle, Willow Way.

Penny's first impression of Diane Davidson's house was that she was trying to fit in with her neighbors. The little ranch house and lawn were painfully neat, the landscaping plants perfectly spaced like soldiers in a battalion, the porch furniture placed at precise jaunty angles. But the serene image was shattered by the words Get Out Witch painted in red on the pristine white siding.

"Looks like the woman's got her own problems," B.J. said as he parked on the street near the end of the driveway.

"Tasteless prank," Penny murmured. "This voodoo festival has everyone stirred up." They climbed out, then walked up the concrete driveway and stepped onto the shallow porch. "The paint looks relatively fresh."

B.J. rubbed his finger against the paint, then frowned and raised his finger to his nose. "This isn't paint—it's blood."

Her heart beat a tattoo against her breastbone. *"Blood?"*

"Probably animal blood. Someone's trying to scare her."

Penny glanced around the serene neighborhood, the perfect little houses, housing perfect little people.

Perfectly evil?

B.J. rang the doorbell twice, but several minutes passed with no answer. "Looks like she's gone."

"She could be too afraid to come to the door," Penny offered.

B.J. pointed to the flattened newspaper in the driveway. "Looks like she backed over it when she left. My guess is she went to buy white paint."

Penny turned and started to walk back to the car.

"Wait for me in the car," he said, then disappeared around the side of the house.

Penny was instantly nervous. What was he doing? She glanced around to see if Diane Davidson's neighbors were peering out their windows, expecting someone to come bounding out any second, demanding to know what they were doing snooping around the witch's house. She climbed back into the messy car and slumped down in the seat, then picked up the voodoo doll she had rescued from her store parking lot, shaking her head at the cryptic note. Some people truly believed that a pinprick could actually set real life events into motion.

She turned her head and stared at the violent words scrawled on Diane Davidson's house. And some people truly believed that Diane Davidson had some kind of otherworldly power, else they wouldn't be trying to run her out of town. Did Diane and other people have the ability to incite events using mere words and thoughts?

B.J. came around the side of the house and casually stopped to cup his hands around his eyes and look in one of the windows. Then he strolled toward the car, his mouth pursed, as if he were whistling. She was struck anew by the athletic way he moved, the informal command he had over his body and his surroundings. Despite his relaxed bearing, she knew he was taking in everything, scanning, memorizing details.

She was torn—grateful that he seemed to be going to such lengths to find answers, but afraid that she was relying on him too much, too quickly. With quiet resolve, she reminded herself that she was ultravulnerable at the moment, fresh from losing Deke and desperate to prove her innocence. It was only natural that she was attracted to B.J. In fact, her desperation was the only thing that explained the attraction—under normal circumstances, she'd never be attracted to a junk-food junkie whose wardrobe seemed to consist of jeans and concert T-shirts and whose car was cluttered enough to conceal a grab bag of weapons.

She remembered the green stiletto, and her thoughts ran rampant as B.J. approached the car. For all she knew about him, the woman who belonged to the shoe could be in the trunk. Maybe he kidnapped and murdered women, then approached their families and offered to look for them. Maybe he—

The door opened and he swung inside. "Diane Davidson's neighbors have reason to be nervous, but not because she's a witch."

"Why then? Did you find something?"

"A gun rack in her living room that houses some pretty impressive weapons."

Penny gasped. "Do you think she was the one shooting at me? But why?"

"Maybe the shooting is somehow connected to your ex. Maybe it was an accident. Maybe it wasn't even Diane Davidson doing the shooting, but it's worth looking into."

The ring of her cell phone startled Penny. She fumbled for a few seconds before locating the Call key. "Hello?"

"Penny? It's Gloria."

And the woman seemed to be hyperventilating. "What's wrong?"

"The police want you to come back to the station."

Penny's heart stuttered in her chest, and her gaze flew to B.J.'s. "Has there been a new development?"

"Chief Davis says they have you on video yesterday morning threatening Deke."

19

Remember to clean up the mess...

"Well, Ms. Francisco," Detective Maynard said with a smile, "here we are again."

Penny felt the gaze of everyone in the interview room—Maynard, Gloria Dalton, and Allyson Davis—upon her. Allyson stood, leaning against a wall, arms crossed over her chest. The smug look on the woman's angular face, combined with the greenish cast to her attorney's face, made the vise around Penny's chest tighten. Ridiculously, she wished that B.J. were in the room with her. A television on a roll-around stand sat in the corner of the room. On the table sat a brown paper bag marked Evidence: D. Black Homicide. Beneath the table, her knee began to bounce up and down.

"I'll tell you what you want to know," she said, her voice thready.

Allyson leaned forward. "Is that a confession?"

Penny frowned. "No, of course not."

Gloria put her hand on Penny's arm. "My client means that she's here voluntarily to answer your questions. She doesn't have anything to hide."

Maynard's mouth pressed into a flat line. "You weren't completely honest with us before, Ms. Francisco."

Penny balked. "I don't know what you mean."

"We found your fingerprints in the bedroom of Mr. Black's home."

"Considering that Penny used to live there," Gloria said, "it's only logical that her fingerprints are all over the house."

"But these fingerprints were on a photograph of Mr. Black and his girlfriend, and they contain the same type of glittery material that was on your hands last night."

Penny's lips parted in panic—she'd forgotten about the photograph. Damn that metallic makeup. How damaging (and pathetic) would it be to admit that she'd broken the photograph on purpose? "I . . . yes, I was in the bedroom." Moisture gathered on the nape of her neck. "When I walked by, I saw that the picture frame had fallen off the dresser. I, um, picked it up and saw the glass was broken."

Maynard squinted. "So you didn't break the glass in a fit of rage?"

A fit of rage? In hindsight, it had been more like petty spite—which was even more humiliating. "No, I didn't break the photo in a fit of rage," she said, her voice stronger.

"So if you picked it up, why was it still on the floor when we found it?"

"I don't know," she said, getting the hang of lying.

"So you weren't upset with your ex-husband last night when you entered his house?"

"No," Penny replied.

Maynard picked up a remote control and aimed it at the television. The screen erupted in static fuzz, then a grainy black-and-white picture appeared, unrecognizable. Trees? A section of a house?

"What is this?" Gloria demanded.

"You'll see," Allyson said, the tone of her voice bordering on gleeful.

Suddenly something appeared on the screen—something moving. A person, walking, down a path. Wearing overalls, carrying a stick. "That's me," Penny murmured.

"Where?" Gloria asked.

"At the museum."

"What museum?"

"The voodoo museum next to Penny's store," Allyson offered. "She was trespassing."

Penny scoffed. "Is that what this is all about? I squeezed through an opening in the fence to deliver some mail that wound up in my box by mistake."

"Keep watching," Allyson said.

Penny squirmed, her eyes glued on the television. It looked as if the camera had been mounted on the eave at the rear of the Archambault mansion, pointing up the side of the house where she'd walked yesterday morning. She watched herself turn, then Deke appeared on the screen.

Her heart jerked sideways to see him alive and well, unaware that he had only a few hours to live. He stood still, and she walked closer to him. The body language wasn't lost on her—he would have walked away had she not engaged him in conversation. They exchanged words—she remembered having made a crack about Sheena, and he had accused her of being jealous. Then he turned away, and she raised the stick she held and shook it at his back.

Her stomach plummeted as she watched herself stride after him, her mouth moving angrily—it was, she remembered, when she'd asked him why he'd painted the house pink. His body language, as opposed to hers, was calm and controlled. He turned toward her, the camera registering her face and his back. They talked for a few seconds, then her expression turned to one of pleading. It was when she had asked for his help with Mona, she recalled. But Deke shook his head, clearly dismissing her. They exchanged a few more words, then she leaned into him and said something, her body language aggressive before she turned and walked off camera. Deke spoke in her direction, then he turned and walked toward the camera until he disappeared from the screen.

When Maynard stopped the tape, tears stung Penny's eyes. Without the audio, she saw what everyone else in the room must: She looked hostile and vindictive.

Allyson put her hands on the table and narrowed her eyes. "What do you have to say for yourself, Penny?"

"It wasn't the way it looks on tape."

"You didn't know Mr. Black was at the museum?" Maynard asked.

"No—the museum wasn't even open yet. I went to drop the mail in the door slot."

"So why was Mr. Black there?"

"He said he was there on business. He was holding a file folder. Deke's father handled all the museum's business, and Deke took it over when his father died. He has a key to the office."

"On the tape, it looks like the two of you were arguing."

She pressed her lips together to regain a measure of calm. "Deke chided me for slipping through the fence, I made a comment about him painting the house pink, then he told me that Mona was going to have the city council stop me from planting the garden I needed to grow my business." She gestured toward the television screen. "We had words, then I asked for his help with Mona."

"And what did Deke say?" Allyson asked.

Penny's throat constricted. "He said . . . no."

"And you were furious?"

"No . . . I was . . . hurt, I guess."

"Because he chose yet another woman over you?"

The woman was hitting below the belt. "Maybe. But I wasn't angry enough to kill him."

"What about the club you threatened him with?"

Penny pinched the bridge of her nose and sighed. "It was a *stick* I picked up in case I ran into a snake as I crossed my property." She looked at Maynard. "You were there this morning—you saw how wild the underbrush is. And I didn't threaten Deke. He'd made some crack about me being jealous, and I was . . . irritated."

"Irritated?"

"That's right," Penny said. "And that's all."

"So you weren't jealous?"

Penny shook her head. "Not jealous. Just . . . sad, I guess."

"And you wanted to get even?"

"*No*," she said with as much conviction as she had in her. "Like I said, I wanted us to be civil. I even congratulated him on his engagement."

Allyson backed up, but her tongue was in her cheek. Penny could tell she didn't believe her.

"And how did Mr. Black respond?" Maynard asked.

"He seemed surprised."

"Surprised that you knew of the engagement?"

"I suppose."

"The video is hardly incriminating," Gloria cut in. "All you have is a divorced couple running into each other, and Penny just told you what happened."

"So you still maintain your innocence?" Maynard asked Penny.

"Absolutely. Either this was a random act, or someone is trying to frame me."

"Speaking of which," Gloria said, "did you ask the officers where they found the handgun they allegedly removed from Penny's apartment?"

"Yes," Allyson said. "It was hidden beneath the dry moss around the bottom of a potted tree." She angled her head. "Does it ring a bell *now*, Penny?"

Penny's eyes went wide. "The ficus tree . . . it was sitting in the foyer of the house. I took the tree with me when I moved out." She glanced from face to face. "I had no idea about the gun. Deke must have put it there."

"So you're saying it's Deke's gun?"

"I never saw a gun in our house while I was married to Deke."

"Did Mr. Black own a gun?"

"Not that he ever told me."

"Who is the handgun registered to?" Gloria asked.

"It's unregistered," Maynard said.

Penny covered her mouth with her hand. "Maybe the gun is what Deke was looking for. Maybe that's why he kept calling me. Maybe he realized I'd taken the tree."

Maynard looked at Allyson, and Penny felt the first glimmer of hope that they might be thinking there could be more to Deke's murder than a simple crime of passion.

"Maybe Mr. Black was afraid for his life," Gloria said, obviously warming up to the argument. "And he suddenly needed the gun."

Allyson pursed her mouth. "Maybe it was Penny he was afraid of, especially since she'd stolen his gun."

Penny swallowed. "I didn't steal his gun—I told you, I didn't even know it was there."

"But you did steal the tree?"

Penny sighed. "It was a lousy *tree.*"

"Ms. Francisco," Maynard said, "your employees told us some interesting things this morning."

Penny bit down on the inside of her cheek.

"They both said that you were quite upset over the divorce."

"As anyone would be," Gloria said. "What's your point?"

"Marie Gaston told me that you spent a great deal of time spying on your husband's house across the street."

Penny's stomach lurched. "Th-that's not true." She managed a little shrug. "I glance out the window occasionally, just to see what's going on along Charm Street. Marie was thinking of yesterday, when I realized that Deke was having the house painted pink. I was . . . offended. Did Marie happen to mention that her friend Melissa boasted of having an affair with Deke?"

He nodded. "We talked to the woman, and she has an alibi."

Penny closed her eyes briefly—so much for that theory.

"Ms. Gaston also informed me that she told you at the divorce party that Mr. Black's paralegal had told *her* that Mr. Black had hidden assets during your property settlement."

Penny's knee bounced erratically. "That's right."

"And you were understandably angry," he pressed.

She wet her lips. "Yes . . . at first. And then I decided I would give the information to my attorney and let her handle it."

Maynard opened the brown paper bag and removed the voodoo doll sealed in a plastic bag. Penny's stomach pitched and rolled. The pin that she'd driven into the doll's chest strained against the clear plastic. Maynard carefully removed the stabbed doll and laid it on the table in front of Penny. Details that had escaped her at the party now leaped out at her. The doll had been fashioned out of plain burlap fabric, and the little raveled edges in the head seam were a remarkably good imitation of Deke's recent hair plugs. The eyes were hand-stitched black *X*'s, spookily prophetic of Deke's blank stare when she had found him in his office. The miniature pin-striped suit was made from strips of dark fabric tucked and folded. Someone had put a lot of time into crafting the likeness.

"Ms. Francisco, did you make this doll?" Maynard asked.

Penny frowned. "What? No—I told you that I got it as a gag gift."

"And so far, no one we've talked to admits to bringing the doll."

"Maybe they're frightened," she said. "After al
was supposed to be a joke."

"Maybe not." Maynard used the tips of his finger
pull back the front of the tiny jacket on the doll. Ins
was a stamp-sized, gold-embroidered monogr
D.A.B. Penny inhaled sharply. Part of Deke's new
age had been having his monogram added to the ins
pocket of his suits when he'd bought them. "Th-
was made from . . ."

"From one of Mr. Black's suits," Maynard said, n
ding. "So it seems to me that this doll was intende
be more than just a joke. It seems like a threat."

"And it had to be made by someone close to De
Allyson added. "Someone who had access to
closet."

"You, Ms. Francisco," Maynard added.

She shook her head. "No . . . I didn't make
doll . . . and for the hundredth time, I didn't kill De

Maynard grunted. "I think you made that doll to
out your revenge. When you learned that Deke had
during the property settlement you were even more
set. Stabbing the doll got you all worked up, gave
the idea to take care of him for good. You went to
Black's house last night not because you wanted
help him but because you wanted to confront him.
told him what you'd discovered, and you had a big,
fight."

"No. I told you he was dead"—Penny choked on
word—"when I arrived. Besides, I couldn't have ov
powered Deke even if I'd wanted to."

"Your blood alcohol test came back—you w
legally drunk. Are you sure you remember everythin

"That's even more of a reason for my client physically not to be able to do what you're insinuating," Gloria said.

"Not if he was drunk, too," Maynard said. "There was a half-empty bottle of bourbon on Mr. Black's desk, and an empty glass." He clasped his hands behind his head. "We should have everything back from the M.E. and the crime lab in a couple of days."

"Good," Penny said, hoping she sounded strong. "Maybe you'll realize I've been telling the truth about the bloodstains . . . and everything else."

"Meanwhile," Gloria said, "what have you found out about the attempt on Penny's life this morning?"

Allyson's smile was flat. "I sent an officer out to look around, knock on doors, ask a few questions. He found a guy in Garden Village Heights who shot at a pack of stray dogs this morning to run them off. He produced the handgun, and since it was loaded with blanks, the officer didn't file charges." She gave Penny a mocking glance. "Now are you satisfied that no one was trying to murder you?"

Penny frowned. "Are you satisfied that I wasn't lying when I told you I heard shots fired?"

Allyson lifted her chin.

"Are we finished here?" Gloria asked, and Penny silently cheered her bravado—Gloria, ever how begrudgingly, seemed to be getting the hang of interrogation.

"One more thing," Allyson said to Penny. "That guy you're with."

Penny bristled. "His name is B.J. Beaumont. He's a private investigator from New Orleans. He's . . . helping me."

Allyson's severely arched eyebrows climbed. "And what exactly do you need help with?"

"Let's go, Penny," Gloria urged, standing.

"Just how well do you know Mr. Beaumont?" Allyson pressed.

Penny frowned. "I met him yesterday. Why?"

Allyson shrugged. "Maybe he helped you with something else—like getting rid of Deke."

Penny stood on wobbly legs. "That's ridiculous." Although hadn't she herself questioned B.J.'s motives for helping her?

"My client is not involved in Mr. Black's murder in any way," Gloria asserted, although Penny thought the attorney looked ready to collapse under the strain. "I assume, Chief Davis, that you're pursuing other suspects?"

"Like who?" Allyson asked sharply.

"Like the people who attended Penny's party. Someone gave her that doll, and maybe that's the person who killed Mr. Black."

"We haven't finished interviewing everyone," Maynard admitted. "But we'll get to them."

"What about Deke's business associates?" Penny asked, regaining a little courage. "Or his clients, or another woman he might have been involved with?"

"Or any one of the thousands of eccentric individuals who are in town for the festival?" Gloria added. "People can be animals."

At her attorney's odd tone, Penny again wondered about Gloria's background.

Maynard nodded. "We're following all leads." Then he looked at Penny. "And we'll be in touch. Meanwhile, Ms. Francisco, you should seriously consider taking a polygraph test."

But would the white lies she'd told and the emotional undercurrent she was treading come to light, muddying the overlying truth? She nodded curtly and followed Gloria to the door and out into the hall of the tiny police station. When they were out of earshot of Chief Davis and Detective Maynard, Gloria exhaled noisily.

"We're not out of danger yet." Then she frowned. "So tell me about this P.I. you're working with, this Beaumont fellow."

"He's in town working a missing person's case. We struck up a conversation at Caskey's bar last night and . . . planned to meet up later. When he heard what happened to Deke, he offered to poke around."

Gloria lifted her eyebrows suggestively.

Penny blushed. "I mean, he offered to . . . you know, ask questions where the police might not."

Gloria bit her lip. "Just to be safe, I'm going to make a couple of phone calls around the city to see what I can find out about him. A woman can't be too careful."

Penny smiled. "I think you're getting the hang of criminal representation."

"Oh, no," Gloria said, shaking her head. "Give me the peace and quiet of two people threatening to kidnap their kids and maim each other's pets." Then her cosmetically altered green eyes gentled. "How are you holding up?"

Penny sighed. "I don't know—I guess it hasn't really sunk in that Deke is dead."

"It will," Gloria warned.

"I know. I'm sure I'm in some kind of self-preservation mode. I keep seeing him dead on the floor of his office, the blood everywhere . . . but it's like a movie or something." Penny hesitated. "And I think I've been trying so hard for the last few months to distance myself from him, it just hasn't registered that I'll never see him . . . alive . . . again." She set her jaw to keep the sudden tears at bay.

Gloria made a rueful noise, then gave Penny a quick hug. "Call me if you need me."

"I will," Penny said as they walked into the cramped lobby.

B.J. was leaning on the counter, holding one of his missing persons flyers, talking to a cute blond half Penny's age, who was blushing under his scrutiny. Suspicion barbed through her chest—was he a player? She'd silently condemned Marie for believing her boyfriend Kirk's outlandish stories . . . had she done the same thing herself?

B.J. straightened when he saw them, then nodded to Gloria as she walked out. He stepped toward Penny, his expression serious. "Is everything okay?"

"Sure," she said. "Everything's dandy. You didn't have to stay."

He nodded toward the young woman he'd been huddling with. "I thought I'd ask about some of my other cases while I was here." He gave her a wry smile. "And stick around in case you needed someone to post bail."

"Not yet," she said sourly.

"So what's up with the video?"

She sighed. "They have a security video of me running into Deke yesterday at the museum—remember I told you about seeing him?"

He nodded. "Was the video damaging?"

"It's misleading. And with no audio, it's my word against a dead man's."

The door suddenly swung open and Mona Black appeared, dressed in her standard uniform of—what else?—black. When the woman's gaze landed on her, Penny took an unconscious step backward even as Mona descended on her.

"You!" Mona shouted, her face contorted. "Why aren't you behind bars?"

"Mona," Penny said quietly, "I know you're upset, but I didn't have anything to do with Deke's death."

"Liar!" Mona screamed, spittle flying. "Wasn't it enough that you ruined his life, you selfish little piece of trash? Did you have to *take* his life, too?"

Penny shrank against the wall, and B.J. stepped up to grasp her arm. "Come on, Penny, time to go."

"You'll pay for this, one way or another," Mona said, her face blood red. She clutched at the silver cross around her neck. "I have more power around here than you could *ever* know."

Penny was frozen, scorched by the unbridled hatred spewing from the woman's eyes.

B.J. gave her arm a yank and pulled her away, ushering her outside into the cool air. "Wow, I assume that was your ex-mother-in-law."

Penny nodded and shivered, still shaken. A solitary black cloud had moved in front of the sun, scaring up a chilly gust of wind that sent leaves hurtling toward the square. Two blocks away, the smoke from the *peristil* and the incessant drum beating were still going strong. It was as if the rituals were sucking the energy out of Mojo and drawing it all toward the ceremonial shelter.

"There's something strange going on in this town," she murmured, half to herself.

"I'm starting to think the same thing," B.J. said.

Then he held up one of the flyers portraying a young brunette named Giselle Taylor, who had been missing for over a year. "The dispatcher says she thinks she remembers this woman stopping her on the street during last year's festival and asking for directions to the voodoo museum."

Penny took the flyer and studied the woman's face. "Wow, that's some memory the dispatcher has."

"She said she only remembers the woman because she looked like her sister."

Penny handed back the flyer. "Maybe Hazel would remember her, too."

"Has she worked at the museum for a while?"

"For as long as I've lived here."

"And the museum was a client of your husband's?"

"That's right."

Penny could see the wheels turning in his head—no doubt slowly because of the cholesterol poisoning, but turning nonetheless.

He folded the flyer and stuffed it inside his jacket. "What do you say let's go check out this infamous voodoo museum?"

20

Sniff around to make sure all is well...

"Something smells good," B.J. said with his nose in the air.

Penny sniffed her sleeve to make sure it wasn't her permanent doughnut cologne.

"Would you mind if we got a bite to eat before we hit the museum?"

"I don't mind," Penny said, buttoning her coat to ward off the chill that the encounter with Mona had left in her blood.

"The diner's close—is that okay?"

"Sure." She wasn't that hungry anyway.

"Hey," he said, his gaze turning solemn. "Are you okay?"

She nodded. As they walked toward the square, she tried to lose herself in the crowd, her head pivoting, on the lookout for reporters and cameras.

"The vultures already got their daily scoop," he said. "Hopefully they're gone for a while."

"Marie said it wasn't safe to go back to the store.

Half the population thinks I'm a murderer and the other half thinks I'm some kind of witch doctor." She gazed toward the shelter, where several women in colorful costumes were dancing in sync, twirling flaming batons. Today a gray-bearded man wielded the *ason,* walking and stomping around the *peristil* with a live snake around his neck, touching the foreheads of those who sought him out and occasionally pausing in midmotion to have his picture taken by tourists.

"You'd tell me, wouldn't you?" he said as they walked into the diner.

"Tell you what?"

He gestured to the bar. "Okay to sit here? We'll get faster service."

She slid onto the stool and swiveled to face the white Formica bar.

"If you were a witch doctor," he said, lowering himself to the neighboring stool.

She gave him a wry smile. "I'd tell you."

"Good." His leg brushed against hers as he passed her a greasy menu. "Because I'd want to know if I was in for some kind of supernatural experience."

A laugh erupted from her throat even as the side of her body nearest him burned. It was a game her mind was playing on her body; it was called distraction. Feel lust and arousal instead of pain and fear.

"So did anything new come to light when you talked to the police?" he asked.

"Marie's friend Melissa has an alibi, so we can strike her off the list."

"Okay."

"And I was legally drunk last night," she said dryly. "They think Deke might have been, too." She frowned.

"The odd thing is, Deke told me he'd stopped drinking the last time I saw him at the courthouse."

A waitress came by and took their orders—chicken noodle soup and water with lemon for her, a double bacon cheeseburger with curly fries and a bottle of Dr Pepper for him.

"So he fell off the wagon," B.J. said with a shrug.

"There's more. The police did find a handgun in my apartment—it was hidden in my ficus tree."

A wary look came into his eyes. "You must have hidden it pretty well if you forgot about it."

"I didn't know it was there. The tree was in the foyer of the Victorian. When I left, I decided at the last minute to take it with me."

"That's ironic."

"So I'm wondering if the gun was what Deke was looking for—if that's why he left me those frantic messages last night."

B.J. raked his hand over the dark whiskers on his jaw. "It would explain why he wouldn't just come out and say what he was looking for."

"I'm starting to wonder if maybe Deke was involved in something illegal. Like drugs."

"What makes you think that?"

"It would explain the change in his personality. When I met Deke, he was so laid back. But after his father died, he became moody and edgy. He was hard to live with sometimes."

"Don't you think that probably had something to do with him losing his father?"

"Probably," she agreed. "But I remember him saying something after his father died—that he felt lost, that for most of his life he had resisted bad things because he was afraid of disappointing his father. When his father died . . . I don't know, but I felt like Deke was afraid he would succumb to . . . something."

"He did succumb to infidelity," B.J. pointed out.

"I know," she said wryly, "but that doesn't explain how he could afford a new sports car and European suits when his practice was supposedly struggling."

"You never asked him?"

"Sure I did. He said he was tapping into his trust fund."

"You don't think he was?"

"Mona still controls the trust fund that was created for him when Deke's father passed away. And she didn't look favorably upon extravagant purchases. She wanted Deke to be . . . classy."

"And under her thumb. So what did his mother think about his new girlfriend?"

"Not much, I'm sure," Penny said. "But Mona kept it to herself. When she stopped by the party, though, I, um, was feeling vindictive."

"And?"

"And I broke the news to her that Deke and Sheena were engaged."

He sucked in through his teeth. "I'll bet Mama wasn't too happy."

"She tried not to react, but I could tell she was shocked . . . and angry."

"Did he go out of his way to do things to annoy his mother?"

"Not usually."

"So were you surprised that he was engaged to the Linder woman?"

She rubbed the condensation on her water glass.

"Frankly . . . yes. I thought they probably would live together for a while. Sheena just doesn't seem like Deke's type . . . not for the long run, anyway." Although what did she know? "The funny thing is, I don't think that even Sheena thought she was Deke's type for the long run."

"You mean the fact that she suspected you and Deke of messing around behind her back?"

"Right. And when I saw Deke outside the museum and congratulated him, he seemed surprised."

"Surprised that you knew about the engagement?"

Penny bit her lip, replaying his reaction in her mind. "I thought so, but now . . . now I'm wondering if maybe he was just surprised."

"As in, he hadn't proposed?"

She shrugged. "Maybe."

"Well, it's possible that Sheena made it up out of desperation. Maybe we're back to the girlfriend after all."

"There's more," Penny said. "The voodoo doll that someone brought to the party . . . apparently the clothes were made out of one of Deke's suits."

He grimaced. "Wow, that's blunt. So whoever made the doll had access to his clothes."

"Right. And since I didn't do it, the most obvious answer is Sheena."

"Did she happen to drop by the party?"

"No, but she was at Caskey's that night, and the gift table was next to the door. I guess it's possible that she put it there without anyone seeing her."

He sighed. "But then so could anyone else who was at the bar that night."

"They would've had to know about the party," she pointed out.

"Did Sheena?"

"Not from me." Then she squinted. "But I did r
tion something to Deke about having the party, s
might have said something to her." Sheena's h
words about how she and Deke had talked about P
resounded in her mind.

B.J. nodded. "So maybe they were having probl
She threatened him, he went looking for his gun
couldn't find it. He called you to see if you knew w
it was."

"And Sheena overheard him calling me," P
added, her adrenaline pumping. "To set me up, she
a stake from my garden. Deke is drunk, so she's ab
stab him."

"Then she panics," B.J. said. "She finds a voo
doll at the festival, dresses it in one of Deke's suits
she cuts up, and puts it on the gift table."

"Then she finds me at the bar," Penny said, "
tells me that Deke is looking for me. She left the ph
off the hook thinking that I'd walk to the house if I
a busy signal."

"Then she conveniently arrives home to find
standing over the body and calls the police," B.J. s

Penny's jaw dropped. "We solved the case!"

But he gave a little laugh. "Just because all
pieces fit doesn't mean they're in the right place.
has an alibi, remember?"

"She was lying in a tanning bed—that alone sh
be a crime."

He laughed. "What would she gain from kil
him?"

"The assets that he supposedly put in her name
in the name of her company."

He nodded. "Pretty good. But you also have something to gain from his death."

"What?"

"Revenge."

She sipped from her water glass. "That's not the kind of person I am."

"That's the kind of person everyone has the potential to be," he murmured. Then he removed a napkin from his pocket. "There were two names on the list of people at the party that you haven't mentioned: Liz Brockwell and Wendy Metzger."

"Friends of mine from college," she said. "Liz lives in New Orleans, Wendy in Atlanta. They came to surprise me."

"Did they know Deke?"

Penny nodded. "We were all in college together, but they were primarily my friends. In fact, Liz didn't particularly like Deke, but I think she's kind of bitter toward men in general because of her two divorces."

"She's the one who lives in New Orleans?"

"Right."

"Could she have brought the doll?"

"I asked Liz and she said no." Penny blushed. "They, um, brought the blow-up man."

He leaned in close to her ear. "A woman who looks like you do shouldn't have to resort to . . . artificial means."

She swung her head up to see if he was flattering her, and suddenly her mouth was mere inches from his. His warm breath fanned her cheek, and desire hooded his eyes. She had the distinct feeling that if they hadn't been in a public place, they would have been going at each other. The attraction she felt for this man was crazy—it had all the hormonal earmarks of a teenage infatuation, but instead of being flush with the curiosity of sex, she was flush with the suspicion that they would be savagely compatible in bed. A current of energy passed wordlessly between them. His lips parted, and she unwittingly mimicked him, lost in the fantasy.

The waitress reappeared, breaking the moment, her hands full, and plates in the crooks of her elbows. B.J. smacked his lips at the cholesterol-laden plate she set before him. "Looks great."

Still shaken by the connection she felt to this man, Penny stared down at her bowl of chicken soup. A pool of clear yellow grease floated on top like an oil slick, suffocating the noodles and little bits of carrot. "Looks . . . hazardous."

"You always been such a picky eater?" he asked before taking a gigantic bite out of his two-story burger.

She dunked the spoon into the grease and pulled it back out, cringing when the lumpy yellow stuff actually congealed against the metal. "I'm not picky—I'm health conscious," she said, abandoning the soup. She scrutinized the cellophane packet of saltines for the sodium content. But when the aroma of his burger reached her nose, her stomach howled, and she tore open the crackers and begrudgingly bit into one. The sodium would no doubt raise her blood pressure. She could practically feel her arteries contract even as she swallowed.

B.J. had already inhaled half his burger and was making a dent in the mountain of curly fries. She pointed her pinky in the vicinity of his well-developed chest. "Chargrilled food is carcinogenic. Free radicals are spinning through your body as we speak, looking for a healthy cell to latch onto and mutate."

"I bet you're always the life of the barbecue," he muttered.

"I'm telling you for your own good. I bet you don't take a multivitamin, either."

"No, that ranks right up there with tofu."

She dug into her purse and removed the little plastic bag that held her daily vitamin pack—twelve pills in all, two of them fairly large. B.J. stared as she swallowed them one by one.

"You're healthy and you take that many pills?"

"I'm healthy *because* I take this many pills."

He shook his head. "That's not natural."

"Really? So tell me, what tree did they pick those curly fries off of?"

He grinned. "That's different. Besides—" He looked her up and down. "You could stand to put on a few pounds."

She frowned down at her baggy clothes. "How would you know?"

"Are you kidding? All I can think about is what you're hiding under there."

Ignoring the spike in her vitals, she narrowed her eyes and ordered a cup of hot water for the emergency bag of green tea she carried with her; one never knew when one might need a booster shot of antioxidants.

He laughed and continued eating. Rankled, Penny sat brewing right along with her tea. Who was he to make fun of her? The health rituals she'd developed over the past year—the meals, the supplements, the exercise programs—had given her life new structure, new meaning. Her body was a lean, mean, autoimmune machine.

She frowned into her cup—that information probably wouldn't look very appealing in a singles ad.

"Don't you miss it?" he asked.

"What?" she asked, and absurdly, sex came to mind.

He gestured vaguely toward the food all around them, the dessert counter. "The fat, the salt, the sugar. It tastes *good*."

"A high-fat diet kills your libido." She regretted those words as soon as they left her mouth.

He laughed. "Couldn't prove it by me."

She chewed on a cracker and tried to force erotic images from her mind and back to the matter at hand. She remembered Gloria's pledge to make some calls about B.J. "How long have you been an investigator?" she asked.

He shrugged. "Five years or so. My brother was a cop who decided to go out on his own. I had a computer job that was slowly killing me with boredom, so I decided to join him."

"You must like it," she observed, although it was obvious from his clothing—and his car—that he wasn't exactly rolling in the dough.

"Yeah, I get to meet a lot of interesting people." He smiled at her, and she squirmed under his scrutiny.

"Lots of damsels in distress?"

"A few," he admitted.

"How long will you stay in Mojo?" she asked, hoping she didn't sound as if she cared.

"As long as I'm needed," he said, withdrawing his wallet.

"Let me pay," she said, reaching for her purse.

"I got it," he said, then winked. "I'll add it to my expense report. Ready to go?"

They decided to leave his car parked in the square and walk to the museum.

"Will you show me the way you went yesterday when you ran into Deke?"

"Sure," she said, glad for a reason not to walk past the Victorian. They skirted the parking lot of her store, and she gazed longingly toward the door, thinking she'd stop in on the way back. At the edge of the brambly field, she looked around for the stick she'd thrown down, then realized the detective had probably found it and confiscated it as evidence. "The stakes are gone," she said. "The police must have taken them."

"Or the tourists," B.J. said.

He was probably right—they were probably already listed on eBay.

She led the way through the brush, stumbling a couple of times on exposed roots. B.J. took her arm and helped her across, but his warm hand was so distracting that she was even more unsteady. When they reached the fence, she frowned at the wire that had been wrapped around the separated areas of the fence, effectively blocking entry to the other side. "Someone patched it up, probably Tilton."

"Tilton?"

"He's Hazel's son. He does odd jobs around the museum."

B.J. stepped up to the vine-covered fence and craned his neck to look at the towering Archambault house. "So that's the voodoo museum?"

She nodded. "Come on, we'll walk around front."

They backtracked to the sidewalk and walked to the

front of the museum. Despite the fact that the day was sunny, the temperature around the tree-shrouded house was always ten degrees cooler than it was anywhere else. Fall leaves clogged the yard, the walkway, and the steps, lending to the spooky appearance of the run-down mansion. Penny gave B.J. some history of the place, including a few bits of the more exotic lore. He studied the house and the landscaping as they walked up the steps behind a small group of tourists, then he surveyed the tall, red-stained door and pushed it open. Penny shivered as she walked through, once again overcome with the feeling that the house had the ability to consume her.

Inside, the atmosphere had been set with low lighting and thick candles behind hurricane globes. The furniture was dark and heavy, the windows tall, the curtains ornate. Murals adorned the ceiling of each room. At first glance, they seemed soft and almost biblical, but upon closer scrutiny, then depicted scenes of torture and sacrifice, each more disturbing than the last. The mural in the entryway showed a man wearing a blue robe with his hands raised to a group of white-robed followers. The man looked angelic and noble, but behind him was a pit of demons, seemingly ready to snatch the followers as soon as they neared.

"Nice," B.J. murmured wryly.

A heavy commercial floral fragrance hung in the air, a not-so-successful attempt to hide the unpleasant scent of mothballs. A carpeted runner spared the creaky wood floors from heavy foot traffic. Hazel stood behind a counter, dressed in a loose black dress, smiling and pleasant, describing the tours to the people who were ahead of them. Then she handed off the group to one of several high school students who worked at the museum during peak times and looked up, her expression immediately turning to concern as she came out from behind the counter.

"Penny . . . my dear." She hugged her briefly. "I'm so sorry about Deke."

"Thank you. And I want you to know that I had nothing to do with it," Penny felt compelled to say to the woman who had been her friend.

"I know that," Hazel said, then she bit her lip. "I have to warn you—when that detective came around this morning, I told him you said you'd run into Deke here yesterday, and he got all our security tapes."

"They've already questioned me about it," Penny said. "It's fine." She introduced Hazel to B.J. "He's in town looking for a missing friend and was hoping you could help."

"Certainly, if I can."

B.J. showed her the flyer of Giselle Taylor. "The dispatcher at the police department says she remembers this woman asking for directions to the museum this time last year."

"Last year?"

"During the festival," Penny added.

Hazel winced. "My memory isn't what it used to be, but let me take a look." She pulled reading glasses from her pocket and studied the flyer, but shook her head. "I'm sorry—I just don't remember her. So many people come through here in a year's time, I just can't remember them all."

"I understand," B.J. said. "Thank you. Do you mind if I look around? I'd be glad to pay for a tour."

Hazel gave them a conspiratorial wave. "Go ahead.

Penny knows her way around." The woman then turned her attention to another group of people who had come in.

Penny smiled up at B.J. "Do you want the nickel tour or the full-blown experience?"

He grinned. "Full-blown."

She took him from room to room, describing the murals and the exhibits of costumes, implements, a few wax figures and a few stuffed goats and chickens (compliments of Lewis Taxidermy). The voodoo displays told the stories behind the myths of the voodoo of Africa and Haiti—the black magic, the human sacrifices, the zombies—but always left the door open for the idea that any dark, horrific thing was possible in the underworld of voodoo.

Penny had read the story of voodoo dolls many times, but she scoured it again. The voodoo doll, to be effective, had to be made of something close to the subject—hair or clothing, for instance. And the person delivering the good or bad "pricks" with a pin had to believe in what they were doing: it was mind over matter, the sign explained. If the person believed deeply enough, then their wish would become a self-fulfilling prophecy. Penny's heart thudded against her chest as a horrible thought seeped into her brain: Had she somehow caused Deke's death just by the bad vibes she had put out into the universe?

"You okay?" B.J. asked, breaking into her dark thoughts.

She startled and looked up at him, wondering how crazy he'd think she was if he knew the things going through her head.

She nodded and tried to shake the heebie-jeebies—

hard to do in such an eerie place. They descended to the musty, moldy basement, where they listened to a tour guide talk, in macabre detail, about the chair of nails, the human stretching machine, and the contraption that prepared sausages mixed with ground glass, which were then fed to victims. Dark stains on the floor suggested blood and other body fluids, but they were probably motor oil and mildew, Penny noted. A myriad of whips and chains hung on the walls, and headless mannequins modeled pain-inflicting clothing—spike-lined vests and garments of barbed wire, necklaces of knife blades and bracelets of wax that would have been set afire.

In the background, a sound track of human screams and other spooky noises played. The tourists shifted from foot to foot, and Penny, as always when she heard the stories, was awash with horror for the people who had been subjected to the sick minds of the masters of torture.

The tour guide led his group out of the room. "Let's go," she murmured to B.J., eager to end their tour. But when she looked back, B.J. was staring at one of the spiked whips on the wall.

"What's wrong?" she said, walking back to join him as she prayed he wasn't into S&M.

"Maybe nothing," he said quietly, then reached up to pull out a long, white-blond hair that was coiled around the end of one of the spikes. "And maybe everything."

21

Store in a dark place . . .

Penny's blood ran cold as she stared at the long, blond hair. Imagining people being tortured was one thing, but seeing the proof of their existence and their suffering . . . that was another thing entirely. "Oh, my God. Do you think the hair is recent?"

B.J. sighed. "It's hard to say—hair breaks down very slowly over time. It could be decades old . . . or left last week. A laboratory could probably date it to some extent by examining the follicle."

"Should we call the police?"

"Don't go jumping to conclusions," he murmured, then he held the twisted hair up to the light, his eyebrows knitted. "Let's see if your friend Hazel can explain why it would be here." He pulled a small plastic baggie out of his jacket pocket and gently placed the strand of hair inside. "Without raising any red flags."

She nodded, and they retraced their steps back to the first floor, although Penny couldn't bring herself to touch anything—not even the handrails. Suddenly every stain on the floor, every peculiar odor, every taped scream took on a new meaning. Chills ran over her skin, and she unconsciously moved closer to B.J. He seemed to sense her unease, because his hand hovered at her waist as they made their way back to the lobby.

Hazel was talking to a tall, slender man with sharp cheekbones and thinning hair, but she turned to smile at them when they approached. "All done?" she asked.

"Yes," Penny said, still shaken.

"Penny, have you met Dr. Troy Archambault?"

Penny extended her hand. "No, but I've heard a lot about you. I'm Penny Francisco. I live nearby."

A wary look came into the owner's eyes as he shook her hand. "I've also heard a lot about you, Ms. Francisco."

Penny swallowed. From the newspapers, no doubt.

"Penny didn't kill her ex-husband," Hazel piped up matter-of-factly. "It's all a big misunderstanding. This voodoo festival has everyone churned up."

Troy Archambault nodded amicably. "But the festival is good for the museum."

Penny turned to B.J. "This is, um, a friend of mine, B.J. Beaumont. B.J., Dr. Archambault's family used to live in this house."

"Call me Troy," the man said and shook B.J.'s hand.

"These two are looking for a missing woman," Hazel said.

Troy's eyebrows shot up. "Oh? What makes you think she's here?"

"Someone remembered giving her directions to the museum during last year's festival," B.J. said, his voice casual.

"Last year?" Troy said, then gave a little laugh. "If she was here, she's probably long gone by now."

B.J. nodded. "Probably. I was hoping Hazel might recall having seen her."

Penny cleared her throat. "Hazel . . . I saw a strand of hair tangled in one of the, um, spiked whips downstairs—it kind of creeped me out."

Hazel sighed. "Tourists, what can I say? I find that and worse all the time when I clean—they're not supposed to take things down from the walls or mess with the exhibits, but they do anyway. No matter how much we try to keep an eye on them, someone will snag their clothes or hair." She reached beneath the counter and came up with a bag of adhesive bandages. "Sometimes they even hurt themselves."

"That's why the insurance on this place is so astronomical," Troy muttered. "We're going to have to raise the price of admission again after the first of the year."

"Interesting place, though," B.J. said. "Did you grow up here?"

Troy shook his head. "No, my father did. I was raised in New Orleans, where my dermatology practice is." He glanced at his watch. "Speaking of which, I have to get back." He nodded to them both. "It was nice to meet you. I hope you find your friend."

Penny and B.J. murmured pleasantries to him and to Hazel. On the way out, they passed the souvenir shop, a cubbyhole off to the side of the entryway that Penny imagined might once have been an enormous coat closet for guests. It was crowded with tourists, many of them dressed in their festival garb. B.J. wandered inside, and Penny followed him, glancing over the array of novelty items, including plastic handcuffs, spongy spiked balls, and generic voodoo dolls stamped with various "target zones," much like a butcher would mark an animal for certain cuts of meat. The woman straightening shelves turned, and Penny blinked. "Diane . . . hello. I didn't realize you worked here."

Diane Davidson seemed surprised to see her too . . . and a little embarrassed. "It's only temporary."

"Of course," Penny murmured.

Diane fidgeted, reminding Penny of a small bird. "I heard about Deke . . . and . . . everything." She stopped and wet her lips. "You've always been nice to me . . . I know you couldn't do what people are saying. And I know how people in this town like to gossip."

"Thank you," Penny said warily, trying to picture the woman wielding one of the guns that B.J. said he'd seen in her house. "Diane, did you happen to bring the gag gift voodoo doll to my party?"

She shook her head. "I wouldn't have brought something like that anyway, but especially not considering the rumors going around about me."

Penny noticed white specks on the woman's wrists—paint?—and felt a surge of sympathy. "I actually came by to talk to you this morning."

Diane swallowed nervously. "To my house?"

Penny nodded. "I saw the graffiti. Did you report it to the police?"

Diane tucked a lock of drab brown hair behind her ear and shook her head. "No use. And it would only stir up more trouble." She looked past Penny and murmured, "Excuse me," then walked over to B.J., who was studying the labels of tiny brown jars on the counter that seemed to be so popular with the customers. "May I help you, sir?"

He held up two small bottles. "Both of these are labeled 'powdered bones.' What's the difference between the ones with the red caps and the ones with the white caps?"

"Just different suppliers." She smiled, then lowered her voice. "You do realize that it's just limestone?"

He nodded and returned her smile. "I'll take both of these—I think my niece and nephew will get a kick out of them." Then he added a pair of plastic handcuffs to his purchases, giving Penny a secret, sexy wink.

She flushed at his insinuation, and foolishly her mind conjured up an image of being handcuffed to her bed and B.J. doing wicked, wonderful things to her, his sensuous, curvy mouth on her skin, rendering her powerless as she strained against the plastic—

"Ready?" B.J. asked.

She jumped, then nodded and exhaled. "Sure." They walked out, and B.J. studied the immense door when they closed it behind them. "Looks old."

"I think it's original," she said, then told him the tale about the door being stained with the blood of the house's victims.

His grin was wry. "This town seems to thrive on the macabre."

"And New Orleans doesn't?"

"Touché."

"By the way, that was Diane Davidson who waited on you. She said she didn't bring the voodoo doll to the party."

"That little mouse is the witch that has people stirred up enough to paint messages on her house in blood?"

"Don't forget, she's the one you said had an arsenal in her living room."

"Maybe she felt like she needed to protect herself." He shook his head. "Wow, when I drove into this town, it looked so innocent."

"Small towns aren't innocent," Penny said. "The people are just better at keeping secrets." She walked down the leaf-covered stone steps and pointed left. "That's where I ran into Deke."

B.J. craned his neck. "What's around back?"

"A three-car garage and a short driveway leading to a gate to drive on and off the property."

"But no customer parking?"

"Right."

B.J. seemed to make some mental notes, then they walked back to the pedestrian entrance in the front.

Penny glanced back at the Archambault mansion and thought she saw a flash in a window, like before. She shuddered, wondering if it was just a tourist or if the people tortured there haunted its halls. Then she looked around and saw it was only the glare from a car coming down Hairpin Hill. She felt silly—she was letting the embellished stories of the tour guides get the better of her. "Are you going to the police with the hair you found?"

B.J. shook his head. "You heard Hazel—thousands of people go through the museum every year, and that hair could belong to any one of them."

"So you're not going to do anything with it?"

"I didn't say that. I only have to prove that it did or didn't belong to Jodi Reynolds. I'll call her grandmother to see if she has a hairbrush of Jodi's. If there's a DNA match, then I'll go to the police."

"How long will that take?"

"A few days at the earliest." Then he frowned.

She pressed her lips together, because she knew what he was thinking—wherever Jodi Reynolds was, she was probably dead . . . unfortunately, a few more days wasn't going to make a difference.

As they rounded the corner of Charm Street, she saw in the distance that a crowd had gathered in front of the pink Victorian, some of them taking pictures. A television news crew was doing a report. Penny glanced toward her store. "I think I'm going to make a run for it and hide out in my office for a while."

B.J. nodded. "Want to grab some dinner later?"

Penny studied the angles of his handsome face, his piercing dark eyes, the sexy set of his shoulders. She was becoming too attracted to this man, too . . . trusting. His proximity and helpful nature were messing with her ability to think logically . . . and on her own.

"I don't think so," she said slowly, hugging herself to resist the urge to touch him. "I need to straighten my apartment, and I need to get some rest."

He nodded. "Sure. How about we meet tomorrow?"

She hesitated. "My store is closed. I was planning to take in the festival, but I'm not sure—"

"I'll drop by around noon."

She bit down on the inside of her cheek, then sighed. "How about two o'clock?"

"I'll bring the doughnuts." Then he grinned and strode away.

Penny watched his retreating figure and groaned. She had no business forming an attachment to anybody right now, especially not to someone like B.J. Beaumont. She cut through The Charm Farm's backyard and walked alongside the building, eyeing the wild brushy field that was to have been her new garden. She had thought that by now, she would be arranging to have the field cleared and would be elbow deep in seed catalogs; that her most pressing problem would be whether to plant the beefsteak tomatoes or the heirloom variety.

Instead she had Deke's death on her hands and a dark-eyed Cajun on her mind.

At least business was good, she thought as she entered the store. She was going to have to pay for Gloria's services to date, and for B.J.'s. A sigh escaped her; if she was going to be arrested, her threat to pay him in vitamins might not be too far off the mark. She nodded to Guy when he looked up, then kept her head down as she walked toward her office.

"Is that her?" she heard someone whisper.

"I think so! It's the voodoo woman!" someone shouted, and a murmur ran through the customers.

Penny darted past Marie and into the office, closing the door behind her. She dropped into her desk chair and put her head in her hands. When would things get back to normal? A lump formed in her throat as tears welled behind her eyes. What would happen to her if she was arrested, if she was convicted? Was this her punishment for being so judgmental when someone else had been in a similar situation, for having no compassion when called upon to forgive?

She swallowed past the lump. A good, hard cry was in her future, but she had to hold it together here. With a mighty inhale, she turned her attention to her desk, sifting through phone messages and mail. *Liz called.* She had forgotten to give Liz her new cell number. *The New Orleans* Post *wants an interview. Liz called. WNNO wants an interview. WOLA wants an interview.*

The mail consisted of bills, seed catalogs, and vertisements. Sheena's Forever Sun tanning salon having a Voodoo Festival special—Get Fried for O $9.95. Penny rolled her eyes, but it made her thoug turn to Sheena and the scenario that she and B.J. talked through at the diner. Had the woman killed D out of anger, then tried to pin the murder on Penny so, then Sheena would have had to already have kil Deke when Penny saw her at Caskey's. She repla the scene in her head, recalling Sheena's brief ou and snakeskin bag. She hadn't seemed out of sorts nervous at all. Was it possible for someone to kill other person and be unaffected?

Yes . . . hadn't she seen proof of that in her o family?

She let the flyer fall from her fingers into the tra wondering what kind of a dysfunctional childh Sheena might have endured that would have made so cold-blooded if indeed she had killed Deke. It did make her any more likable, but it would explain flamboyance and her compulsion to sue anyone she had wronged her.

The murmur of a headache began to stir in Penn temples, and her stomach gurgled. She was hungry, nothing sounded appetizing. She just needed a lift .

Her gaze dropped to the locked desk drawer, and heart gave a glad little jump. Didn't she deserve to dulge? What was she waiting for? If being accused c voodoo murder didn't warrant an emotional em gency, then what did?

She moistened her lips and fished the key out of top drawer, then inserted it into the lock.

A knock sounded on the door, and she exhaled. "Who is it?"

"It's me," Guy said.

Penny returned the key to the top drawer and sighed. "Come in."

He opened the door and slid inside, then closed it behind him. His face creased in worry, he held up an energy bar and a glass of juice and said, "Marie thought you might need some nourishment."

She smiled gratefully and reached for the food. "Thank you."

"How are you holding up?" he asked.

She bit into the energy bar and shrugged. "Okay, I guess. I'm not really sure how I'm supposed to be after . . . everything that's happened."

"Marie told you that the police were here this morning?"

Penny nodded. "When I called her earlier. And I've already been back to the station today to answer more questions."

He winced. "Marie feels really bad for telling them . . . some things."

"It's okay," she said. "I have nothing to hide."

He exhaled, looking relieved.

Good grief—did he also think she'd killed Deke?

He pulled a piece of paper out of his pocket. "I, um, called Goddard's Funeral Home to get arrangements for . . . Deke."

Her heart stuttered. It still didn't seem possible that yesterday morning, Deke had been alive and now he was across town in an embalming tray. She closed her eyes briefly as a wave of nausea hit her.

"I didn't know if . . . I mean you might not want to go—"

"Of course I want to go," she murmured. "Thank you, Guy, for calling." Penny looked at the paper.

DEKE BLACK FUNERAL

MONDAY 2:00 P.M.

GRAVESIDE SERVICE AFTERWARD.

She stuffed the paper into her pocket and lifted the glass of yellow juice to her mouth for a deep drink. It tasted good; she hadn't realized how dehydrated she was. "How are things here?"

"Busy, as you saw."

"But is anyone buying anything?"

"Oh yeah, we've had a record sales day, in fact."

Penny massaged the back of her neck. "Well, I guess there's something to be happy about."

He shifted from foot to foot. "Do the police . . . know who did it yet?"

She shrugged. "If they know, they aren't telling me."

He suddenly leaned over to hug her. "I'm just so sorry you got dragged into the middle of this."

She nodded against his neck. "Thank you."

He pulled back. "You look exhausted."

"Probably because I only got about two hours of sleep last night."

"Want to stay at my place tonight? I'll take the couch."

She smiled at him fondly. "Thank you, but I need to get my place straightened up."

Guy looked puzzled.

"From the police search," she explained wryly, taking another bite out of the bar.

He looked stricken. "God, this is just awful."

"I know," she said, then felt compelled to pat his arm. "But hopefully the police will have some answers soon."

Guy scoffed. "Sheena did it."

Penny blinked. "Do you know something?"

He made an exasperated sound. "What everyone else knows—that she's a gold digger and a slut."

Penny sighed. "That may be true, but it's not against the law."

"Oh, come on, Penny, of course she killed him," he said vehemently, his eyes wide. "Who else could it have been?"

At his vicious tone, she pulled back slightly, suddenly uneasy—she'd never seen Guy lose his temper before. "I really don't know. I think Sheena is a likely suspect, but I'm sure a lot of people think that about me."

He pulled his hand down his mouth, then nodded. "You look exhausted."

She smiled. "You said that already." Then she stood. "But you're right. You and Marie have everything under control, so I think I'll head home and turn in early."

"I'll drive you," he said.

"That's not necessary, Guy."

"I'm *not* going to let you go out there to be hounded by voodoo weirdos and news reporters."

The man did make sense. "Okay."

He smiled. "See, the Ragin' Cajun isn't the only person looking out for you. I'll get my coat."

Penny frowned as the door closed, then shook her

head. She pulled out her new cell phone and punche
Liz's number, downing the rest of the juice Guy
brought her while the phone rang. She got Liz's v
mail and smiled at her friend's seductive voice. She
posed most men, like Ziggy, did find Liz intimidati

When the beep sounded, she assured her friend
she was doing fine, then left the details of Deke's
neral and directions to Goddard's in as steady a v
as she could muster. "If you can't come, I'll un
stand," she said, then hung up. She looked up Wen
number and dialed, fully expecting to leave ano
message, but smiled in surprise when Wendy answe

"Hello?"

"Wendy, hi, it's Penny."

"Penny?" Wendy sniffed. "How are you?"

Penny frowned at Wendy's muffled voice. "I'm
Are you sick?"

"Yeah," Wendy said, then blew her nose. "I r
have . . . picked up a flu bug."

"I'm sorry you're not feeling well. I was callin
give you the details of, um, Deke's f-funeral." In c
bination, the words were surreal: *Deke's fune
Deke's funeral. Deke's funeral* . . .

"Well, I'm probably not going to be able to make
Wendy said, her voice breaking. "I'm sorry—it's th
allergies."

Penny squinted. "I thought you said you'd picke
a flu bug."

"Right," Wendy said thickly. "It's awful. I'm
sorry, sweetie. I'll send flowers."

"It's okay," Penny murmured, shocked at how
she felt. But Wendy was ill, and she probably thou
that since Penny and Deke were divorced, it wasn

necessary trip. After all, Penny had pretty much denounced the man during the party, hadn't she? "I hope you feel better."

"Thanks. I'll call you soon."

Penny disconnected the call, thinking it was strange that Wendy hadn't asked questions about the investigation. Then she chided herself . . . of course Wendy wasn't concerned because she knew that Penny couldn't have murdered Deke.

A knock sounded at the door, and Guy stuck his head in. "Ready?"

"Yeah."

"It's died down a little, so you should be able to make it out without a mob scene."

She shrugged into her coat and slid past him into the showroom. Marie looked up and gave a little wave, and Penny gave her a reassuring smile. Thankfully, they made it through both rooms and to the parking lot with no incident. Dusk was falling—the street lights were already flickering. Guy unlocked and opened the door of the Lexus for her, and she slid in, sinking into the luxurious, squeaky leather.

"This is *nice,*" she said when he climbed in.

"Thanks."

She inhaled. "It still smells new."

"Well, it's only a few months old."

She nudged him playfully. "By the way, how do you afford a car like this on what I pay you?"

He laughed. "I'm very frugal."

"I'll say." She glanced around while he backed out of the parking lot, making silent comparisons to the dumpy green sedan that B.J. drove. The man truly was a slob. Then her gaze caught on something in the back

floorboard sticking out from under the driver seat, an
her jaw loosened. "Guy—is that a *gun?*"

He blanched, then he gave a nervous laugh. "It's n
mine—I borrowed it from a friend." He sighed. "Oka
I guess the whole thing with Deke has got me spooke
I thought it wouldn't hurt to have some protection."

"I thought you believed that Sheena murdere
Deke."

"I do," he said, his voice wavering.

"So what—you think that she's a serial killer?"

He giggled. "That would make a great movi
wouldn't it?"

Penny frowned. "Are you really scared?"

"Aren't you?" He waved to the bustling throngs o
people spilling over the sidewalks. "This kind of fest
val brings out the psychos, Penny. Speaking of whicl
who is this P.I. you're working with?"

"I don't think B.J. is a psycho."

"Really? How did you get hooked up with him?"

She bristled. "He was . . . at Caskey's. It was . . .
chance meeting."

He pulled into the side street leading to her apar
ment and slowed. "Hm. Kind of coincidental, don
you think?"

A warning bell sounded in the corners of her min
"What do you mean?"

Guy wet his thin lips. "Just be careful—somethin
evil is in the air."

A finger of fear tickled her neck as the car fille
with a cloying tension. In the dim light, Guy looked a
most . . . sinister. Her breath caught in her throat. The
he lunged for her, and she cried out. He reached acros

her to tug the door handle. Her door clicked open, then he pulled back and frowned. "Are you okay?"

She put her hand to her throat. "You just startled me. I guess it was all that talk about . . . danger."

He gave her a sad little smile. "Try to get some rest."

She nodded. "Thanks for the ride. See you Monday."

"Want to ride with me to the funeral?"

"Okay." She stepped out of the car and onto the sidewalk, trying to shake the creepy feeling that had come over her. She watched Guy's car disappear, slowly obscured by pedestrians who seemed determined to crowd cars off the streets. She gazed out over the square, where the crowd was even larger, the scene even more uncontrolled than it had been last night.

The people seemed to be caught up in a tangible, convulsive energy. The drummers in the *batri* were relentless, their pounding and beating an almost continuous noise. The costumed dancers were impossibly vigorous, some of them draped with live snakes. The purple smoke from the *peristil* fire seemed to hang itself on everything. The scent of eucalyptus—perhaps an attempt to cleanse the air of the stench of perspiration and animal flesh—burned her nose.

But when she walked around the corner, the sickly sweet odor of beignets cut through everything else. She sighed and fished for her key.

A squatty, sweaty man appeared out of nowhere, invading her personal space. "An interview for the *Post,* Ms. Francisco?"

"No," she snapped, opening the door. "Leave or I'll call the police."

"Call the police—or put the voodoo on me?"

Penny glared at him. "Don't tempt me." She stepped into the tiny entryway and let the door slam behind her, reducing the blare of the festival noise to a muffled hum.

If possible, the dim overhead light seemed even more faint as her eyes tried to adjust to the darkness. She felt for the light switch and flipped it, praying that her landlord had replaced the bulb.

Nothing. She groaned in frustration—Elton was going to hear about this.

She started climbing the steps, silently cursing Guy for leaving her so spooked. Borrowing a gun—what was he thinking? And all his talk about evil in the air. He was making her imagine things. She reached the landing. Things like hearing someone else's breathing in the pitch-black space.

But when the distinct scent of male perspiration reached her, she froze, her nose flaring in fear. Someone was on the landing with her.

22

If something is rotten, you'll smell it . . .

A scream lodged in the back of Penny's throat, but when she opened her mouth to unleash it, a large hand clamped over her lips and nose. Terror seized her, and in the space of a heartbeat, she imagined herself being thrown down the stairs or tossed inside her apartment and having her throat slit . . . or worse. Ravaged, then suffocated? Hacked up into little pieces and skewered?

Her lungs pumped furiously as she tried to drag in air between the man's ironlike fingers. He moved in behind her and put his head next to her ear.

"I'm going to let go," he murmured. "Don't scream. Okay?"

She nodded against his hand, her mind racing. She knew that voice from somewhere.

"It's me—Jimmy."

Her eyes flew wide. Jimmy Scaggs? Was he a madman? A serial killer living on the land?

Slowly he released his grip on her and she gasped

for air, flattening herself against her door. "Jimmy . what . . . are you . . . doing . . . here?"

A click sounded, and suddenly his shaggy face w illuminated by a flashlight. He grinned. "Did I sca you?"

Anger overrode fear as she tried to calm her breat ing. "Answer me!"

He looked hurt. "I just wanted to talk to you is all went by the store, but you weren't there. I thoug you'd come back here sooner or later."

"*What* do you want?"

"To say that I'm sorry."

Fear washed over her anew. "Sorry for what?"

"That everyone thinks you killed Deke. I hate to s you in trouble, Miss Penny. Can I help?"

Her breathing eased a bit—Jimmy's crush on h had led him here, that was all. "No, Jimmy, but tha you."

"I'll give you an alibi," he said earnestly. "Whatev you want me to tell the police, I will. I'll cover f you."

She wet her lips and tasted the salt from his swea fingers. He was offering to lie for her—just like he lied about seeing her push Sheena into the stre "Th-that's not necessary, Jimmy, b-but I do appre ate it."

He looked dejected. "I'd do anything for you, Mi Penny."

She swallowed. "I know, Jimmy. I'll let you know I . . . need your help."

He brightened. "Okay. Good."

"Okay," she said, nodding and breathing, her mi

churning for something to say to get them back on familiar footing. "I still need to pay you for the truffles. I don't have the money with me, but come to the store next week . . . and bring more. Ziggy said they were perfection." She tried to smile.

He made a mournful noise. "Can't."

"Why not?"

"It's Henry—he's sick. Out of commission for a while."

"Oh. I'm sorry—I hope he feels better soon."

"Me, too," he said. "Bye now." Then he turned and tromped down the stairs, just as if he had done nothing out of the ordinary.

Penny went limp with relief against her door and managed to find the keyhole with her key just as Jimmy opened the door leading to the outside and let in a bit of light. The knob twisted and she fell into her apartment, turning the dead bolt behind her even as she lunged for the nearest light switch. The fluorescent bulb over the dining table flickered and caught. Penny gasped.

Everything was . . . in order. Someone had restored everything the police had displaced: The kitchen counter was clean, the drawers and cabinets were closed. The items on the dining room table were neatly arranged, the rugs were straightened. Her CDs were stacked on her TV cabinet, the magazines next to the chair were carefully fanned, the pillows on her couch were precisely positioned.

With her heart thudding in her chest, she walked to the bedroom to find the bed made, her dresser tidy, her closet orderly. She turned in a circle, wondering who

could have done such a thing. Elton? Jimmy? B.J.? E
ton had a key; Jimmy was known for slipping in ar
out of places undetected; B.J. had studied her lock
and could probably pick one as fast as he could sna
his fingers.

If the person had done it to lend a helping hand, th
effect was exactly the opposite. She walked over to th
dresser and opened her jewelry box, only to find h
few pieces of jewelry efficiently sorted. She slid ope
her underwear drawer, tingling with a new sense of v
olation to see her panties and bras folded painstak
ingly. She backed away from the dresser and bumpe
into the bed, suddenly exhausted beyond words. Wi
nothing on her mind except a numbing sleep, sh
pulled back the comforter and the cotton quilt, stop
ping when she saw a small, dark object against th
white of her pillowcase.

Leaning closer, recognition barbed through her—
was the little red Hot Wheels car that had been at
tached to the hand of the voodoo doll she had receive
at the party. When she'd stabbed the doll, the car ha
come loose and smashed to the floor, crumpling th
front end. She'd lost track of what had happened to th
toy, but apparently someone at the party had thought
important enough to keep—the person who had give
her the doll?

Her pulse thumped in fear. Was it a message?
promise? A threat? She considered calling B.J., bu
Guy's response when she told him how she'd met B.
came back to her.

Kind of coincidental, don't you think?

Was B.J. somehow more involved in this situatio
than she realized? Than she wanted to believe?

She rushed back to the door, prepared to go . . . where? To B.J.? To the police? Who could she trust? She jammed chairs under the knobs of both doors, then, too weary to think, Penny slipped off her shoes and crawled under the covers fully dressed. She buried herself as deeply into the mattress as she could. Every muscle ached, every nerve ending screamed. She didn't even have the energy to cry or to be afraid. Her eyes fluttered shut to the tune of drums and feet pounding out in the square. Evil was in the air. . . .

She was in the peristil, *watching the masked priest dance around . . . except she was watching from a cage . . . she was a chicken . . . waiting to have her head removed . . . to be sacrificed to the celebrated* lwa *in order for the tribe to remain in good favor . . . the priest danced all around her cage . . . she could feel the vibration of the drums . . . the shimmy of the* ason *full of snake bones . . . he came closer and closer to her cage . . . she was paralyzed with fear . . . he ripped off his skeletal mask and it was Deke . . . he looked angry . . . you were too good for me, Penny . . .*

She jerked awake and blinked gratefully at the daylight streaming through the windows. The priest . . . Deke . . . she'd been dreaming for long, gluey hours, her nightmares going in circles, bizarre enough to disturb her, familiar enough to frighten her. She sighed and waited for the dredges of the anxiety to dissipate. But when it did, she was left with the profound ache of realization that Deke was gone . . . murdered. She had thought she'd known what being alone was when they had first separated. But then the aloneness of being separated had been topped by the aloneness of being divorced. And now the aloneness of being divorced had been *trumped* by the aloneness of being survived in death.

You were too good for me, Penny . . .

She closed her eyes and conjured up the image of Deke's face, the exact intonation of his voice when he had uttered those words . . . the last words he would ever speak to her . . . as if he'd been trying to make amends.

Her eyes popped open. Had Deke known then that he was in trouble? Had he feared for his life? Is that why he had said those words to her at such a bizarre place and time?

She sat up, then grimaced when an ache erupted in her head. Her face felt slick and crackly . . . glazed. It was the hot sugar from Benny's that had somehow made its way into the ductwork and her apartment. She swung her legs over the side of the bed, still woozy from a long, troubled sleep. One look over the neat bedroom brought back the chilling events of the night before. Someone had broken into her apartment to . . . clean.

And to leave the little Hot Wheels car, she recalled, staring at it sitting next to her lamp. She pondered calling the police, having them dust for prints, but what if it had only been Jimmy and what if they questioned him and he told them about her pushing Sheena into the street?

She stumbled to the bathroom for aspirin, only to be faced with more orderliness—her medicine cabinet, her vanity. The thought of Jimmy Scaggs handling her birth control pills and her toothbrush made her skin crawl.

Was it possible that Jimmy was more than just a little . . . skewed? Could he be behind the women who had been reported missing in the area? Did he happen upon them, offer them a ride, take them back to his cabin in the woods of which no one seemed to know the exact location?

She tossed back three aspirin with a glass of water. It was close to noon. She had slept for . . . fifteen hours? Was that possible? Her head felt fuzzy from the pain, and she thought a shower would help revive her. But as the water poured over her pounding head, questions about the mysterious events over the past couple of days churned in her mind until things began to muddy. The incident last night with Guy was a case in point: He had offered her a ride home, and she had begun to question his motives. She was starting to suspect everyone in Mojo of evildoing.

By the time the water ran cold, her headache had eased a bit. She left her hair wet while she flipped through her newly organized closet. The more she thought about it, the more she thought that the person who had done this couldn't have been B.J.—the man was a mess. No, it was a compulsive individual, probably a woman, or maybe a gay man.

She bit her lower lip—Guy? He did have a key to her apartment, for emergencies and to water the ficus tree if she happened to be out of town for more than a few days. No, he and Marie had been working, and he'd seemed surprised when she'd told him that her apartment had been searched.

Regardless, she had to admit that the prowler had done an amazing job with her closet.

She put on a pair of dark jeans and a lime green sweater that she'd forgotten she owned, then dried her hair. Only when she caught herself slicking on pink lipstick did she admit that she was looking forward to seeing B.J. The realization had her reaching for a tissue and wiping off the lipstick. It was one thing to have developed an unhealthy lust for the man as a distraction from her dilemma, but to consciously foster it was something else altogether.

She fixed a bowl of yogurt and blueberries, then turned on the television to catch up on world events, sticking to CNN because she was relatively sure that Mojo wasn't on their radar.

Wrong.

Twenty minutes in, she saw the words LOUISIANA MAN FOUND KNIFED AFTER HIS EX STABS VOODOO DOLL scroll across the bottom of the screen. And a few minutes later, the "local cable news update" featured Deke's death prominently. The woman was the reporter who had been waiting for her when she'd left the apartment to go to work yesterday. They showed a clip of her dodging the camera, then jogging away.

Penny swallowed hard. She looked . . . guilty. And the story was just too juicy—a wife dumped for a younger, blonder version. When she saw the coverage, she, too, was surprised that she hadn't been arrested. There was another clip of Sheena leaving the pink Victorian, wearing a tight black dress and huge sunglasses. Penny rolled her eyes—the woman's mourning clothes, no doubt.

Although . . . Sheena didn't look at the camera or talk to the reporter. In fact, overall, she had been pretty low key with the media. Penny would have thought the woman would be granting countless interviews and slipping in a plug for her tanning salon.

Penny pursed her mouth. Hmm . . . curious.

The doorbell rang, and she allowed herself a spike in her pulse—but not a quick check in the mirror. She pushed a button on the intercom next to her door. "Yes?"

"It's B.J.," he said. "Can I come up?"

She hesitated. "I'll meet you down there."

"I've got something for you."

"If it's doughnuts, I'm not interested."

He laughed. "It isn't."

Despite her resolve to resist him, a smile curved her mouth. "Okay, I'll buzz you in."

She pushed a button to release the lock on the outer door, then opened her apartment door and looked down the stairs. B.J. appeared in the doorway carrying a box. The sight of him alone gave her a sobering little jolt—wow, if she wasn't careful, she might fall for this guy.

And something told her that falling for B.J. Beaumont would take her to a new level of aloneness when he left.

"What's in the box?" she asked.

"Something you desperately need."

Her mind raced with the possibilities as he reached the landing.

"No, it's not *that*," he said, reading her mind. "Something you need even more—130-volt lightbulbs."

She grinned. "Thank you."

"If you have a stepladder, I'll change them for you."

She retrieved a stepladder from the pantry and fol-

lowed him around as he changed every bulb in
apartment. Such a domestic thing to do, she realiz
watching him make short work of the chore. Her he
beat with appreciation . . . and something else.

"You've been busy," he said, gesturing to her pr
tine apartment.

"Uh-hm," she murmured vaguely, wondering whet
to tell him about Jimmy Scaggs and her suspicions.

He squinted as he climbed down from the stepl
der. "Are you okay?"

She looked into his dark eyes—trustworthy eyes?
just convincing?

"Did something happen?"

She took a deep breath and told him about Jim
Scaggs waiting for her, and what she'd found when
had entered her apartment. She showed him the li
car and explained its connection to the doll. B.J. h
the toy by two fingers. Too late, Penny realized she
probably obliterated any fingerprints.

"Jimmy is that woodsman of yours?" he asked.

"Right."

"Did you call the police?"

"No."

"Why not?"

She hesitated, then exhaled noisily. "Because I .
don't want the police to question Jimmy."

His eyebrows climbed. "Why not?"

"Because . . . Jimmy saw me . . . do something .
that I'd rather the police not know about."

B.J. crossed his arms. "I'm listening."

She closed her eyes briefly. "I . . . might have tri
to . . . kill Sheena."

His eyebrows flew up again. "Excuse me?"

"It was an accident," she said. "Well, I meant to do it, but—"

"What did you do?"

"I . . . pushed her off the sidewalk in front of a car."

He pressed his lips together. She couldn't tell if he was smiling or grimacing. "And when was this?"

"Friday."

"Friday, the day your ex-husband was murdered, you pushed his girlfriend in front of a car?"

She winced and nodded.

"And what precipitated this, um, push?"

"She told me that she and Deke were engaged . . . among other things."

"Ah. And what makes you think she didn't tell the police what you did?"

She lifted her chin. "Because . . . I threatened to tell Deke that I saw you at the house."

He frowned. "Me?"

"Remember? I saw you at the house Friday morning. I assumed you were lovers and that she didn't want Deke to know."

His frown deepened. "No—I told you, it was the first time I'd met her."

She wet her lips. "Then why were you there? What was the dead end lead?"

"The Reynolds girl liked to tan, so I stopped by the tanning salon in the square to show her picture, and the kid working there told me the owner lived down the street. I thought I'd check with her."

Penny squinted. "From what I saw, she seemed angry."

"She *was* angry, but damned if I know why. Said she'd never seen the girl and how dare I disturb her at home, then she practically slammed the door in my face."

"So why wouldn't she want Deke to know you'd been there?"

He shrugged. "Maybe he was a jealous guy."

She started to deny it but bit her tongue—just because Deke was jealous where she was concerned didn't mean he wasn't jealous where his mistress was concerned.

B.J. pulled his hand down his face. "Do you think this Scaggs guy could have murdered your ex?"

Penny grimaced. "I don't know why he would."

"Maybe he has a crush on you, and he thought Deke had treated you badly."

She recalled Jimmy comparing Deke to a polecat. "It just seems so—"

"Crazy? Look around. Everyone in this town is a little cuckoo."

"I beg your pardon?"

He gave a little smile and leaned in close. "Sorry—except for you, of course."

His nearness made the breath catch in her lungs. If standing next to him fully clothed could make her body do such crazy things, what would it be like to make love with this man?

He pulled her to him slowly, as if he expected her to resist. But she didn't, lifting her mouth to his for a long overdue exploration of what he felt like, tasted like. He slanted his mouth over hers and flicked his tongue over her teeth, moaning as he delved deeper and slid her body against his. She sank into his arms, her senses electrified as his erection grew against her stomach. She slipped her hands beneath his T-shirt and ran her fingers over the expanse of his back. When he cupped her bottom against his sex, an age-old tug on her womb answered, setting off warning signals in her brain. *Slow down . . . proceed with caution . . . bumpy road ahead.*

She wrenched her mouth from his and stepped back, breathing hard. She brought the back of her hand to her mouth and swallowed. His eyes were hooded, his lips parted, his body in an obvious state of arousal.

"I . . . can't," she said.

"But you want to," he said bluntly.

"It doesn't matter," she said, then turned away. "I'm in trouble . . . big trouble. I have too many things going on in my life for . . . another complication." She drew in a cleansing breath. "I need for you to . . . concentrate." She lifted her gaze to his, and he blinked, as if she'd slapped him.

"Okay," he said, pulling on his chin. "No problem." He cleared his throat and straightened. "If the Scaggs guy comes around again, call the police . . . or call me, understand?"

She nodded, still trying to regain her composure.

He sighed, clearly frustrated. "Are you still up for going to the festival?"

After a moment's hesitation, she nodded. "I want to talk to the woman at the voodoo doll booth."

He winked. "Good thinking. Let's go."

"Thank you for changing the bulbs," she said as they walked down the stairs.

"No problem," he said, although she had the distinct feeling he was thinking that maybe there *was* something she needed more than lightbulbs after all.

Out in the square, the festival was rolling along,

marred only by a few churchgoers holding signs that said Jesus Saves, not Voodoo.

"I wonder if someone in that crowd is behind the graffiti at Diane Davidson's house," B.J. murmured.

Penny studied his profile and felt a warm rush in her chest that dismayed her. B.J. Beaumont truly championed the underdogs of the world . . . and he stirred her like no man ever had.

Then he sniffed the air. "I'm starved," he said. "Want a sausage on a stick?"

And then again, there were the man's eating habits. She laughed and shook her head no. "I'll be over there," she said, pointing to the booth she sought.

On the way, she skirted the *peristil,* wondering about the masked priestess who had so spooked her Friday night. Did the woman know that something bad was about to happen to Penny . . . or could she have caused it?

Penny tried to shake off the silly thoughts of black magic but found it difficult not to be drawn into the mystique when she was surrounded by the sights and sounds of voodoo, where she could witness how seriously the people took their religion. She approached the booth with the voodoo dolls, noticing that the inventory had nearly been depleted.

"You were here the other night," the woman said when she saw Penny surveying the dolls.

"That's right. What can you tell me about voodoo dolls?"

The woman smiled. She was missing a tooth. "What do you want to know?"

Penny squirmed. "Do they work?"

"Of course," the woman said. "If something is attached to the doll that belongs to the person . . . and if the person who uses the doll believes in what they're doing."

Penny wet her lips and glanced around to make sure that neither B.J. nor anyone else she knew was within hearing distance. "Is it possible to . . . accidentally make something happen that you didn't mean to happen?"

The woman nodded. "Yes, if the passion is there—anger, love, jealousy."

Penny swallowed hard. She had certainly been passionate when she'd stabbed that doll.

"Did you find what you were looking for?" B.J. asked. He was chomping a sausage that was almost as big as her arm.

She frowned. "You don't want to know how many preservatives are in that piece of meat."

He grinned. "You're right—I don't." Then he nodded toward the park where two guitarists were setting up. "Come on—let's go have some fun."

For the rest of the afternoon, Penny tried to put Deke's murder out of her mind and focus on the living that was going on all around her—the children who were laughing and singing, the people who danced and clapped to the music, the families who walked with their hands chained together. She watched the families with envy, wondering how different her life might have been if she'd been sandwiched between a loving mother and father. At one point, she caught B.J. staring at her.

"Where's your family?" he asked.

"I don't have any," she said. Her rote answer. "I heard you mention a niece and nephew in the souvenir shop. Do you have a big family?"

"Nope," he said lazily. "Just me and my brother and our mother."

"So where do the niece and nephew come in?"

"In the future, hopefully," he said with a smile. "I thought it sounded better to say I was buying those things for my niece and nephew than to say I was buying them for myself."

She frowned. "Why did you want bottles of crushed limestone?"

He shrugged. "Just curious, I guess." Then he winked. "Same with the handcuffs."

Penny burned with more questions about his family and his background, but she was afraid that he might ask questions about *her* family and background. They sat in the grass and listened to the music until the day's festivities began to wind down, with Penny fighting the growing realization that she simply enjoyed B.J.'s company. "I should be getting back," she said. "The funeral is tomorrow, and I know it's going to be a long day."

He nodded and pushed to his feet, then extended his hand. She clasped his warm fingers, then allowed him to pull her up, close to his body. A thrill of awareness traveled through her; the attraction between them was hard to deny. It would be easy, she thought, to spend the night in his arms. But it wouldn't be right to go to the funeral tomorrow with another man in her mind. He held onto her hand longer than necessary, but she pulled free and maintained extra distance between them as they made their way back through the square.

They walked by a booth that sold more of the little

brown bottles that had attracted B.J.'s attention at the souvenir shop in the museum. The booth was packed, and Penny recognized at least one of the women from her shop.

"That's the woman who asked for bat brains," she whispered to B.J.

"Maybe she needs them for a spell," B.J. said.

"I'm not judging her," Penny said. "I just hate to see people get scammed and spend their money on ridiculous potions."

He laughed. "Is that really so different than buying vitamins?"

She gave him what she hoped was the evil eye. "There's more limestone dust," she said, pointing.

"Mine aren't limestone," the man behind the booth said. "It's real bones—chicken bones, of course."

B.J. walked closer to take a look, and Penny observed other customers at the booth.

"I'm a chemist," the man told B.J. "My mixtures are all authentic and guaranteed. This stuff isn't souvenir grade."

A customer next to Penny uncorked one of the bottles, and an unpleasant odor filtered out. "Ew," she said, covering her nose even as a memory chord stirred. She prided herself on knowing the fragrance of herbs, but she couldn't recall where she'd smelled this scent . . . it was recently . . . and in an unexpected place, she somehow knew. Then it hit her—Deke's cologne the day she'd seen him at the museum. God, it had been awful—no doubt some trendy blend derived from something exotic, like animal pheromones.

She picked up the bottle. "What is this stuff?" she asked the man.

“Dimethyl sulfoxide,” he said.

“But what does it do?”

He leaned in conspiratorially. “It preserves human organs. Got a body you want to keep fresh?”

23

Keep everything bottled up . . .

"It could be nothing," Penny said as they reached the outer door of her building.

"Right," B.J. said. "But I'll probably check it out tomorrow, while you're at the funeral."

She nodded, the disturbing information about Deke and the chemical she'd smelled on him only adding to her discomfort about tomorrow's service.

"Unless you want some company tomorrow," B.J. said.

She glanced up sharply, but his eyes were unreadable in the dusk, his voice barely audible with all the noise behind them in the square.

"You can bet Maynard will be there," he added. "Sometimes a funeral will shed new light on a murder case."

Oh—of course, he'd offered to go for the good of the case. "Guy is going to pick me up," she said. "Besides, I'm not sure what kind of reception I'll get, but people are bound to talk if they think that you're . . . that we're . . ."

"Right," he agreed, his gaze holding hers. "I guess they'd really talk if I were to spend the night."

Her eyebrows went up. "P-probably."

"Still, I'd like to . . . if that's okay with you."

Her throat tightened, and while her body screamed Yes! she knew that she was too vulnerable for anything good to come of their sleeping together tonight. "I don't think—"

"On the couch," he said quickly. "To be on the safe side, until you get your locks changed tomorrow."

Oh—of course, he'd offered to sleep over for the good of the case. She felt like an idiot and tried to save face. "Do you charge time and a half for after hours?"

He grinned. "If I charged for my skills after hours, you couldn't afford it."

She pursed her mouth and tried to ignore the little firestorms igniting all over her body. "Okay . . . but just for tonight." She stepped inside, flipped the light switch, and was met with beautiful white light flooding the stairwell. Such a small thing, but she was disproportionately grateful.

Slowly she climbed the stairs, conscious of him behind her, warmed from his concern. But when he stood close behind her on the landing while she tried to open the door, something changed. For a split second, she felt the tiniest finger of unease, the merest hint of danger. Working with B.J. on the case was one thing, but allowing him to spend the night in her apartment was another. How well did she really know this man?

"Having trouble?" he asked, then he slipped his arms around hers, covering her hands with his, guiding the key into the keyhole. Penny's breath stalled in her lungs as his chest pressed into her back. She allowed him to direct her hand, but suddenly the act of inserting the key took on a new connotation. He seemed to hesitate over the opening, waiting for her to complete the task. But when she pushed the key forward, he put his weight behind it and sent the key home. Desire whipped through her body, heightened by the tendrils of uncertainty where B.J. was concerned. Perhaps the man didn't mean her danger intentionally; perhaps she was only picking up on the transient vibes the man exuded.

Besides, she'd been willing to spend the night with him within hours of knowing him, hadn't she? Why the hesitation now—because she knew him better?

The door swung open, and the lamp she'd left burning in the living room was still going strong. She stepped inside, both relieved and vexed to be away from him. Then a new panic set in—what were they going to do until bedtime?

"Do you mind if I get my laptop from my car?" B.J. asked.

"No," she said, immensely relieved.

He left, then returned a few minutes later. He settled in at the dining room table, dwarfing the furniture. "Don't feel like you have to entertain me," he said. "Do whatever you normally do."

Penny flushed and glanced around her apartment. How embarrassing for a stranger to see how little she truly had going on in her life. She could read a magazine, or watch television, but neither seemed particularly appealing. "Actually, I'm hungry. Can I fix you something to eat?"

His head popped up. "Don't go to any trouble."

A smiled curved her mouth—he was hungry, too.

And perhaps if she was able to satisfy one appetite, the other wouldn't get out of control. She went to the tiny kitchen, and while he typed on the keyboard, she prepared a spinach and arugula salad with garbanzo beans, sprouts, and flax seed, served with whole wheat rolls and, just for B.J., a side of soft tofu drizzled with lemon juice and olive oil.

"Soup's on," she said, setting their plates on the table around the laptop.

He was absorbed in something on the screen as he scribbled notes on the back of one of his missing persons flyers. He looked up and studied the salad and gelatinous tofu gingerly. "Where's the soup?"

"Figure of speech," she said, suddenly enjoying herself. "I thought this would be a perfect opportunity for you to try tofu."

One side of his mouth slid back. "If you wanted me to leave, all you had to do was say so."

"Just try it," she said with a laugh. "What would you like to drink?"

"Strong coffee or beer, if you have it."

"How about green tea or water?"

His mouth twitched downward. "I'll have water, thanks."

She poured a glass of filtered water for him and one for herself, then sat at the table and spread a napkin on her lap. B.J. followed suit, still wary of the food on his plate.

Penny cut into her tofu, to set a good example. "What are you working on?" she asked, nodding to the screen.

"Doing some research on dimethyl sulfoxide. The chemical has, shall we say, a checkered past." He put a forkful of the tofu in his mouth, then stopped, grimaced, and swallowed.

"It grows on you," she said encouragingly.

"I'll bet this stuff would grow on just about anything," he said, turning to the salad.

She bit back a smile. "So what did you learn about the chemical?"

"It's a by-product of wood pulp, used commercially in paint thinner and antifreeze."

She made a face. "I thought the man in the square said it was used to preserve body organs."

He nodded. "The medical grade of the substance was used for organ transplant preservation in the 1960s, but there were side effects, and the close kinship of the chemical to harsher commercial grades made it suspect. Apparently the cheap and potentially harmful grades were popping up at roadside stands and general stores." He grimaced. "I imagine it tasted like this tofu."

She laughed. "But it's good for you."

"What is it exactly?"

"It's made from soybean milk."

He scratched his temple. "And I didn't even realize soybeans had nipples."

She burst out laughing; he was so . . . male.

"But," he said, taking another bite, "I'm always willing to try something new. The salad is good," he added. "It's probably the most healthful thing I've had to eat in . . . my entire life. Thank you."

"You're welcome," she murmured, struck once again by his easygoing manner. B.J. Beaumont probably had a woman in every town in Louisiana. She averted her gaze to her plate. "So, this chemical isn't used in the medical field anymore?"

"Not widely. But the commercial grades are still available. And they wouldn't necessarily raise suspicion if someone was using them for . . . illicit activities."

She drank from her glass, trying to digest the implication of his words. "You think something horrible is going on at the museum?"

"I don't want to jump to conclusions, but I've got a few missing girls, one of whom we have on good authority was headed to the museum. And we have a blond hair found in the museum, which might or might not belong to one of the women. And we have your ex-husband coming out of the museum with the scent of this chemical on him. And then he was murdered."

Penny swallowed a bite of salad past her tightened throat. "You think that Deke might have been murdered because he found out something illegal was going on at the museum?"

"I don't know, there are just too many pieces of the puzzle missing. I wish we could get into the house to see the crime scene, maybe get a look at Deke's files."

She frowned. "That's not likely to happen. I have extra keys somewhere to get in, but I've heard that Sheena has practically barricaded herself inside. Which surprises me because I thought she'd be all over the media."

He worked his mouth from side to side. "Maybe there's a logical explanation for all of this. Maybe the hair isn't Jodi Reynolds'; maybe the other woman didn't make it to the museum after all, or went and then left on her own volition. Maybe Deke was murdered by his girlfriend, or by some psycho who likes crowds."

B.J.'s words when they'd first met came back to her. *I go where the crowds are—festivals, concerts.*

Penny kept eating, wishing she could make sense of

everything going on, including the push-pull feelings she was having for B.J. He was so believable in his role as protector . . . was he too good to be true?

"What do you know about the woman who runs the museum?"

"Hazel Means? Salt of the earth. She and I have been friends for years." Penny flushed. "I confess that I've always been a bit fixated on the Archambault mansion. It reminds me of the big manor houses of Gothic novels I read growing up. Hazel has been nice enough to humor my interest."

"You mentioned someone else working there—a handyman?"

"Tilton Means, Hazel's son."

"How old is he?"

"Midthirties, maybe. He's mentally disabled."

"To what extent?"

"He's communicative and productive, and he drives, but he doesn't like to socialize. He works for the two local funeral homes when they need him."

B.J. was instantly alert. "So at least one person at the museum has access to cadavers."

A chill slid down her back. "But that could also explain the existence of the chemical, right? What if Tilton spilled it and Deke just happened to be around it, or stepped in it?"

B.J. nodded. "Or if Tilton was doing some kind of painting or work on one of the machines we saw, that could also explain the presence of the chemical." He made a rueful noise. "Which is why I can't go to the police until I do some more checking around."

She wet her lips. "So what are you thinking—worst-case scenario?"

He shook his head. "My mind doesn't even want to go there."

Hers either. Hair in the torture equipment . . . missing women . . . a chemical to preserve organs . . . and Deke dead. Was Deke involved in some kind of depravity? Without the moral guidance of his father, had Deke, as he had feared, succumbed to an evil buried deep within him? It was when he had begun to change, when his personality had gone from congenial to conceited, and when his stress level—and temper—had rocketed higher. Had he been conflicted about something he'd been doing?

Other than Sheena.

"So we still don't know who made the voodoo doll," B.J. said.

"Right."

"Did Deke have a maid or someone who ran his errands, dropped off dry cleaning?"

"There's no maid," she said dryly, remembering the mess in the entryway—Sheena's shoes, the unread newspapers. "I used to run most of his errands," she admitted sheepishly. "And when I couldn't—" She stopped as an alarming realization occurred to her.

"What?"

"When I couldn't run Deke's errands, Steve Chasen did."

"So Chasen had access to Deke's suits."

"Right."

"And he's cozy with Deke's mother."

Penny frowned. "I can't imagine anyone being cozy with Mona the Stone, but if that's who he was talking to on the phone yesterday, they seemed friendly. But why would Mona be friendly with the man who murdered her son?"

"Simple—either she doesn't know he did it, or he didn't do it. Maybe he murdered Deke and told Mona he found the body and decided to make it look like you'd done it."

"But what could be Steve's motive?"

"Something business-related perhaps, something illegal. Or maybe he didn't do it, but found the body and decided to make it look like you'd done it."

"Buy why would he do that?"

B.J. shrugged. "Maybe he thought Mona would help him get a job if she felt like she owed him."

"But why wouldn't Mona want her son's real murderer captured?"

"Maybe she knew that Deke was up to something and is afraid that if the real murderer is caught, all of his activities will come to light."

Penny put her hands to her temples. "I think my head is going to explode. Can we talk about something else for a while?"

"Sure," he said, then gestured toward his empty plate. "How long have you been obsessed with health food?"

She bristled. "I'm not obsessed. Just a little . . . compulsive."

He pursed his mouth. "It's my experience that when people are 'compulsive' about something, it's to mask something else."

Irritation spiked in her chest, and she had the unsettling feeling that he could see into her private places. "That's not true in my case."

"Whatever you say." Although he didn't look convinced.

Penny stood to clear their dishes, her nerves jangling. All the St. John's wort she'd taken over the past few months to calm her nerves didn't seem to be working. Maybe she was past the threshold of over-the-counter assistance. Maybe she was on the verge of a nervous breakdown. Maybe that explained why her emotions and urges were all over the place.

To her surprise, he joined her at the sink and helped clean the kitchen. But he must have sensed her extreme anxiety, because he kept the conversation light, asking about her business and about living in a small town. Penny remembered a bottle of merlot that someone had given her. B.J. opened it, and they drank while she leisurely washed dishes and he dried. She asked him about some of his favorite cases, and when he talked, his eyes came alive—the man loved what he was doing despite the fact that he couldn't be making much money. They chatted like old friends, and when Penny felt a warm rush of connection coming on, she had to remind herself that B.J. made a living out of drawing people out, of getting them to talk.

She drank the last mouthful of her second glass of wine, then folded the dishtowels, her body throbbing in awareness of him. "I think I'm going to turn in."

He drank from the wine remaining in his glass. "Okay."

Penny wet her lips, then walked past him. "Let me get you some linens."

Feeling like a teenager at a coed sleepover, she went into her bedroom to get the extra pillow from her bed and put on a fresh pillowcase. When she returned to the living room, she stopped. B.J. had removed his T-shirt.

"You don't have anything to get out wine, do you?" he asked, holding up the stained shirt that read Jet. Get Born.

She shook her head carefully, riveted by the sight of his muscular chest, covered with a layer of black, black hair that whorled down his flat stomach to disappear into the waistband of his jeans.

"Darn, this was one of my favorite shirts." He made a rueful noise. "That's what I get for being distracted."

Penny could only nod.

He walked toward her and took the linens. "Are you sure you're okay with me staying here?"

She managed a little smile. "Why not? It's safe. After all, you don't sleep with clients."

Suddenly the mood in the room changed. His eyes grew hooded and he stepped closer, lowering his mouth to within an inch of hers. She could sense the aroma of the wine on his tongue. Her breasts grew heavy. Her knees threatened to buckle.

"No, I don't," he said. "But for that reason alone, I'm determined to solve this case." He kissed her, just a whisper of a kiss—anyone watching would have missed the brief touch of his lips across hers. By the time she opened her mouth, it was over . . . and she was left aching for more. He uttered a little moan like he wanted more, too, but now wasn't the time or place.

"Goodnight, Red."

"Goodnight," she whispered, then turned and fled to her bedroom. She undressed in the bathroom, pulled a long gown over her head, and crawled under the covers, wondering which man would wind up causing her the most heartache—the man she would see buried tomorrow, or the man currently snoring on her couch.

24

Don't keep things buried . . .

Penny gingerly slid into the front seat of Guy's car, hoping she wasn't going to be sick.

"You don't look well," Guy said, his expression worried, as if he knew he'd never get the smell of vomit out of his car. "Are you sure you're up to attending the funeral?"

She nodded but swallowed hard, trying to block out the noise of the festival on the square. It seemed ludicrous that anyone could be celebrating when Deke was only hours away from being interred. She broke off another antacid from the roll she'd nearly consumed, then smoothed a hand over her simple navy blue dress. "Do you think I'm dressed appropriately?" She had debated on whether it was special, yet somber, enough for the service. Not that anyone would notice, but she wanted to look nice out of respect for Deke and the good years they'd shared together.

Guy reached over and squeezed her hand. "You look wonderful. Just relax. It'll all be over soon."

If only that were true, she thought. Maybe B.J. was

right—perhaps the funeral would fuel someone to do or say something that would advance the case. It would be the first time that the people closest to Deke—and closest to the investigation—would be together in one place. Thoughts of B.J. sent completely inappropriate impulses through her body. He had been gone this morning when she'd woken up, having left a note that read, "Raided your pantry, found a couple of 'Happy Divorce' chocolate bars. Didn't think you'd mind if I ate them since they were full of nasty sugar and preservatives. B.J." The linens had been folded neatly on the couch, which meant the man could be tidy when he wanted to be.

And speaking of tidy men, she glanced over to Guy, who wore a spiffy turquoise coat over apricot-color slacks, and dark Gucci glasses. And he was looking rather . . . tan.

"Guy, have you been to the tanning bed?" After she'd ranted about how dangerous Sheena's device was—and surely he wouldn't be giving *her* business anyway.

He shifted guiltily. "No."

"Have you been to the Bahamas since I saw you last?"

"It's self-tanner," he said quickly. "I know how you feel about tanning beds." He sighed. "Everyone in town knows how you feel about them."

"They'll give you cancer."

"Everything will give you cancer," he said in a long-suffering voice. "I can't help it if I look better with a tan."

"How are things going with Carley?" she asked.

"They're not," he said in a clipped voice. "Do you

believe the woman had the nerve to ask me if I'm gay? I mean, do I seem gay to you?"

She took in his gelled spiky hair, his designer sunglasses, turquoise sport coat, and deep tan. "No."

"Thank you," he said, nodding curtly.

"Guy, did you happen to come by my apartment Saturday before you took me home?"

He frowned. "Before I took you home?"

"Yeah. Someone . . . left something for me inside. I've been trying to figure out who it was, and since you have a key . . ."

He pushed at his glasses in a way that made her think of Wendy and her nervous habit. "I wish I could take credit for it, but it wasn't me. Sorry." Then he grimaced. "Someone was in your apartment?"

"Must have been my landlord," she said easily.

"What about that P.I. guy?"

A flush climbed her neck. "What about him?"

"Does he have a key?"

"No," she said evenly.

"Well . . . he could probably pick the locks."

She decided to change the subject as they drove past the store. "It was nice of Marie to offer to work this afternoon."

"She's been selling that juice of hers to everyone who walks in the door. You know how she likes to tinker—I hope she's not poisoning people."

"Me, too," Penny said, then leaned her cheek against the cool glass of the window.

They rode the rest of the short trip in silence. Goddard's Funeral Home was located past the Charmed Village strip mall, on a plot of residential land. Formerly home to the Goddard family, the structure still fit in with other houses on nearby lots. Except for the sign, the circular driveway, and the hearse sitting out front, one wouldn't know that it was a funeral home. And except for the two TV news vans sitting at the curb, one wouldn't know that this funeral was different from any other.

Her heart jumped to her throat when she saw the marquee: Deke A. Black, Beloved Son.

So, apparently Mona had wrestled control over the services from Sheena, else the marquee would have read, Beloved Adulterer. Penny fisted her hand over her chest. A few months ago it would have read Beloved Husband, and she would have been prostrate wondering how to go on. Suddenly she was thankful that the separation and divorce had given her a bit of emotional distance from Deke. Meanwhile, Mona was making a statement to the women in Deke's life: Wives and girlfriends would come and go, but a mother's love is forever.

They parked among many other cars—she recognized Mona's Cadillac and Steve Chasen's white BMW, plus Sheena's yellow Miata. She looked for Liz's silver Mercedes but didn't see it. She had hoped to hear from her friend, but she realized that people had other pressing issues in their lives.

A police car sat next to the hearse, and next to the police car was a dark Ford Crown Victoria—Maynard's car, no doubt.

She hadn't realized she was still sitting until the passenger door opened and Guy gallantly offered his hand. She took it, grateful to have someone to lean on, since her legs felt unreliable. On the way in the front door, they passed Tilton Means, who was walking out. He stopped and held open the door, keeping his gaze averted, as was his way.

"Hi, Tilton," she said.

"Hello," he said in a monotone, probably in deference to his severe underbite. He was a big man, with thick limbs and no neck. Penny's heart went out to him—his life, and Hazel's, couldn't have been easy.

When they walked into the entryway, the strains of a hymn were playing over speakers. The sickening scent of preserved live flowers hit her, causing her stomach to roll. Greg Goddard, portly elder son of the family, stood next to the door to greet visitors. When he saw Penny, he blanched a bit under his tanning bed tan—not a good sign, she decided.

"Penny," he said with false cheer. "We, um, wondered if you'd be coming."

"Why wouldn't I come to my ex-husband's funeral?" she asked politely, taking Goddard's offered hand. Real or imagined, there always seemed to be an underlying metallic scent on the man.

He chose to answer by coughing violently, then he said, "You didn't talk to the newspeople, did you?"

"No," she said evenly.

He looked almost disappointed, then said, "Right this way," and led her and Guy to a pew in the back of the crowded chapel. "The service will begin in five minutes."

Her arrival caused a stir, she noticed. Heads turned and whispers ensued. She looked around and saw that Mona sat like a stone on the front pew, staring at the closed casket in the front of the room, with Steve Chasen sitting next to her. Curious. On the other side

of the aisle, Sheena sat in the front pew, dressed ou
rageously in yellow—to match her car, no doub
Next to her sat a few people whom Penny didn't re
ognize, but judging from the odd orange glow of the
skin, she guessed that they worked for Sheena at t
salon.

Hazel lifted her hand to Penny from about midwa
and Penny smiled back gratefully. She saw people s
recognized as Deke's clients, or colleagues from Ne
Orleans. Jules was there, sitting off to herself on t
other side of the chapel. She looked at Penny, th
shook her head mournfully and looked away, rubbi
the head of her carved walking stick.

Chief Allyson Davis and Detective Maynard sat
the same pew as Penny and Guy, but down a few fe
They both were watching her intently as she sat a
seemed to observe how other people reacted to h
presence.

The wood seat of the pew was hard and cold—li
Deke, she thought suddenly, unable to reconcile t
warm, fun-loving man with the body that was benea
the spray of white roses over the lid of the deep purp
and bright gold casket—the colors of LSU. It was
surreal that she could almost believe he wasn't dea
that he'd simply gone on a trip or moved away. Exce
she'd seen his stabbed body, rid of much of its bloo
his cold, dead eyes staring at nothing . . .

She shuddered, and next to her, Guy gripped h
hand. Gloria Dalton appeared at the end of the pew a
shimmied down to sit on the other side of Penny. A
just before Greg Goddard closed the chapel door, L
arrived, seeking out Penny with red-rimmed eyes. Gl
ria moved down so Liz could sit next to Penny, wh

smiled at the other two women, feeling fortified by their presence.

The service was heartbreaking . . . heartbreakingly short, that is. There was no minister, which was strange, considering how religious Mona propped herself up to be. Greg Goddard gave the eulogy, which mentioned Deke's college days, his law degree, his practice, his father, and his mother, even his "companion" Sheena Linder . . . but his eight-year marriage to Penny Francisco was noticeably omitted.

She choked back tears to think that their marriage hadn't even warranted a shout-out in his eulogy. Guy squeezed one hand, and Liz squeezed the other. She stared at the back of Mona's head, wishing for once that she had the ability to telepathically convey what she was thinking into the mind of another. At this moment, she hated the woman who had smothered her son, resented his choice of bride, and on occasion, bullied him.

After the eulogy, there was a short prayer and the announcement of a graveside service at Garden Hills Cemetery. Then, as a hymn played, visitors lined up to file past the closed casket to pay their respects. Since those seated in the back went first, Penny had to walk past Mona and Sheena. She glanced at her ex-mother-in-law, whose face was immobile, but her eyes were practically shooting fire. On the other side of the aisle, Sheena the "companion" was wailing like a banshee, crying, "Oh, my Deke! Oh, my precious, darling Deke!"

Penny bit her tongue—where was a moving car when she needed one?

As Penny approached the casket, she leaned on Guy's arm as the finality of Deke's death at last washed over her. The man she had loved for her entire adult life . . . gone, like a season that had slipped through her fingers while she wasn't looking at the calendar. The impact of the loss echoed in the canyon of her heart, exacerbated by the fact that she felt like an outsider, while his mother and his mistress held court over his casket and most of the people in the room thought she was responsible for putting Deke here. But, shored by the support of her friends, she didn't break down. Instead, she touched the casket lightly and sent a loving prayer heavenward.

And the casket tipped over, crashing to the floor and resting on one corner.

The room chorused with gasps and startled cries. Penny jumped back and stared at the casket, half expecting it to open and spill Deke out at her feet.

"Haven't you done enough?" Mona screamed at her.

Penny pulled herself up. "Couldn't you at least have acknowledged our marriage in the eulogy, Mona?"

"Get out!"

Guy positioned himself between Penny and Mona, but Penny was relatively sure he would bolt if Mona charged. Sheena was freaking out. Greg Goddard rushed to right the casket, shouting for men to help. Detective Maynard gave him a hand, as did Allyson, who was as strong as any man there, Penny conceded. When all was settled, the spray of white roses looked a little worse for wear, and the corner of the purple casket was a bit . . . crumpled.

The sight of it stirred a memory in her mind, but she couldn't place the significance of it before Guy swept her down the aisle and outside.

"That was memorable," Guy declared.

"Are you okay?" Gloria asked.

Penny nodded, although she was shaking. She glanced around for Jules Lamborne, but the old woman must have left, because she was nowhere to be found.

"I almost had a heart attack when the casket fell," Liz said, fanning her tear-streaked face. Then she winced. "I don't suppose you're going to the graveside service?"

Penny shook her head. "I don't think that would be such a good idea. I'll take flowers to the vault later." Privately.

Liz gave her a one-arm hug. "How about let's grab a drink before I head back?"

Penny nodded, thinking she could use one, and Gloria and Guy agreed to join them.

"Just a moment, Ms. Francisco," Detective Maynard said, striding up to her. Gloria edged closer to Penny's side.

"What is it?" Penny asked, wondering how the day could possibly get worse.

"That was quite a show in there," he said mildly.

"What do you want?" Gloria demanded.

Maynard grunted. "We got the autopsy report from the M.E.'s office. Turns out that Mr. Black was unconscious when he was stabbed." He angled his chin at her. "But then, you know that, don't you?"

Penny shook her head. "I don't know what you're talking about. Are you saying he'd passed out?"

"No. He was struck on the back of the head, and postmortem bruising showed that before he died he was struck on other parts of his body as well, with a cane—the cane that Ms. Linder said you threatened her with when she arrived."

Penny's mind raced, thinking back. "The cane was sitting in the umbrella stand by the office door. When I heard a noise downstairs I picked it up."

He made a clicking noise with his cheek. "If you're telling the truth, that's too bad, because you might have obliterated any other fingerprints that might have been on it."

She bit down on the inside of her cheek to stem her tears of frustration. Why had this happened to Deke, and why was this happening to her?

"Penny admits she held the cane," Gloria said, "but that doesn't mean that she hit Mr. Black with it." Then she glanced around at the people who were staring in their direction. "Detective Maynard, this is hardly the place for this discussion."

"You're right," he said amiably. "And I suspect we'll be asking Ms. Francisco to come back to talk to us *real* soon." Then he frowned. "By the way, Ms. Francisco, I can't seem to find any record of you or your family in Kingston, Tennessee."

"No?" Penny squeaked, trying to remain calm.

"No," he said, watching her intently.

Her throat convulsed. "That's because I grew up in Kings*ford*."

"Kings*ford*?"

She sighed in relief. "That's right. You must have misunderstood."

He gave her a tight smile. "My mistake."

Gloria tugged at her sleeve, pulling her away. Her eyes were clouded with concern. "Are you okay?"

Penny nodded, although she was far from okay. She walked to Guy's car a bit unsteadily and climbed in, sinking into the seat. "I don't know how this situation could get more crazy."

But Guy didn't answer—he was staring at Liz's Mercedes as she pulled out of the parking lot. "Is that the car your friend always drives?"

"Yeah," Penny said. "Why?"

"Well, for starters, it's the car I'm going to trade this one in for some day."

"That's nice."

"And it's the car that was sitting in the parking lot of the store Friday night when I drove by to take Carley home."

Penny sat up. "Friday night? After the party?"

"Yeah. It was maybe . . . ten o'clock, or a few minutes past."

"Are you sure?"

"Positive. That car, or one just like it."

He pulled onto the street, and Penny unwittingly looked directly into a rolling news camera. She cursed under her breath and frowned, her mind clicking. That would have been right after Liz and Wendy had left the party. Why would they have parked in the store parking lot?

Then she froze—to walk across the road and visit Deke? Her breath started coming faster as the possibilities unwound in her head. Could her friends have stopped by with the idea of telling Deke what they thought of him? Why else would they have wanted to see him, unless . . .

Penny closed her eyes briefly. Unless Liz was having an affair with Deke. That would explain her friend's attitude toward Deke—maybe she was trying to pretend she didn't care for him to throw Penny off. Maybe that's what she and Wendy had been arguing about as they'd left—Wendy had known that Liz had wanted to stop to see Deke. Then another memory clicked into place: Ziggy saying he'd seen Liz at his restaurant. Penny opened her purse and dug out her cell phone.

"What are you doing?" Guy asked.

Penny ignored his question as she called directory assistance, then called Ziggy's restaurant and asked for him.

"*Chère*, Penny! How are you?"

"Not so good, Ziggy." She pinched the bridge of her nose to stem a headache building there. "When you saw my friend Liz the other night at the party, you said you recognized her from your restaurant."

"That's right," he said slowly.

"Who was she with when you saw her?"

"Penny, I—"

"*Who* was she with, Ziggy?"

He sighed. "Deke. But that was a couple of months ago, and it doesn't mean anything fishy was going on."

"Right," she said, her heart shattered. "Thanks, Ziggy."

"Don't jump to conclusions, *chère,*" he begged. "Deke is gone, forget about it, okay?"

"Right," she repeated, wondering how many different ways Deke could have betrayed her, how Liz was able to look her in the eye.

"And don't forget to call me when you have more, um, you know."

She sighed. "That might be a while—my woodsman said his helper is out of commission."

Ziggy made a frustrated noise. "They will be out of season before long."

Penny bit her lip. She had so many things to worry about other than black truffles. "I'll keep you posted, Ziggy."

"Take care, *chère*."

She disconnected the call and laid her head back on the seat.

"What was that all about?" Guy asked.

"My life just turned on end," she murmured. "Again." She wondered, if it kept turning, might it someday be right side up again?

"Do you still want that drink?" he said.

"Want it?" Penny asked. "I might never *stop* drinking." What had happened when Liz and Wendy had stopped at Deke's? Had they argued? Fought? Was it possible that Liz had murdered him, and was Wendy somehow involved?

When they arrived at the square, the festival was in high gear. By the time they threaded their way through the crowd to Caskey's, Penny was light-headed and dizzy from the thoughts running through her head and the heady scent of the smoke from the *peristil* fire.

"Don't these people ever get tired?" Guy asked, nodding toward the dancers whirling to the music of flutes.

"Apparently not," Penny said. And as far as she was concerned, the festival couldn't be over quickly enough; when the crowds left, the news media would lose interest in the "Voodoo Murder." To think that the festival would go on for the rest of the week was almost unbearable.

The bar was just starting to get crowded in anticipation of happy hour and free appetizers. Gloria and Liz were sitting at a table, but Liz stood when Penny walked up.

"Penny, could I talk to you, in private?"

"No," Penny said, her voice deadly. "I have something to talk to *you* about, and I want witnesses."

Liz sat down hard, her face tight with apprehension. "So you know?"

"About you and Deke?" Penny asked. "Yeah, I know."

Liz's eyes rounded. "*Me* and Deke? No—it was Wendy and Deke who had the affair."

Penny practically fell into one of the vacant chairs and put her head in her hands. "*Wendy* and Deke? When? For how long?"

Liz sighed, and her shoulders rounded. "College. You were off on some field trip, and the two of them hooked up." She wet her lips. "When I found out, I was furious with both of them."

Penny closed her eyes. "How . . . how long did it go on?"

Liz hesitated. "A year . . . or so."

Penny inhaled sharply at the stabbing pain behind her breastbone. "And since then?"

"Not that I know of," Liz said. "But Deke called Wendy after your separation, wanting to see her. She called me asking for advice, and I told her to stay away from him."

"So . . . you both knew I was getting a divorce before Marie called you about the party?"

Liz nodded.

Humiliation burned her from the inside out. "And the dinner you had with Deke in the city?"

Liz looked surprised, then apologetic. "I asked Deke

to meet me. I was hoping I could appeal to his morals." She made a rueful noise. "I asked him to leave Wendy alone, that . . . she wasn't as strong as you are . . . that when he eventually left her, she wouldn't be able to recover like you have."

That still remained to be seen, but warm appreciation washed over Penny at Liz's confidence in her emotional fortitude. "So that's why you were always so antagonistic toward Deke?"

"I didn't realize it showed," Liz said. "But yeah, I couldn't stand him. He didn't deserve you."

Liz's eyes grew moist, and Penny's chest welled with fondness. She reached across the table and touched Liz's arm. "You have to tell me what happened Friday night. Did you stop to see Deke on your way out of town?"

Liz hesitated.

"I saw your car sitting in the parking lot across the street," Guy said.

Liz puffed out her cheeks and nodded. "Yes—Wendy insisted. She'd met someone in Atlanta, and she said she wanted to see Deke, that she wanted to get him out of her system."

Penny shook her head in disbelief. "Was it Deke calling her on her cell phone?"

Liz nodded. "Once. Wendy had left him a message on his cell phone that she wanted to see him, but when he called her back, he told her not to stop by, that he was expecting a client to come by the house."

"But she wanted to stop anyway?" Gloria asked.

"Right," Liz said.

"That's what you were arguing about as you left the bar," Penny said. "I saw you."

Liz nodded. "I shouldn't have let Wendy talk me into stopping, but I was hoping that seeing him would be the release she needed to move on." She looked at Penny. "I'm so sorry."

"Did Wendy kill him?" Penny asked thickly.

Liz gasped. "What? No, of course not! Deke wouldn't even let her inside the house. I watched from the parking lot. He came to the door, they talked for a minute, then Wendy came back to the car. She was angry with herself. She said she couldn't understand why she'd ever been hung up on him and that she was glad you were rid of him, too." She reached into her purse and pulled out an envelope. "Wendy wrote you a letter—that's what I wanted to talk to you about. It's all in here, for you and for the police. She couldn't face you."

Penny recalled Wendy's claim that she was ill when she'd called, but in hindsight, Wendy could have been crying.

"And you're willing to take a polygraph test?" Gloria asked Liz.

"Sure," Liz said, lifting her hands. "Wendy and I agreed—anything to help clear this up. Deke was definitely alive when we left."

Penny took the envelope, her chest tight with mixed feelings. The affair had occurred before she and Deke had been married, and if Wendy had carried a torch for him all these years, she had certainly been punished for her transgression. "Was Deke alone when you were there?"

Liz bit her lip. "Wendy said that Deke insisted he was alone, but she had a feeling that he wasn't."

"Maybe it was the client who was supposed to come

by," Gloria said, then removed a prescription bottle from her purse and tossed back two pills.

"Yeah, except Wendy said she smelled a woman's perfume."

"Could have been Sheena's," Guy pointed out.

Or the faceless "other woman" that Sheena was concerned about, Penny thought to herself.

"Isn't that your phone?" Guy asked.

Penny jumped. "Mine?"

"It's coming from your bag," he said, pointing.

Penny pulled out the cell phone, and her heart did a little jig at the incoming number: B.J. She flipped open the mouthpiece. "Hello?"

"Hey, Red, it's me. How was the service?"

She frowned at his assumption that she'd know who "me" was. "Fine," she lied.

"Did you get the locks changed on your doors like I told you?"

"My landlord was changing them when I left. Why?"

"Because I'm on Hairpin Hill."

"And?"

"And I just pulled a .38 slug out of a tree where you told me you were running. If this is what you dodged, babe, it's no blank."

25

Be careful—the potion has a bite to it . . .

The next day at the shop, Penny was still antsy from B.J.'s call, but she wasn't sure what bothered her the most—that she'd truly been shot at, or that B.J. had called her "babe." Or maybe the fact that he hadn't offered to sleep on the couch last night?

The chime on the door sounded, announcing a customer. Business was still booming, and she'd decided the most constructive use of her time was to work in the store.

Besides, here she was less likely to get shot at.

Jules Lamborne strode in, leaning on her walking stick.

"Hello, Jules," Penny said, glancing around for Marie, hoping to get out of waiting on the spooky old woman. She wasn't in the mood for more bad mojo.

"*Bonjour,*" Jules said, although her voice wasn't its usual strong warble. She climbed up on a stool but seemed to be moving more slowly than normal. "I came for my morning elixir."

Penny spotted Marie handling another customer and groaned inwardly. "Coming right up." She filled a glass with Vigor Juice, managing to spill some on the floor in her nervousness. She set the glass in front of the old woman and reached for a paper towel. "I saw you at Deke's funeral yesterday, Jules."

"Saw you, too," the woman said after a hearty drink. "Saw what you did to the *cercueil.*"

Without her translator, Penny was confused, but she took a guess. "You mean the casket?"

Jules nodded.

Penny frowned. "I didn't do anything to it. I barely touched it, and it fell. It was just an accident."

Jules wagged her finger. "Nothing is an accident. The *cercueil* fell because you wished it to, or because it had to."

"Okay," Penny said, still skeptical. She certainly hadn't "wished" it to fall, and why would a coffin *have* to fall?

Jules drank the rest of the juice in one gulp, then set down the empty glass and abruptly stood to leave.

Penny observed the woman's agitated body language. "What's your hurry, Jules?"

"There is a serpent underfoot," Jules murmured, glancing from side to side, her eyes wide, her tongue darting in and out as if she was unwittingly mimicking a snake. "I must go—I'm weak from using my *Cajun* and will be susceptible to the serpent's evil." The little old woman scrambled toward the door unsteadily.

Penny strode ahead to get the door for her. "Watch your step, Jules. See you tomorrow."

But when the woman didn't respond with her normal "*Bon Dieu* willing," as she walked away, Penny bit her lip. Was Jules's age finally catching up to her? Had the woman slipped into senility? Were the voodoo festival and all the bizarre events making her more agitated, more neurotic?

Just as Penny was closing the door, it was shoved open, catching Penny on the heel. While pain shot up her leg, she looked around to see Sheena Linder standing there in snakeskin jeans, a gold shirt, and four-inch stilettos. Her orange skin was slick with some kind of oil, her white hair as poufy and dry-looking as straw. Didn't the woman realize that when she fried her skin, she was also frying her hair? One of these days, she was going to burst into flames. "Hi, Sheena."

Sheena planted her hands on her generous hips and glared at Penny. "I'm going to sue you."

Penny sighed. "What for now?"

Sheena's eyes narrowed. "Don't get smart with me, Granola Girl. Do you know what kind of pain and anguish you put me through yesterday when you knocked Deke's casket off its stand? I had to take a handful of Xanax just to make it through the rest of the day."

Customers began to stare, and Penny swallowed her retort. "Maybe we'd better take this, um, discussion into my office?"

Sheena's chin jerked up. "Okay by me."

Penny led the way, then glanced back to see if Sheena was following her . . . just in time to see Sheena step in the Vigor Juice that Penny had spilled, which had seeped from behind the counter. In one awful second, Penny realized she was still holding the paper towel that she'd meant to use to wipe up the spill . . . before Jules had distracted her with all of her ramblings. Sheena had been strutting full steam ahead, so she'd hit the green Vigor Juice with maximum momentum. Her legs flew up in the air as if they'd been pulled by a rope, and she landed in a yoga v-sit, directly on her tailbone. Penny heard the crack of bone from where she stood, and she winced—that had to hurt.

Sheena was still screaming when they loaded her into the ambulance, but all Penny could hear was the sound of her insurance premiums soaring over the moon. She did feel sympathetic for the woman . . . a little. But filing so many bogus personal injury claims was bound to come back and bite her sooner or later. Penny sighed. She just wished it hadn't been her negligence that had taught the woman a lesson.

Just before the ambulance door closed, Penny noticed Sheena's pants—snakeskin. Penny's body tingled. Jules had said there was a serpent underfoot . . . had she foreseen the accident?

"It couldn't have happened to a nicer person," Marie said sarcastically, watching the ambulance pull away.

"Careful," Penny said. "If she takes my business away from me in court, you might be working for her."

Marie made a face.

Penny wet her lips and tried to inject a casual note into her voice. "Jules was in this morning, and she wasn't making sense to me."

Marie frowned. "Jules is the smartest person I know. What did she say?"

"She said that a serpent was underfoot."

The young woman shrugged. "That just means she thinks that evil is all around."

"But then she said she had to leave—that she was weak from using her Cajun and was 'susceptible' to the serpent."

"So she thought she was susceptible to the evil."

"From speaking Cajun? Did I misunderstand?"

Marie bit her lip, then shook her head. "No . . . in that context, Cajun isn't a person, or a language, or even a culture. The word can be more loosely translated to mean *magic*. Jules was weak from using her magic." The woman wagged her eyebrows, then walked back inside the store.

Penny pressed her mouth together—just what had Jules used her magic *on?* A voodoo doll? Hadn't Jules offered to put a hex on Deke? And Jules had been in the square Friday night—perhaps she was the one who had placed the doll on the table at Caskey's. And she had been at the funeral home yesterday, when the casket had practically leaped off its stand. . . .

No. Penny shook her head to rid it of nonsense. There was no such thing as voodoo or black magic.

She stared at the pink house, and B.J.'s words about wishing they could get in to look at the crime scene came back to her. Sheena would be in the hospital for a while, so what better time to snoop around? He had returned to New Orleans yesterday to drop off some items at a lab, and he'd said he'd be back soon. She pulled her cell phone out of her pocket and hesitated. Was she calling because she wanted to tell him about the house being empty, or because she missed him?

She closed her eyes and groaned, and her phone rang.

When she saw his number pop up, her heart lifted

higher than it had a right to. She flipped down the mouthpiece. "Hello?"

"It's me," he said. "I miss you."

Surprise and pleasure sparkled through her chest. "So come back," she said breezily. "I have a job for us." She explained about the house.

"I was planning to come back this evening," he said. "But I'll bring my cat burgling clothes."

She smiled into the phone. "Are you a master of disguise?"

"If the situation calls for it," he said, and for some reason, his admission niggled at her.

"Where shall I meet you?" she asked, changing the subject.

"At your place," he said. "We'll walk to the house after dark. Wear all black clothing. Preferably tight."

She laughed, then disconnected the call, mystified over her reaction to the man. And had she, in Jules's words, "wished" him into calling her?

"No," she said aloud. "There's no such thing as magic, voodoo, or witchcraft."

Steeled with resolve, she marched back into the store and drank a glass of Hot Voodoo Sex. Two of them, in fact.

"I can't believe he didn't change the locks after the divorce," B.J. muttered as they entered the house through the back door. "That's rule one."

A whining noise sounded, a warning to disengage the security system before an alarm went off. She punched in a code, and the whining noise stopped.

"Rule number two," he said. "Change the code on the security system."

"Lucky for us, Deke was a creature of habit," Penny whispered into the hush of the house.

"You don't have to whisper," he said.

"Sorry," she said. "I've never broken into a house before." The latex gloves felt strange and cold on her skin.

"Which way to the office?"

Using her loaner P.I. penlight, she led the way through the foyer and up the stairs, her pulse ratcheting higher with every step. At the top of the stairs, she pointed. "There."

He opened the office door and walked in. Penny hung back, the idea of seeing the room again, of visualizing Deke's body on the floor, overwhelming.

"You don't have to do this," he said.

"No . . . I'm fine," she lied and followed him inside the room. The bloody rug was gone and the room was relatively neat, without the disarray she recalled. She exhaled.

"Do you remember any files being on the desk or being open?" he asked.

She squinted, thinking back. "No, sorry."

"What about the file he had when you saw him at the museum?"

"Blue," she said. "I think it was an accordion file."

For over an hour, they looked through drawers and file cabinets, but they came up with nothing.

"Maybe the police took the file," she offered.

"Could be. Did your ex-husband have a secret hiding place—other than the ficus tree?"

"What do you mean?"

"You know—the drawer you wouldn't necessarily want people to open after you're gone."

She started to shake her head, then she remembered

the place where she had once found some men's magazines. "The garage."

They backtracked through the house. "Nice woodwork," he mused, shining his light on the crown molding.

"Thanks," she said. "I refinished most of it myself."

"I shouldn't be surprised, but I am."

"Why?"

"Because you're . . . resourceful," he said.

His words were smooth and velvety in the darkness, strumming her libido . . . or maybe it was all the voodoo juice she'd drunk. "I don't think I'll ask for clarification."

She opened the door leading to the garage, closed it behind them, then flipped on the overhead light. "No windows," she explained, then walked past Deke's red Lotus Elise and Sheena's yellow Miata to a metal toolbox that Deke had bought one weekend when he'd been feeling particularly ambitious. But Penny had used the toolbox more than he had, thus finding the stash of girlie magazines. She opened the bottom drawer, then lifted out the tray that held wrenches of all sizes imaginable. Underneath it were magazines and videos, but not the more innocent, pinup kind she'd found before.

"So Deke was a kinky guy," B.J. said.

"Not with me," she murmured, picking up an S&M video picturing a man having his bare bottom welted with a leather strap. The rest of the items were more of the same and worse, with a particular lean toward spanking and punishment by lashing. Near the bottom, they found a plain video case with no markings.

"Looks homemade," B.J. said. "If it's something the two of you did—"

"It isn't," she assured him.

B.J. put the tape in the bag he'd brought along, then held up the magazines by the spine and gave them a shake. "Just checking for notes or letters," he said, but he didn't find any. "Let's hope the tape tells us something." They replaced the items and closed the toolbox. On the way out, B.J. stopped to look at Deke's car.

"I hated that thing," she said. "And now it seems petty."

He crouched down. "Was Deke a bad driver?"

"Yeah," she said. "He loved to talk on the phone while he was in the car, and he drove way too fast. Of course, when your mother's the mayor—"

"You don't have to worry about speeding tickets," he finished.

"Exactly."

"Looks like he hit something," B.J. said.

Penny leaned down to look, then stared at the crumpled fender. Waves of recognition rolled over her, colliding with denial. The little car the voodoo doll was holding . . . the crumpled edge of the casket . . .

"What's wrong? You look like you've seen a ghost."

She jerked back and stepped into a garden tool organizer, toppling it with a mighty crash.

B.J. winced and reached for the tools to right them, but Penny fled, back to the foyer, back to where she could breathe and assimilate. But everywhere she looked, she imagined evil spirits hanging in the corners, just waiting for her to let down her defenses enough to—

"Hey."

She screamed, then realized it was B.J. "I'm sorry," she said. "I'm a little freaked out."

"Let's go," he said quietly, "then you can explain. If the neighbors heard us, they might have already called the police."

She nodded and followed him to the back door, where she reset the alarm and they made their escape. During the three-block walk to her apartment, they kept to the inside of the sidewalk to escape notice as much as possible. Using careful words, she explained about the smashed Hot Wheels car, the bent casket, and the crumpled fender.

B.J. was quiet for a few seconds. "And you're telling me that there's some kind of supernatural connection between the three things?"

"Don't you think it's too much of a coincidence?"

"Not if the alternative is believing in voodoo."

When they approached the square, the beat of the *batri* drums was so loud to her that she clapped her hands over her ears; the dancers so frenzied that she had to look away; the stench of the smoke and animal blood so offensive that her stomach roiled. She ran to her apartment door and up the steps, distantly aware that B.J. was behind her.

Once in her apartment, she dropped onto the couch and pulled her knees up to her chest, rocking to hold back the wall of tears that pressed on the back of her eyes. She felt desperate.

"Hey, it's going to be okay," B.J. soothed, sitting next to her and drawing her into his arms.

"I think I'm losing my mind," she whispered, reveling in the warmth of his skin, the comfort of his body. "There's no such thing as voodoo, I know that."

"Someone is trying to scare you," he said, stroking her back.

"Someone is trying to make me look crazy. So that no one will believe me."

"I believe you," he said earnestly, then lifted her chin with his fingers. She looked into his eyes and clenched her jaw against the feelings that swelled in her chest. Falling in love with someone so quickly, and under such duress, was as false as voodoo.

He kissed her, gently at first, then harder when she responded, until their tongues lashed feverishly. He pulled her onto his lap and ran his thumb over the peak of her beaded breast. She closed her eyes and arched into him, clutching at his back, pulling at his clothing as desire pooled in her midsection.

Their clothes came off slowly until a pile of black fabric lay on the floor and they were completely nude, lying mouth to mouth, sex to sex. "You're beautiful," he breathed, then lowered his head to take a rigid nipple into his mouth while caressing her other breast. Incredible sensations exploded in her body as his mouth traveled over her skin. His erection surged against her thigh, and she reached down to stroke the length of him. He moaned and lowered his hand to her stomach, then lower, to tease her wet folds, and she nearly came apart in his arms.

"Easy," he whispered. "Take your time."

He massaged the most sensitive part of her until the stabs of pleasure became swells of bliss, carrying her higher until she cried out and thrashed against his hand. At the pinnacle of her orgasm, he thrust inside her, taking her to another plane of excitement and complete stimulation. He began to move slowly, allowing her to set the pace. She opened her knees to give him full access to her body, grasping his lean hips to pull him even more deeply inside. He kissed her, plunging his tongue into her mouth, and laved her breasts until she thought she would come from the prompting of his tongue alone.

They found an easy, long rhythm, taking pleasure in the breadth and width of every stroke, clenching and relaxing, each glide of their bodies more pleasurable than the last. When the tremor of another orgasm rose and swept her away, she cried out his name and contracted around him. He shuddered and thrust deep, wedging their bodies together until the shared vibrations subsided.

Penny wanted to stay in that rosy, languid place of recovery, when the body is too weak to do anything except feel, for as long as possible. But too soon, sounds from outside her window began to cut through the pleasant sexual haze, and the aroma of Benny's Beignets overrode the scent of their satisfied bodies. Gingerly, B.J. shifted until she was lying next to him. "That was tremendous," he murmured into her ear.

"Mm-hm," she said, her eyes barely open. "Let's go to my bed."

He grinned. "I thought you'd never ask."

"Carry me?"

He laughed and stood, then pulled her to her feet and threw her over his shoulder. "This isn't what I had in mind," she said, hanging upside down and being jarred with every footfall into the bedroom.

Still holding her, he leaned over and pulled down the covers. "Penny . . . do you have a pet snake?"

She scoffed and smacked him lightly on the behind. "No, but I'll adopt yours for a while."

But he didn't laugh. "I'm not kidding. Don't move. Where's the light?"

She froze, her heart thumping wildly. “B-back up.”

“I’m going to have to set you down.”

He backed up, hit the light switch, and swung her to her feet in one movement. But when she tried to stand, she nearly fainted from the head rush. She blinked the bedroom into focus and wished she hadn’t.

The only thing more scary than seeing the man you love face off with a full-grown venomous snake is seeing the man you love *naked* while facing off with a full-grown venomous snake.

26

Stir with an olive branch . . .

"Well, that was a big waste of time," B.J. said as they left the police station.

"Allyson doesn't trust either one of us," Penny said. And she had to admit, in the light of day, that the allegations that someone had broken into her apartment and left a snake in her bed were pretty outrageous, especially with new locks and no signs of forced entry. Allyson had said in that infuriatingly reasonable voice of hers, since the snake's fangs had been removed, it was more likely that one of the snakes from the *peristil* had escaped and climbed up a tree to her balcony, then crawled in through a window.

More reasonable, for instance, than putting stock in Jules's prediction about serpents being underfoot.

"Then it's a good thing we trust each other," he said with a wink. "What was all that business about where you grew up?"

"I don't know," she said lightly. "Detective Maynard asked where I grew up and I told him, but he keeps getting it wrong."

"Kingsville, Tennessee?"

Penny nodded but dropped her gaze. Did she truly trust B.J.? She hadn't told him everything because it would only muddy the water and implicate her further. And some secrets were just better kept. Last night had been wonderful . . . until he'd had to kill the snake, of course. She wanted to leave it at that.

"I'd feel better if you went with me to the city," B.J. said, nodding toward his car.

Penny glanced up at city hall next to the police station and up to Mona's office window on the third floor. "This is something I need to do."

"I can wait," he said lightly.

She looked into his eyes, saw the invitation. *Fall for me . . . we'll have fun . . . for a while . . .*

"That's okay. I might not get in to see her for a while. Besides, my employees are going to wonder what's happened to me, and I don't think I should leave town right now, even if it's just overnight."

He nodded. "Okay. I have a lot of things to run down, and I have to stop by the agency to do some paperwork. I'll see you tomorrow?"

She smiled. "Sure. Call me if the video is . . . enlightening."

"Will do."

But as he pulled away from the curb, she couldn't help thinking that if something on that tape would incriminate someone else for Deke's murder, she was letting the one piece of evidence that might exonerate her drive away. Then she chided herself—she was projecting her own behavior onto B.J.

It was safer to believe that he couldn't be trusted rather than acknowledge that he just might be worth loving.

She sighed and walked into the city hall building, then pulled the ring that Deke had given her from her pocket—a gold ring with a black onyx cross. A family heirloom, he had said. It was a lovely piece, but she'd rarely worn rings because of her garden work. She had almost forgotten about it, rediscovering it after the phantom maid had rearranged her apartment, including her jewelry.

It was only right that Mona have it back. Maybe the woman would see it as a peace offering; that they had both loved and lost Deke, and that Penny had had nothing to do with his death.

She rode up to the third floor and smiled at Mona's clerk, a timid, plain girl of about eighteen. Immediately, the girl looked terrified.

"I'm Penny Francisco—"

"I know who you are," the girl said, her eyes wide.

Great—now she was scaring young girls. "Is the mayor in?"

The girl shook her head solemnly. "No . . . she said she'd be in, but no one's seen her."

Penny glanced down at the ring. Maybe it would be better if she left it for Mona so the woman could ponder the gesture without the pressure of a confrontation. She held up the ring box. "Would it be all right if I left something in her office? It's a family heirloom—I'm sure she'll be happy to have it back."

The girl looked around nervously, then nodded toward the office door. "Go ahead. But hurry."

Penny smiled in gratitude, then walked into Mona's spacious office, impressively outfitted with the best furniture. The woman had certainly built her own little world here in Mojo. Penny walked over to the desk and set the ring in the center where Mona would find it, then decided she should write a note. Penny scanned the desk for a piece of paper, but Mona was compulsively neat.

What was it that B.J. had said—that when people are compulsive, it's to mask something else?

She slid open a top drawer but didn't find any paper. Then she slid open a bottom drawer and jerked back in shock. The *ason*, the rattle that the masked voodoo priestess in the square had wielded, was lying there in a velvet-lined box. With her heart thumping against her chest, Penny lifted the rattle to make sure it was the same one. It had the same beadwork, the same little bell on the handle. She gave it a slight shake, a shiver skidding over her arms at the knowledge that the shimmy noise was loose snake vertebrae.

Fear rose in her chest. Jules had said that only the priests and priestesses were allowed to use the *ason*. Her hand began to shake. So that meant—

"*What* in the hell do you think you're doing?"

Penny turned and nearly fainted at the sight of Mona standing there, looking as if she'd just as soon kill Penny as look at her. *There is a serpent underfoot.* Penny wet her lips. "I . . . brought you something," she said, nodding to the ring box on her desk. "I was looking for a piece of paper to write you a note. I didn't mean to pry. This, um, shaker is lovely." Mona didn't have to know that she was aware of its significance. "Is it Native American?"

"No," Mona snapped, then walked over to her desk and slammed the drawer closed. "How dare you come here, how dare you come into my office and rifle through my things!" Her voice escalated to the point of shouting.

"I didn't mean to," Penny said, moving toward the door.

"Get out before I call the police!"

Penny ran out of the office, past the trembling little clerk, and left the building, shaken at the new revelation: Mona was a voodoo priestess? She'd been the one the other night who had singled her out of the crowd and torn the chicken's head off with her bare hands?

Could she have created a voodoo doll for her own son and left it at Penny's party? Then orchestrated the murder to frame Penny? But why would a mother kill her own son?

With her hands shaking, she called B.J.'s cell phone number, but it rolled to voice mail. After a deep breath, she dialed directory assistance for the New Orleans police department and asked for Detective Maynard.

"Ms. Francisco," he said, "this is a surprise. Mona Black is on the other line accusing you of breaking into her office and harassing her."

Penny swallowed hard and told him what had happened and what she had found, wondering if it sounded as bizarre to his ears as it did to hers.

"So let me get this straight—you're saying that your ex-mother-in-law, the mayor of Mojo, is a voodoo priestess?"

She hesitated. "Maybe."

"And you think that she might have killed her own son and framed you for the murder?"

She wet her lips. "Possibly."

Maynard gave a little laugh. "Ms. Francisco, now I've heard it all. I thought you didn't believe in voodoo."

"I d-don't," she said, suddenly feeling as if she were unraveling.

"Ms. Francisco, I think you should leave this investigation up to the police."

She inhaled for strength. "Did you talk to Liz Brockwell and Wendy Metzger?"

"Yes, we took statements from them both, including"—paper rattled in the background—"both of the women quoting you as saying on the night of the murder that you had plans for your ex-husband, and that he was going to regret screwing you over."

She closed her eyes, her mind racing back to their conversation just before Liz and Wendy had left the bar. "I only meant that I was planning to have my attorney sue him for hiding assets." She let out a frustrated cry, wondering if her friends had turned on her under interrogation. "Why doesn't anyone believe me? I didn't kill Deke—there's a murderer out there somewhere! And B.J. found a slug in a tree near where I was running."

"The slug could have been there for ages," Maynard said calmly.

"Someone left a snake in my bed last night."

"Chief Davis informed me of your report."

"And?"

He sighed. "Frankly, Ms. Francisco, you could have planted that snake yourself to divert attention from you as a suspect."

Her mouth watered to mention Jimmy Scaggs, but at this point, she was afraid it would only lead to the fact that she'd pushed Sheena into the street, and where would that leave her? Besides, Jimmy didn't have a motive for killing Deke . . . not as much as some other people . . . not as much as she did.

"Let us do our job, Ms. Francisco. I'm convinced

that as soon as the forensic results are back, we'll be making an arrest. My guess is that'll be happening about Friday. Do you have any plans for Friday, Ms. Francisco?"

"N-no."

"Good. Meanwhile, stay away from Mona Black. You've got enough trouble as it is."

She disconnected the call with trembling hands and wondered if she had gone a little mad. Maybe the trauma of finding Deke and attending the funeral was just now catching up to her.

Her phone rang, and it was B.J. She answered and tried to inject a note of normalcy into her voice.

"What's up?" he asked. "How did it go with your ex-mother-in-law?"

She told him what had happened at Mona's and the conversation with Maynard.

"Are you sure of the meaning of this rattle?" he asked, sounding dubious.

"Jules told me that the *ason* is used only by priests and priestesses."

"Maybe in the old days," he said. "Now you can probably buy them online."

"It would explain some other things," she argued. "Like Deke's aversion to animals, for instance—maybe he saw her behead one too many chickens. And then there's Mona's general weirdness."

The silence on the line told her that her argument was weak, at best.

"Maybe Maynard's right," he said casually. "Maybe you should just lie low for a few days. Go to work, stay out of your mother-in-law's way." He cleared his throat. "Or maybe you should go home and get some rest."

"Are you forgetting that someone put a snake in my bed?"

He was quiet again. "Look, I've been thinking. Maybe Chief Davis is right about how the snake got into your bedroom . . . it could happen."

Her heart bumped against her chest. "Okay." So he thought she was nuts, too.

"Try to relax and I'll see you tomorrow, okay?"

"Sure," she mumbled, then disconnected the call. She felt ridiculously let down that he didn't believe her, although she wasn't sure what she was asking him to believe. She hugged herself and headed toward the store, her rock in the storm. If Maynard made good on his threat, she had only two days of freedom left to get her affairs in order.

27

The taste might come back to haunt you . . .

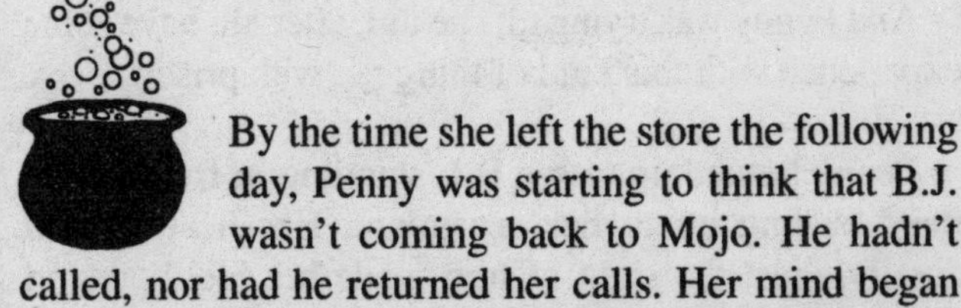

By the time she left the store the following day, Penny was starting to think that B.J. wasn't coming back to Mojo. He hadn't called, nor had he returned her calls. Her mind began to weave wild stories—maybe he was working undercover for the cops, building a case against her. Or maybe he was like Marie's "Kirk," a phantom too-good-to-be-true con man who went from town to town looking for adventure and easy women, then moved on when things became too complicated.

The latter seemed far more likely.

She took a circuitous route home and wound her way through the voodoo festivalgoers, ever watchful for a stray news camera. Tomorrow, Friday, would be the last day of the festival—thank God. Not that things would be getting back to normal, not for her anyway.

Gloria had called her with one bit of good news: The DNA from the blood spatters on her clothing had come back as animal blood—chicken blood, to be exact. As soon as she heard Gloria say the words, Penny remembered having walked by the *peristil* when an unlucky chicken had been getting its head whacked off. In the darkness, she hadn't realized that she'd been sprayed with the blood. She shuddered, still sure that it had been Mona behind the eerie skeletal mask.

But, Gloria had added, with Penny's fingerprints on both murder weapons, the link to the voodoo doll, and the fact that she'd found the body . . .

"I have the names of some good criminal attorneys," Gloria had said quietly. "You should prepare yourself."

And Penny was trying to; she did, after all, have some experience with this kind of thing . . . with prison.

"Hello."

Penny looked up to see B.J. standing in front of the door leading up to her apartment. Her heart jerked crazily—just the sight of him made her feel better in the wake of what she faced. At least he had tried to help her . . . had given her some very good memories.

"Hello, yourself. Have you been waiting long? I took my time walking home, it's such a nice night."

"I've been here a while," he said, his voice thick. "Thinking."

Something had changed, something for the worse. Her chest tightened with apprehension. "Do you want to come up and talk?"

"I think I should."

They walked up the stairs and into the apartment, the mood solemn. Penny took off her coat and sat on the couch. "What?"

B.J. bit into his lip, his eyes intense. "You didn't grow up in Kingsville, Tennessee."

She looked at her hands and sighed. "No, I didn't. And I didn't grow up in Kingston or in Kingford."

"And your last name isn't really Francisco."

"No . . . it's plain old Frank. Penny Frank. I had it changed when I was sixteen."

"The year your mother went to prison."

She nodded again, the pain and shame welling up in her chest. "That's right."

"Nobody around here knows?"

"No . . . not even Deke knew." She gave B.J. a little smile. "I told him and everyone else that my parents were dead, which was half true."

"Your mother is in prison—"

"For murdering my father," she finished. "Yep. And my two older brothers are in prison—drugs, armed robbery." A little laugh escaped her. "I'm from rotten stock."

"Don't say that," he murmured.

"It's true. See—you already think differently of me. Imagine what will happen when the police and the D.A. and everyone in town finds out." She stood and walked to the window and stared out over the crowd, which seemed more subdued tonight . . . or maybe it was just her. "This information will be the pièce de résistance for the prosecution."

He came over to stand next to her. "No one can hold you responsible for the things your family did."

"I know, but it will make a difference." She shook her head. "I feel like somehow I've brought this on myself."

He frowned. "How?"

"By lying, by trying to block out that part of my life. By denying my mother's very existence." Her chest ached with misery. She choked, and he pulled her into his arms, kissing her so gently that tears squeezed out of her eyes.

"Make love to me," she whispered. "Tonight I want to forget everything."

He undressed her slowly, kissing every inch of skin as he exposed it to the air. When she was nude, he kneaded and suckled her breasts until the tips were rigid and singing with pleasure. Then he knelt and kissed her flat stomach down to her thighs until she quivered for more. He thrust his tongue into her folds, flicking at the jewel of her essence until she pleaded with him to end her suffering and make love to her. "I want you inside me," she murmured.

He flung off his clothes in record time. She tried to memorize the lines and the textures of his lean, muscular body and his rigid sex, shiny with his desire for her. He pulled her to the couch, straddling his lap. She lowered herself onto his shaft slowly, then took him fully in one final motion. Their moans mingled. She adjusted to his fullness, then began to ride him slowly. He put one hand on her hips to guide her, and with the other, he stroked her, kissing and licking her breasts. Her body was one long nerve ending—every breath, every nip, every caress intensified. He seemed to know intuitively where and how she wanted to be touched. She fell against his chest in powerful climax, clenching her feminine muscles to maximize the pleasure for both of them. His breath rasped out, and he ground her down on him, uttering his own guttural groan of release.

She sighed against his neck, feeling . . . gratitude . . . and love. It was false love, she knew—infatuation. But she clung to it like the desperate woman she was.

As if he sensed her urgency and her fear, he made love to her twice more before dawn, each time more emotionally and physically gratifying for her than the last. She had never enjoyed this kind of physical connection with Deke, nor with any other man. They didn't even have to talk to communicate what they wanted. She thought about his mouth on her breast, and it was already there. It was a magical night, with no voodoo in sight.

It was only after she stepped out of the shower the next morning that she remembered to ask about the videotape.

He was already dressed, and he refused to make eye contact. "It's amateur quality. Deke with . . . two women. Bondage type stuff, soft core. Can't see the women's faces and there's no sound, so it doesn't help us. If we turn it over to the police, we'll have to explain how we got it." He finally lifted his gaze. "But you can decide."

She nodded, surprised that the information didn't hurt her. Maybe she was numb; maybe she was shutting down, preparing herself, as Gloria had said.

But then she looked at B.J. and realized that no, she wasn't numb, not by a long shot.

Penny cleared her throat of emotion. "Gloria told me that I'll probably be arrested today."

His lack of reaction told her that he already knew. Maybe his brother still had contacts at the New Orleans P.D. "I'm sorry," he said, then lifted his gaze to hers. "I thought I'd be able to uncover something that would keep you from having to endure an arrest."

She feigned nonchalance. "Now I understand how people can be convicted on circumstantial evidence."

He reached her in two strides, his face stricken. "Don't say that—don't even think it. Gloria will help you find a good attorney. You can offer to take a polygraph test."

Penny pressed her lips together. "But I wasn't truthful about where I grew up or my family history, and the incident of me pushing Sheena into the street is bound to come out. Plus . . ." She stopped, her eyes welling up.

His eyes darkened with concern. "Plus what?"

"Plus . . . maybe on some subconscious level, I did want something terrible to happen to Deke." She bit into her lower lip to stop it from trembling.

He raised his finger to her mouth. "Shh. You wouldn't be normal if you didn't have thoughts of revenge against someone who lied to you, who betrayed you." He wet his lips. "Especially when that person was supposed to be someone you trusted most."

She swallowed as tears rolled down her cheeks. "My husband."

He nodded.

"And my mother."

He pulled her into his arms and she went, crying softly against the solid warmth of his chest. He held her tight and rubbed her back, kissing her hair. "It'll be okay," he murmured. "You'll get through this. You're a strong woman."

At his words, she closed her eyes tightly. *You'll get through this. You*, as in *by yourself*. She chided herself for wanting him to care enough to stick around—they barely knew each other, and he had other commitments, commitments that were less . . . sticky. She inhaled deeply, savoring the musky maleness of him a few seconds longer, then pulled away with a nod and a sniff. "You're right," she said, trying to sound upbeat. "Of course I will. And I appreciate all of your . . . help."

"My pleasure, Red." He smoothed her hair back from her face. "You know the investigation will go on, even after an arrest is made. The police still have a lot of leads to follow—Sheena, Steve, your friend from Atlanta."

The police—meaning he was definitely moving on. "Right." She angled a jaunty little smile up at him. "I assume you'll be sending me an invoice for your time when you get back to the city?"

He dropped his hand, then nodded. "Sure, if that's what you want."

"I think that would be best," she said, and they both knew she was referring to more than just his billing process.

"I'll probably be in town through the rest of the day," he said. "Walking around the festival, asking questions."

She smiled cheerfully. "Great. So maybe I'll see you around."

He lowered his mouth to hers for a sweet, sexy, sizzling good-bye kiss that resurrected every twinge and tingle from their night of lovemaking. When he lifted his head, he said, "Yeah. Maybe I'll see you around."

He left, and Penny stood at the window, hugging herself and watching him walk away. Then she went to the kitchen to count out her vitamins.

28

Make sure you have a stomach for it . . .

When Penny arrived at the store, she felt remarkably calm. In a way, she was looking forward to the arrest, like coming up for air after being underwater so long your lungs hurt. If B.J. had uncovered her past, it would be only a matter of time before the police found out . . . or maybe they already knew. Maybe Maynard had been able to tell the minute he'd seen her. She always felt as if she wore the shame of her family on her sleeve.

She wondered how they would take her in—with much fanfare and television coverage, or would they put a brown paper bag over her head? Wouldn't it be ironic if she wound up in the same prison as her mother?

Guy was morose this morning, burrowing into the stockroom behind paperwork. Marie was artificially cheerful. She had gotten an e-mail message from Kirk, who was supposedly on a medical mission to help the tsunami survivors. Penny let her prattle on, since customers were few and far between, many of them already heading out of town on this last day of the festival. Marie was looking out the window, in the direction of the pink house. Penny wondered idly how much longer Mona would allow Sheena to live there. Since their divorce, Deke had undoubtedly willed everything to his mother, and since Sheena and Deke hadn't yet married, the woman would be entitled to nothing except gifts.

But the Sheena Linders of the world seemed to land on their feet. The Penny Franks, on the other hand, seemed to land on their heads.

"Hey, doesn't that P.I. guy that you're sleeping with drive a green car?" Marie asked.

Penny frowned. "Who said I was sleeping with him?"

"Oh, please."

Penny moved toward the window. "Do you see him?"

"He just drove up to the Victorian and got out. He's waiting for someone to come to the door."

Curious, Penny grabbed her mini binoculars and peeked through the blinds, a sense of déjà vu settling over her to see B.J. standing on the porch, waiting for the door to be opened. She frowned. What could he be doing at Sheena's?

As she watched, the door opened, and Sheena appeared in a sexy, gauzy getup. Penny rolled her eyes—the woman's tailbone was broken and she still couldn't help herself. They appeared to be talking rather seriously, then suddenly B.J. removed something from beneath his coat and handed it to Sheena. If not for the color, Penny might not have recognized the lime green stiletto that she'd dug out from under her hip when she'd ridden in his car.

Wonder how long that's been there?

Behind the binoculars her eyes stung—it was Sheena's? He'd been her lover all along?

Then B.J. handed Sheena another item—a black videotape.

Penny stepped back from the blinds as if she'd been slapped. Hurt and betrayal washed over her. Had he been working for Sheena all this time? Was there something on the tape that would help Sheena in some way? More disturbing thoughts battered her. B.J. had been at Caskey's the night of the murder—it would have been easy for him to have placed the voodoo doll on the table for Sheena, especially since Penny had made such a fool out of herself falling for his charm.

Her heart hammered. B.J. could have killed Deke for Sheena . . . B.J. carried a gun—he could have shot at her while she was running, then gone back and dug out the slug under the guise of warning her. B.J. could have planted the snake in her apartment—he'd certainly killed it handily enough. B.J. knew every little incriminating thing about her. Would he testify against her? And wasn't she the biggest fool ever born to think that he had actually cared about her?

"Penny?" Marie asked. "Are you okay?"

"I'll be in my office," she managed to get out. She closed the door and leaned against it, tingling with shame. What about her made her such an easy target for deceitful men? Did she reek of desperation? Did she emit vibes of gullibility? On her desk, her cell phone rang, and Gloria Dalton's number came up.

Penny steeled herself, then flipped down the mouthpiece. "Hello?"

"Penny," Gloria said, her voice breaking. "The D.A. just issued a warrant for your arrest."

Penny closed her eyes as fear filled every cell of her body. "How long do I have?"

"Maybe thirty minutes. Do you have that list of attorneys I gave you?"

"Yes, thank you, Gloria, you've been wonderful during all of this."

"I'm not going anywhere," Gloria said. "We'll see this through, okay?"

"Okay," Penny said, feeling guilty for dragging the woman into the mess, then disconnected the call. She locked her office door and withdrew the little gold key for the secured desk drawer.

She slid it open and gazed upon bag after bag of Boulder Potato Company Malt Vinegar & Sea Salt potato chips. She tore into one bag and placed a mouth-sized chip on her tongue, flinching when the sharp tang of vinegar hit her taste buds. She pressed the chip against the roof of her mouth, breaking it into tiny pieces to release all the pent-up taste. Then she chewed slowly and swallowed, flush with pleasure. She always ate the first bag that way.

The second bag, she lined up the chips on her desk and ate them by size, stacked in little sandwiches of three or four. The crunch was intense, and the tart rush of flavor made her mouth pucker.

For the third bag, all bets were off—she crammed in as many as she could get into her mouth. By now, her tongue was raw from the sea salt, but that didn't keep her from licking her fingers to get every last grain out of the corners of the bag.

Forget black truffles—she'd take these fat- and salt-laden delicacies over any kind of fancy fungus.

Suddenly Penny froze, her finger in her mouth, as a thought slid into her head so solitarily brilliant that she could almost hear the gonging noise in her brain. The blending of two memories . . . of Jimmy Scaggs saying that his beloved and valuable truffle-hunting dog Henry was out of commission, and of Deke's crumpled front bumper.

She could still hear the squeal of tires as Deke had pulled away from the museum Friday morning, driving like a teenager. Henry had escaped from the truck bed once that morning—what if Henry had gotten loose on the road? What if Deke had hit the dog, maybe killed it, and driven on? What if Jimmy had seen it all? Would he have killed Deke over his dog?

Penny swallowed the last salty bite. Yep.

A knock sounded on the door. "Penny?" Marie's voice quavered. "Detective Maynard and Chief Davis are here to see you."

She jumped up and stuffed the crackly, empty potato chip bags in the trash can, then licked her fingers before wiping them on her jeans. She flung open the door to see Allyson, Detective Maynard, and two uniformed New Orleans police officers.

"Penny Francisco," Detective Maynard began.

"Wait," she said, holding up her greasy hands stop-sign fashion. "I know who killed Deke."

Allyson Davis cursed. "So do we—*you.*"

"No," she said, then looked at Detective Maynard. "Please—hear me out. Just walk across the street with me. If you don't find on the bumper of Deke's car what I think you'll find, then you can arrest me."

"This is bullshit," Allyson said.

"Please," Penny said to Detective Maynard. "It'll take only a few minutes. This is my life we're talking about."

The man wavered.

"Please?"

Then he sighed. "Okay, Ms. Francisco, you've got ten minutes for your little field trip."

"Follow me." She jogged past them, then outside, where she bounded across the street to the pink Victorian. B.J. and Sheena were still on the porch and pivoted their heads as the entourage of Penny, Detective Maynard, Chief Davis, the two officers, Marie, and Guy came onto the property.

"What's going on here?" Sheena shouted from the porch.

B.J. squinted at Penny and lifted his hands in question.

"Tell her to open the garage," Penny said to Detective Maynard.

He sighed. "Open the garage, Ms. Linder."

"Why?" Sheena shouted.

"Just do it," he said in a tired voice.

B.J. left the porch and joined them in front of the garage. "What's going on?" he whispered.

"I have a theory," she said, still smarting over his obvious lies about Sheena.

"What kind of theory?"

"Just watch."

Sheena returned with the remote control opener and pushed a button. The double garage door rose slowly, and Penny was thankful that Deke liked to back in when he parked. His crumpled bumper shone beautifully in the sun.

"Now what?" Maynard asked.

"Check the bumper," she said. "See if you find any blood or fur."

"Fur?" Maynard said.

"Fur," she repeated.

Maynard crouched down, then craned his neck and squinted. "There's something . . ." He pulled out a penknife and scraped at it. "It's blood, I think."

Penny's heartbeat picked up.

Then he removed a small plastic bag and scraped something into it. "And . . . looks like fur. Reddish—maybe a dog?"

She nodded. "Bloodhound."

"So?" Allyson asked, clearly inconvenienced.

Maynard was quiet, but his arched eyebrows echoed the chief's question.

Remorse pulsed through her for the information that she possessed and whom it would hurt. Jimmy Scaggs had offered to give her an alibi for Deke's murder . . . because he had actually committed the murder. She didn't want to believe that the oddly gentle man could do something so heinous, but it all made horrific sense.

"Penny," Allyson prompted, "we don't have all day."

Penny closed her eyes briefly, then sighed. "I think that Deke hit Jimmy Scaggs's dog, maybe killed him, sometime Friday, and Jimmy went to Deke's Friday night for retribution."

"Over a dog?" Maynard asked.

"It's a very valuable dog," she assured him.

Maynard looked at Allyson. "Do you know this Scaggs character?"

"Yeah, but I don't think—"

"Let's bring him in," Maynard said. "I want to see where this takes us." Then he looked at Penny. "You're coming with us, too . . . just in case your theory backfires."

29

Beware of a missing ingredient . . .

Penny and B.J. sat alone in an interview room at the police station while Jimmy Scaggs was being questioned in another part of the station. Gluey silence stretched between them. Penny wasn't even sure why B.J. had come with her.

"That was good thinking back there," he finally said.

She lifted her eyebrows. "Thanks."

"So what is it that this bloodhound hunts that makes him so valuable?"

"I'm not at liberty to say."

"You're angry."

"What?"

"You want to know why I was talking to Sheena Linder."

"That's none of my business," she said, studying her nails.

"It's not what you think," he said.

"Oh? What else could it be if the woman's *shoe* is in your car?"

He blanched.

"I saw you give it to her," she said.

"You were spying?"

"No. I just happened to be looking out the window." With her binoculars. She frowned. "I saw you give her the videotape, too."

His eyebrows went up, then he pursed his mouth. "And what do you suppose that means?"

Penny crossed her arms. "That you're . . . working for Sheena."

"I am?"

"Yeah." She narrowed her eyes. "What else could it be?"

"I'm not at liberty to say."

"Good."

"Good."

The door opened and Detective Maynard walked in. "You were right, Ms. Francisco. Mr. Black apparently hit the dog and kept going. Jimmy Scaggs just admitted to going to Mr. Black's residence Friday night, arguing, then hitting him over the head with the cane. That's backed up by some partial fingerprints we found on the cane."

Penny winced. "How's the dog?"

"Scaggs said he almost died, but he's improved in the last couple of days."

"What about the garden stake?" B.J. asked.

"He says he doesn't remember doing it," Maynard said. "But he admits that he probably did. Seems like the man had a pretty low opinion of Mr. Black to begin with, and a pretty fair crush on Ms. Francisco, so the hit-and-run probably just pushed him over the edge." He clapped his hands. "Looks like we got us a solved case."

She went limp with relief.

"I'm sorry, Ms. Francisco, for the anguish you've gone through. Please accept our apology on behalf of both police departments. I hope you know that we were only trying to do our jobs."

She nodded thoughtfully, relieved beyond words to be off the hook for Deke's murder, but grief-stricken by the knowledge that Deke had lost his life because he'd been a bad driver and a jerk, and now Jimmy would likely spend a good chunk of the rest of his life in prison. "I owe Jimmy some money, if he needs to make bail. And if he needs a character witness, please let me know."

B.J. frowned and scratched his head. "So Scaggs copped to the voodoo doll?"

"No, but that's probably just a coincidence, whipped out of proportion because of this voodoo festival going on," Maynard said. "One of Ms. Francisco's friends probably brought it, and now is afraid to admit it because of what happened."

B.J. nodded slowly. "I guess you're right. If Scaggs had a crush on Penny, he wouldn't have been trying to frame her."

"Right," Maynard said. "Ms. Francisco, you're free to go."

Penny and B.J. walked outside, and she breathed in the cool air as deeply as possible, then exhaled noisily. "God, what a week."

"Yeah," he said. "Seems longer, doesn't it?"

She nodded and smiled at him, glad it was ending this way, on a friendly note. "Did you ever hear back on the hair you found at the museum?"

"Not yet."

She gave a little laugh. "We were really letting our imaginations run away, weren't we?"

"Yeah."

"I guess that's what happens when you want something to be true so badly—you make up the middle."

He met her gaze. "So true."

"I hope you find those missing women."

"Me, too," he said, then his eyes turned pensive. "But meanwhile, I'm glad I found you." He leaned forward and gave her a kiss next to her ear. "It was fun."

"Yeah, it was," she said with a sunny smile, but inside she was heartbroken. She had been too needy last night, too . . . intimate. Intimacy scared men more than war. Still, she'd known from the beginning that B.J. Beaumont wasn't the settling down kind of guy, so it wasn't like she was surprised.

"We could still take in another afternoon of the festival," he said.

Tempting, but she'd binged enough for one day. "I think I've had enough voodoo to last me for a while," she said. "I might restake my garden—with surveyor's paint this time."

"Sounds . . . productive," he said. "Okay, well, I guess I'll see you around, Red."

"Sure. The next time you're in Mojo, look me up."

"I will," he said, then strode away, his step carefree.

"No, you won't," she murmured, watching him walk away. "But I'll never forget you."

Her cell phone rang, and Gloria Dalton's number popped up. "Hello, Gloria? Did you hear the good news?"

"The D.A. called me," Gloria said, her voice sounding strained. "How frightening is it to think that the wrong person was almost prosecuted for Deke's murder?"

"Pretty frightening when it's me," Penny admitted.

"So, um, the D.A. mentioned he might have a place for me on his staff."

Penny smiled into the phone. "Criminal law? Are you considering it?"

"I'm considering it," Gloria said. "It's certainly more exciting than family and divorce law, and I'm looking for a change."

"Keep me posted?"

"Absolutely. Oh, and Penny, I kept forgetting to tell you. I ran a background check on that P.I. that Chief Davis was so suspicious of, Baron Jeffrey Beaumont."

Baron Jeffrey? "Yes?" Penny said, her pulse clicking higher. She could still see him in the distance. Was he a con man? Criminal? Fugitive?

"He's legit. And he works pro bono."

Penny frowned. "What? How does he make a living?"

"He already did that—made a small fortune in the dotcom industry. He and his brother started an agency and take on missing persons cases. Sounds like a real stand-up guy."

Penny closed her eyes briefly, her heart aching. "Yeah, sounds like it." She disconnected the call and watched him until he disappeared into the crowd.

30

Don't kill it all in one sitting . . .

When Penny returned to the store, she did restake her garden (with surveyor's fluorescent spray paint) and spent the rest of the afternoon stepping off what would go where. Mona and the city council would just have to get used to a cornfield in the city limits—she would break ground next week. She noticed that the opening in the fence was still wired shut and wondered if she should talk to Hazel or Troy about having a stone path from her parking lot to the museum. It seemed silly to have such rigid fences between businesses that thrived on the same type of customer.

She took off her gloves and stretched her back. In the distance, she heard the ceremonial drums in the *peristil* pounding the slow, monklike rhythm and chant of their closing ceremony. She shivered. Even from here, it sounded like a death march.

Deke would never be more than a few seconds from her mind, she realized. And she would forever mourn the emotional distance she had maintained in her marriage that blinded her to Deke's dark tendencies. But she would have to accept his untimely death just as she had accepted her father's. The alternative was madness.

She turned back to the Archambault mansion, and a movement caught her eye . . . in the cupola, like before. It had to be a bat. But the longer she stared, the more focused the image became. It was too big to be a bat. Perhaps an eagle or a vulture had made a nest? She pulled out her binoculars and tried to find the image among the foliage. There. She focused on the object . . . and nearly swallowed her tongue—a hand? A hand extending from the cupola, waving a red cloth. Penny looked at her watch. The museum was closed for the day. Had someone accidentally been locked in?

She lowered the binoculars as another, darker thought came to mind—or was someone being held against their will? She pulled out her cell phone only to find the battery dead. Penny looked back over the distance to the shop, biting her lip in uncertainty. What if she raised an alarm and it turned out to be a cleaning lady?

She raised the binoculars again, but saw nothing. Was her mind playing tricks on her? She toyed with the idea of returning to call B.J., but he would be back in the city by now, and besides, she would mostly be calling because she missed him.

No, for time's sake, and the fading light, she'd investigate alone. She decided she couldn't scale the tall fence without risk of impaling herself on one of the spikes on top, so she went back to the original opening in the fence she had discovered under all the foliage. With pruning shears from her garden tool belt, she hacked at the repair wire. She made it through with only a few scratches but realized she might need some of her tools, so she squeezed back through, quickly picked through the more useful implements, then tossed her tool belt over the fence, and squeezed through again. By now she was bleeding, but adrenaline kept her moving forward. Darkness had fallen quickly, and here among the trees, the air was as black as India ink. Her old phobia nagged at her—the boogey man came out after dark, along with other, more tangible evils. If she hadn't traveled this path so many times, she wouldn't have been able to find her way. Finally she burst through the foliage and onto the path that ran alongside the house, where she had run into Deke only a few days ago.

In her mind, she was plotting the quickest way to the cupola. She had been there once, years ago, before it was boarded up. Hazel had allowed her to go up and look out over the town, but the structure had been crumbling even then. Penny reasoned that the lower-level windows would have security alarms, but she remembered a second-story window that she might be able to climb to if only she had a flashlight.

Then she realized she was wearing the black coat she'd been wearing when she and B.J. had explored the pink Victorian. She shoved her hand in her pocket and was almost giddy to find the penlight that B.J. had given her. She strapped on the garden tool belt, and, holding the penlight in her mouth, she did a chin up (thank you, Pilates) to pull herself up to sit on the windowsill, holding her breath while she tried to raise it. It wouldn't budge; with the penlight, she could see that the closure on the inside was secure. But one of the panes was loose, and after a bit of pressure, she was able to slip it out, then reach in and open the window from the inside.

She was in the animal exhibit room, she realized when she dropped to the floor. The stuffed and resin animals seemed more sinister in the dark, especially when her penlight made their eyes glow with a greenish cast. She took a few seconds to orient herself and calm her breathing, then she took a step toward the hallway. But she knocked over an animal, falling with it. In the process, she managed to trigger some kind of automatic recording of animals screeching and cawing, which blasted into the air. Panicked, she felt for an off button, and finally found an electrical cord, which she yanked from the wall. Suddenly, all was quiet again, except for the sound of her own labored breathing. And . . .

She closed her eyes so she could focus on the sound.

A faint pounding noise way above her, as if someone was . . . stomping their feet.

Spurred into action, she found the stairway to the third floor, then made her way up to the attic, through which the cupola was accessed. The attic door had been padlocked, but after several minutes of sawing, she was able to cut through it with a large pair of garden shears. The door led to a set of dusty stairs and up to an enormous room that was as big as the main part of the house. But the attic, like so much of the old mansion, had fallen into disrepair, and her penlight was becoming dim. She had taken only a couple of steps when the wood beneath her foot gave way and she fell through to her ankle. She cried out, but mostly in surprise. She freed herself, shed the weighty tool belt, shoved a small pair of shears into her coat pocket, and pressed forward, testing boards before putting her weight down.

When she reached the door that led to the cupola, she was met with another padlock. This one was thicker and would be harder for her to saw through with her small, dulled shears. She pounded on the door three times and put her ear up to it.

After a few seconds, she heard a distinct *thump, thump, thump*. She gasped—someone was there. The knowledge made her almost frantic to cut through the padlock. When the small shears were exhausted, she went back to get her tool belt and the larger shears, which made the trip back over the rotted floors more precarious. By the time she had cut through the padlock, her hands were blistered and bleeding. She swung open the door, her heart thudding in anticipation. The door opened into a cool blackness, a stone hallway of sorts that led to the cupola. The scurry of dozens of feet told her that many rats were about. She swallowed hard.

"My name is Penny," she said into the darkness. "I'm here to help you. Where are you?"

Muffled noises sounded, and she used the penlight to find her way, almost hysterical now. Suddenly she tripped over something and fell . . . onto a person. The penlight went flying. She cried out, and the person beneath her struggled, making muted sounds. Penny scrambled on her hands and knees to find the light and encountered at least another person before her hand closed around it. She was practically sobbing with fear by the time she clicked it on.

It illuminated the hollow-eyed face of a dark-haired woman, bound in chains and gagged. Next to her, a thin woman with white blond hair cowered against the wall. She was gagged and was bound by some kind of chained leash, like a dog run.

"Oh, my God," Penny breathed. "Oh, my God. Are you Jodi Reynolds?"

The woman's eyes widened, and she nodded frantically.

"People are looking for you," Penny said. "I'm going to get you out of here." She removed the tape and gags from their mouths, and the women began to weep.

"They've been holding us," Jodi croaked. "Torturing us . . ."

"Who did this to you?"

"We don't know—they wear masks." She broke down sobbing.

"Shh," Penny said, trembling. "Save your strength." *They wear masks.* She couldn't take the time to think about what these women had been through, or she wouldn't be able to think at all.

But one look at their chains and she knew she didn't have the tools to get them loose. "I have to go back and get help." Both women begged her not to go, but she had no choice. "I'll be back as soon as I can."

She ran as if the demons who had tortured the women were behind her. She pounded her way across the attic floor, splintering the wood. She ran down the attic stairs, then down to the third floor and to the second floor, stumbling and catching herself every few steps. Just as she reached the second floor, the penlight went out, plunging her into darkness.

She cried out in frustration.

"Need a light?"

Penny froze with terror because the voice was so

close, and so familiar. A flashlight came on, illuminating Allyson Davis's face, painted with dark, severe makeup.

"Penny, dear, do you know the fine for trespassing?"

Penny searched for her voice and found it down around her knees. "Allyson . . . what's going on?"

Allyson pursed her dark lips. "Didn't you see upstairs? We keep pets." She smiled. "Actually, we only keep the good ones. The bad ones . . . well, the bad ones are recycled."

"R-recycled?"

"Killed, dissected, chopped up, ground up, sold," she said, as if she were talking about pork sausage.

"S-sold?"

"Sure—we sell worldwide. The Internet is amazing."

Penny swallowed, rigid with horror when she realized that Allyson was completely insane. "Wh-who is we?"

"There are a few of us."

"Hazel?"

Allyson scoffed. "That deaf old granny? No way. We only keep her around because she can't hear enough to be suspicious. Deke was in our club for a while."

Penny felt sick. "Deke?"

Allyson sighed. "He liked the money, but he didn't have the stomach for it."

"Is . . . is that why he's dead?"

Allyson nodded. "Pretty much. And because he couldn't control you."

Penny's jaw loosened. *"Me?"*

"Yeah. We've been operating for years in isolation, and suddenly you move into the house next door, start clearing the property, breaking through the fence, sticking your nose in where it doesn't belong."

Penny's mind raced. That was why Deke had discouraged her from going into business, had been so vehemently opposed to the garden; it put her even closer to danger, and their group even closer to being discovered.

"We had some good times, Deke and I," Allyson said with a grin, then sobered. "But not while you two were married, Penny—I'm not an adulterer."

Penny's stomach rolled. *Just a sick sadist.*

"I was waiting for the right opportunity to get you both," Allyson said. "Kill Deke, frame you. I thought the voodoo festival would be a good time." She laughed. "I went to Deke's to give him a spanking, and he told me that Jimmy Scaggs had barged in, hit him on the head with the cane, and left."

"So . . . Jimmy didn't kill Deke."

"No. He just knocked him out." Then she smiled. "Just an appetizer, really. By the time I got there, Deke was in the mood for some real pain. I used that cane on every part of his naughty little body. He told me all his dirty little secrets, like how he'd cheated you in the property settlement. You'll be glad to know, Penny, that I thrashed him for that."

That explained the postmortem bruising that Maynard had mentioned. Penny struggled not to faint.

"Then I whacked him on the head and shoved one of your garden stakes through his chest. Don't you love the symbolism?"

Bile backed up in Penny's throat, gagging her.

"Deke told me that he had looked for his gun after Jimmy left, that he'd called you because he thought you'd know where it was. I had a feeling that you'd drop by . . . because you were still in love with Deke."

Penny shook her head.

"Sure you were," Allyson said, then laughed. "Love is nothing to be ashamed of, Penny." She licked her lips. "Deke died happy."

"The v-voodoo doll?"

"Coincidence." Then Allyson scoffed. "Come on, Penny—you don't really believe in voodoo, do you? We've made a fortune off the black magic freaks, selling them remains that they think will give them some sort of magical powers." She put her hand up to her mouth in a conspiratorial gesture. "Between you and me, they're just plain old cannibals. Sickos, if you ask me."

Apparently, it took one to know one.

Penny moistened her dry lips. "Why . . . why are you telling me this?"

Allyson looked confused. "Well, so you'll know what to expect, of course."

Ice cold terror set up in Penny's veins.

"Surely, you don't think I'm just going to let you go? You and your clever theory about Jimmy Scaggs and his half-baked confession ruined everything. This is actually a fortunate turn of events. Now you, Penny are going to just . . . disappear. There will be a note, some missing clothes, a suitcase gone from your closet." Allyson angled her head. "Well, it's not as if you have anyone to come looking for you, do you?"

Tears welled in Penny's eyes. On that account, the madwoman was correct.

Allyson raised a gun and pointed it at Penny's heart. "Let's go."

"Wh-where?"

"To the basement—that's where all the fun stuff is."

A bullet through the heart versus years of torture? Penny would have taken the former but for the fact that she was the only hope for the two women manacled upstairs. She made her feet move, keeping her eyes open for a way to escape. "Were you the person who shot at me?"

"Yes. Skinny bitch—you weren't a big enough target to hit."

When they reached the basement, Penny could almost feel Allyson's energy level rise. The woman turned on the lights, revealing her dominatrix garb of robe, corset, and boots.

"Take off your clothes."

"What?" Penny asked, horrified.

"Take. Off. Your. Clothes."

Trembling noticeably, Penny removed her clothing down to her panties and bra. Her mind reeled. She saw spots behind her eyes—what would the woman do to her if she fainted?

"That'll do," Allyson said, then gestured at the devices in the room. "What's your pleasure?"

A lump formed in Penny's throat, but she refused to cry—it would only play into the woman's sick fantasies. "You pick."

"Ooh, you're a pleaser," Allyson said. "I like that. Hm, how about the chair of nails? It's good for beginners."

Penny almost buckled, and out of the corner of her eye, she noticed a shadow on the stairwell. At first she was afraid it was more of Allyson's cronies, but then she realized that those people had no reason to be quiet. Hope billowed in her chest. She almost cried out.

"Why don't you turn on the sound track?" Penny asked. "It's too quiet."

Allyson smiled. "I know what you mean—there's

nothing like the sound of people screaming to put me in the right mood." She walked to a panel and flipped a button, turning up the volume until the sounds of screeching and agony vibrated to Penny's bones.

But it worked to mask the person's approach. Because on the stairs behind Allyson appeared a familiar set of boots, then faded jeans, then holey T-shirt and leather jacket, then B.J.'s face. He held his gun at the ready.

Penny used her peripheral vision because she didn't want to alert Allyson to his presence, but it was hard to hold back the tears of relief . . . and fear. Allyson would think nothing of shooting B.J. And Penny was sure that that was one death she would not be able to withstand.

"Come here," Allyson said, nodding to the chair.

Penny surveyed the sharp tips of the six-inch nails set into the seat of the chair at quarter-inch intervals, and swallowed. "Do you think you can put the gun down to help me into the chair?"

Allyson smiled. "Only if you promise to behave."

"Where would I go?"

"True." Allyson set down the gun, then beckoned her forward.

Penny moved slowly to give B.J. time to advance.

"Now it's important that you get into the chair very easily," Allyson said, then smiled. "We don't want a lot of blood the first time."

B.J. put his gun to the back of Allyson's head and shouted over the sound track, "Freeze or I'll blow your head off!"

Allyson went rigid with surprise, her painted mouth rounded. Then she cursed violently under her breath and put up her hands. "I prefer the giving end of pain over the receiving end." She rolled her eyes at Penny. "I knew this guy was going to be trouble the minute I saw him."

Quaking with relief, Penny ran to turn off the sound track. By the time she came back, B.J. had handcuffed Allyson and bound her ankles with a cable tie, all of which she seemed to enjoy. He turned to Penny, and she fell into him, sobbing.

"Are you okay?" he asked fiercely, covering her with his coat. "God, I was terrified of what I would find."

"How . . . did you . . . know?"

"The DNA results came back—the hair belonged to Jodi Reynolds."

"She's being held upstairs, with another woman."

He nodded. "I brought a team of people with me. They're swarming the entire building and grounds."

"They've done horrible things," Penny said, choking.

"I know," he said. "Some of that crushed bones mixture they're selling is human bones."

"Premium product at a premium price," Allyson said.

B.J. pointed his gun at her. "If you say another word, I will shoot you, do you understand?"

Allyson nodded meekly.

He looked back to Penny and his jaw hardened. "Did she kidnap you?"

"No. One of the women being held managed to get to the cupola and wave a rag. I saw it from my garden and . . . came to investigate."

He frowned. "Why didn't you call someone?"

She smirked, her energy returning. "A lot of good it would have done to call the police."

He leaned his head closer. "Why didn't you call *me?*"

A hot flush made its way up her neck. Because it was the first thing she'd thought of, and the instinctual response had spooked her. "I . . ."

"It's okay," he said gently. "You don't have to explain. What matters is that you're okay. When we found the opening in the gate, and the tools you'd left behind . . . I thought the worst."

"I was . . . terrified," she admitted, still reeling over what could have happened and no one would have been the wiser. "Thank you, B.J., for . . . coming when you did."

He bit into his lip, then winked. "Get dressed, babe. This nightmare is over."

31

If the recipe is a success, pass it on . . .

Marie and Penny sat at the juice counter and watched as the voodoo festival banner that had been stretched across Charm Street was taken down.

"This town will never be the same," Marie said, sipping from her juice glass.

"So true," Penny said. And neither would she.

"Do you think they'll have the festival next year?"

"I don't know." The fact that Allyson and her little club had been using the festival as a way to attract victims and to fence their gruesome contraband wasn't exactly Chamber of Commerce ad copy.

"I can't believe that Jodi Reynolds is Sheena's sister."

Penny nodded. "Apparently, Sheena changed her name when she was a teenager and moved away from her family. Jodi came to Mojo looking for her."

"And was kidnapped and tortured." Marie shook her head. "I just can't believe this was happening in a town like Mojo."

It was national news. The little town famous for its Instruments of Death and Voodoo Museum was now infamous for the things that had gone on within the museum's walls. The governor was sending a task force to have the entire house analyzed for any DNA that could be linked to open missing persons cases.

"And Sheena Linder is really Ruth Reynolds. Wow, I would never change my name—would you?"

A little smile curved Penny's mouth. "I certainly understand why some people do it."

Jodi was the reason B.J. had stopped at Sheena's house the first day Penny had seen him. He'd asked Sheena if she was Ruth Reynolds, and she'd slammed the door in his face. The next time, he'd gone back with personal items of Jodi's that her grandmother had given him—a pair of shoes that Sheena had sent to her sister and a videotape of Jodi's graduation, to try to soften Sheena and convince her that Jodi might have been in the vicinity of Mojo when she'd disappeared. Sheena had been afraid that Deke might discover her history and had shunned the cameras so that no one from her past would recognize her. But the sisters were together now, and from what Penny had heard, Sheena was a changed woman. Indeed, she had changed her mind about suing Penny for the broken tailbone when she'd learned that Penny was the person who had rescued her sister from the Torture Tower, as it was being called. And more surprisingly, Sheena had handed over all the documentation on the assets that Deke had hidden during the property settlement.

Penny squinted. Maybe there was the possibility that she and the woman would become friends. Then she made a rueful noise. Nah.

The only glitch in the case was that Allyson Davis wasn't giving up other members of the "club," so for now, she and Dr. Troy Archambault were the only people being charged, and Troy had abjectly denied knowledge of the cadaver enterprise that was being run out of his family's former mansion. Jodi Reynolds and the other woman, Giselle Taylor, told of unspeakable acts on up to a dozen people they had been held with and who had subsequently "disappeared." Penny wondered if Mona was somehow involved, but she would leave the rest of the detective work to the police. Still, it was odd that Mona had withdrawn her opposition to Penny's garden.

Jimmy Scaggs had been freed, and the last Penny heard, Henry would be well enough by next year to hunt the bumper crop of black truffles that Jimmy was expecting. Diane Davidson had taken care of Henry while Jimmy had been incarcerated, and the couple had been seen around town together. Admittedly, they seemed like a good fit.

Although what did Penny know about relationships?

"So, who made the Deke voodoo doll?" Marie asked.

"I don't know . . . we may never know." Although Penny had someone in mind.

Guy walked through the showroom wearing a John Deere ball cap and a camouflage shirt, a la Jimmy Scaggs. But the look was somehow compromised by the pink iPod clipped to his military belt.

"Some mysteries will never be solved," Marie muttered.

Penny smiled. "Did you hear that Gloria Dalton is moving to Mojo?"

"Your divorce attorney?"

"Yeah. She's decided to turn down the D.A.'s job offer and take over Deke's practice."

"Think she can make it in a small town?"

"We'll see."

"Guess we're going to be getting a new chief of police."

"Looks like it," Penny said, shuddering. Allyson Davis's depravity was almost inconceivable.

"Are you going to sell your story?" Marie asked. "You are the bravest person I know."

"Save all your admiration for the cops and investigators who exhaust every lead to find a missing person. I just happened to be in the right garden at the right time."

"Speaking of investigators, have you seen B.J.?"

Penny's heart gave a little tug every time she heard his name. "Not since the day of the bust at the museum." It had been traumatic for both of them. Emotions had been running high . . . too high for any rational conversation. "I've talked to him on the phone a couple of times—sounds like he's very busy with all the sudden attention his agency is getting."

"He looks like that *and* he's filthy rich," Marie said dreamily. "He's too good to be true."

"Kind of like Kirk?" Penny asked, taking a sip from her glass, but Marie suddenly seemed fascinated by her cuticles.

The door chime sounded and Jules walked in, seemingly light on her feet this morning, swinging her walking stick.

"Good morning, Jules," they said in unison.

"*Bonjour*, ladies," Jules sang, her voice strong. "I came for my morning elixir."

"Coming right up," Marie said.

"How are you doing this morning, Jules?"

"Right as rain," the old woman said. "How about you?"

Penny thought about it, then nodded. "I'm good, actually."

Jules pointed her finger. "Take care of your unfinished business and you'll feel better."

Marie looked at Penny and lifted her eyebrows.

Penny leaned into the counter. "Jules . . . you wouldn't happen to know anything about a voodoo doll made in the likeness of my ex-husband, would you?"

Jules pursed her wrinkled mouth and shook her head. "Not me."

"Or a little red toy car?"

"Nope."

"Someone breaking into my apartment and cleaning?"

"Nope."

"A snake in my bed?"

"Nope. Although I believe I warned you about a serpent being underfoot."

Penny frowned. "What about Deke's coffin falling?"

"Nope."

"Hm," Penny said, studying the woman intently. "I guess it was all just coincidence."

"Nothing is coincidence," Jules said. "Things happen because you want them to happen—"

"Or because they need to happen," Penny finished.

"Right," Jules said. "So maybe those things happened to help you figure out the puzzle of your life."

Penny narrowed her eyes. Figure out the puzzle—like when she hadn't taken the hint of letting the crumpled toy car lead her to Deke's car, the coffin had been compromised as a second hint? Like if Allyson hadn't used a garden stake to frame Penny, Penny might not have been restaking her garden at just the right moment to see the distress signal from the cupola? And wasn't she in a better, calmer place now than at any other point in her life?

"Excuse me," Penny said, then went to her office where she paced for a few minutes, practicing deep breathing techniques. Finally, she picked up the phone and dialed. As the rings mounted, she wiped her clammy hands on her jeans.

"Cumberland Federal Women's Facility."

"Hi," Penny said. "I . . . I'd like to arrange a phone call with an inmate, please. Anita Frank."

"I'll need the inmate number and date of birth."

Penny recited the information.

"And what is your name?"

She closed her eyes briefly. "Just tell her it's Penny."

"And when should I tell the inmate you would like to arrange the call?"

Penny wet her lips. "As soon as possible, please."

Penny was given instructions on when to call back for a response, and she hung up, feeling as if a weight had been lifted from her shoulders. If her mother didn't want to communicate, that would be her problem . . . but at least Penny could rest in the knowledge that she'd done everything to make an effort to forge some kind of relationship.

She picked up a bag from her desk, then walked out into the showroom. "If anyone needs me, I'll be in the garden."

She walked outside, thinking how quickly the weather

changed this time of year. Cool and dry, it was great for late fall planting. She looked over the expanse of the newly tilled black soil and sighed with pleasure. This time next year her garden should be yielding produce every single day. She expected to hire more people, attract new commercial business, and become a mainstay for the community. She bit her lip as she stared at the roof of the Archambault mansion. She only hoped the town would be able to compensate for the tourist dollars it would lose while the museum was shut down—especially if it never reopened. And until the full extent of the torture and cadaver ring was revealed, everyone in Mojo would look at their friends and neighbors a little differently.

Then she inhaled deeply and expelled a cleansing exhale. No matter what the future brought, she was going to embrace it. She picked a nice fresh spot of dirt near the end of the plot and crouched down, running her fingers through the fertile soil.

The Charm Kit to Bury the Past instructed her to place items representing situations that she wanted to be reconciled in her life in a burlap bag (with the aromatic packet provided). She had selected a picture of her and her brothers when they were little, her father's pipe, a single earring that her mother had given her when she was little to play dress up, the letter that Wendy had written apologizing for her affair with Deke, the pewter lovebirds ornament that said Deke and Penny, forever, and a packet of vitamins. Satisfied with her assembly, she put the items in the bag as instructed, then dug a hole as deep as she could with her hands and buried it with handfuls of black soil, repeating positive mantras like, "The past is gone, the only thing I can change is the future."

Maybe voodoo and magic were just a figment of one's imagination, but if the belief brought peace, what was the harm? Afterward, she stood, content with where she was headed with her life, resolute to mend broken relationships where possible . . . and ever hopeful for a strong relationship with a loving man.

"Hello."

Penny turned to see B.J. walking toward her on the perimeter of the garden. Her heart, frivolous thing, starting beating wildly. "Hello," she managed in a relatively calm voice.

"Looks nice," he said, nodding toward the cleared land that went up to the fence around the Archambault mansion.

"Thanks, I'm really happy with it."

He smiled. "Good. I like to see you happy." His mouth turned down suddenly. "I can't stop thinking about what might have happened if I hadn't gotten there when I did."

She turned to face him. "But you did get there . . . and I'm fine." She smiled.

"I would have looked for you," he said suddenly.

She frowned. "Hm?"

"I was listening to the conversation between you and Allyson before you walked down to the basement. I wasn't in position to get to you, but I heard . . ." He looked up. "I heard what she said about you not having anyone who would look for you if you disappeared, and I wanted you to know that . . . I would've looked for you. And I wouldn't have stopped looking until I found you."

Tears welled in her eyes—he couldn't possibly know what those words meant to her. She didn't know what to say, didn't want him to think that she thought it meant he was in love with her. "Thank you," she said.

He cleared his throat and looked out over the garden again, this time gesturing. "This isn't going to work."

Proud of her garden, she bristled. "Why not?"

"Because I was just asked to lead the task force that the governor is sending to the museum to try to solve open missing persons cases."

She gasped, uncaring if her feelings for him were too obvious. "You'll be working in Mojo?"

"And living." He grinned sheepishly. "I realize that I have to be near you, or I'm never going to get any work done."

Her heart took flight, but she reined it back in. "What does that have to do with my garden?"

"I don't plan to walk all the way around every time I want to see you," he said, pointing toward the fence. "So I was thinking if we put in a gate right about there, it would make life easier." Then he shrugged. "If you want."

She leaped into his arms and kissed him with all the pent-up energy of missing him, wanting him, and needing him. When they pulled back, they were both flushed, and she was anticipating being in his arms tonight.

"I love you, Penny." His voice was full of wonder, as if he himself were surprised. "I think you worked some voodoo on me."

"I love you, too, Baron Jeffrey." At his surprised expression, she laughed. "You're not the only one who can investigate." She pressed her face into his shirt, so happy she was afraid to move.

"Hey, did you know that if you crumble up a bag of Frito's in tofu, it's not half bad?"

She laughed. "That kind of defeats the purpose."

"Hey, I'm trying to learn to compromise. But that means you have to eat a bag of potato chips occasionally."

She thought of the stash in her desk drawer and grinned. "I can do that."

They walked over the garden holding hands. And Penny . . . she was showing a lot of gum.

Can Gloria adjust
to being a small-town attorney?
What handsome devil in Mojo
suddenly needs an attorney?
Is Mona really a voodoo priestess?
Does Marie really have ESP?
Is Kirk a real person?
Is Steve a real cad?
Who is making voodoo dolls
of local residents?
Will Jimmy ever take a bath?
Who will Sheena sue next?
Is Guy really gay?
Will the end of the voodoo museum
mean the end of Mojo?

Look for

VOODOO OR DIE

from Stephanie Bond and
Avon Books in 2006!

The first sign a man is into you

He gets nervous at the thought of being around you!

In Jacquie D'Alessandro's September 2005 release, *Not Quite a Gentleman*, Nathan Oliver, the youngest son of an earl, comes face-to-face with the arrival of Lady Victoria Wexhall. On the surface they have *nothing* in common: he's content as a country doctor; she's considerably put-out at having to leave fashionable London Society for some pretty scenery and farm animals. But then she can't help but notice Nathan's strong arms and tempting ways . . .

Colin waved his hand in a dismissive gesture. "Perhaps it was a table in the drawing room. How did Lord Wexhall put it in his letter? Oh, yes. 'I expect you to take care of Victoria and see that no harm comes to her,' " he recited in a sonorous voice. "I wonder what sort of harm he believes might befall her?"

"Probably thinks she'll wander off and fall from a cliff. Or overspend in the village shops."

Colin cocked an eloquent brow. "Perhaps. Note how he said *you*. Note how I was not mentioned *at all*. The chit is completely *your* responsibility. Of course, if she's as lovely as I recall, I perhaps could be persuaded to assist you in looking after her."

Nathan blamed the heat that scorched him on the unseasonably warm afternoon. Bloody hell, this conversation was bringing on the headache. "Excellent. Allow me to persuade you. I'll give you one hundred pounds if you'll watch over her," Nathan offered in a light tone completely at odds with the tension consuming him.

"No."

"Five hundred."

"No."

"A *thousand* pounds."

"Absolutely not." Colin grinned. "For starters, given the fact that you're routinely paid with farm beasts, I doubt that you have a thousand pounds, and unlike you, I've no wish to be paid with things that make 'mooing' sounds. Then, no amount of money would be worth giving up seeing you do something you so clearly do not wish to do, as in acting as caretaker to a woman you think is a spoiled, irritating twit."

"Ah, yes, the reasons I stayed away for three years all come rushing back."

"In fact," Colin continued as if Nathan hadn't spoken, "I'll give *you* a hundred pounds—in actual currency—if you're able to carry out your duty to Lady Victoria without me witnessing you fighting with her."

Well accustomed to Colin's tricky nature, Nathan said, "Define fighting."

"Arguing. Exchanging words in a heated manner. Verbal altercations. I'm assuming you would not enter into any physical altercations."

"I've no intention of getting within ten feet of her," Nathan said, meaning every word.

"Probably for the best. She's unmarried, you know."

He stilled. No, he hadn't known. Not that it mattered. He shrugged. "Can't say as I'm surprised. I pity the poor bastard who finds himself leg-shackled to that puffed-up bit of talkative goods."

The second sign a man is into you

His mission is to tempt you to leave your own party!

In Stephanie Bond's October 2005 release, *In Deep Voodoo*, Penny finds herself with a deadbeat ex-husband who soon turns into a dead ex-husband! Some people think that she's to blame, and it sure seems like she's being followed by a handsome, rough-around-the-edges, but oh-so-sexy P.I. But does he want to apprehend her for the crime—or capture her for his own pleasure?

"Is this a private conversation, or can anyone join in?"

She swung her head around and the mystery man was standing there, holding a bottle of beer. And he was still breathtakingly sexy . . . all muscles and male, leather and Levi's.

"I, uh . . ." Her brain was pickled.

He looked at the flyer she'd been studying. "Do you know her?" His smooth Cajun cadence was like a down pillow for her ears.

"No. I was just . . . wondering what might have happened to her."

He took a drink from the bottle, still reading. "Looks like a good kid, I hope she's found safe."

"Or not."

He arched one eyebrow. "You hope she isn't found?"

Penny shrugged. "She's seventeen. Maybe she doesn't want to be found."

He pursed his mouth. "Is that the voice of personal experience? Do you have secrets, Penny?"

Her mouth went dry as his gaze bored into hers. One minute in and he was already too close for comfort. "No," she croaked.

"Ah. So it's the cynicism of someone newly divorced." He grinned and took another drink. "You left your own party?"

"I just stepped out for a few minutes."

"I'm ready to leave, too. So why don't we leave together?"

She blinked, wondering if she'd misheard him, but the sexy glint in his eyes and the curve of his mouth was unmistakable—he wanted to get busy . . . with her. A tug on her midsection answered his call, and her breasts tingled, but her good-girl training kicked in. "I don't even know your name."

"It's B.J.," he said. "And don't worry—I'm not a serial killer."

She smirked. "I'll bet that's what all the serial killers say."

He laughed, a pleasant noise that stroked her curiosity. "I promise that as long as you're with me, nothing will ever happen to you . . . that you don't want to happen."

She swallowed hard. Strangely, she believed him, trusted him . . . with her body anyway.

He leaned forward. "You smell good."

"Thanks . . . it's, um, almond oil."

"Really? Smells like doughnuts."

She pushed her tongue into her cheek. She had to find a new place to live.

erly settle you. She probably meant to come back and finish with you after, but forgot."

Greg didn't have a clue what she was talking about, except that she seemed to think her mother had brought him here and he was positive she was wrong. "The woman who brought me here was too young to be your mother. She looked like you but had dark hair. Your sister maybe?" he guessed.

For some reason his words made her smile. "I don't have a sister. The woman you're describing is my mother. She's older than she looks."

Greg accepted this with some incredulity, then his eyes widened at the ramifications of what she was saying. "Then, I'm *your* birthday gift?"

She nodded slowly, then tilted her head and said, "That's an odd smile. What are you thinking?"

Greg was thinking he was the luckiest son of a bitch alive as his mind automatically readjusted his earlier imaginings of a large, ugly woman stripping and climbing on top of him, to this woman doing so. He allowed himself to enjoy the fantasy for a moment, but then realized that his body was enjoying it way too much, a noticeable bulge growing in his pants. He gave his head a shake. As delightful as a night as this woman's sex slave might be, he had plans: a trip full of sandy beaches, palm trees and half naked women gyrating on a dance floor. And it was already paid for.

Now if after his trip this woman wanted to go on a date in the normal way, then tie him to a bed and have her way with him . . . Well, Greg liked to consider himself an obliging sort. Besides, in this case, he thought being a sex slave might not be so bad. Realizing his thoughts were wandering into areas better left alone, Greg gave himself a mental kick and forced a stern look onto his face. "Kidnapping is illegal."

Her eyebrows rose. "Did Mom kidnap you?"

"Not exactly," he admitted, recalling how he'd climbed into the trunk under his own impetus. Kidnapping generally required being forcibly taken away. Greg supposed he could have lied, however, he was a poor liar. "But I don't want to be here, and really I don't have any idea why I climbed into the trunk of your mother's car. It seemed the most natural thing to do at the time, but I've never . . ."

Greg's voice trailed away as he realized that the blonde wasn't listening to him. At least, she didn't appear to be. She was staring at his head with concentration and a deepening frown. She was also moving closer to the bed, though he suspected it was a subconscious action. She seemed wholly concentrated on his hair, but then she shook her head with apparent frustration and muttered, "I can't read your mind."

"You can't read my mind?" Greg echoed slowly.

She shook her head.

"I see . . . and . . . er . . . is that a problem?" he queried. "I mean, can you usually read people's minds?"

She nodded, but it was an absent action; her thoughts were obviously elsewhere.

Greg tried to ignore the disappointment suddenly pinching at him as he acknowledged that the woman was mad, or at least delusional, if she thought she could read minds. He supposed he shouldn't be surprised. The mother couldn't exactly be normal or she wouldn't allow strange men to climb into her trunk—for she'd been behind him and had to have seen him climb in. Anyone else would have run screaming for building security instead of taking him home.

He bowed. "Miss Witfeld. Pleased to meet you."

Caroline Witfeld nodded back at him. "I advise you to save the bowing till the end, or you'll end up dizzy," she returned in a low, amused voice. Since her mother had moved on to the next daughter, he was probably the only one who'd heard it.

"Susan," the matriarch was saying as she traveled down the line, "then the twins Joanna and Julia. Grace is just eighteen. The youngest are Anne and then Violet."

Zachary shook Harold, the dog, off his foot, waited a moment to be certain Mrs. Witfeld was finished with the introductions, then bowed again. "It's good to meet all of you," he said, glancing again at the oldest girl, who seemed to have forgotten her wit of a moment ago and was now staring at his left hand. He experimentally wiggled his fingers, and she blinked.

"You've all grown so much," Aunt Tremaine commented to the brood. "And into such lovely young ladies. My niece married a month ago, and I'm afraid I've been a bit starved for a good chat and a look at the fashion plates."

One of the twins rushed her, clasping her hand. "Then you must stay! Mama, tell Lady Gladys she and Lord Zachary must stay!"

"Of course they'll stay. I wouldn't have it otherwise, and I'm certain Mr. Witfeld would agree."

Aunt Tremaine smiled. "If it's not imposing, we would love to visit for a few days."

Caroline hung back a little as her sisters swarmed around Lord Zachary, each vying to be the one to show him to a guest bedchamber. She watched as he smiled again, diplomatically offering his arm to Violet, the youngest, and gestured the rest to lead the way.

Deep brown, almost black hair, with a slight glint of bronze in the afternoon sunlight, eyes that seemed to vary between a dusky charcoal and cloudy gray, and a pleasing figure both tall and athletic, Lord Zachary was an exceptionally handsome gentleman. In addition, his face, with its high cheekbones and aristocratic brow, had some very nice angles to it. Caroline would have smiled, but it wouldn't do to announce victory until she'd made a few preliminary sketches and discovered whether she could do him justice on canvas.

At this moment, though, it seemed as if her prayers had been answered. She'd asked for an aristocrat, and Lord Zachary Griffin had practically sprung to life on her doorstep. And with him, her way out of Wiltshire.

Passion, Thrills, and Suspense

from award-winning author

STEPHANIE BOND

In Deep Voodoo

0-06-082057-8/$6.99 US/$9.99 Can

hen Penny Francisco receives a voodoo doll of her recently divorced usband, she sticks it with a pin as a joke. But when he winds up fatal- stabbed, the police aren't laughing.

Whole Lotta Trouble

0-06-05642-X/$6.99 US/$9.99 Can

three women plot to get revenge and humiliate bad-boy literary super-agent Jerry Key and their scheme goes off without a glitch . . . until they discover the next morning that Jerry is dead—and not of humiliation.

Party Crashers

0-06-053984-4/$6.99 US/$9.99 Can

fter hooking up with a pair of retail fashionistas who have made rashing society bashes an art form, Jolie Goodman and her gal als have become the toast of the town . . . until a body turns up t a sexy soiree the women have crashed.

Kill the Competition

-06-053983-6/$6.99 US/$9.99 Can

ood girls finish last is Belinda Hennessey's new philosophy in life, vork, and love after moving to Atlanta for a fresh start. But before he can say "corner office," a coworker is murdered, and evidence oints to a carpool conspiracy!

AVON TRADE... because every great bag deserves a great book!

Paperback $12.95
($17.95 Can.)
ISBN 0-06-059038-6

Paperback $12.95
($16.95 Can.)
ISBN 0-06-081587-6

Paperback $12.95
($16.95 Can.)
ISBN 0-06-076250-0

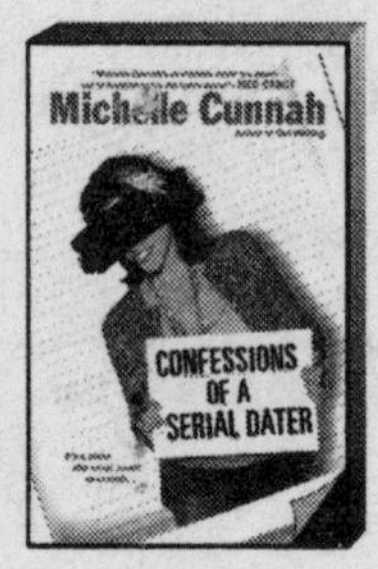

Paperback $12.95
($16.95 Can.)
ISBN 0-06-056037-1

Paperback $12.95
($16.95 Can.)
ISBN 0-06-075322-6

Paperback $12.95
($16.95 Can.)
ISBN 0-06-075591-1

Don't miss the next book by your favorite author.
Sign up for AuthorTracker by visiting *www.AuthorTracker.com.*

Available wherever books are sold, or call 1-800-331-3761 to order.

ATP 1005